i

Also by Mae Schick

A Life of Her Own
Lila
Minna

The Lookout Woman

Mae Schick

Library of Congress Control Number: 2019919597

ISBN-978-1-944504-01-4

In Memory Of

Hallie M. Dagget who came first

And to
Ella E. Clark and Harriet Linn

And the other "Two-fisted" women who followed

Aurora Borealis

Suddenly
Is the night made luminous
A rain of white fire falls in a wavering curtain
Above the dark and sleeping hills
-Dolores Cairns

Contents

Foreword

The date was May 12, 1913. The place was Sawyer's Bar in the rugged Siskiyou Mountains of northern California. The letter was addressed to Mr. W. B. Rider, Supervisor, Klamath Forest. The writer was Mr. M. H. McCarthy, Assistant Fire Ranger.

His purpose in writing was twofold: first, to inform Mr. Rider that W. R. McDowell, who had served "so well" as Fire Lookout at Eddy's Gulch Lookout Station during the fire season of 1912, had declined the invitation to serve in 1913, having found a "better paying job." and, second, to review the qualifications of three new applicants.

The first applicant, McCarthy's letter continued, was a man "whose reputation for the various cardinal virtues that go to make up a desirable employee of Uncle Sam's is not of the best. It's liable to 'run' in warm weather." Concluded McCarthy, "I could not conscientiously recommend him, even in a pinch."

The second applicant, wrote McCarthy, was:

…a passably good fellow…whose eyesight is reported to be not of the best, but who is also said to be one of the best rifle shots in the country, he having shot more holes in game laws than any other man on the Salmon…For various other reasons…I should prefer to defer recommending this applicant until I had to.

"The third applicant is also 'no gentleman,'" continued McCarthy:

…but has all the requisites of a first-class Lookout…The novelty of the proposition which has been unloaded upon me, and which I am now endeavoring to pass up to you, may perhaps take your breath away, and I hope your heart is strong enough to stand the shock. It is this: One of the most untiring and enthusiastic applicants which I have for the position is <u>Miss Hallie Morse Daggett,</u> a wide-awake <u>woman </u>of 30 years, who knows and has traversed every trail on the Salmon River watershed, and is thoroughly familiar with every foot of the District. She is an ardent advocate of the Forest Service, and seeks the position in evident good faith, and gives her solemn assurance that she will stay with her post faithfully until she is recalled. She is absolutely devoid of the timidity which is ordinarily associated with her sex as she is not afraid of anything that walks, creeps, or flies. She is a perfect lady in every respect, and her qualifications for the position are vouched for by all who know of her aspirations.

From: A Novel Experiment: Hallie Comes to Eddy's Gulch, by Rosemary Holsinger, first published in Women in Forestry 5:2, Summer 1983.

Acknowledgments

In the July 1946 issue of *National Geographic*, Ella E. Clark writes an article entitled: Forest Lookout, "Yes, I was entirely alone, but I was never lonely...No, I was never afraid."

Harriet Linn wrote that being a "smoke-spotter" in the Superior District of the Lolo National Forest, "Maybe doesn't deserve too much credit, but in almost every way the work is superior to most other so called 'patriotic war jobs.'" *Reproduced at the National Archives at Seattle.*

I am grateful for the recorded stories of these women, and to those whose stories must remain untold. I live in Montana, a land of people with powerful tales filled with grit and purpose just waiting to be told. The many unique characters that live in this land contain the gold for a willing writer.

I owe many thanks to Janice Kooiker who faithfully asked hard content questions, and didn't let go as I worked my way through several editions. I greatly appreciate the ongoing support from Sharon and Rich Franklin, and the technical expertise from Aimée and John Zupicich, and Isaak Winkelman. David Reese, photographer, fellow writer, and good friend added the finishing touches.

To my family, I thank you for your love, encouragement, and your trust and belief in the work I do.

Note: to follow Martin's trek, a map is available at maeschick.com

Part One

Florence–One

A bottleneck highway winds through the canyon east of Missoula in between five-thousand-foot Mount Jumbo and Sentinel. Left over from the Ice Age, the two giants guard the valley floor and its many ancient secrets. In the early 1800's, French Trappers, *coureurs des bois*, stumbled over the remains of human bones on their slopes and named it Hells Gate because the Blackfoot frequently ambushed the Flathead Salish there.

After the natives were safely consigned to the reservations, a century later, boys from the town's expanding population built forts and scavenged the steep slopes among the knapweed for arrowheads. Lumber mills buzzed, railroad cars rumbled, and at Mount Sentinel's bucolic foot, the university took root.

Florence walked out the front door while those mountains still slumbered and tentatively pulled the handle behind her. She ducked under the lone maple tree half as old as her forty-two years a few pods falling onto her gray felt hat. It had been not much more than a stick when Fred brought it home.

"Lookit I got!" Strangled in his fist, its beleaguered roots pulled up from the construction site where he worked.

"Do you think it's going to grow?" She tilted her head back to close the foot between their heights.

"Hard as a rock, dammit." He handled the pickax like a toy. "What d'ya mean? You ain't got no faith in me, Flossie?" She stood on her tiptoes to pat his shoulder, his face was in shadow and she squinted against the halo of light glowing around his head. That year, the fall they got married was unseasonably warm with cool nights and leaves only hinting at turning. If Fred's starter turned into a real tree, in a few autumns they would rake up palm-sized leaves.

"Of course, I do. It just looks so…you know." She shrugged.

She tucked the wool collar of her coat tighter around her neck and thought of Freckles who had been a pup when her dad brought him home out in Frenchtown. The dog had golden fur that saluted whenever it rained. He'd bark when the kids tormented him putting maple pods on their noses. He didn't like things out of order.

"Hey Freckles. Look at this." Giggling until the pods fell off. They'd turn their backs to him making him circle round. He'd growl until another pod fell.

Poor Freckles. When Florence was fourteen, a grizzly came off the mountains to chomp a new crop of apples and chomped Freckles instead. "Not fool enough to get another dog." Her dad buried her mother a few years later next to where Freckles was buried.

When their son Homer was twelve, he brought home a black lab with a tiny perfectly shape white heart on his chest. "No!" It wasn't her way to raise her voice and Homer winced but he didn't move.

"A dog will break your heart, Homer. You remember what I told you about Freckles."

"But Mom." Its rib bones hung like wire coat hangers so she fed him some pieces of fat from their stew, and some broth. Put it in an aluminum tin that it kept licking after the food was gone.

"Buddy." Homer announced and made a bed of rags for him in the back entrance. His breath frosted into a balloon when he put the dog out before bed. "I'll just sleep here with him."

"My kid don't sleep with no stinkin' dog. Enough the mangy bugger's takin' up half the goddamn doorway."

"He'll be all right." Florence said under her breath. "He's warm and his belly is full."

The arthritic gate groaned on its rusted hinges. "Shh." She inched it open commanding its allegiance for she'd left Fred stretched out and smiling in his sleep sated like a cat after his evening's bender. When she climbed out of bed folding the quilt back, he grunted. She went rigid but his mouth went slack again and the black spikes of impish hair sprouted on the pillow. In the dim light his skin looked green as a frog. He snorted at the box springs squealing when she had one foot on the floor so she perched like a statue until his breathing grew steady again.

Tucked into the closet next to the front door was a pillowslip stuffed with toothbrush, comb and hairbrush, clean underwear, two pairs of heavy socks, a long-sleeved plaid shirt, bandana, two bars of

Castile soap, and a towel. Fred snored away in the bedroom as she retrieved it.

She lay in her street clothes the night before and when he crashed into bed he was too far gone to notice. She heard him cough when she got to the front door. A deep crackle from something he'd caught working outside in February when Montana temperatures dipped below zero. It still nagged when he was on his back. April came and instead of getting better it got worse. He wouldn't go to the doctor.

"Here, drink this."

"What the hell is it, Flossie?" He made a sour face after one swallow. "You trying to kill me with one of them crazy elixirs on top of everything?" The liquid was hot but not sweet. "Not enough honey left." It couldn't mask the lemon tang or the cayenne bite.

"Just let it cool down and sip it. It'll ease your cough." He shook a bottle of whisky in her face. "

"For medicinal purposes. He smiled after the first shot. "Now, that's a cure for you, Flossie." He didn't stop after two more shots.

She paused at the door. He'd stopped snoring. If he got up, he'd curse and fumble for the light switch but instead he coughed and he settled into a contented snore. It nagged that the living room needed a coat of paint.

Twenty years ago they'd been like two fresh pups on their own starting out. "I'll build you an even bigger place than this, Flossie. Just you wait and see."

Homer's high school basketball award sat obscure on the shelf in the still dark room. She slipped on her boots and pulled her coat around her.

If it hadn't been for Homer's announcement, she'd be waiting for dawn lying next to Fred, counting his snores, and in her mind already fixing his breakfast. The week before, Homer put a period at the end of her world. She had just cleaned out the fruit room, and that day the Farmers' Almanac said to put in the cold crop of radishes, beets, carrots, and peas.

He should be starting at the college in the fall with a scholarship and gratefully Fred hadn't threatened to put the boy out when he

3

turned eighteen like his dad had done to him. If Homer studied at the library, they'd get along and stay clear of each other.

On that early spring day, the mammoth letter "M" on Mt. Sentinel, freshly white-washed by the college students, glistened against the Kelly-green hillside. A mound of slow to melt snow lingered at the doorway although buttercups blossomed in the open fields, and in a few weeks the bitterroot would bloom. Homer sucked his breath in before crossing the stoop and marching through the sticking front door almost an hour later than usual.

She was sitting at her rocker by the door where she often waited for him to return from Missoula County High, a sandwich and glass of milk on the table to see him through until supper. He couldn't look her in the eye, stared up at a corner of the ceiling and in less than a minute wiped any glow a woman in her fortieth decade has right off her face.

She should have had more kids. That was her first thought as he stood over her, nearly a foot and a half taller than she and gave her the news. Her only kid had joined up, gone to the recruiting station and signed his name on the dotted line. She should have kept the radio off when she fixed his breakfasts instead of letting it blare on and on about how proud the country was of the young men who put off their futures to go to war. Read their names out, one by one, calling them patriots.

The Army center exploded with enthusiasm, guys bragging about how many Nazis they were going to get, and when the officer shoved the paper in front of Homer he hesitated maybe a second longer than some because he was sorry she wouldn't understand it had taken him weeks to decide to fight the Nazis.

Just one word of praise from her was all he wanted. Instead, like the treasured porcelain cup with hand-painted periwinkles, an heirloom from her mother, with the hairline crack, the tears leaked.

He left before Palm Sunday and wouldn't get his diploma. She left at the end of May. The wind snapped at her collar carrying on the air the smell of earth waking up. A few lights winked from kitchen windows and she caught a whiff of bacon frying.

4

"Don't come to the station, Mom." His broad back had become a stranger's. He waved by the maple tree and took off at a jog. She counted raindrops smacking against the pane until she ran out of numbers. When the train tooted an hour later, she started counting again.

She planted peas too deep in soil that seemed as hollow as she, crammed carrot seeds together, and forgot to put salt in her bread. For two decades she'd chopped onions and carrots in the small rectangle of a kitchen, her knives had become extensions of her fingers in a room with too small a window.

The ceiling light draped like a shroud over her as she picked at her solitary meals of potatoes and a bit of meat. Fred drank more of his suppers at the Elbow Room. If he had been there to eat with her maybe it wouldn't have come to mind. The advertising poster at the post office looking for women to man the fire towers during the summer.

It wasn't Rosie the Riveter and her companions building airplanes and ships but they needed women not daunted at being on their own for three months on top of a lone mountain. Women who could bear the monotony and isolation. It was a perfect fit.

The post office bustled. Mothers dressed in their church clothes, beige-colored gloves handing over their precious letters and boxes with molasses cookies and warm socks for their sons, and making new friends in line. Florence waited fifteen minutes to get the application, rushed home, wiped the kitchen tablecloth down twice before filling it out but only got past name, address and age before coming to her work history. She folded the paper into quarters, tucked it into the back of the recipe box. Her one job as a secretary had lasted only until she got married.

That evening she was browning stew meat. Spits of oil bit into her bare skin.

"A working man has to have meat, Flossie. Regular like. None of them stinkin' goo lashes you try to push on me."

The advertisement showed a lookout tower perched on a solid rock. "It needs sunflowers on those bare walls." Butter rubbed into the burns eased her pain.

5

Martin-Two

He stood tall and forbidding as the stone walls of the imperial palace of Henry II, later designated Saint Henry the Exuberant, in the medieval town of Goslar in Lower Saxony. A spy must be convincing and to the Abwehr trainers, he wasn't. An operative should blend into a crowd, slip in and out of roles, and be a chameleon, the very opposite of who this middle-aged eye-catcher was. Because of the number of women who in vain ogled him in attempts to catch his eye, his trainers were also jealous.

No doubt some incompetent military general recommended him for intelligence work. The training was harsh, excessive, and often vicious. "Arrogant son of a bitch." They couldn't break down the walled off barrier despite the yelling and humiliation. He ate his meals of *Braunschweiger* sausage with mustard and hearty cheese made in the Harz Mountains alone. He'd been culled from the list of potential candidates because of his prestigious geology professorship and for having lived his first decade in northern Canada.

When his assignment came through, a ranking officer told him he was being sent to Sudbury, Ontario to blow up the nickel operation there. Martin managed to cover the flicker of surprise lighting a cigarette, inhaling deeply and through his self-made cloud conjured up the image of he and his pals building forts in the mining town of Timmins in northern Ontario, racing ahead of the volume of snow coming down. When winter crawled into spring over the tundra, they'd played war games in the boreal woods.

After the family moved back to Germany, his typical Schwabian mother inching just over five feet if she stretched hard, kept her two feet firmly planted in her domicile. Martin's ubiquitous boyhood got squeezed like a green lemon under her vigilant eye. He hadn't thought to notice if she'd been happy abroad but back in Germany her laugh was never more than half throttle. If she laughed it was with a cautionary glance over her shoulder, a plump woman devoutly following village rules and exacting the same from her boy.

His objective in Canada would take time. The first step after getting hired on at the nickel operation would be to recruit a few likeminded men on the inside. "Sympathetic to our cause" Embittered men, angry at management and the company's blatant mistreatment. "There's always that. Working like dogs and barely holding a family together. Just lay low. Listen and act when the moment is right. Win them over, play them until you're sure, and only then hint at something you've been thinking about." None of that could happen unless he got hired on at the plant, however.

Timmins sits fairly like the crow flies between St. James Bay on Hudson Bay to the north and Sudbury to the south, and in his memory, it would always be a place unobstructed by fences or dividing walls, and where horseplay happened almost entirely out of sight of parental prying. He was nine when they ran through fields in search of hideouts to practice the fine art of smoking. One perfect afternoon after he turned ten, he came home for supper. It was the last day of his fourth year in school and he and the boys busted out of the oppressive academic doors and headed to their favorite spot to make plans for a summer fort. It was because of the packed boxes and suitcases piled at the front door that his fists went wild and he was on the wrong end of a punch to the gut from his dad that knocked him flat against the wall. His friends wouldn't hear about the ship or of his father's village of Oehringen-Baden-Wurttemberg.

It was a quaint village with ancient walls constructed during the Crusades and there the half-tamed boy was curbed and confined, hid his tears at night in his pillow, and yearned for his unbounded steppes and the biting wind against his face. Historic Roman forts, castle and church dominated the panorama. Orderly rows of vineyards, meticulous orchards with precise spacing between trees stippled the landscape and crowded out his daydreaming.

In her kitchen nest, Mother labored over dumplings and tapped her finger at the table to keep him from flying away from the studies he must master before *Gymnasium* started in the fall. The clouds percolated past the window until sunlight broke into the kitchen around lunchtime, and he ate *Brötchen* with sausage. She released him briefly to take the trash out between math equations and German grammar, the necessary stool legs of the exams. He rushed to finish the easy problems and hid the drawings of his forts beneath his papers.

He tried to make friends with a boy his age from the apartment building who sometimes hung out by the trash cans. Martin made a joke his Canadian pals would have hooted over but the kid didn't even blink, just shook his head and walked away. They ended up sitting next to each other at school but the kid ignored him and made faces to his friend behind Martin's back and put thumb tacks on his seat.

"Don't use the left hand when the right is always right." Mother lectured after a meeting with his teacher, her twisted way of saying he needed to do a much better job of getting along.

It wasn't so simple to steal cigarettes in the village tobacco shop, so he made a stash from his father's taking only one out of an opened pack. Eventually, he alleviated his mother's qualms bringing home good marks, and some Saturdays she released him to wander near the Kocher River where he discovered the limestone cave systems that helped ease some of the emptiness from his forever lost friendships.

The *Abwehr* recruits with thick heads of hair who had been gleaned from their studies at the universities called him Old Baldy. During calisthenics when they snickered, "Come on, old man," he pumped and pushed harder and sometimes put them to shame. If any of them reached the age of forty, managed to make it through the war, one or two might be lucky to be as fit.

Three packs a day numbed the memory of the unfinished boyhood of his life. With the strike of the match sometimes a flashback came with it of him and his buddies sneaking into the Hollinger Mine company store to lift a few packs of Cravens. Two of them distracted the clerk and the third did the actual thieving. They drew sticks for it. As winters gradually advanced toward a partial thaw, they lazed on the soggy banks of the Mattagami River leaning into the warm mud, puffy clouds drifting above, practicing smoke rings.

The cigarette fascination grew into an addiction by the time he got to university where he boasted that even blindfolded, he could identify any brand they lit. The distinctive French *Gauloises* were his favorite although it was an unpatriotic choice with the Germans.

Whenever women pursued him, he hid his sneers behind pinched lips. Despite Mother's cross examinations once he'd achieved his position at the university and she demanded demand he make her *Oma*, he blew smoke clouds to obliterate her image of family and home which to him was a dull box, a cubicle of walls, floors and doors, screaming kids, and a gray mouse flattened in a trap with cheese stuck in his mouth.

The Abwehr armed him with explosive devices, camouflaged sabotage equipment he would carry to Canada. The inventions were exciting and stirred a boyish delight of imagination crisscrossing over into reality. The scientists in the Abwehr demolition lab experimented with a genius and cunning that Martin admired and he slyly scoffed at the half-witted, shortsighted judgment of the trainers and their anemic efforts to thwart him.

He'd carry seven chocolate bars, disguised bombs, steel covered by a thin coat of dark chocolate in his pack, explosive throat lozenges, a shaving brush, and an incendiary time bomb designed inside a thermos. "Seven seconds." They warned. After breaking off a piece of the chocolate a canvas detonator would be pulled giving him a few seconds before exploding.

"In case you're in a pinch, use it as a hand grenade." Straight forward and simple and just the opposite of the distasteful discussions about entanglements that could deter a successful operation. When and how to avoid contact and smiles from women because the numbskull trainers were blind. It galled him that he might have to encourage someone if it served to help him reach his objective.

"You know how women can be. Especially a scorned woman." He smirked. "Could they be any more dangerous than blowing up a plant?"

When he arrived in Sudbury, the apartment was situated over an appliance store with a clear view of the main street at the broadest intersection. A window led out to the rooftop and could be used as an escape route. The other boarder, a woman near his age, worked in a department store in ladies' apparel. After she brought him a casserole, he studied her comings and goings to avoid meeting her on the stairs.

He hadn't invited her in, didn't ask her name, and didn't give her a chance to ask his. "Thank you." he shut the door and dumped the dish into the trash. When he realized she might be one of those women who could cause him a problem, he went to a bookstore and bought a book on trout fishing, put it inside the empty dish retrieved from the garbage and washed clean, and propped up it at her door across the hallway.

Florence-Three

In April, ice scraps wore thin as patches on the knees of a boy's pants but continued to hang on around Missoula's side streets. It was business as usual on Higgins Avenue but the rest of downtown was stalled either waiting for the weather to brighten or the worry of a protracted war to come to an end.

For a moment and on impulse, she had a girlish yen to slide on the strips of ice and be carried along on the whim. The grim post office hijacked that notion with its stony-cold steps that led up to the glass doors and inside, the pinching odor of varnish imprisoned the fresh air. Three glass booths separated the riffraff from the civil servants but only one had a worker behind the bars.

The application fluttered as she passed it under the glass window to the deadpan face of a man whose inheritance had been robbed of height. Her fingers felt like ice cubes and to avoid staring at his shiny scalp, she tapped them on the marble counter until the Lilliputian's pinpoint pupils glared at her. The five minutes spent blowing on her hands outside hadn't warmed them at all. If it had been her usual trip to the butcher's, she wouldn't have noticed the cold and would have dismissed the surliness when she asked for plump chicken thighs.

"Sit there." He spoke at her through the round hole in the glass and she followed his finger to a bench. Her feet sweat inside her shabby boots but the Ogg Shoe Store hadn't run a spring sale yet and probably wouldn't with the war on. When the clerk managed a glimpse her way, she tucked her feet underneath the seat. Maybe he didn't like her gray coat or that she was taller than he.

The second hand on the regulation clock clicked off the seconds, each one laboring in thought and effort. Under her breath she counted, one, two, three. When she got to sixty, she started again. After five minutes, the drumming drilled inside her brain. The garden needed work and she needed to get up and move around, but the little man looked at her again, this time staring at her and she squeezed her legs together and stayed on the bench. After fifteen minutes, she stood up. "Enough of this." It was daft to fool herself

11

about a job at a lookout. Why hang around waiting for a handout like the bums outside the Oxford Bar?

"It shouldn't be too much longer." The little man's voice echoed in the hallway like he actually cared.

"That's all right." The lamb stew and the kitchen would smell of garlic, onions, pepper, and sage when she got back home. Fred would like that. If he came home for supper.

A door on the other side of the clerk's window flew open just then and a person the extreme opposite of the little man appeared. Mutt and Jeff in real life and right down to the full head of hair! She covered her mouth to hide her smile.

"Mrs. Hickson?" He glanced at her paperwork.

"Yes. That's me." There was no one else in the sterile lobby.

"Come this way." His room had no window and she felt sorry for this rangy comic book Jeff, bookish, absent-minded and surrounded with paperwork that ran out of space on his banged up wooden desk, at some ancient point giving in and drifting to its permanent place on the floor.

"I could use a secretary." That sounded like Homer mocking himself. "But I guess you want to be a smoke spotter."

"Yes, sir." He hadn't introduced himself and until he said otherwise, he was Jeff.

"I'm Mr. Winston." Maybe he'd read her mind. "Now, tell me why you want to be a smoke spotter, and why you think you're suited for this job. You know it's not for everyone. In fact, it's not for most people. What makes you different?" He squeezed his eyebrows as he quizzed her.

Her tongue froze up like the icebound fingers in her lap. "I...I...like to be outdoors." She stuttered.

"Well, that's a good place to start. How do you feel about being on your own for days and days on end? You know, you won't see no people most of the time. Every now and then a packer'll haul some supplies up. That might be it for three months."

"I'm used to being on my own. I like it."

Mr. Winston studied her face for a good minute. "You're not runnin' away from somethin', are you?"

12

"Oh, no! No." Good grief.

"You got any illnesses or handicaps?"

"No sir, Mr. Winston."

"Well, you look a strapping woman. You ain't too young and you ain't too old, neither."

"I'm strong."

"You got a husband?"

"Yes, sir." There it was.

"He's not off fightin', is he?"

"No." If only he was. "My son is." She smiled and then frowned.

"Well, that must make you proud, Mrs. Hickson. What's your husband gotta say about you runnin' off to the hills for the whole summer?" There it was again.

He'd be livid and it would serve him right. "He's just fine about it, sir."

"Wants you to do your duty, too? Like you son? Is that it?"

"Yes, sir. He's got so much work he won't have time to notice I'm gone."

"Okay. I've looked over the application. You got any references?" He looked at her application again.

None except for the secretarial experience listed on the application. "No, sir. I haven't worked since my boy was born."

"You go on home, now. I'll be sending you a letter in about a week to let you know how things stand."

He picked up some of the other paper work and was looking at it when she left. He wasn't impressed. How could he be? She shook her head. "What an idiot you are." She didn't even know what he was looking for. "Oh, that was a waste of time." She headed to the market for a bag of salt.

"Not gonna be enough rain this year." The grocer whined the same greeting to everyone coming in.

"Maybe we'll get it in June." He watched her walk down the crammed aisles. She felt his eyes undressing her from behind and pulled her coat around her.

"You're looking mighty juicy today." All dressed up with no place to go?" He leered when she handed him the dollar and the cash

13

register jingled while she waited with outstretched hand for the change and pulled her coat collar over her bosom.

It was already late to put in cold weather seeds, but when she returned home, she planted two more rows of snap peas.

Martin-Four

His birth name was Johann Meidenger but when the Abwehr extracted him from his position in the Physical Geology Department at Tubingen University he became Martin. There were no farewell parties or good luck celebrations for the professor who discreetly cleaned out his desk and slipped away.

His Habilitation dissertation had secured a place for him at the university and had taken eight instead of the full ten years to complete. Its results shifted the study of mineral deposits in a significant and new direction, as well as drawing international praise from the scientific community. But his colleagues were skeptical at what they perceived unwarranted and undeserved publicity, reputing his work to be flawed since it had been completed in less than the traditional time and by logic could not be sufficiently comprehensive or rigorous. Martin, they gossiped, had sacrificed quality over speed, was only out to make a reputation for himself, and could not control all the variables in his field work. Mustachioed, pipe-sniffing men huddled in the professors' lounge parsing his thesis word for word with missionary zeal to tease out its weaknesses. After four years of mistrust and relentless criticism, and ceaseless reviewing but finding nothing untoward, the military drafted him.

The *Schadenfreude*, the snide asides, the rancor, and the gossip he left behind in the empty desk. His mother clucked like a setting hen on unhatched eggs when he was awarded the position.

"My Johann is the youngest tenured professor in the Geology department! In Tubingen!" At the bakery and butcher, the hired help ducked behind their counters to avoid eye contact. She expected even grander titles when he went into the military. "Just you watch. He'll be a general soon." Her head despite the short neck thrust over the shop counters.

Initial training in the Harz Mountains was followed by a stint in Petsamo, Finland where nickel was mined and refined for the manufacture of arms and munitions. As Germany's ally, Finland traded its natural resources for protection against the Soviets who

15

drooled at their shared border. As early as 1935 the Canadian and French companies had also mined the ore there.

Germany lacked the resource deposits which forced the country to go abroad to acquire them, especially nickel with its beneficial properties to resist rust and protect stainless steel at high temperatures. Only a few countries had deposits of the ore, but Canada was the world's principal source of both crude and refined nickel. Since the Nazis couldn't get their hands on the Sudbury production, sabotage was the next best option to slow down the Allied manufacture of airplanes and tanks.

In Canada, the ore had been discovered by accident when the Canadian railroad laid down its tracks north from Sudbury. The province was resource rich and for ten years Martin lived 300 kilometers from the nickel mines and Sudbury, an ugly town with blatant tailings that snuffed out living things clear to the edges of its boundaries.

The slagheaps were higher than he had remembered when got hired on at the nickel plant as a steam hammer operator, and his new employers didn't ask why he was not in uniform serving his country like the many men who'd left for the service. A forged medical report listed a severe allergy to wool, the material made into military uniforms that can cause severe rashes and interfere with the duties of a regular soldier.

Immigrants populated the province because of the jobs available on the railroads, in the mines, and lumber mills and although his accent was difficult to pinpoint it didn't raise any alarms. It wasn't unusual for people coming from a shared country to find it difficult to understand a local accent so his language didn't draw suspicion.

The U-boat dropped him near Gaspé on an almost moonless night. He wobbled ashore, a staggering boozer until the ocean's motion ceased rocking him and he headed away from the beach gaining distance before daylight. Patrol boats had sunk two U-boats in the bay in the last three months, and the high winds his had encountered delayed the plan to drop him until the weather improved.

His hands trembled terribly in the frigid air. In Finland, the Nordic winter nights began at 3:00 in the afternoon and the street lamps were lit. For months, he'd chain smoked through the chilling and suffocating darkness and pored over the steam hammer operating manual. In Canada he'd suffered frost bitten toes but his father called him a crybaby for screaming when they started to thaw and the stabbing pain was being prodded by hot irons. Strangely, he rarely felt cold after that.

Night and day ran together at the Arctic Circle painting perpetual twilight that fueled his smoking addiction and an annoying cough. Without the cigarettes and the manual, he would have spiraled into internal night despite having found respite for the darkness in the limestone caves, and treasuring its protection from an intrusive mother who regularly poked her head into his room before bed to catch him unguarded and peer into his soul. The Nordic other world heightened the beloved memory of the Canadian tundra and the Mattagami River.

The night air off the Canadian coast clamped its teeth down on him because his woolen navy cap and pea jacket were buried at the base of a scrappy tree near the imposing cliffs hovering like antediluvian fortresses rising out of the sea, so he ran to warm up. The loose fibers in his French suit couldn't insulate him from the biting gusts.

The narrow road to Gaspé was deserted but that town was where he'd catch the train for Montreal if the schedule he'd memorized was up-to-date. He dared not smoke. A solitary red ember in the darkness would arouse a patrol. He could tolerate the cold but burying the cigarettes had been akin to leaving one of his arms behind. On the U-boat he'd pushed the bits of food around with his fork and knife when they'd served him a last meal, and he smoked ten Gauloises to finish off a pack.

A noise, a foot crunching on the gravel sounded behind him but when he turned to see, no one was there. He'd buy his first pack of Cravens at the nearest store in Gaspé.

A long line of women stood before him to interview at the Sudbury plant when he applied and got hired on. A clerk assigned

17

him a dormitory room and gave him a suspicious look when he said
he   didn't   need   it.   He'd   rented   a   room   in   town.

Florence-Five

At eleven o'clock three letters clacked to the bottom of the green mailbox nailed to a board next to the front door. The mailman, as usual, punctual. Florence fed the last of the laundry, Fred's long-sleeved plaid work shirt, through the washing machine wringer that spit bubbles onto the cracked yellowing linoleum. She shook the wrinkles out and hung the shirt on the back of a kitchen chair. Even on rainy days and wrestling with his raincoat, trudging in heavy boots, the mailman was prompt.

To this day, a year after they'd buried Buddy under the same maple tree where he'd delighted in making the poor man jump whenever he entered the yard, he routinely clutched his mailbag for safety. It was simply reflex.

"He likes you." Homer had grinned at the carrier, defending his dog. "If he didn't, he'd bare his teeth and growl." The mailman gave the animal a wide berth anyway stepping off the path and making an arc around the dog.

"I'm not takin' no chances." The man shook his head but he didn't complain.

Homer was in his junior year of basketball training season when Buddy took sick. "I think it's the horsemeat." Florence puzzled about giving him the leftovers from a stew but he'd looked up at her with pitiful brown eyes, whining. "Oh, here you go, you little beggar. You're probably going to be sorry."

He didn't chase the mailman for three days after that, then he revived and seemed fiercer than ever. That lasted for two days. When Buddy died she wished she could blame the butcher. At the end, the dog couldn't get up on his hind legs to greet Homer when he came home worn out from dribbling and shooting.

Maybe the loss of Buddy, a wound that didn't heal over the months, had something to do with Homer joining the army, like the dog had somehow by dying given him permission. Florence dried her hands on her homemade flower-printed apron and went to the door. Days went by with no letters from him and then three or four came in one delivery playing catch-up. She'd put paper and stamps in his suitcase.

He laughed. "Come 'on, Mom, I'm not going to need all this. The Army's gonna give us everything we need." She laundered and ironed his shirts folding them into his suitcase like egg whites into a cake batter topping it with the paper, envelopes, and the stamps.

The stoop was wet but the rain had stopped when she finished the laundry and the spring air felt like that first bite into a crisp, just-picked apple. The letter on top had his straightforward script with the tight, cursive thick letters on it. In grade school he'd balked at learning the cursive capitals with their frilly flourishes.

"So, look whose writing like a girl now." Fred had stood over Homer at the kitchen table one evening while the boy practiced his capital "G's and "F's."

That afternoon when Homer came home and towered over her in her rocker near the fireplace, the sun poured like lemon curd through the living room window. It had been such a promising day, too. She'd rushed around that morning to tidy the kitchen and put on her work boots to get into her garden needing only a light spring jacket for the first time that season. Afterward, her back ached bent too long over plentiful weeds and from ignoring the complaining muscles that had been in hibernation. She made herself a cup of coffee and was attentively mending a hole in a pair of his pants when Homer came home. When he told her what he had to say, he bent down and tried to look her straight in the eyes. She poked her finger with the darning needle but wouldn't cry out.

That afternoon and before he'd come home, the weather had turned, the wind howled and snow followed him through the door. The flakes landed on the braided rug over the wood planks and puddled from the heat. A uniform wouldn't keep his ruddy freckled arms warm in a driving snow storm.

"I'm shipping out next week."

"Goddammit, Flossie! Cut it out! Quit acting like a big baby." Fred had showed up early, of all days, because the boss sent him home. He'd been coughing for weeks. But the fear of lost wages kept him going.

20

"You gonna hack up a goddamn lung, Fred. Go home till you can do a decent day's work for me." For weeks he hauled himself out of bed exhausted after each night's suffering and the piercing aches in his back and chest. There was no arguing when the boss put his foot down.

"That's just the ticket for Homer. Right thing for you to do, kiddo. Get off your duff instead of chasing a goddamn ball around. Finally make a man of you." Fred straddled the kitchen doorway, half in, with one foot planted out in the entryway. Florence's tears fell into the potato peelings. She was making dumplings and Homer stood between them his hands stuffed in his pockets.

The few blond feathers on Homer's upper lip made him more, rather than less, an adolescent as did his arms and legs hanging out below his long-sleeved shirt sleeves and pants. When he told his favorite teachers his decision, they gave him optimistic faces, patted him on the back, and didn't ask if he knew he was throwing away his chance for a university education. His algebra teacher gritted his teeth and spoke to the door after Homer walked out. "He should have graduated college."

His basketball coach was grateful he'd waited until the season finished. They'd made it to the finals and took home the trophy. When June came and his classmates walked across the stage to receive their diplomas, Homer would be abroad. Florence had already sewed a dress for the occasion, reworked the decorations on her Sunday hat and regretted she couldn't have a new pair of white gloves. The dress got tucked in the back of the closet out of sight.

Three weeks had passed since her post office interview. It had been a long shot anyway, the moments in the interview awkward, Mr. Hickson couldn't even keep up with his paperwork, and probably considered her a second-rate candidate. By the time she'd gotten the application filled out, he'd already decided who they would hire. Any number of people, single women with job experience and references, a lot better candidates, most likely, or men too old to go into service but young enough to man a lookout.

The mailman shuffled his feet three houses down lugging his brown leather bag over his shoulder flopping against his hip. The front door as always rubbed against the floor when she closed it. Fred said it was only temporary but that had been almost twenty years ago.

Martin-Six

Someone was watching him. The seamen had sneaked him ashore over the choppy sea during a muddy night, and when they slipped back into the dark leaving him in shadow, he detected a presence. The sailors were brusque with him itching to get out of the bay and back into the safer waters of the Atlantic. The quiet motor coughed a few times, then what remained was a nerve-wracking silence in the murky gloom desolate as Finland's winter– and the eyes. He was sure of it and although still wobbly he hustled to get off the shoreline.

He picked his way over the pockmarked lane with its dips and ruts for a half mile with no help from the nugget of a moon before he stumbled into a pothole from looking over his shoulder. His pack weighed him down with disguised explosives and a perfectly good flashlight that he dared not use. He landed on his knee but twisted the ankle and kept moving, favoring the foot and leg. His mission would end with a whimper if he was detected near the seacoast in the middle of the night.

He'd memorized the Abwehr aerial photo of the road to Gaspé that ran parallel to the bay, and committed the names of towns and cities, railway routes, their schedules and fares, where to make connections and changes, the major and minor highway arteries, to memory. He'd practiced phrases to use in restaurants, and the proper way to pour his tea or coffee, when he should request one beverage over the other, how the silverware and dinnerware were placed, and how to use each utensil. If someone asked him if he was left-handed it would be a dead giveaway that he was from the continent and maybe a German. His wallet was as crammed as his brain with the Canadian dollars they called bucks. He remembered that from Timmins days.

Significant and insignificant details they'd drilled into his brain floated in and out of his mind as he shuffled along the road. He could feed back everything the Abwehr had thrown at him even in his sleep. The mock scenarios, stilted and overplayed by sharp-throated Teutonic women who meant to curb his obvious lack of interest. "What will you do if you're train is delayed?" They pressed him, their elbows jutting from their generous hips.

"What and how do you answer if you are taken in for questioning?"

"How do you handle a long layover? What about a cancellation? How do you make yourself disappear?" That was easy enough. Their shared glowers didn't perturb him. He was as unreadable to them as he'd been living in the flat with his parents and his father had embarrassed him when he returned to the tiny flat and wasn't sober.

Gaspé he discovered was the poor man's thin drink, lacking gusto, an unsatisfying substitute for quality liquor. The odd name seemed to have come from the Algonquin word for Land's End. He loitered on the perimeter of the village until the residents began to shake off their sleep watching from the outskirts and growing irked by their lethargy. He needed a cigarette and their collective ambivalence peeved him. At 7:30 a.m. they emerged by inches like turtles. He counted backward the number of minutes before the general store opened.

"Two packs of Cravens." Even sardines would feel crammed in that store. He'd seen the light on earlier, the clerk there stocking the wire tobacco shelf. His French was good enough, almost as good as his English. She stood on tiptoe to reach the packs. He entered behind an elderly woman who waddled and he matched her steps careful not to startle or overrun her. He tipped his hat when she turned to leave but she didn't acknowledge him although he held the door for her.

"You ain't from the fort?" The clerk liked him. "Looks like a warm day." He nodded still chilled from the night.

"I hope." He was halfway out the door by then.

He smoked two cigarettes and then went a few doors down to the café ordering what passed for coffee and a hard roll with cheese. He wished he'd ordered the tea. It smelled damp and fishy in the place, the windows filmy forever assaulted by sea salt. A valiant person could wash them daily but the glass would always be blurred. He had a window seat and discreetly studied the customers who came in after him. He could see the depot from where he sat and looked for the type of men who would be looking for him, probably two or three men in trench coats wearing bowlers, skulking and obvious.

"You ain't from around here." The waitress sneaked up behind him like she was stalking a deer. He jumped and that made her jump. It rattled him and he smiled to cover it. Had he made a careless mistake? Her smile with its crummy looking teeth detracted from an otherwise open, innocent face.

It rankled him, the way nature had cheated her, stolen her chances. She caught the brief sad glance when he returned her smile but he turned toward the window. It was an ideal spot for watching the comings and goings of the village but with three more hours to kill until the midday train to Montreal, he paid the bill, smiled again at the girl before leaving to stroll down the main street where he found a small park with a bench. The weather was mild, half clouds and sun, a slight breeze, and with the depot in his line of sight, he smoked and tipped his hat to walkers passing nearby.

The train's intermittent schedule had complicated the U-boat captain's decision for getting him ashore. It ran three days a week and the boat couldn't safely linger in local waters. The cap Gaspé lighthouse, perched seven hundred feet over the sea, had spotted other German boats in the bay and destroyed them. Fortunately, the wind got calmer and he was put ashore as planned. Otherwise, he would have had to fend for himself.

The train arrived on time and an old deaf man shared his seat. He nodded when Martin sat down and pointed to his own ears and shrugged apologetically. Not long after, his head tilted back, his mouth went slack and he snored. With a copy of Roger DuGard's *Les Thibault* as a prop, Martin studied the passengers. He no longer had the sensation that he was being followed. That changed once on board, the twinge at the back of his neck returned. A half hour after the train pulled away from the station, someone laughed very loudly and he turned around to see who else was in the compartment. A large, jovial lady and her pig-tailed daughter were playing a fast game with their hands, slapping each other's and giggling. The woman's eyes had the squint lines of the Sami in Finland. Her skin and hair were like theirs, and to some extent so was the little girl's.

At intervals he studied the landscape but not letting down his guard. The old man got off and was met by a younger woman,

25

perhaps his daughter, at a nondescript town, his seat replaced by a middle-aged woman reeking with perfume. Martin nodded, went back to reading after accounting for everyone aboard and took short catnaps.

Florence-Seven

Homer went off to the army on Good Friday, the same day Jesus was crucified. On Sunday, the First Methodist church smelled of Easter lilies and damp wool. Navy crackerjacks and army greens dotted the pews punctuating the Easter bonnets and Florence's festive hat meant for Homer's graduation. The organ dragged its feet humming a dirge and the pastor used up his sermon time rambling about a heavenly home far removed from strife and conflict.

Every year Florence set the holiday table with her good china and at Easter decorated each plate with a pastel egg. Sitting in the church pew, a uniformed man lucky to be on leave sat with his family a few shoulders away from Florence while Fred, still in bed, slept off a bender and a stuffed chicken roasted in the oven. Tender legs and moist thighs would fall off the bone, the kitchen window steamed over, the room saturated by potent sage, only this year two places were set at the table with everyday plates.

The letter in his unpolished handwriting, half professional, the other half declaring the youthful strain of a grade school kid, felt too light. The green letter box either benevolently delivered up welcomed letters or turned a cold shoulder or worse, smirked about the inevitable bill from the Montana Power Company or Mountain Bell. Recognizing the awkward script, she breathed out the air she didn't know she had been holding, the backward scrawl bringing her son to life.

A dog howled incessantly the next block over, tethered on a chain connected to his dog house left to fend for himself all day. She resisted ripping the envelope open, nudged the sticking door with her hip to close it and went to get a sharp kitchen knife to fillet it. That letter would go into a shoebox at the top of her closet along with every one that would come placed in sequence by date with virtually intact envelopes, until he returned.

He was doing terrific, a word he'd never used before. "Eating great. You wouldn't believe how much they feed us. At this rate, I'm gonna get fat! Their biscuits aren't as good as yours, though." She sighed. He'd made friends with some recruits. "One of the guys I

27

bunk with is from New Jersey and the other's from Georgia. They talk funny, Mom, but they're great guys. They say the same about me. If I'm really from Montana where is my cowboy hat and six-shooter?" She grinned. "My stomach hurt from laughing so hard." She pressed the paper against her heart and read it three more times before lunch.

Fred slept through Easter. The juices sizzling in the roasting pan were usually a happy sound for her on holidays, but at 3:00 she picked at the drying meat on her plate and afterward prepared sandwiches and chicken soup to send with him in the morning.

The day the three letters dropped to the bottom of the mailbox, she drank a third pot of coffee at the kitchen table. Magical gold dust from the late morning sunlight filtered into the room and onto Homer's envelope propped against the salt shaker. She studied it while wiping nonexistent salt crystals off the red checked oilcloth tablecloth then traced the letters of her name addressed only to her. She'd put it away before Fred came home.

The Forest Service letter waited near her elbow unopened and under the bill from the Montana Power Company. She pushed back the chair to wash her coffee cup and tend to the garden. Tomatoes and the cabbage plants came up spindly but as more sunny days came on, they'd sturdy up. She patted the straggly bushes. The radishes and spinach had bright green leaves almost ready for harvesting to add to the supper salads.

The weeds as always flourished among the vegetables. After pulling up the intruders, she planted marigold and nasturtium seeds along with cosmos and stayed outside too long to organize supper so she stirred up a pancake batter with sausages. If Fred was in a decent mood, he'd tell her his story, as he always did. "When I was a boy, Mom made this for me because I loved them so much." It was the easiest and quickest meal to fix.

The Forest Service letter still waited for her on the table. Her hands were dirty and she smeared the envelope opening it and tempted to toss it into the trash without reading it.

The walls in the living room needed painting and Fred had leftover cans of blue and green and yellow salvaged from work. She'd do all the painting, the kitchen too, then the bathroom and bedrooms.

28

Homer had promised to help her when summer came. Maybe a face-lift would make Fred cheerful. She ran her thumb under the flap not bothering this time with a knife. Without experience, no references, a short work history, it made sense that the stationery was thin. One page with just a few sentences.

Someone knocked at the door just as she read, *Dear Mrs. Hickson*, and the letter dropped to the table. The pastor was out doing his weekly calling to the invalids, the old, the families of servicemen. There was dirt under her fingernails and she tucked her fingers under her apron, crossed them, and asked if he'd like coffee hoping he'd be pressed for time.

He drank three cups and ate two slices of bread with homemade strawberry jelly. At almost five o'clock he hadn't budged and Fred would be home soon, if he came directly from work. Fred had a few words about the pastor. "What's the son-of-a-bitch hanging around you for, anyways, Flossie?" Until Homer went into the army, she didn't know why he stopped in while he made his rounds other than that she belonged to the church. "He wanna get up your skirt or something, Flossie?"

Fred drove up the driveway and the pastor jumped up, brushed the crumbs off his pants and rushed to the door. "I'll see you Sunday, then?" She thought he winked at her as she closed the front door. Fred was coming in the back entry before she remembered the letter. While he muscled off his boots, she grabbed it and ran to the bathroom.

Dear Mrs. Hickson. Her hands shook. The capital *M* on his typewriter was out of alignment which after visiting Mr. Winston's office, seemed to fit. He needed a secretary to fix it or get someone to do it.

I am sorry…there it was. He apologized. She didn't want his apology. Fred yelled down the hallway. "Where the hell is supper?"

"It's almost ready." Through the closed door she told him her stomach was upset but she'd be out in a few minutes.

In the second sentence, Mr. Winston offered her the job, *if* she still wanted the job, he added. He apologized three times, sorry about the delay getting back to her and sincerely hoped that in taking longer than he had wished, she had not gotten another job in the meantime.

She clapped the letter between her hands and quietly did a little hop on the linoleum, tucked it inside her apron pocket, patted her hair down, and put her shoulders back. "Now, what do I do about Fred?"

Martin-Eight

Montreal buzzed and he immediately joined a crowd at Union Station staying to the middle and letting it carry him along. Stragglers, the ones on the edges of the crush, stood out, easier to pick out and follow. During the train ride from Gaspé he'd shaved at the lavatory's tiny mirror before the other passengers stirred and then examined the window's size, unhooking the latch to see how far it swung open if needed.

He matched the pace of the other travelers taking the public transportation system. In Berlin, Munich, Helsinki it was the same, probably true worldwide, a throng hurrying to catch a connection, or rushing to meet an arriving passenger. Train stations swarmed and emptied with clockwork regularity like a repeating stage play. When his crowd dispersed, spreading out like the threads of fraying fabric, he merged into smaller and then smaller clusters, ever careful not to become completely alone.

The one available seat to Toronto was next to the same perfumey woman who was at the moment engrossed with a silver compact. She applied Victory Red lipstick and wiped the excess with her little finger and tongue, and as he sunk down into the cushion she glared at him for knocking her elbow. Her hat with its floppy black flower obstructed his view of the platform to see if anyone was searching for him. As the train pulled away, he peered over the top of his novel and once again sized up the passengers.

For five interminable hours, three rambunctious children ran up and down the aisle playing tag. Their mothers unable or unwilling to contain them, mouthed, *Shush*, but were ignored. Four soldiers on leave wore their uniforms with CF green berets and passed around a flask laughing and singing, *We'll Meet Again*.

At the Toronto depot, a sparse group headed for the connecting line to Sudbury leaving him little cover. After checking the arrival time and all the exits and entrances, he ordered a sandwich, a somewhat less than foul affair of old cheese, salami, and a limp piece of lettuce. He took three bites and threw the remainder in a trash receptacle. His mother would *tsk tsk*, an otherwise brilliant only son who didn't enjoy her meals nearly as much as she did. It bordered on a nearly unforgiveable slight, a blunt insult to her culinary skills. His father snapped at her, told her to shut up about it.

"Your idiot son runs the other way if someone even looks cross-eyed at him. He'd hide in the closet if you'd let him, and never come out." The father beamed at his insight and for trumping her whining with the boy's much more serious faults.

The highly scented woman didn't board the Sudbury train and since he had his choice of seats, he took one next to a window. A woman across the aisle facing him soon punctured his solitude. She smiled and nodded before turning and looking out the window. The softer tone of her lipstick, her agreeable red tam and matching red bow at the crown, made him think of a marzipan cake with its layers of raspberry preserves. *Trust no one!* His Teutonic role players no doubt at this very minute hovering over another intelligence trainee in some hidden corner of Germany pummeling their receptive brains with careful directions.

Twenty minutes later she smiled at him again. He read a sentence, read it again, then again, the French words didn't make sense, no matter the Du Gard novel's reputation for riveting attention. He forgot to turn pages periodically, glanced at his watch, and surveyed the landscape. Maybe she'd get off before Sudbury.

A hundred yards from the track, some boys were running across the fields. Their wildly pounding heartbeats echoed in his ears, his legs, once again adolescent and toned, ran with them sweeping through the tall grasses, his feet pounding the ground like African drums. He sucked in his breath refilling his hungry lungs. They were rushing to a copse at the edge of the field before he completely lost sight of them, looking for a blind, somewhere to light up their pack of cigarettes in private. He smiled slightly toward the book and started reading the same line yet again.

A sister of Wilhelm, one his former students at the University, smiled like this woman on the train. Clotilde let certain people call her Tilly. Not Martin, however, just her brother and his friends. She applied her makeup in steps like she was preparing a soufflé after

Martin made love with her. He smoked two cigarettes while she primped on the edge of the bed.

"Don't watch me like that."

"Like what?"

"Like, I don't know. A peeping Tom."

Clotilde started flirting with him, waiting outside the classroom where her brother studied. The first time she approached Martin, she pretended to be looking for Wilhelm.

"I don't know where he went." She made him uncomfortable and he was abrupt. Then, she came up to him, that lipstick mouth half open. He stood opposite her at the lectern until she put her hand on it, leaned over it and brushed her breast against the elbow of his Houndstooth jacket.

"What's geology about, anyway?" She asked looking out the window of his apartment after the second time they made love. He'd jumped up from the bed as soon as she began to apply her makeup, refrained from lighting a cigarette, put on his shirt and studied the wall. "It's just about silly rocks, isn't it?"

Clotilde's smile however had one difference from this woman's. It had come attached with a stipulation. He'd been aroused, fascinated and had succumbed, but later found out Wilhelm and his friends had placed bets on how many professors she could seduce in one year's time. Wilhelm knew his sister. She received monetary payment as part of the bargain for each one she conquered, and her payments grew exponentially as her numbers increased.

The following year she went on a Grand Tour around the world.

Florence-Nine

She didn't tell Fred. Had she intended to do so? The sentences she practiced in the kitchen just never came out of her mouth.

Mr. Winton wrote that fire spotter training started the following week and he needed to know her intentions. If she couldn't arrange it on such short notice, he would have to hire someone else. He apologized for the third time in the letter about the delay that had arrived on Monday and on Thursday she walked briskly to the post office wearing her church hat, garnering stares from women passing by. But formal dress seemed appropriate and even critical for accepting a new job, and it would show to Mr. Winston he had made the right choice.

On Tuesday and Wednesday, she watched the snap peas send up graceful tendrils while the recipe box on the kitchen counter cradled her acceptance letter. A few warm days had brought the rhubarb on early, juicy, thick stalks soon ready to go into a pie, the kind that Fred's mother made for him. Tucked in the back of the recipe box, the mother-in-law's scrawly handwriting on a faded piece of paper stayed next to the letter. When Florence opened it she nodded and grinned.

The following Monday, training would begin. The Friday before, she fixed Fred's favorite roast beef with onions, carrots and potatoes fairly begging the butcher to give her a fine cut.

"Not horsemeat." She forced a smile but kept her shoulders back. He muttered but complied with his faithful customer's request. The wedding china, two plates, on the Easter tablecloth gleamed in the modest kitchen table that evening, an inviting and homey sight only missing a candle or early wildflowers, but nothing too fancy to arouse Fred's suspicions.

"What's all this nonsense?" He'd say, or worse. He wasn't a fool and wouldn't be duped by a story about how he deserved a really good meal because he worked so hard. "Who died and left you a million bucks, Flossie?"

"I have some really good news." Straight forward, that' how it had to be.

"Okay. Cut the crap, Flossie." No hesitation, no sweet talk, and the reason for the fancy table to make up for Easter.

"Are you totally off your rocker?" That's what he'd say if he got wound up, a second's hesitation maybe to let it sink in before he threw one of their wedding china plates, maybe two against the wall. The tableware for special occasions that she painstakingly packed up after each use to avoid chipping.

But maybe he'd be in a good mood, come in laughing and itching to tell a story about some goofball at work who didn't know the head of a nail from a hammer. That's what she hoped. In good humor he brought the sunlight in with him and they laughed together and the aroma from the roast would add to that gaiety. The moment to tell him was just after he took a bite of rhubarb pie.

He didn't come home for supper. After 11:00, he blustered through the back door from the Elbow Room. She'd undressed the table, stored her good dishes back in their cardboard box, folded up the tablecloth and put it with the other linens, and set the roast in a covered dish in the ice box.

On Saturday, laundry routinely done on Mondays and ironing on Tuesdays were added to her other chores of scrubbing and waxing the linoleum floors, dusting the living room and bedrooms, and shaking out carpets. On Sunday, once more donning her fancy hat and walking the ten blocks to the First Methodist Church, Florence chose a back pew distant from eye contact with the pastor and after the service slid between two parishioners shaking hands with him at the doorway.

She made Fred his favorite suppers that weekend and baked rhubarb crisp with extra crunchy topping. Sunday evening, he sat on the stoop after the meal and smoked until the sky grew dark and the earliest stars appeared.

The vegetables would wilt and die unless they had a rainy summer, and the weeds would overtake the garden in a matter of a few weeks no matter. Any produce that came on would rot. Still, the carrots and beets needed to be thinned before leaving, the dirt between the corn stocks hoed. As the days became hotter, the ten

35

potato plants would require more of the straw for mulching that lay in a corner of the garden.

Fred didn't ask about Homer, didn't seemed bothered they hadn't heard from him. The shoebox contained the letters free from greasy smudges and careless creases and dog-eared edges. Florence read over the ones that had come whenever she had the chance.

Once her training started, Fred's meals were served on time and as luck would have it, he did not arrive back at the house before she did. For the first time ever, she welcomed the fact that the Elbow Room was his second home. Otherwise, he may have commented, more likely, griped about the number of slow-cooked meals.

"It's because of the rationing." If he asked. The poor quality of meat required longer cook times and stews and soups stretched other limited supplies.

The Saturday evening before the training started, they sat side-by-side in their rockers in the living room in silence. It was wet out, uncomfortably damp. He wasn't able to settle so he lit a fire to take off the chill.

"No surprise this damn weather. Hate to be using our wood this time of year but I don't think we're gonna have a summer, Flossie." The night air aggravated his cough making him fidget in his rocker and shifting to find a comfortable spot. The crackling fire gradually warmed the room and radiated a halo of soft yellow light. His cough eased finally and after a time she absently counted his regular snores and gurgles. Tired after combining three days' work into one, her shoulders felt tight. Monday would be her first day of training. Fred's head rested against the rocker's cushion and occasionally when he snorted he lifted his head and mumbled, "It ain't straight, goddammit." His dreams were always about work.

It was better he didn't know. The next two weeks were critical, being in a classroom after so many years, and then balancing her responsibilities at home. One more fight, one more tantrum, was one more reason not to tell him. She'd slip out of his life, not let him tell her what she was allowed or not allowed to do. While mending the sleeve of his workshirt in the dim light, he swallowed wrong and woke himself up.

36

"Goddamn it. I'm going to bed. I gotta get some sleep." He'd been asleep for nearly an hour in the rocker.

The weekend rain soaked the garden down and after church she put a bit more straw around the potatoes. They were growing fast, as was the rhubarb, with enough stalks for one more pie.

Martin-Ten

The Intelligence officer had missed the flicker of wonderment. In the windowless, dimly lit room, he had to squint to read out the code name they assigned him.

"Martin Clarke." Martin stared into his lap. A bland, unremarkable name that would blend wherever he was sent, a perfect replacement for Professor of Geology, Johann Meidenger. Their cleverness mildly impressed him, the surprising insight that the name could be British or Canadian, German or even Austrian.

Night after night at 1:00 am or 3:00 or 2:30, they shook him awake yelling at him, demanding instant answers. "What's your name?"

"Martin Clarke." They couldn't catch him in a mistake when they woke him. One time, some muscular blond officer with a toothbrush mustache not two inches from his face with teeth like a gopher spit on him. "What's your real name? Why are you lying."

They dragged him down the brilliantly lit hall without letting his feet connect to the floor. Inside a similarly bright cubicle they hit him, beating him just enough not to leave tracks. "What's your real name?" Not every night. Maybe on the third night or the fourth, they'd start again. The worst of it was being deprived of his cigarettes. "This is what's gonna happen to you if you're caught." As if they relished the idea. "They'll wipe that smug smirk right off your face. For good." They enjoyed this assignment too much.

"Martin Clarke." He embraced Martin Clarke and was born anew. On a metal table, a pack of fags between him and the interrogator taunted at him. "I'm Martin Clarke." Aggressive, dimwitted pigs. His family name, Meidenger, the name he hauled behind him like a miserable bag of rocks all his life, now instantly erased, vanished and replaced on a single official document. Behind his inscrutable expression he buried his satisfaction.

Six weeks into his training and roused unpredictably from a deep sleep, he'd spout, "Martin Clarke, Sir." Martin Clarke, the man without a past, a blank piece of white paper, starting over, free from a doting mother, a regimented education, bullies and gossips, a humiliating father.

Who was Martin Clarke? The Abwehr described him as a genial if somewhat reclusive, a reliable worker, always trustworthy and generous with his co-workers. They shrugged, threw up their hands in despair at their failed attempts to make him seem less a hermit. As for being reliable, that was a woefully inadequate word for a man whose obsessive attention to detail annoyed to the point of making him hated and isolated. But the commonplace name with its vague roots had the possibility of reinventing who he was.

The woman's glances coincided with the train's whistle. An elderly gentleman helped by a solicitous daughter got on the train at a brief stop and settled next to Martin.

"He's a little blind." The daughter confided, smiling hopefully. "He's getting off in two stops. I'd be grateful if you'd help him."

The nearer they got to Sudbury, the more frequent her glances and more than a hint of the coquet behind her eyes. In thirty minutes they'd pull into the Sudbury station. Martin scanned the coach, letting his eyes fall on her so briefly he should have missed her licking her lips. To cover the awkward moment, he opened his valise and with deliberate slowness fumbled with the latches, intending to stow his book. The hefty steel door at the rear of the coach built to hold back the noise from the clacking wheels, opened and then slammed shut with the sucking sound of a pneumatic tube. Someone had slipped into or out of the coach and he'd missed it. He'd noted a man earlier wearing a dark gray suit sitting on the left side of the coach. He'd disappeared. Then, there was the other man sitting directly behind him two rows wearing a black bowler who was still there.

Martin helped the old man off at his stop but when he returned to his place, the woman had changed seats and was smiling up at him from the one just vacated. She smelled of lavender. More passengers boarded and wiggled past him because he hadn't move out of the aisle.

"Excuse me." A grandmotherly woman with a satchel overflowing with carrot greens said gently needing room to pass. Her hair, gray and straggly as the vegetable tops, seemed to be fleeing from under her woefully inadequate hat.

"Here, take this one." Martin pointed to the vacant seat next to the woman.

"No, honey. I can't take your seat. But, that's a kind gentleman, you are."

"Not at all." He was surprised how easily the English flew off his tongue. "I need to stretch my legs, anyway. Sitting too long."

"Well, don't you have a lovely smile. And a generous nature to go with it." He accidentally knocked her hat when she brushed past him and it now sat cockeyed on her head. She didn't bother to right it as her produce was drifting into the aisle so he offered to put it overhead. "Honey, I won't be able to reach it if you do that."

"That's okay. I'll get it down for you." His Marzipan lady sniffed and turned her head toward the window. He'd had been warned not to make enemies and his valise rested on the floor on the other side of her knees. After the grandmother was settled, he tapped her on the shoulder.

"How far are you going?" His cheeks crinkled pleasantly. The gung-ho trainers in Germany would be mollified.

"Calgary." She talked like she was holding a clothespin on her nose.

"You've got a long ride ahead, then. I've been admiring your hat. It really suits you." He spoke over the older woman's shoulders.

"Where you going?" She turned with some hesitation toward him.

"I'm visiting relatives up Timmins way." He lied.

"Oh. Getting off at Sudbury then." Her pretty lips pouted.

"That's right."

"Well, have a good trip."

"You, too." He smiled, but she'd turned head to watch the front of the train curve as it came back to meet itself.

Florence-Eleven

Uneven bureaucratic flooring inside the training facility's unventilated hallway squealed when treaded upon, a perfect place for lurking gnomes to hide in its shadowy crannies. The passage was empty and had the institutional feel and smell of the halls at Missoula County High School where Homer should be graduating. Her footsteps echoed off the pallid walls and she felt self-conscious. Fluorescent bulbs tucked into the ceiling panels blinked and buzzed between ones that had simply given up. Walking along was like a bad dream inside a strange house, looking for a way out only to discover more rooms and no exists, each room odder than the one before it.

A sudden burst of boisterous male laughter came from the end of the corridor, guiding her to a doorway that opened into a brightly lit but windowless classroom. Every chair was taken except one next to three women. Florence peeked at her Sunday church wristwatch dreading that after careful planning even down to the last minute from before and after Fred left the house, she had arrived late.

The women sitting in the left back corner either had claimed that spot for themselves or it had been assigned. The most matronly among them caught her eye in the doorway and gestured to the empty chair beside her. The men stopped talking and turned their heads to watch Florence go to her seat. A few smiled kindly, the others grimaced and shook their heads. The instructor came in immediately after her, shutting the door hard and slamming their former lives behind them and closing them in with the smell of stale air and the perfume of one of the women.

"Hang on to your hat. Here we go and honey, you'll do just fine." The matron raised an eyebrow and patted her knee.

"Let's get started." His facial expression, if any, was lost behind wire rim glasses, the cheekbones pasty under the fluorescent lights, and the light hairs on his forearms glistened where his sleeves had been rolled up. He quickly moved to the blackboard and described with his back to them the day's agenda. The room felt stuffy but he brought a whirlwind of energy into it, and despite wearing heavy field boots he shifted and swayed as if he wore ballet slippers.

41

By lunchtime, they'd learned his name was Ken, because a forest service person ducked in briefly to speak to him. Later, they learned Ken had pioneered on forest fires and was among those earliest spotters who had worked out of tents or lean-tos on the mountains before special equipment was invented. "It takes some getting used to. This fandangled stuff. That, and a little math." He chuckled to himself. "It's the most precise tool for locating a fire invented. Don't worry. You'll be able to operate it after a few lessons."

"Time to send them ladies back to the kitchen, then." A leathery man in the second row with a grizzly beard that hung down on his chest turned halfway around, sniffing the air at the women in the corner. His chair couldn't contain all his girth so it spilled over the edges. Another woman named Hattie McCloud tittered but stopped when the matron gave her a teacher's scowl.

"Harrumph!" Like a block of ice, the matron had no recognizable waist but unlike the bearded man sneering, neither was there any flab. Her interjection was a not subtle warning to the women to stand up for themselves and each other from this point forward. Ken ignored the exchange, charged ahead describing the most difficult piece of equipment they would have to master. "The Osborne Fire Finder. But believe me." He blinked several times behind his thick lenses. "You'll get enough practice on it. You'll know it forwards and backwards and be dreaming about it to boot."

On the wall next to where the women sat, an oversized Forest Service map stretched out like a mural. After lunch, Ken told everyone to fold up and stack their chairs on the opposite side of the room. He proceeded to hand out assignments, a single piece of paper with their individual names on it.

"This is it, ladies. Get familiar with where you're going to work." The matron clucked. Her little flock instinctively gravitated to the circle around her after the chairs were put away. The men lined up against the wall opposite the map leaving a space of three feet between them and the women.

"Mrs. Hickson?" Florence stepped out of the safety of the women's sphere, the first woman called up. Two men before her, the bearded one and another near her age, studied the positions of their

42

lookouts on the map while Ken pointed out where hers was. The bearded man growled when she stood on her toes and leaned his direction, but if he meant to intimidate her, she didn't move away although he reeked of tobacco and stinky sweat.

"Let's not have any of that." Ken spoke so quietly only she and the bearded man heard him. "There is a war on, understand, and we have to work together. I don't want to hear any more of this." The bearded man picked his nose and shuffled back to the other side of the room.

"Is your husband going to collect your pay?" The youngest of the women, Grace, noticed her wedding ring during their afternoon break. Florence smiled weakly and shrugged. She'd be eating suppers and staring out at sharp peaks and into valleys below her cabin, sunflowers and tomatoes growing against the lookout walls. Not sending money to Fred.

"The most important other piece of equipment is your phone." The chairs were back in place and everyone had gotten their assignments. The wooden wall phone was a necessity for the spotters and Ken emphasized that they must use it, he held up his fingers. "Three times a day," to communicate with the ranger station. Their reports would note changes in the weather and any lightning strikes. The Osborne Finder would assess the accurate location of a strike and potential fire. Florence was paired with Grace to practice using the Finder that displayed the topographical map of their specific lookout assignments.

"McGregor Peak." Ken repeated her assigned location. A Lookout in the Flathead National Forest, three miles from the Canadian border. "Your speed in making reports, and your accuracy is critical to the Smokechasers at the base camps." Ken reminded them that those men lived in tents and slept in quilted bedding just waiting to be told where to rush to put out a fire.

"You'll get the hang of it soon enough." The matron really was a schoolteacher the rest of the year. Everyone addressed her as Miss Conrad and the men mostly avoided her because she knew what she was talking about as a third year smoke spotter. "The mountaintop. A reprieve from twenty-six knuckleheads." She laughed.

43

"I'm here because I want to help out with the war." Miss Conrad could carry Hattie McCloud on her back for a mile or more if she had to. Florence wondered how someone so delicate could live and work at a lookout tower. If this was the kind of people they'd interviewed, she'd been foolish to think she wouldn't get the job. "They hired a pipsqueak." She said it under her breath. "The Forest Service must really be in a pinch."

Martin-Twelve

Sudbury sat atop the Precambrian shelf above the igneous rock of the Canadian Shield, one of the world's richest areas for mineral ores, especially nickel, gold, silver and copper. A meteorite once crashed there and its impact formed a huge bowl known as the Sudbury Basin. In this treeless landscape, a traveler would first see the slag heaps and exposed permanently stained rocky outcrops charcoal black from the putrefied air from the roasting yards. Its first view is depressing and immediately imprinted on the psyche.

A creeping melancholy, a stormy cloud drifted over Martin's mind by degrees obscuring his personal sun as the train passed boldly through the changing landscape. In Germany, the Abwehr had interrogated him, questioning his drive and loyalty. "What do you remember about Canada? Were you happy there? Do you have any attachments, any contacts, any friends?" He gave their silly questions one word answers.

"No." His pal Billy might still be living in Timmins.

"Are you lying?" Lying about what? He didn't have any loyalties.

"No."

"Can you carry out your assignment faithfully?"

"Yes."

They shoved photos in front of him, one of the house where he'd lived until he was ten. He remembered it had been painted blue. A cracker box, but as a boy, it seemed much larger. There was even a picture of the back yard. He'd forgotten there wasn't a fence, and then several gritty black and white photos of the nearby fields where he and Billy and the others played ball. The last photo of the Sudbury Basin, a barren and unforgettable image for a ten-year-old.

"How do these make you feel?" He shrugged, lit a cigarette and blew the smoke impolitely near their faces.

The train tooted at intervals on the outskirts of Sudbury winding down as if lamenting its entrance to a graveyard. An ancient sadness caught him off guard, a mixture of feelings from having been thrust into a new life in Germany's confined spaces and intrusive cultural mores after the sudden and unexplained uprooting from his friends and Canada's expansiveness. Sterile Sudbury, resembled a volcanic eruption with skeletal orphaned-trees.

He lit a cigarette puffing on it in rhythm with the train's motion. The desolate environment mirrored his psyche. When he was overly tired, or if he let his guard down it sneaked in and threw him into a depression that could last for weeks. The boys from the train window running through the field had aroused a sadness. Then, the lavender woman who reminded him of Marzipan and first flirted and then gave him the cold shoulder, and there was that sense of unseen eyes piercing into the back of his skull on all the trains he'd boarded in Canada.

Germany was frothing, in the throes of a patriotic epileptic fit. Martin had mostly sidestepped the Hitler clatter, the screaming and swooning, the adulating crowds. He sequestered himself in his university office between classes to avoid fervid students shouting slogans. His Swabish mother exalted, "The Fuhrer is what we have been waiting for. God has listened and finally answered our prayers." She clapped her hands and put up a flag as did her neighbors.

The marionette salutes, pompous parades, the spider flags fluttering even above chalets in remote hamlets, didn't entice him. The intemporate emotional fever only embarrassed him, as did his mother's. When informed he was going to Canada, he barely nodded. Canada, the repository of his best memories.

A saboteur, the antithesis of his professorial career, intrigued him. He had no loyalties. He'd studied geology because he was good at it and needed a position but he hated the classroom tedium and the tiresome students. In ongoing research, he'd been able to explore exotic places that gave him the kind of independence he knew as a young boy in northern Canada.

World politics always repetitive, always unfinished, would come and go, the unstoppable pendulum that shifts from one extreme point to its opposite. He scoffed at people like his mother who believed a forceful leader's promises to bring about necessary and legitimate changes and improve the quality of their lives. Because of it, however, he'd been handed an assignment he could never have imagined, one that transformed his colorless professorial life into one of intrigue. He would have to rely on his instincts and that stirred something that had been hollow in him. His stoicism unnerved his trainers, however, made them question his motives, over and over they asked, because they weren't ever sure where he stood or what loyalties he had. He was a risk but they were putting him at risk, a risk that might cost him his life. On the whole, it didn't seem a remarkable sacrifice and they'd given him a purpose, something he hadn't realized he was missing.

He rented the room above the appliance store where he could watch the comings and goings at the Balmoral Hotel and café. The rental owner didn't want to rent to him. "Most of them workers up there at Falconbridge lives up there, too." The man waited for a persuasive reply but Martin didn't answer. The portly man shifted his weight back and forth from one leg to the other, waiting.

"Christ," Martin said under his breath. "How much a month?" The owner snapped out the price and quickly pocketed the dollars for two months' rent.

"That how long you stayin', then?"

Faded blue wallpaper of Parisian café scenes peeled away from around the small sink in the miniscule kitchenette that included a gas two-burner stove, an icebox, three plates, two cups, one glass, and a hobo toaster. The bed was too soft and too narrow but long enough to accommodate his frame, and smelled dank. A metal table in the middle of the room had two chairs and was covered with an oily cloth that disguised the dents.

For the next three days he scouted Sudbury and the company towns of Copper Cliff, Lively, Onaping Falls picking out the major landmarks and learning the names of streets and where they went and how they ended. He surveyed the immigrant populations, especially the Finns. That's where he would find an ally, either among them or the Italians.

He took the street car lines memorizing each stop and its schedule. He verified all the Canadian Railways timetables across the provinces, learned the business hours of cafes and stores and crafted a place to stow explosives beneath the linoleum in the kitchen.

In the department store he went in search of a wool blanket but spotted his neighbor clerking in the ladies section. She saw him before he saw her and smiled when he looked her direction. He nodded and left the store without buying a blanket to replace the one on the cot that was saturated with unwholesome odors from previous tenants.

Florence-Thirteen

As luck would have it, the second day of Florence's training coincided with Fred's new job down in Lolo which added ten miles to his travel time. It meant a bonus of a half hour for her. Before he had his pants on and shirt buttoned, a breakfast of two sunny-sides up eggs, two pieces of homemade toast with her year-old raspberry jam, and a slice of fried spam waited for him. He looked glum as the weather under the similarly glum ceiling fixture and between bouts of hacking cough fixated on the salt shaker and wolfed down one whole egg before taking a swig of coffee.

"Dammit, Flossie, why didn't you tell me it was so goddamn hot? I just burnt my tongue. Fine way to start a job. Goddammit!" He slammed his fist down and a dollop of jelly fell into his plate as he bit off half a piece of toast.

Rain that started during the night and hadn't stopped made the twenty-minute walk to the training facility an obstacle course with puddles the size of wheelbarrows. Her umbrella sagged at one corner and the loose hair sticking out under her felt hat twisted into miniature corkscrews.

"I must look a sight." The raincoat hadn't kept the rain off her legs. Once inside the building, she wiped her feet on the mat creating her own puddle and attempted to tame the wild hair with her fingers.

Muddy footprints left by someone who hadn't bothered using the mat at the entrance made a trail leading down the hallway to the classroom and the floor was slick. Her boots were half the size of the tracks she slipped into.

Going from the gloomy weather and the dim hallway into the training room was like emerging from a cave. Ken's color matched the gray of the wall at the front of the room where he laid out devices on a long folding table. Because of the damp weather, his plan to demonstrate and practice on the equipment outdoors had gone by the wayside. He was fluid as a penned coyote running along its boundary. The grizzled man was one of three people who'd come earlier and underneath his chair the floor was soiled and damp. Miss

Conrad came in after Florence, who had already taken her seat by Hattie.

"Aha!" The matron seemed pleased and hurried over to hand them a list of instructions.

"La de da. Here comes Miss-Know-It-All." Ken shifted items around the table while the other man who had arrived ahead of Florence cleared his throat and went over to Ken to help out. The scoffer was near in age to the matron and although Ken had chastened him the previous day, it didn't improve his manner. He had chosen Miss Conrad to target and goad. She, however, having spent the last twenty years with rambunctious boys whose sole objective was to get a reaction from her, dismissed him like a pesky mosquito. What seemed to drive her was a desire to set an example to the women that if ever there was a time to stand up for themselves, it would be on the mountain.

"Come hell or high water." Miss Conrad smiled at "my ladies." They were getting a quick and important lesson in how to take charge of unruly behavior.

Ken spent the morning explaining the parts of the equipment, the mechanics for adjusting the Osborne Fire finder, and how to make and record measurements. "Remember, three times a day you report to the ranger station." He repeated this phrase throughout the day. They started raising three fingers each time he said it.

"You gotta be as accurate as you can about where you spot smoke. And don't knee-jerk it. Be accurate first!" It must have been worth repeating three times. "Those smoke chasers are gonna be running up and down trails to get to your smoke and if it turns out you've sent them on a wild goose and it's just fog or a mirage that could cost them three important days somewhere else."

The following day Miss Conrad ushered the women into an adjoining room. "That Pipsqueak," as Miss Conrad called him, was the only man to titter when the women filed out. "You gonna talk about that woman thing, ain't you?" The men got to leave early.

"Okay, ladies. I hate to admit it, but Mr. Pipsqueak is correct. We are going to talk about how to deal with female matters at your lookouts. I don't want to scare you, but animals in the wild gravitate toward the smell of blood. Stay off the trails early morning and late afternoon when you are menstruating. Plan your days accordingly."

The women hung their heads and blushed. Miss Conrad was not deterred. "I know. Awkward as it is, it is *that* important. Let's get the worst out of the way. Use your shovels, ladies! And I don't mean spreading a bit of dirt on top. We're not planting carrots, you know. You've got to dig a good-sized hole, and be at least a hundred yards away from your cab." They would have to come off the hill to take care of their business.

"The cab." What the forest service called lookouts, the exclusive group to which Florence had in just two days become a member.

"You don't want an amorous grizzly getting cozy some night now do you?" Florence shook her head. She'd shared a bed with Fred for twenty years.

"I get the idea," Miss Conrad winked at her.

Because the spring had been cool, it was to their advantage, Miss Conrad told them. They could collect snow and put it in their holding tanks by the cabins to use for washing. Later on, as the days grew warmer, they would have to rely on the creek or springs, whatever was nearest their facility. "With good luck ladies, that won't be more than a mile away."

How Hattie McCloud would be able to haul herself up to her cab let alone a 5-gallon bag filled with water on her shoulders was a puzzle. She was headed for a lookout near Superior in the Cabinet Mountains.

"Just remember," Ken repeated several times. "Haul your water early as you can in the morning. Make sure you get your reports in on time and stay near your phone."

"Reckon no fires start before six in the morning," one fellow chuckled. Ken didn't change expression and Miss Conrad constrained her bewildered teacher's face. "Fires are hard enough to pinpoint during the daylight hours." Ken later explained patiently.

"There are two reasons, and two reasons only, to abandon your post at the lookout. "One. "A toothache." The second reason would be a death in the family. Since the war was going on, others like Florence didn't want to say it out loud.

"The men won't do so well in isolation." Miss Conrad told them privately. For three years as a spotter, she'd seen more than one up and bolt after a few weeks on the hilltop. "We're better equipped, aren't we, for being alone?"

Martin-Fourteen

Rumor had it the women they were hiring at the nickel company would end up in the machine and blacksmith shop. The operators grumbled. "No place for a dame." Allied forces needing nickel for tanks, ships, and airplanes appealed for output to be expanded by 50 million tons for the year. Many able-bodied men had gone off to the war and women had to pick up the slack.

It was true that the work was filthy and the heat insufferable, conditions not ideal but decidedly preferable to the labor going on deep underground in the mines. Relentless pounding from the steam hammer rattled the floor drowning out even basic dialogue so hand signals substituted. Outside of work the men spoke in short, abrupt sentences and strained to understand each other. "Aye? What's that, you said?" "Say again?" Constant booming quashed any solitude or daydreaming or appetite for conversation.

If the rumor was accurate about the women, it was sure to disrupt Martin's timeline. His attempts to recruit had been hopeful so far, incrementally taking shape, but it was early days yet. Building trust with his co-workers didn't come easily. The nitty-gritty men wouldn't take to courting or wooing nor would Martin consider doing that. It was a balance knowing when to utter some frustration about the company or make a small but effective complaint or raise a doubt. Here an off-hand remark about some laxity or a safety infraction the company had ignored, or a subtle but effective gripe, gradually growing seeds of mistrust, creating skepticism, building tension. During their shift, five men rotated fiery metal side-by-side and depended on each other to stay sharp and vigilant shifting the heavy loads. Adding a woman was a sure way to ruin his plans.

Callouses rose and hardened on his once scholar's hands, the muscles in his legs and arms had grown taut and were bulging from his slim frame. The ruggedness added to his good looks but made it all the harder to fade into the background. Petsamo had readied him for the work, roughened him up, schooling him on the ins and outs of nickel production. If his father were living, he might be less disappointed in his son.

53

During his interview with NICCO, the company insisted he sign a promise not to leave the job without permission, a prerequisite for getting hired. Martin Clarke quickly penned his name to that piece of paper and immediately became an employee of the nickel works. To temper his drive he had to moderate himself and not out-produce the others. Furtive glances from the men who watched for a mistake would give them the upper hand. But, as he was precise and cautious, doing his fair share of the work and only a bit more, he began to win them over. He added an extra step here, an assist there but just enough to earn preliminary acceptance.

Unlike the trainers in the Intelligence Services, the men took to him. He didn't bullshit. He wasn't haggard and worn down but he sweat like them and became a part of the team. They agreed he wasn't a laggard nor was he trying to avoid the army. Not a Conchie who didn't believe in fighting wars. They would despise him if he proved to be a malingerer or a conscientious objector.

"Let's get a beer." The biggest of the two Finns slapped him on the back on Saturday evening of the second week. The ceaseless pounding drummed behind them seeped out into the yard beyond the forge.

"What'd you say?" Martin knew exactly, but made him repeat it.

"A beer?" The big Finn wrapped his hefty fist around an imaginary mug. Martin nodded. The Finn clapped him on the back pointing down a coarsely pebbled alleyway that curved through a row of dismal buildings. When they arrived at a corner, a red neon sign advertising LaBatt's winked from the pub's one grimy window. In the doorway they ducked under the low ceiling that tilted upward to get inside, the highest point ending up over the bar. A strand of weary Christmas lights sagged above corner tables, someone's attempt to cheer the place up. The three other workers had arrived beforehand and were standing around a high table hunched over their beers. One barely waved, the others stared vacantly into their mugs.

"What'cha havin'?" The woman behind the bar had tree-trunk arms and was giving a haphazard swipe with an unsightly cloth to the counter in front of him. She flashed a toothy grin.

"I'm buying tonight, Lilly." The Finn tapped Martin on the arm and then proceeded to count out his coins examining each one in the dim light before handing them over to her open hand. Martin tipped his pork pie cap to Lilly and the Finn.

A noisy bunch of Creighton miners, their cheeks, noses, and foreheads permanently etched black were tucked up in the corner under the Christmas lights and well on their way to soaking their misery. Seismic activity had been quiet for them that week a relief after working down in the world's deepest hole.

"What are those sons of bitches doing here?" The big Finn asked the other Finn, thumbing at the miners. He nudged Martin. "This here is our pub. Not for no stinking moles." Martin shook his head contributing to the Finn's disgust. If there was a brawl, Martin would come out swinging. To make the point obvious, he clenched his fists and the big Finn and the others saw he was on their side.

"Hey, boys." Lilly smelled trouble. Lightly tossing the dirty dishtowel over her shoulder she sauntered over to the miners' table. "Enjoying yourselves? Nobody deserves it more than you, poor fellows, but do me a big favor, would ya?" After she left the table they laughed quietly and spoke barely above whispers until one fellow started to bawl and the party was over. "Awful tough work them fellas have." Lilly breezed past Martin's table on her way to the bar raising an eyebrow aimed at the big Finn.

Martin strained to learn about their grievances. If one of the guys made a complaint, he'd agree without offering his opinion. Gradually the grumbles slipped out, cheating on wages, shoddy work conditions, crummy housing and expensive groceries, and the miserable Allies screwing up the world. He did his own mining to unearth discontent, to find who was susceptible and amenable to a well-placed suggestion.

They'd drunk five beers a piece when the big Finn started cursing in Finnish. "Goddamn Russians taking over our country." There were tears in his eyes. The other Finn nodded and looked around to see if any of the others understood. Martin studied the bottom of his beer mug.

"And we're propping them up over there." The other Finn scowled. The men had come to Canada from Petsamo because they needed the work.

"All right now, boys." Lilly interrupted just when the Finns got going. "Hate to have to remind you, but you got homes to go to, and it's time." She tapped her watch and collected their glasses and one of them swatted her butt. She giggled. The men fell out the door and zigzagged down the alley, arms over each other's shoulders. When they got to the first man's house, they yelled, "Good Night!" He waved back. Martin walked the others home and went back to his apartment.

The stairwell was dark and he fumbled for his key. He wasn't drunk but his balance was off. It was past one o'clock.

"It's very late." The lady renter mildly chided. He squinted at her in the doorway of her apartment. He nodded while searching for his key.

"I wanted to thank you for the book." Her face lightened. "How did you know I like to go fishing?"

He'd gambled and lost.

"I wonder if you would go to mass with me at 8:00. This morning?" She was still smiling.

Florence-Fifteen

Florence paced under a lackluster street lamp at the designated pick-up location. The misty late-spring air lay on her skin like a wet cloth, but as she'd rushed to put distance between her and the house, after six blocks had to stop to unbutton her red plaid Pendleton jacket. Daylight had yet to crack open the sky over Mount Sentinel and she tucked her chin into the collar. Suddenly, a paperboy emerged out of the fog his bike rattling past her to the pick-up point for the daily *Missoulian*. He was whistling *Dry Bones* and the earflaps on his cap fluttered suggesting they might fly right off his head. Breakfast, no doubt, would be waiting for him after he tossed fifty papers onto their respective stoops and before he headed off to school.

She'd put leftover rhubarb crisp out for Fred's breakfast having made his lunch the night before. By the time he realized his coffee wasn't made, she hoped the forest service vehicle would be climbing up the Evaro Hill, north of town at least fifteen miles away. "Where the hell did she go to?" He'd be perplexed but angrier that his thermos wasn't filled. He'd let her have it that evening.

Miss Conrad arrived precisely ten minutes later and tapped her wristwatch indicating it was five minutes before the agreed upon departure time. Hattie stumbled up behind her hauling her pack like a child hobo, and the men arrived all at once and then the head lights from the forest service trucks rolled out of the fog.

"Don't do a lot of traveling, do we?" Miss Conrad chuckled at Florence's stuffed pillowslip. The family suitcase, stored in the attic until Homer had hauled it down producing a cloud of dust that made her cough, was stashed somewhere in an army barrack now. Every item on the list the trainers handed out was in Florence's kit stuffed among Homer's letters, his high school photograph, sunflower seeds and a variety of vegetable seeds. Hopefully, some of the seeds would sprout, but if the soil wasn't productive, she'd find dirt where other plants grew. Given the high elevation the sun would scorch even the hardiest of plants. She'd thought to pack a shade cloth for those hot afternoons.

Grace was late. A clunky car rumbled ahead of its arrival and then swerved to the curb on the opposite side of the street. She jumped out arms flapping over to the women clustered around Miss Conrad to say their goodbyes. "Just remember, ladies, don't let anyone push you around when you're up there alone on your lookout. Nobody is going to take care of you except you, yourself, and you. Her smile had caution behind it. "Keep the rifle handy."

Silent as submissive churchgoers, they piled into their respective vehicles, one heading south into the Bitterroot, another to the west, and Florence with a few others toward the north where she would be the last to be dropped off because her lookout bordered Canada. Other spotters manning lookouts in her area were coming from another facility.

"Ladies, let's show the Forest Service what we're made of." Miss Conrad tapped the hood of the truck headed for the Cabinet Mountains and grandly shut the door after her. They returned uncertain smiles but Florence would recall the matron's words many times in the course of three months, once during a fierce stormy night when thunder sounded like bombs and she agonized that Homer was in danger somewhere.

Any hint of a sunrise or a view of the Mission Mountain peaks was quashed as clouds flowed like skirts, their hems hanging above the tiny town of St. Ignatius. At the Nine Pipes a hole in the sky let through a single squiggly line that ran across the ponds and into their faded cattails. Old mounds of nearly melted snow clung to the sides of the road here and there, and at the overlook to Flathead the men took a stretch and had a smoke. Florence stayed in the cab. The lake seemed forbidding and aloof without sunshine to brighten its cold gray water and left her feeling empty.

North of Columbia Falls the fields held onto winter. She had on her wool jacket and the truck's heater still didn't keep her toes warm despite thick socks. The mountains, if they even existed, were holed up behind the weather and for the first time she wondered if she had made a horrible mistake. Backcountry isolation didn't feel anything like being alone for hours in her warm kitchen. Hemmed in by unseen but foreboding peaks, the rutted road skirted the angry river with its menacing snarl, and gloom hung over the valley.

"Sun'll be pourin' down soon enough. More than we want and we'll be good and sorry then." She and the driver were the last two in the truck and he hadn't said a word to her until then leaving her at a loss for an answer. Less than a mile later, he dropped her off at the trailhead to McGregor Lookout. The packer was leaning against a tree smoking and hardly acknowledged them pulling up. The three mules and two horses munched at woeful bits of grass next to the road.

This man had to be counted on to bring up supplies and mail once a month. She'd written Homer with instructions where to write. For Fred, she'd left a note in the breadbox to find when he went looking for what there was to eat.

"I'll be gone for three months so take care of the garden." She'd left the ration books with the note and mentioned the canned vegetables in the fruit cellar. "When I come back, we'll talk. I won't go on living like we have. Florence."

"I haven't packed no lady up to the lookout before." The packer gleamed, eyeballing her shape while handing her the reins to a sassy black and white pinto. "Need some help gettin' up there, do you, missy?" So, it began, and Miss Conrad's words were already ringing in her ears. The matron would hold her ground and she expected them to do likewise.

"Don't put up with anything or anybody you don't want, ladies." She'd flashed a grin at her tenderfoots.

Martin-Sixteen

It took four flights of stairs for the faithful to reach God, the priests, and the entrance to Sudbury Christ the King Catholic Church. Humbling the worshipper, to reiterate his unworthiness when coming into the presence of the Almighty. In Europe, the magnificent architecture of the cathedrals handily accomplished what the religion itself couldn't do for the disenfranchised...the ability to inspire. In awe, even the unholy surrendered to the sheer enormity and the ingenuity of its soaring buildings.

Up to the age of fourteen, Martin had climbed such steps along with his mother until he refused to go any longer. He still held the grudge, and inwardly with Mary Alice next to him, scoffed at Sudbury church's inferior structure with its bargain-basement attempt to replicate the grandeur of the great cathedrals.

Early morning light was drifting through the apartment's tacky window curtain when precisely at 7:30 Mary Alice knocked at his door. He buried his head under the pillow and held his breath willing her to go away. She knocked again.

"Are you awake in there? You must be by now." She spoke to the door, rapping once more. "I don't even know your name, so whoever you are, it's time to get up for Mass."

He threw cold water over his face, but didn't shave. "Screw her. Serves her right." Still, he dressed in his travel shirt and good shoes and jacket.

"Well, you look a lot better than you did in the middle of the night." She had been floating about his door while he got ready. "It's getting late." She gestured at her wristwatch. His day-old beard didn't seem to bother her as he'd hoped.

Her gloves and hat and coat were of soft gray, the sturdy heels and pocketbook dangling at her elbow matched her ebony hair. Every detail would pass the test of a persnickety priest slipping through the crowd wickedly drooling at the prospect of dressing down offenders. No frills called attention to her person except for a slightly rebellious scarf with its tinge of red. Her underwear had to be strictly Catholic, no lacey lingerie. Sacred in that department.

Martin, in a half-awake state, struggled to keep up with Mary Alice's military stride. "Where's the fire?" He was puffing hard.

"Tsk. Late nights." She shook her head and tapped her watch again.

He was still panting inside the church where she lit a candle to some departed person and then waited for him while he caught his breath to put a coin into the slot and light his own. When the candle burst to life, he silently cursed his father's memory because no one else came to mind. At a middle pew she stopped and genuflected, making the sign of the cross simultaneously while he attempted a feeble bow longing to sit down. She promptly knelt with prayer book and rosary fingering the beads and adoring the crucifix hanging pitifully at the front. The incense made his cheeks ache and reminded him he had not had his first cigarette due to the abrupt wake-up call.

Catholic women emulating the virginal Mary, pretending to be free from sin and the stain of sexual intercourse aroused an old wound, more a hatred, for the hypocrisy. Mary Alice held her head and shoulders in the manner of the sacred statue feigning what had to be a demure demeanor, but behind that a façade of steel, and an edginess from having to protect her Catholic purity.

His mother had faithfully gone to Mass every morning before he and his father woke. She idolized the Virgin Mother and permanently regretted the act of giving in to his father, thus spent her waking hours trying to redeem her transgression. Martin was the reminder of what could never be fixed, her expression toward him often one of disgust mingled with affection. Her face torn in half by opposing feelings.

After Mass they strolled back toward the apartment. "Shall we have tea?" Her attempt to sound spontaneous felt contrived. It was a tiny place with only six tables, three taken by others who'd endured the priest's exhortation about their complacency. "Times are tough. Don't whine and complain. Skip meals if you run short of money during the week. Be like Jesus." The priest had no such worries and looked like he hadn't skipped a meal in his entire life.

They squeezed past two elderly women and Mary Alice nodded to them. Regulars, all of them, he noted. The table was away from the window. "Makes a nice change." He looked at her quizzically. "Coming for tea after Mass." She was showing him off and he was the fish caught and lifeless at the end of the hook.

Her hands fidgeted with the clasp on her purse until their order came and started again on the handle of the teacup. She ran her index finger in and out of its circle. At one point, her shoe bumped against his leg.

"Would you like to take me to a movie?" So, that's what she'd been working up to say. That was the paradox. Gradually the doors would open for Martin, one by one, but when they got to the final door she would utter a resoundingly, No!" That one would only open with a certified document.

He'd fallen into bed after midnight following his initial success with his Finnish comrades, Taavi and Erno at the beer hall, but not before discovering their fault lines. He was anxious to get started on the plan for his next moves but Mary Alice had other ideas.

How easily it came to him though once he decided what to do about her. He certainly couldn't be the first man she'd targeted. He had become her next opportunity because he roomed across the hall.

"That would be nice. But there's one problem."

"What is it?" She smiled patiently and leaned forward, ready and eager to tackle whatever could stand between them.

"I'm sorry to say." He sighed in feigned disappointment. "I am married." It was so simple.

"Oh." She turned red and looked down at her watch. "Is that really the time? I have to go…My mother is not well. Please forgive me." She left a half cup of warm tea and a biscuit behind. He ate the biscuit and thought he'd not ever had a better one.

The remainder of the day he drew up a plan of the forge locating the best positions to lay explosive devices. Instead of slipping up the stairs, he heard her plodding footsteps as he made his supper. He held the spatula still until he heard the door shut behind her. He didn't expect her to knock but he put his sketches under a loose board beneath the linoleum.

Much later, he peeked out the door to see if her lights were off and then worked a bit more. His room was thick with cigarette smoke and he went to bed only after he'd come to a decision on how to approach Taavi and Erno. In their drunkenness they had raised their complaints. He'd capitalize on those once he heard them raised again and knew they were authentic.

The pub made him nervous. Lilly was too canny for him. She may have figured him out but he couldn't read her. Nevertheless, he'd go there and drink regularly and wait and listen. He'd find the right men and the right time. Sooner or later something would open up for him.

Florence-Seventeen

On August 21 and 22 in the year 1910 the Great Fire burned over three million acres in Montana, Northern Idaho, into Eastern Washington and British Columbia. An area as large as the state of Connecticut lay charred after being fanned by strong winds. Often referred to as the Big Blowup, it left 87 people dead as well as wiping out several entire towns along the Montana/Idaho border. The whole crew of 28 men caught in the dead man zone died and perhaps because of their heroic action and the publicity that followed, the forest service was finally able to implement strategies to provide better protection to the forests.

Prior to the Big Burn, the agency teetered on extinction due to the huge expense involved and questionable return on the dollar. "Let them burn themselves out naturally." Fires were unpredictable but dry forests struck by lightning and emboldened by high winds caused vast damage to the supplies of lumber and severely damaged national forests. Instead of being eliminated, the Forest Service expanded its role and with it the "10 a.m." policy with the impressive goal of suppressing any fire reported by 10 a.m. the day following the report.

The unemployed of the Great Depression were instrumental to the suppression efforts due to the Civilian Conservation Corps (CCC) and the many people hired to build fire tower lookouts. However, Florence's lookout had been built a whole decade earlier in 1922, constructed as a D-1 log cupola cabin with a floor plan measuring 14 x 14 feet not counting the glass topper. It was sentinel toward the east into the North Fork of the Flathead River and Glacier National Park, Canada to its north, and the Kootenai National Forest to the west.

Unlike the more common fire towers, it was situated on a natural rock platform known as a ground cab. Many of the smoke spotters worked in wooden towers and climbed twenty five or thirty steps to get into them. That was case for both Miss Conrad and Hattie and Florence considered herself lucky to have this assignment.

Her first view of the quaint building reminded her of a miniature rural schoolhouse with a bell tower except that it was perched atop the tallest point of the ridge at 6,744 feet. Each of the four walls had windows and in the cupola there were double windows on each side.

A cold wind was blowing and got stronger as the pack train neared the top, and between the chill and the altitude, Florence lost her balance and nearly tumbled against her horse when she dismounted.

"You'll get used to it after a few days." The packer put his hand under her elbow. She took a few deep breaths.

"I'm all right."

He'd muttered to his animals on the way up but said nothing to her after they crossed the swollen creek an hour earlier.

"This is where you're gonna go for water when the snow runs out in your holding tank. Should be 'bout two more weeks for that happens."

He unloaded and dumped her provisions at the door of her new home. The month's worth of staples looked rather meager in its pile. Miss Conrad had urged the women to learn how to fish and shoot a rifle. With all the advice she'd given them, they'd not learned her first name and she hadn't volunteered it. Given that she was an authority, it seemed fitting to address her as Miss Conrad.

"Keep that rifle handy and you can feast on a delicious rabbit stew some suppertime. Or grouse. When you get sick and tired of beans and rice and dehydrated potatoes." She laughed. "Oh yes. You will *yearn*," she emphasized, "for fresh meat after a few weeks of canned corn beef." Florence's dad had taken her fishing and hunting and she hated both activities.

She watched the tail end of the packer's mules disappear down the trail and clapped her hands at the door of her new home. "First things first." She dusted and cleaned the cobwebs off the ladder to the cupola and at the windows before she brought in her stock of goods. Soap and cleaning materials were set by the sink, salt, flour, coffee, rice, peanut butter, and canned goods on the shelf over the window nearest the stove.

"You sure you know what you doin'? It can get mighty lonely up here." The packer had been hell bent cajoling the animals along up the trail and then was reluctant to leave.

"I'll be just fine." She walked along the ridge later, took her first jaunt to the outhouse and surveyed the soil where she could plant her seeds. The wind had settled down but she pulled the collar up on her jacket.

"You get into trouble up here, you get on that phone. Fast as you can." He warned her. He'd lingered too long. Finally, his hesitation got the best of him. "You a married lady?"

"I am." He clamored up on his horse after that and was soon gone.

"Take a while to get here if you was in trouble." He called from the back of his horse before the path disappeared from view.

"I won't need help."

She unpacked the 125 pounds from their wooden crates and upturned them for shelving. The side of bacon, eggs, a bag each of potatoes and onions stored separately. Miss Conrad told them butter would last forever submerged in a strong salt solution and kept in a cool location. Her water supply consisted of four ten-gallon water cans. If the packer returned in a month with more supplies as he said, she had enough water for twenty cups a day.

She'd already decided on a location to plant her seeds. The following morning she'd get started. The large can now full of tomatoes would come in handy for watering when the days got warm and dry. With luck, afternoon showers would help.

The stove sat in a corner and as the sun turned low, she got familiar with how it heated, making a syrupy mixture of sugar with two cups of water along with dried apricots, prunes, and raisins for a dessert. For supper, there was fried spam and a can of vegetables.

"Just a little treat after my first meal. To celebrate." The compote was still warm. The leftovers would be tasty for breakfast. Afterward, she recorded how much water she'd used. A sliver of orange sunlight in the west shone through the dark bank of clouds as the phone rang. The clang burst into the room like a sudden and unexpected intruder making her jump up from her chair.

The three other smoke spotters in the area got very quiet when she introduced herself. "Hello. Hello?" She looked at the phone to see if she'd somehow disconnected them. They hadn't expected a woman to be on the other end.

"You bring an instrument?" One of them finally asked her.

"What? What do you mean?"

"I got my harmonica." That was George. "By the way. What's your name?"

"Florence."

"Anybody ever call you Flossie?" Joe asked before he started an Irish lullaby on his violin. The tears sprang in her eyes for her mother had sung that to her.

"You get yourself a couple of sticks and you can bang on a tin can." Henry offered and did a squeeze on the concertina.

The sun disappeared behind the banks and she sat in the dark listening to them make music and feeling melancholy and happy at the same time. She'd shut the door of her old home and passed under the maple many hours earlier and fatigue was catching up.

"You get your instrument together by tomorrow night." George said gently. "Then we'll have us a real band." He chuckled.

The cot was not a feather bed and she spent part of a fitful night tossing. She couldn't get enough air into her lungs and imagined she was suffocating.

Martin-Eighteen

"I'm giving you stinkin' fellows fair warning." Lilly set down the fifth round of five beers at their table. "If I have to, I'll grab an ear and toss you sons-a-bitches out. Maybe you don't have a home to go to, but I do."

"Ah, come on, Lilly." Erno teased and she shot him a glare before pointing up at the clock. "A half hour." He whistled at her backside when she walked away. "That's some ass." He burped.

Before Erno got distracted by Lilly, Martin had had some unexpected luck with the Finns that couldn't have been any more favorable. He chuckled thinking how the Abwehr would choke on their oatmeal if they witnessed his good fortune.

By the third beer, Martin slurred his words and as he hoped, tongues started to loosen, but then Erno shifted his focus to Taavi who got up to play darts. He and Taavi had lapsed back into Finnish after the three beers and before Lilly showed up.

"You're a real schemer." Erno said in Finnish. "Maybe you could figure out how to blow up the damn steam hammers. Now that'd be somethin' to see."

"I could do it." Taavi stuck his chest out. Martin stuck his nose deeper into his beer glass and hummed quietly.

"So, why don't you?" Erno dared him. Martin looked up at them smiling like a drunk so he could get a read on whether they were joking. By the fourth beer he had to pee in the worst way. He gripped his glass and counted backwards from 100.

"Your turn." Erno said in English to Martin. Taavi had quickly destroyed the other dart player in a game of "Around the Clock."

"Gotta go first." He pointed to the bathroom laughing.

"You do that. Can't hold your beer like us Finns." Erno bellowed.

The question for Martin at this point was timing. Lilly would be shutting the place down soon and he didn't have enough time before the pub closed to raise his own doubt about the nickel works. The tricky thing was to know when to lob his first gripe about NICCO and what it should be. As a newcomer, it would piss them off if he complained about wages since they'd swallowed that injustice long before he came along. He couldn't say anything about housing cr the exorbitant prices at the company store since he lived alone and away from the others, didn't support a family, and did his shopping in town.

He was thinking too hard and taking too long. "Where the hell are you? Tryin' to duck out on Taavi?" Erno poked his head into the toilet.

"Jesus. Can't a guy even take a leak in peace?" Erno laughed.

When the time was ripe, he'd start griping about safety conditions. Not this night. He needed solid background, a concocted but fool-proof story of where he'd worked before and the several co-workers who had been killed due to careless and inhumane management.

"How come you livin' up there over Sudbury way?" Erno asked. He was waiting outside the toilet. Martin jumped back but he'd been waiting for that question. "Got my eye on a dame there." He laughed.

Erno grinned. "That so?"

"No. I just didn't know where I'd get hired on. I took a chance and put down two month's rent cn a cheap place. Just in case."

"Is there really a dame there?" Erno's eyes glistened.

"Just an old one."

"Hell. How old is that? Never too old if you ask me."

"Old enough to run away from." Martin laughed.

"Maybe want to move down here to Coniston then."

"Yeah. Makes sense." He and Taavi started a round of "Around the Clock," and Martin was beating him. Erno hooted.

"You got some competition now, Taavi." Taavi glared at Martin who deliberately missed the board with the next throw pinning it to the wall.

"Maybe not." Taavi snickered. Erno picked up the darts after Martin lost.

"You hit the board anyways." Taavi chuckled smiling broadly after Martin's wild throw.

"Too many beers to shoot straight." Erno was out after his first throw.

"Get out of here." Lilly joked following them to the door so she could lock it behind them. Erno, Taavi and Martin left together, Taavi on one side of him, Erno on the other. They zigzagged down the road with their arms over each other's shoulders.

"Damn forge never sleeps." Erno spoke over the pounding racket that newcomers could not abide until they got so used to it they couldn't go to sleep without its repetitive beat. People suffered for months if they moved away, no longer regulated by the cacophony.

"I'd like to blow the place up," Martin said before they go to Erno's place. He even surprised himself. Maybe the beer had been stronger than he realized. "What the hell did I just say?" He slurred the sentence letting the drink be what was talking.

"That's what we should do." Erno patted him on the shoulder. "Show them buggers a thing or two." Erno hugged him.

"That'd be some show." Taavi laughed.

"Sure would." Martin bent over like he was going to puke to see if they'd say anything more. When they didn't, he stood up. "Take a bunch of explosives." He looked at them blurry-eyed. "That's the hard part." He slapped Erno on the shoulder.

He stumbled when he left them and headed down the dark road toward Sudbury.

Florence-Nineteen

Miss Conrad, ever the pragmatic teacher, had armed the women with an encyclopedic list of suggestions, shortcuts, hints, and warnings but even she couldn't think of everything, like advising Florence how to get through a horrible first night when Fred's reliable snores were missing. Or the belching and flatulence, the nightmares, the coughs, and the snorting. On the nights he came home tight, his balance off, he'd fall on top of her and immediately commence snoring.

She had tiptoed away from her family home, hustling on foot in the dull-dawn mist to the drop-off point, and ended up bouncing around in a truck with no shock absorbers for mile upon mile through dispiriting weather. She'd been cold and cramped and then fended off a bawdy packer on a remote mountain top which would give anyone reason to be wary and sleepless. But it was the absence of Fred's snoring that had her fitful.

It took a week for her lungs to grow accustomed to the thin air. She fairly giggled at her peculiar pre-dawn alarm clocks, the Columbia ground squirrels cavorting over her wood pile pinging and squeaking indignantly while the noisiest of early birds, the Clark's nutcrackers, buzzed like tubas. Her lightheadedness became worrisome when it got worse rather than better and went on for several days. During some moderate activity she found she had to sit down and put her head between her knees until a spell of dizziness passed. The second night went better, less unsettling than the first except for the lack of oxygen. She'd no sooner fall asleep and jerk awake gasping for air. The fourth night she expected the same, wondered if she would be able to endure the summer if it went on much longer. The packer told her she would get used to it but he didn't say how long it would take.

She awoke bright and ready at 5:00 am on the fifth morning following a restful night to discover the ridge had been fairy-dusted with frost making the path to the latrine perched very near the edge slick. Even with her wool Pendleton plaid on she hurried through the new daily task of hauling snow to the tank.

"Keep it filled to the brim as long as you have even a bit of snow." Miss Conrad preached. "You'll be glad you did when you have to haul your water from the creek." Someone said, "crick," instead of creek which she didn't correct but behind her teacher's eyes she flinched. "I can already hear you ladies now, come July, thanking me for this sage advice." Her eyes twinkled.

If the sun came out later it might warm the earth enough and be possible to till a spot for the garden. Although it was not likely her beets and peas had been given any attention in her Missoula garden, they would have substantial leaves by now and were many weeks ahead of whatever she would be able to grow on this ledge.

The stove warmed her chilled fingers while she made coffee, and the used grounds ended up in a jar for the future garden to enhance the soil. The oatmeal was hearty and with the remaining tablespoons of fruit compote in it the routine began for what would be a customary day at the lookout.

The men in the other towers were cautious. They hadn't expected to spend the summer ending up talking to a woman. It was a man's job with a female on the other end of the phone. "How you doin' over there, Ma'am? Not too lonely for you?" They spoke to her like she was an egg that would crack from a misplaced or swear word. Joe broke the ice after the fourth day. "You awake over there, Flossie? You're awfully quiet."

"I'm here. Don't you worry about me." At 6:00 am they had to be within earshot of the phone. In the evenings, they took turns being lookouts and eating their suppers.

"Don't look like no fire gonna come up today." George did a glissando on the harmonica. "Not with this stinkin' weather.

"Looks to be a pretty quiet long as it stays this cold. I'm gonna cozy up with Phillip Marlowe." Henry had packed in a stack of ten detective books and two atlases.

"What you gonna do, Flossie?" Henry followed Joe's lead on the nickname since she didn't seem to mind.

There was an awkward silence. She wasn't used to being asked what her plans were. Henry coughed. "Good grief. The wet air is getting to my lungs."

"I'm...I'm going to write to my boy. Homer." She immediately crossed her fingers fearful that because she'd said his name aloud to total strangers, she might jinx his safety.

"You gotta a boy in the army?" Joe soothed.

"Yes. Yes, I do."

"Where is he?" George's voice dropped an octave. "My boy's on a ship. God knows where." He hesitated. "Somewhere in the Pacific." None of them spoke for a time. The silence spoke for them.

"Best get started on the day. Keep your eyes peeled. These quiet days can sneak up and bite you when you're not looking." Miss Conrad would say the same, remind them often of their important task.

Each day she would write something newsy to Homer. After thirty days he could expect a fat letter, she promised. She described her tight but cozy room with the ladder to the cupola. She mentioned the packer who would bring his letters once a month on the pack train and that she had a good supply of food and lacked for nothing. Her companions were the squirrels and birds. She drew the floorplan of the cabin, noted where her cot and stove were, and tried to capture the view from her windows. It was a disappointing rendition. "Can't capture it at all." She described the peaks, the dense valleys, and the vast view into Canada.

Afterward, she washed the windows and scrubbed the floor. When the sun came out for a bit, she took her seeds out and covered them in precise rows where they would get the most light. It wasn't even lunchtime, yet so she made an inventory of her stock drawing pictures by each type of good, identifying it by name with the number of items in that category. She had six large cans of stewed tomatoes. Each time she used one up, she would cross one of the pictures off the chart tacked up next to her stove.

At 1:00 she got a bucket of water from the holding tank and washed two garments and hung them on the chair near the stove. After that, she washed her hair in the frigid water and got a headache from the cold. So she sat next to the drying laundry by the fire.

"Well, it's been an exciting day here." Henry chuckled that evening." Phillip Marlowe is in quite a pickle, I can tell you."

73

"Flossie, you go ahead and fix your supper." Joe had things organized. "When you're done, George you go next."

"Hey. When's it my turn? Me and Marlowe will be out of our fix by then. At the rate I'm going, in two weeks I'll have read everything I brought."

Martin-Twenty

People were bumping into each other at Lilly's Pub, spilling beer. Just the scene for a fight to break out, a too common occurrence on payday. "Too damn many of you buggers in here tonight." She mopped up puddles and bawled out whoever was in earshot at that moment. Generally, she didn't curse. She left that to her customers but she was as upset as everyone else, maybe more so. She kept the beer coming because that's what she did every time it happened, and it happened often enough, another accident at the forge. Another crushed body, what was left of it anyway, lying on a kitchen table, then moved to the family living room before the corpse took its final trip to a hole in the ground.

She'd tear herself apart if she paid attention to the hardened, overburdened shoulders, she needed consoling herself, or to scream in rage at NICCO, or empty the dam of tears she held back. The crowd was in a sullen mood and she refilled glasses and wiped up the spills. Her boys. Even the ones who didn't drink in her establishment. To keep her personal ship steady she griped about the elbows that poked into her ribs.

It was one of the Finns. Not Taavi or Erno but a fellow called Esa. NICCO immediately took the upper hand dictating a statement about how deeply sorry they were to announce the demise of a worker who had caused his own death. Standard fare. "He was reckless, we regret to report. Didn't follow regulations." They could pinpoint his fatal error, they vouched, a careless and mortal mistake for which unfortunately he paid the ultimate price. "God rest his soul. May he lie in perpetual peace." Not one sentence in condolence to the widow and five children.

"They stopped the goddamn machines for one fucking half hour." Taavi's words spit out rat-a-tat. Out of generosity, however, NICCO would pay funeral expenses. Someone in the pub started the hat around for Esa's widow for next month's rent and food. The oldest of the five kids had already been pulled out of school and sent to work.

"One free beer for anyone who puts in five bucks." Lilly yelled over bent heads. Martin put in ten. "Give the beer to Taavi and Erno."

"I'm puttin my own ten in." Erno curled his lip.

Following the burial, the Finns held a potluck at the Lutheran Church. The wives divided up the meal schedule for Esa's family which for a month's time meant bringing a hot dish each evening. It was an expense they bore as true Lutheran Christians and because it could have just as likely been one of them. Martin stood at the edge of the homespun crowd at the cemetery making sure Taavi and Erno saw him there. Then, to build on the resentment toward NICCO, he hurried to his flat and drew up a finalized plan. Timing was critical now. It couldn't happen too soon after the funeral. The anger was raw and senseless mistakes were likely. No. The anger must turn to seething resentment and sobered by their sorrow, their judgment again restored.

Martin thought he'd offended Erno when he told Lilly to give the beers to them, so to repair that , he privately told Erno he would like to contribute more to the widow's fund. "I don't have a family to support. Only my mother." He lied. "I'd like to see Esa's widow gets a fair start again." He'd misread Erno's terse snarl which came down to bitterness and grief. Erno clapped him on the back at the sizable wad of cash, many more times than ten dollars, but didn't ask where it came from and Martin shrugged and then grinned because Erno's eyes flooded into muddy pools.

For the next several weeks, the men didn't go to Lilly's. They stayed close to home leaving the place half-empty most nights. She understood. It could be anyone next time round, ground up like sausage meat and then blamed by NICCO posthumously to top it off. The men sunk into their families' bosoms for comfort so Martin poked around Little Italy to see what he could pick up there. They must be fascists, Nazi supporters, but he'd never understood the Italians, their language or why they waved their hands and shifted their bodies continually when they had so little to say.

He wound up in a storefront café with six tables crammed together. Mama and Papa were in the kitchen making cheese ravioli and small loaves of crusty yeasty bread, their top-heavy daughter serving table. On black pumps her popping steps echoed over the linoleum from one customer to the next and the big question that hung in the balance was if or when she would land chest first on someone's plate of spaghetti.

The meal was exceptional. The papa in the back room yelled at his daughter from the kitchen when she went in the back for orders. "Hopelessly trying to keep her virginity intact." How ridiculous parents are to think they have some power to direct the impulses of their adult children. He rhythmically smoked two cigarettes to the heated banter, a pair of roosters jockeying for the upper hand behind the kitchen wall, and then went back to his room.

Mary Alice was coming down the stairs as he went up. She barely nodded at him when he said good evening. He wondered where she was going at that time of evening. She wasn't unattractive, he decided, and something gnawed at him after they crossed paths. He shrugged the feeling off and pulled out his sketches. He was so absorbed he didn't notice the footsteps so when the knock came at the door he jumped up and knocked a full ashtray onto the floor.

"Just a minute." He pushed the papers together and stuffed them in his hiding place.

She couldn't ignore the butts by walking over them and bent down to pick them up. "I know you're married. And I don't expect anything to come of it, but would you hold me tonight?" She was on her knees using one hand as a brush to wipe the fine ash into her other hand. It turned out she really did have a mother she visited every Sunday after church. Only the mother had died two evenings before.

They pressed together on his cot and it sunk down to the floor in the middle. "Maybe we should go to my room." She sounded so sad. "The bed is bigger." But they didn't get up. The dread of touching a woman, for fear of losing his way once he stroked tender skin, freshly washed hair tickling his nostrils, got drowned out by her delicate perfume.

She cried a bit afterward. He held her and whispered in her ear. "It's all right. It's all right."

She was gone when he woke up. The faint scent of her lingered on the pillow. She'd left hobo toast and a cup of coffee for him. Apparently, he'd slept hard but felt uneasy the entire day.

Florence-Twenty-One

June is a month of rain in Montana. "Don't plan a wedding till July." She and Fred didn't. They went to the Justice of the Peace in Frenchtown and her dad wouldn't talk to her for two months. "If your mother was alive she'd a bat that *stupid* out of you." That's what he said when he finally gave up on being mad and came into town for his Thursday milk run.

He didn't like Fred, not up to the very end, but he made up for it with Homer. He'd drive the cantankerous seafoam green milk wagon into town and pick up Homer for a weekend here and there. Taught him everything there was to know about cow, and then because Homer kept pestering him, about horses. First how to groom and feed them, then how to ride. "They's humans, just like us, Homer. Treat 'em that way."

Florence couldn't keep her stove lit. It worked fine if the sun was out which wasn't very often. Not on rainy days. She muscled up the courage to ask why. It was either that or forego cooked meals until the weather cleared.

"Not drafting enough, Flossie. Give it more air."

"What you cookin' over there, anyways that you need the stove? Just open a can of beans." George chuckled. "That's what I'm gonna do pretty soon."

"Baking powder biscuits."

"What?" The trio drooled in unison.

"Baking powder biscuits today, if I can keep the stove going long enough to finish them."

"Now, Flossie. You got my mouth watering." George again. "You gotta be a woman to do that kinda thing."

"No you don't, George. It's easy and you can do it just as well as me."

"Well, I ain't no cook, Flossie. I'm too busy. Son-a-gun if I didn't bring me a Dashiell Hammett along. Surprised myself! Thought it was just me and Marlowe this summer." Henry was halfway through the *Maltese Falcon*.

"Want me to tell you how, anyway?" They murmured agreeably.

"Okay. It's very simple."

"That's what you say."

"Maybe you want to write this down so you have it the first time." Paper rustled in the receiver.

"Okay, Flossie. We're ready." Joe could charm a mouse out of its hole.

"Got your mixing bowl? Now take 1 cup flour and 1 teaspoon baking powder. You'd need more if we were off the mountain."

"How much more?" George liked things precise.

"I'd add another half teaspoon down in the valley. Got that?"

"Uh huh."

Now, add a quarter teaspoon salt to the flour and stir it round with a fork."

"That don't look like nothin'." Henry felt Hammett calling to him.

"You're right. Nothing yet until you take a tablespoon of shortening and mix it into the flour with your fingers." Dead space on the line.

"Okay. Got it. What's next?" George pressed.

"Did you all do that?" They mumbled yes like schoolboys about an assignment and she nodded as Miss Conrad would to her students.

"Okay, now you can add either water or milk at this point, or a combination of both, but this is the tricky part. You don't want to add too much so do it gradually. You won't need more than a half cup but don't dump it in all at once. What you want to do is just add enough liquid to pick up all your flour." Quiet on the line as they went to retrieve the liquid.

"Okay. I'm doin' what you say, but it's sticking to my fingers." Henry fussed.

"That's okay, but if it feels too sticky add a bit more flour. Now roll the dough out on your table. Use one of your large cans and roll it to a quarter inch thick." A whistle in the background.

"Dang it, Flo. I thought you said this was easy." She laughed.

"Now take a lid from a jar and cut out circles in the dough. Snuggle them inside your Dutch oven and bake them for about fifteen minutes. But watch them! Each stove is different. You don't want them to burn."

To Homer she confided. "Here I am telling men how to make biscuits, and over a phone line, no less." She ground a period to the end of the sentence with her pencil then held it against her temple and gazed out at her kingdom. Until now, her life history fit on a classroom chalkboard, and could easily be erased. She felt a bit motherish toward the fellows and pleased with them. Fred would never have stood still for a cooking lesson.

Organization with a daily schedule would be key she determined to dealing with the monotony. First task of the day: collect snow, then make coffee, take the readings and call in the report, fix breakfast. While snow water was still available, she had plenty of time to clean windows. No smudges on the glass to cloud or confuse the field of vision. "No obstructions!" Miss Conrad. The outside cupola windows were trickiest and a little terrifying. To get to that side of the glass she sat propped on the ledge, crossed her legs around the top of the ladder, leaned out backwards and held her breath.

"Keep those windows sparkling." Ken, their trainer was a weak voice after Miss Conrad's instruction.

Did George and Henry and Joe do that, like she did? Did they actually wash their windows? Keep them sparkling? They were men. With stunning courtroom speed she ruled against them in absolute judgment. How would they go about washing cupola windows? And what if they were on towers, how would they keep the windows ship-shape? Henry wouldn't know a smudge unless investigated by Phillip Marlowe or Sam Spade.

Glacier lilies, hardy lemon-yellow petals supported on insubstantial stems, suddenly began poking out around the D-1, stars exploding golden fireworks over the ridge line, the more stalwart pushing up through rapidly diminishing snow and between rocky outcroppings. She was no artist but attempted to capture the fragile, exotic flower for Homer in her daily record. He must be overseas by now, six weeks of basic training well behind him.

The *isolation!* It still rang in her ears. The evangelicals down in Missoula sermonizing what to do when the anxiety on the mountain raised its ugly head after being cut off from the rest of the world, suspended from real life. Their apostolic warning turned out to be

80

nothing but empty words. She'd never felt freer except maybe when riding bareback on her palomino near Frenchtown, speeding across whiskery fields in late fall, sucking in the pungent smell of decaying leaves, her jacket wide open and the chilly air flowing over her neck and onto her cheeks. Ruddy-faced, she raced back and into the steamy kitchen redolent of deer meat with garlic her mother had in the oven.

There was purpose. In an odd way, she was shoulder-to-shoulder with Homer however and wherever he was doing her duty. Before falling to sleep on her cot though, the truth peeked undeterred at her through closed eyelids. It was more than purpose, more than duty. Something she would need to address. Later. Sometime before September.

"You been holding out on us, Flossie." Joe played the ending notes of an old Irish ballad.

"What do you mean?"

"Why didn't tell us about your singin'?" Henry jumped in.

Had she sung out loud, over the phone?" Her face felt hot.

"Well, you ain't gettin' away with that no longer." George's harmonica bleated.

"No, you ain't. You're gonna have to sing to us from now till September." Joe plucked a high "A.". "What's say we do a duet. Right now, Flossie." He started the familiar melody again not bothering to wait for her assent.

At least they couldn't see her blushing.

"You ready?" Joe stopped and waited. "Okay. You ready now?" He began again.

"Ready." The sweet soprano wafted through the evening air exquisite as pine scent on the breeze.

Martin-Twenty-Two

The stale air fogged up the room from a surfeit of smoked cigarettes. With windows shut, a towel stuffed at the crack under the door, he worked within the circle of a flashlight beam. If he used the stove, it was only after he heard the key in her lock and then the diminishing clack of her black pumps down the stairs. In the evenings, he ate bread with salami and listened in reverse for her tread up the stairs, and then the hesitation outside his door, holding his breath until footsteps again, and the key in her lock. Finally.

The week before, Mary Alice had unburdened her grief and pent up sexual longing and temporarily addled his brain, and after that he had the headache of finding ways to miss her comings and goings. On Tuesday evening at 9:00, he was pretty sure she was sobbing outside his door.

On Sunday evening, she completely put him off the last bites of salami and cheese the way she stopped and started coming up the stairs like an old woman with a bad hip, and to top it off, on the landing issuing a plaintive sigh. It wasn't his fault she'd ended up an old maid who couldn't find a husband and had lost her old lady.

He waited until 11:00 before turning the light on supposing she'd gone to bed. Her schedule, her routine, going to her job Monday morning would get her mind off things, work was always best for what ails you, and the harder it is, the better. He'd remain in the shadows and hopefully she'd forget about him before he'd finished the job he came to do.

A light knock at the door. *Shit.* A muffled double tap, pleading, not her one sharp thump. He flinched but didn't move, snuffed out the butt of his cigarette but the light was on. With luck, the towel sopped up its shine before it slid under the door. Another muted tap, more insistent, this time. *Jesus.* She must have heard him, smelled the cigarettes, or seen his light. He looked at his watch. 11:30. She should have been asleep for an hour already.

He didn't have a strategic step to counter her moves. The Brunhilda trainers should have armed him for this kind of woman. What he had thought was a brilliant plan, the preemptive attempt to keep her at a distance by producing a nonexistent wife had failed miserably. Why is it people lose their inhibitions when someone dies? A way to ward off their own final curtain? She would be abashed if she took a good look at herself, practically begging. Wasn't there anyone beside him she could find to go to for solace?

Another knock, double time. More strident. Impatient or more desperate? "I'll tell her she's ugly. No. I'll say I don't like older women. No, no. I'll say my young, emphasis *young*, wife is coming in a few days."

The Abwehr expected him to complete his mission in three months. Get in, make the necessary contacts, put the plan together, blow the damn thing up and get back to Gaspé. Never linger. Each Wednesday starting in September if the weather held and Canadian surveillance could be jammed, a U-boat patrolling the North Atlantic would slide into the bay after dark and wait for his signal. Three long, two short flashes of light. What assignment would he get after the job in Sudbury and submarined back to Germany?

She had been vulnerable, grieving, and lonely and he'd taken pity on her. Now she was going to be in the way if she got it in her head to push him. If she knocked once more, goddammit, he'd act cold as ice, curt. But maybe she couldn't get to sleep so she got up and made him another of her tasteless casseroles. Okay. He'd be pleasant enough when he opened the door, but if she got soppy on him again, started whining, he'd send her packing. It was a short hop for her to be waiting every evening for him to get back from work. She'd get jealous if he didn't spend his off-hours with her, want to know what he was doing when he wasn't there. He wasn't having her around asking questions, sticking her nose into his business, hanging on him, pouting if he didn't come back to her home cooked suppers.

Insistent. She knew he was in the room. He nearly felt her body heat radiating through the door. He waited for the defeated footsteps to surrender and walk back across the hallway. No more taps but no footsteps either.

The sketches like an architect's blueprints papered the oily tablecloth. If he gathered them up she was sure to hear the rattle. The knocking started again, and this time it didn't care if God heard it.

"Goddamn." He cursed loudly and stuffed the sketches into their hiding place.

"This is it!" He threw the door open saying just that. The scowl caught Erno and Taavi off guard "You wasn't expecting visitors, I guess." Erno put his thumb up like he was going to hitch a ride back to wherever he'd come from. "Maybe we shoulda said we was coming ahead of time."

"We come back another time." Taavi had pleaded with Erno not to show up in the dead of night in the first place.

"What?" Martin confounded thinking he was facing Mary Alice in the doorway. "No, no. Glad to see you." Mary Alice up to her chin in a grandmother's nightgown watched from the end of the hallway half inside the doorframe, critiquing his visitors. He pretended he didn't notice her. "Just wasn't expecting visitors, is all." He meant for her to hear it. He slapped them both on the shoulders. "Come in. Come in. Good to see you."

"Jesus, Mary, and Joseph." Erno sniffed. "Smells like a whorehouse in here. You ever open your damn windows or they painted shut?"

Martin laughed. "Guess I forgot." Pulling out a bottle of whiskey for just such an occasion. "I got some of the good stuff. Warm our spirits and our heart!" He waved the bottle at them and winked. He heard Mary Alice shut her door a few minutes later.

"By God. You is full of surprises." Erno grinned but Taavi looked like he wanted to be someplace else, maybe anywhere else.

Florence-Twenty-Three

"By Golly, Flossie, you got me plain addicted to them powder milk biscuits of yours. I got enough for a week. What else you get up that sleeve of yours?" The hours turtled along. Only a fool who couldn't find something to keep busy counted raindrops and that quickly turned into a fruitless effort.

"I shoulda brought thirty books." He'd finished *The Big Sleep* and Henry was suffering the all too painful reality of running out of Phillip Marlowe stories. Every avid reader's conundrum, either limit the time spent reading or run out of books and face the readerless abyss.

"You can always start over again." George whittled something on a piece of firewood.

"Or how about it, Flossie? What else you cookin' up over there you can teach us?" His previous summers at fire towers, instilled in Joe, like Miss Conrad, a long view. Stay optimistic, stay busy and the days will move along.

"Them biscuits turned out like cow patties." It was an effort to put up with Henry's perpetual gripe about life's continuous grievances.

"Don't judge your efforts so harshly. If you keep it up, with practice you'll get the hang of it." Miss Conrad's words wafting on the air currents. How did she encourage disappointed students? She willed it, Florence thought, set her mind to it just as she willed the hostile man out of their training group. One bad apple, her father would say although he never said that about Fred, much as he didn't like him.

"You just don't put an aggressive stallion in with a lead mare that don't want to mate. That don't make no sense." His way of saying she and Fred were not meant for each other and his one piece of advice after he got over being mad at her for going off to get married. "Your mother, god rest her, shoulda been here to see you through this thing. I thought you'd figure it out. You always did, always had the common sense." Until Fred.

"He ain't a bad fellow." If he wasn't married to her. Her father promised not to bad mouth Fred now they were married. "But don't expect me to like him. Good, steady worker, that's for sure." True. He never lacked for a job, kept a roof over their heads, food on the table. "It's the way he was raised, Florence. His ma always coddling him like he was two years old because his pa beat him up regular like. Mean bugger. Just because he could. Poor guy don't know if he's comin' or going in that brain of his and that ain't ever going to change. I don't begrudge him a good life, Florence. Just wish he wasn't with my daughter. And I ain't gonna ever say no more on this." He didn't. Stayed true to his word to the end.

"Tell me again why we are sittin' up here? Are they out of their cotton-pickin' minds? Waste of the government's money. Shoulda waited till July to send us up here."

"You never know, Henry." Joe cautioned. Still, you couldn't argue since it was the third straight day without let up. Anyone with half a brain, Henry said, could figure out no fire was gonna burn down the damn soaked woods.

"How you getting along, Flossie?" Joe hinted about another recipe.

"I'm fine." In fact, she was pleased. The holding tank was full and she would have water longer than she had expected. In Missoula they'd cautioned that by mid-June they'd have to haul water. It was now the middle of the month.

On one halfway decent morning she went down to where the packer had showed her where to access the stream. It would take some getting used to hauling the pack up but at least now she knew what she was up against when the time came.

She slept deeply. Felt strong. Her lungs expanded to capture more oxygen. The muscles in her calves and thighs were taut. She wondered how Hattie was getting along and what she was doing to stay busy on rainy days, if it was raining in the Cabinets like it was here on the Canadian border. Homer, too. What was he doing? Where was he? Her letters to him were cheery and about her garden's progress, the antics of a Clark's nutcracker that visited her in the cupola very early in the mornings having adopted her, and the amusing phone conversations with the men who entertained her in the evenings.

86

I taught them how to make sour dough starter for their pancakes because it's raining like crazy and they need to stay busy. They'll have to tend to it every day and that gives them something to do. She talked about Miss Conrad, too. *I never thought about how hard it must be to face a room full of students. Every day. I can't think how you would teach stubborn or ornery kids. She'd have these men on the end of my line figured out. They're very nice to me now that they's gotten used to me being a woman. They listen to me and, Homer, they are about as different from each other as you can imagine. One of them, that's Joe, well, your grandpa would say he's like a Border collie. I don't know if he's been assigned to do it, but he makes it his business to know before everyone else what they're thinking and points us in the right direction if we go haywire. That's easy enough because we're like birds up here on our perches locked in the clouds and rain. He's so easygoing, doesn't get upset if we grumble or, like Henry, want to throw in the towel every other day, maybe every day! Henry is the poodle. Things have to be just so. I bet you wouldn't find anything out of place ever in his cab. If everything is not right, and I mean everything, he fusses and goes on fussing after he's fussed. Sometimes I'd like to wring his neck but I don't say anything. I wait and hope he gets tired of hearing himself complain. When he's done with that we hear about Philip Marlowe. I didn't know anything about mysteries before Henry. I might get myself one of those stories when I get off the mountain this fall. Then, there's George. He's kind, like Joe, and smart in his own way, but different than how Henry is smart. His son is in the Navy and he doesn't know where and that's all we know except that he makes the harmonica sing. I guess he's a bit of both of them which makes him the mutt. Then, there's me. I wonder what kind of dog I am.* And what about Fred? What would he be? Her dad would know.

Thoughts about Fred came at the oddest moments. Not when the morning creatures woke her with their noises that somewhat resembled his snoring. Nor when she was doing her reports or washing the windows of the cupola. No, but when she ferried water from the tank to the cab, she imagined him hauling a board or hammering nails on a ladder. Or, when the fellows came on the line at the end of the day she pictured his shadow in the rocker, not drunk just swaying back and forth contemplating the mantelpiece.

Soon it would be July. On the fourth day of rainy afternoons, she sat at her table and wrote as she did every afternoon, but not to Homer. She wrote to herself, words that dripped like droplets from a pinprick. She wrote about the chair. The one Fred launched at her when she came home with horsemeat from the butcher. Its leg gouged into the arm she put up to protect herself. It was beastly warm in church that next Sunday but she kept her coat on to hide the ugly gash.

She remembered that she hadn't gotten angry. How could she be? He deserved decent food even when there wasn't any to be had and it had been her fault for making the joke. "You know how you can tell there's a war on? Horsemeat's the special at the butcher's." She laughed. He might not have even known what it was after she had it prepared if she hadn't said so.

It rained for a fifth day and she wrote. Every day it rained her list of grievances grew going so far back as Homer's birth, and something began to shift in her. A peculiar sensation, like a hand that falls asleep and prickles when it is shaken as the blood flows back into it.

"Flossie, sing one of them Irish tunes. Cheer us up before we drown." Poor George lamented. "I ain't never seed so much rain. We ain't going to spot a fire this summer."

"Don't count your chickens just yet, George. You'll forget all about this when those hot July days dry out all them nice tall green grass." Joe had worries. This much rain pointed to a firecracker season.

Her injustices piled up, too. The high altitude was no longer causing her fitful nights. Old bruises and insults did.

Martin-Twenty-Four

Sweat bubbled up from the roots of Erno's graying hairline, a random drop plopping onto his one good shirt from the short-clipped hair. "Jesus, Martin. Nobody told you it's summer in Sudbury?" Martin opened the three windows but the night air hung flaccid, the room still a reeking sauna.

For a man used to sweltering work conditions, the complaint seemed misplaced but Erno paced like a caged wolf. Between shots of whiskey he hopped up traipsing past the sofa then flopping back down. "You got somethin going with that woman?" He nodded toward Mary Alice's door and slugged back his fifth shot. "That why you live here?" Erno smirked. "She ain't half bad looking, neither. Is she, Taavi?" Not a twitch from him, not even a blink until Taavi remembered his glass and threw back another shot.

A third was left in the bottle before Erno got around to mentioning why they'd come to see him. Martin had played the good host not pressing for some explanation. "We wanted to know if you was serious." He pointed to Taavi who was studying the wall behind Martin's head waiting it seemed for some crawly creature to reveal itself.

It was after midnight by then. A breeze tapped the tacky curtains but the air didn't clear out with the three chain smoking. Mary Alice was on the stairs when Martin poured out the next shots. He heard her door open, the angry feet punch down on each step, the door to the street crack open, the trashcan lid in the alley shout out a single bullet that made Taavi jump up his eyes drowning in a languid dark pool.

"Someone dumping their garbage at this time of night." Martin shrugged. He wondered if she would go to mass before work. Light a candle for her mother? Say a prayer for her? For him?

"Serious about what?" Martin held the glass by the rim casually leaning in toward Erno. Taavi sat back down and twirled his whiskey in a hypnotic daze chasing the amber color around the sides of his glass. Erno gulped the liquid and held the empty out for Martin to refill. Neither explained how they'd found out where Martin was living and Martin didn't ask. He'd get the story sooner or later.

"Your neighbors hear you through these walls?" Erno asked in a low voice.

"One neighbor." Erno was puzzled. "Only one neighbor." Martin held up his index finger and motioned toward Mary Alice's apartment. "Probably. Yes, probably."

"Then we gonna talk a little quieter." Erno pulled his chair closer to Martin's. Taavi, inert as a butterfly collector fixated on the wall waiting for his prey to make a move.

"About what?"

"Bout what you said the other day. You know. Bout needing them explosives." Erno turned his head from side to side in case someone who shouldn't be hearing this was nearby.

Martin picked up the pack of cigarettes, the match flared as he studied the tip. After some long puffs he looked to Taavi now gazing at the empty glass nestled in his lap. Erno sat wide-eyed as a child at Christmas.

Erno suddenly started mopping his forehead with his Sunday handkerchief wadded in his great big paws, and the red-faced Finn leaned in. Martin felt Erno's sweat dribbling on his pants. *Like a pig.* The Finns had their peculiar ethic, like other Scandinavians. Hard workers but emotionally stunted. Not one word more than necessary. How far could he trust them? Perspiration seemed to be Martin's one clue. Otherwise, the pair were inscrutable.

"What'd I say?"

"You don't remember?" The bridge of Erno's nose crinkled. He whispered in Martin's ear. Taavi studied his shot glass. "You said you wanted to blow the place up. Remember? After Esa got killed?" He spat into Martin's ear.

"Did I say that?" He acted phlegmatic which perturbed Erno, his shoulders hitched up and he shifted away from Martin.

"Oh, yeah. I remember now." He had played it too close. "I was pretty damn drunk then, wasn't I? Did I say too much?"

"Yeah, yeah, yeah." Erno moved closer to him again. His eyes shining. "You was mad as hell. I thought you was mad at me at first.

Like it was my fault Esa got killed." Erno laughed. Taavi squeezed his eyebrows together suddenly recollecting the game of darts he'd played with Martin.

"I won fair."

"What're you talking about now, Taavi? We're having a serious talk here." Erno curled his fingers like he was going to knuckle Taavi on the head.

"I said I won fair." He retorted and stuck his jet-jaw lower lip out even further.

"Jesus, Taavi, we ain't talking about darts here. Get it? Why you think we come on over here?" Erno gave a disgusted shake to Martin, the pair at once in league against their mutual numbskull. Martin nodded but something didn't fit. He couldn't put his finger on it. It was only a hunch.

There was a sharp thump at the door and Martin and Erno jumped up spilling the remaining few ounces of whiskey. Taavi sat too stupefied to move. It was after one o'clock. An agitated Martin flung open the door to Mary Alice standing in her prudish nightgown in the dull hallway light gathering the cloth of her high-necked collar to hide any exposed flesh.

"I thought you might want some more whiskey." She waved a full bottle toward them. "Someone gave it to my mother before she died. I'm not going to drink it." She looked so downhearted Martin had to stop the urge to reach out and touch her.

"Thank you, Mary Alice." *In more ways than one.* He waited for her to get to her door but she didn't turn to look when she closed it behind her.

Florence-Twenty-Five

In western Montana, when the sky's lugubrious drapes decide to give an inch, they fly apart and the azure heavens stretch to the far horizons. The brilliance is astonishing and literally painful to the naked eye. Like a hibernating bear lumbering out of his cave, the observer is transformed by a wondrous and overpowering light.

At the lookouts, the foul moods quickly evaporated. The nasty, often difficult to bear attitudes mutated into steamy vapors that floated into the ether leaving downright goodwill. Most surprising was Henry who on impulse credited Florence for the turn in the weather. "It was that sour dough, Flo. That's what did it. Just the ticket. *I was as empty of life as a scarecrow's pockets."*

"What for criminy sakes does that mean?" George made an effort to temper his bark while Florence stayed mute. Some convoluted explanation would go on for five minutes and by the time he got to the end of it, Henry would no doubt give credit for the pleasing weather to something entirely different.

"Philip Marlowe, of course. *The Big Sleep.*" Henry chuckled.

"So, finally we have a chance to practice the Osborne Finder. Today we can put it to work and find out where the kinks are."

"Heck, Joe. I was going to put on my swim trunks and bask in the sun with Dashiell Hammett." Henry's mood had lifted but not the sarcasm.

Joe laughed. "Well, make sure you and what's-his-name cozy up to the fire finder while you're at it."

After a run of powerful sunlight, the peas and beets were stretching up more than an inch and thriving. "I swear." The packer had shown up with supplies and mail eyeing her tiny garden. "Nobody done that before."

"Well, here it is July already. I hope I'll be able to harvest something before September." A crop was looking like folly. By middays now she covered the plants with the cloth from her pillowslip suitcase Miss Conrad had joked about to shield them from the intense afternoon rays. The sunflowers showed no promise nor did the lettuce.

"Pete's the name." He'd dismounted and stretched out his back before putting his hand out for her to shake remembering to take off the rawhide glove on his right hand. She shook his but didn't give him her name. "I guess you're Florence. That right?" He squinted although he wasn't facing into the sun. She slightly nodded.

She'd run low on flour and until he showed up it was anybody's guess when more supplies would arrive. The sight of the 24 pound bag he hauled off the mule was more thrilling than a holiday feast, and there were oats, rice, butter, spam, a side of bacon, ham, a hefty bag of potatoes, sugar, canned milk, beans, canned vegetables and fruit, eggs, vinegar, toilet paper, matches, soap, cornmeal, and corn starch.

"Almost forget the tin of honey, and salt and pepper." He'd moved to the other side of the animal where he'd tucked it in.

"They's a little short on coffee." He shrugged. "It's that damn war. Sorry, Florence." She guessed he must have seen her name on the letters. Why didn't he address her as Mrs. Hickman? Nevertheless, she fixed him lunch to spare him eating from his rucksack full of hard biscuits. "Is that all you carry for your meals?" She shook her head.

"What?" She didn't say it seemed a pitiful way to live.

The casserole had beans, rice, canned corn, tomatoes, and canned corn beef and he ate it as Buddy had devoured the leftovers when Homer first brought the skinny dog home. *No one cooking for him.* He wasn't like Fred at least who grumbled about the mishmash of food and insisted his meat be separated from his potatoes and vegetables. Fred drew boundaries around each food group on his plate into little islands that had to fend off their neighbors.

It was just a month since the packer had gone down the path and waved back at her. She had been so lightheaded then. When she heard him whistling coming up over the ridge this time she chuckled remembering back to early June. She could manage with the supplies she had on hand, but she was starving for a letter from Homer.

The packer carried two letters and she wanted to dive into their contents but held back her eagerness acting the good host to her first human visitor in a month. In addition to the Clark's nutcracker, a family of mountain goats had arrived and stayed until the last of the snow was gone. Hawks and eagles often cast shadows over her when she was watering or weeding or washing, and squirrels, even shy marmots, chirped at her and scampered around her. The "Boys," as the spotters called themselves, had bears rummaging around their lookouts recently but she hadn't seen any. They'd warned her, though.

"Just wait, Flossie." George seemed a little in love with her. It was her clear, lilting voice in the evenings that tugged at him. "They're gonna want to get a good look at you. Just make sure you got your rifle handy when you're out and about." He wondered what color her hair was and her eyes. He willed them to be blue.

"If it's a black bear, you make a lot of noise, Flossie." If it was a grizzly, Joe warned them, do the exact opposite. "Be humble and move away slowly. Don't make eye contact."

"How can we be sure we know the difference? I don't want to end up in some fat furry stomach. *Dead men are heavier than broken hearts.*"

"That you're Philip Marlowe again, Henry?"

"Yep."

It might be easier to get rid of the packer than a bear. "Mmm." The packer smacked his lips. "You got one lucky husband. Somewhere." He had devoured two-thirds of the meal she had planned to eat the next day. But he had brought her fresh eggs, more bacon, a supply of onions, and real potatoes. The dehydrated ones tasted like chalk.

"Darkness descends a little when you are down to only boxed potatoes. Believe you me, nine months of eating chalk in my classroom is more than enough." Miss Conrad warned them. "Do yourselves a favor. Use them in your stews and casseroles to stretch the staples that have some taste at least until the packer shows up with real ones."

"What your husband got to say about all this?" Pete waved the fork at the room.

"What do you mean?" He grinned. She ached to read her letters from Homer. She could shoot a bear, she would if she had to, but could she defend herself against a man?

94

After lunch he asked if anything needed repair, rolled a cigarette at the table but went outside to smoke it. Then, he came back in and watched her climb into the cupola to do her observation. *If he hangs around thinking I'm making him another meal, he's going to wait a long time.* Henry, for once, turned out to be the helper, inadvertently.

"What's going on over there, Flo? You seen a bear, yet?"

"No bear, Henry. Just the packer." The sun would be down in two hours. Pete had enough light to get off the mountain before dusk.

Martin-Twenty-Six

The Crown Royal whiskey bottle discarded and tossed on its side had succumbed to defeat, but the Canadian Club from Mary Alice still held its own. "Explode the whole works?" It was three o'clock and two short shots hugged the bottom of the second bottle. Taavi's eyes fluttered and he wavered between a snuffling snore and slurring in monotone a Finnish ballad.

"Look at that big sucker. Who'd think that goddamn ox couldn't handle more than two shots. Jesus. He's done in." Martin had filled their glasses twice as often as his own but was sure he'd caught Taavi eyeing him. The meaty Finn wasn't as drunk as he feigned.

"She ain't bad looking. Huh?" Erno winked at Martin after Mary Alice closed the door behind her. "She got pretty hair. Maybe she wants a drink with us?"

"Never mind about her."

"You in love with her or something? Maybe she's a real party girl? What d'ya say we go ask her?"

"You heard her say she doesn't drink. Besides, her mother just died."

"Well, hell, then. No better time than that to get all liquored up. We done that after we put Esa in the ground. Didn't we, Taavi? A real to-do. You shoulda been there. Let's go an ask her. C'mon. We got her full bottle here."

One minute Erno was whispering in his ear about putting off explosives and the next going off the rails when he saw a woman. Was it the nightgown? *Christ*. What kind of apes was he dealing with?

"We were talking about blowing up the nickel operation."

"How old you figure she is?" Martin had wasted good whiskey on a pair of donkeys. "You seeing her? On the sly?" He grinned. "She ever married? I got you figured." Erno shook a knowing finger at Martin. "That's why you living here, ain't it?"

Martin was about to shelve the Canadian Club and call it a night. But, Erno pushed his empty shot glass toward the bottle.

"She keeps to herself. A spinster. She's Catholic, you know." That stopped Erno the churchgoing Lutheran dead in his tracks. A forbidden mixing of blood.

"Gimme another shot, would ya?" Erno settled back on the flabby sofa. He threw the drink back and it seemed to clear his brain. "Yeah. Let's get back to talking about blowing NICO's forge up." He leaned toward Martin again. "What you got in mind? Frankly, me and Taavi don't have the brains to pull it off on our own."

"What do you fellows have in mind?" Erno was playing dumb and using a lame excuse.

"We wanna get it done. Blow that sucker sky high."

"What about you?" With his one-note song, Taavi had been serenading the door following Mary Alice's brief appearance. He sounded like a lovesick hound dog.

"Knock it off, Taavi." Erno had drunk himself into soberness. "We talking serious here." Erno whispered loudly.

"I dunno."

"Yes, you do, Taavi." Erno prodded him. "Quit it. You know why we come here tonight. He's just scared." Erno shrugged at Martin. "That's all. Ain't you Taavi?"

"I ain't scared. Don't you keep saying that, Erno." His barrel chest expanded like bellows. He lifted the heavier loads.

Erno was no small man, either. They needed the bulk to work the steam hammer. Martin's finer frame dwarfed alongside them and went against him for the torquing work.

"Don't want to see nobody else gets killed." Taavi hung his head like it had already happened.

"Esa was his best friend. That's why he ain't saying nothing tonight." Erno spoke for him. "Ain't that the truth, Taavi?"

"What we gonna do for work if we blow it all up?" Taavi studied the floor. A remarkable question, Martin thought.

"You're crazy. You know that, Taavi? I already done told you, they gonna pay us more to put it back together."

"What if they don't? Do you think they will?" Taavi looked Martin straight in the face for the first time. He seemed sober now.

97

"Well, Erno's right. They need the nickel to win the war, Taavi. They're gonna need more men than they've needed up to now to get it back on its feet. Most likely, you'll get the better jobs when that happens since you know the work."

"I don't want no more of my friends to get killed."

"Okay. I'm going to think this over. See if I can come up with some plan for your *idea*." He enunciated the point that it was their idea. "Taavi's right. We don't want to kill anyone if we can help it." He looked toward his kitchen hiding place.

"Well, you do that. We'll talk more at Lilly's tonight." Suddenly Erno was in a hurry to leave. Mary Alice was moving about in her apartment. Early light would be glowing like soft coals over the Sudbury slagheap when she left for Mass.

Florence-Twenty-Seven

The sun hung suspended above the Western horizon while Florence watched the packer's bobbing Stetson recede bit by bit below the ridge. In some ancient time the hat had been a shade of white but was currently in its phase of sloppy gray. When the cone of the hat disappeared from her line of sight, she concentrated on the steady beat of the pack animals' hoofs not putting it past him to turn around somewhere down the path. The way he looked at her, like the grocer in Missoula, made her want to run for her Pendleton and crawl inside it.

The mules' rhythmic padding grew fainter and when the drumming faded altogether she suddenly felt ravenous and hurried back to the cab and cooked up a skillet of cowboy potatoes with onions from her fresh supply. The mixture spilled over the sides when she scrambled eggs into it and to justify the extravagance she divided it in half for morning leftovers.

The rifle hung just above the doorway. She could reach it on tiptoe, had dutifully cleaned and oiled it early in June as had been advised but it was an alien contraption. Unlike Miss Conrad who admired it as "a most helpful tool with many purposes," Florence reluctantly accepted it in her living space to use if need be. Sometime. Hopefully, not ever.

The bears were regular pests at the other lookouts. Joe suggested they be more careful about their trash. "Best not to throw it off the cliff around the cab." But what other means did they have for disposing of garbage? Apparently, a slope of fifty yards littered with empty bean or soup cans was an attraction, not a deterrent. The prowlers grunted around the cabs in the middle of the night, scratching and biting with the single purpose of getting inside.

"I bout jumped out o' my skin last night. Bugger wanted to kiss me, I think." Henry had slept with his head next to the window screen one night and woke to a bear snout sniffing at him from the other side of it. Marlowe's problems suddenly seemed inconsequential.

"Not even a bear would wanna do that." George tittered.

"Anything that rots or stinks should be buried." Miss Conrad was militant. "No mistakes. No problems. Don't be careless or let an idle thought sway you. Think about your actions and their consequences." Joe, Miss Conrad, and Ken in Missoula sang the same melody. "And, keep your rifle handy. At all times!"

Miss Conrad wasn't just talk. She took her women out into a field with shovels and had them dig holes deep enough to deter the predators. However, the long bout of rain in June caused negligence except for Florence who, with gear on and shovel in hand, dutifully disposed of potential bear bait.

Although it seemed certain the packer had left the area, she couldn't quite settle. Writing to Homer at night was detrimental because sleep would be impossible. Too many gruesome ideas floated behind her closed eyes. To tend to her uneasiness, she stacked the latest supplies around her, listed the quantity of each, and divided by the number of days before the packer should again arrive. This gave a solid picture of the number of servings on hand and a chart allowing items to be checked off as they were used. *That way I won't have to eat chalky potatoes.*

Two nights after the packer had come and gone a wail jolted her from a sound sleep. Despite the balmy temperature, the skin at her neck prickled and her armpits felt sweaty. The rifle! She fumbled to get into her pants, then her boots, and to the door but by then the noise had stopped. Not even an owl hooted, or an annoying squirrel bickered about not getting its fair share. She got the rifle down, leaned against the door, and waited. If it was a bear, it must be in pain which would be more dangerous than accidentally meeting one on the trail.

A singular howl shattered the lull. She pulled the rifle butt tight against her body, finger on the trigger, the nose aimed at the door. Except for the thumping from her heart, the blood pulsing at her temples, there was no other sound.

Some animal was in distress. The cry had come from where the trail turned out of sight and disappeared behind the thick brush. The giant flashlight of a moon shone on the giant legs of ponderosas with wispy boughs dangling at their knees in a light breeze, and the woods conjured dancing ghosts amongst ponderous trunks.

100

She held her ear up against the door. A lifetime later an intermittent whimpering, not shrill, and after that, again silence. She waited. The night was mild but she shivered and draped the Pendleton over her shoulders. And waited. Finally sliding down to squat against the door.

"Oh, no!" She gulped. A morning sunbeam woke her. She hurried to take her readings rubbing the crick in her neck from having used the door for a pillow.

The squirrels gossiped and hopped across the path on the way to the latrine. In her garden, the faithful beets mushroomed with plump green leaves gone wild and in time to be picked. The day was radiant, so clear and dazzling as if God visited during the night and washed it down with a solution of ammonia and water. The horrific night sounds were scrubbed away, too. Perhaps two trees rubbed against each other pushed by a breeze the friction generating the squeal.

Homer was overseas and she existed on a mountaintop without news updates reaching her. In the afternoons she fought the strong inclination to imagine the worst when she wrote him. The journal was deliberately chirpy and informative, littered with humorous comments from the previous evening. The detailed list of supplies from the packer with the weather-beaten Stetson, guessing the features of Henry, George, and Joe built on their robust exchanges.

"How'd your day go over there, Flossie? You spot any smoke?" They all chuckled. It was the standard joke. "I'm telling you. We're wasting the government's money. "I suspect we won't get so much as a whiff of smoke for all the watching."

Every evening Joe reminded them. "We're not gonna get off scot free. Just wait 'til them lightning storms shoot out their fireworks."

"We're waiting, Joe. And we're hoping." George was seriously afflicted from the lack of action. "Otherwise, I'm going to have some explaining to do about what I did all summer up in this dang treehouse." It was quiet for a minute. "Sorry, Flossie. Didn't mean to swear."

"Something strange happened last night." She didn't say anything else and they waited. Joe jumped in.

"What was it, Flossie?"

"There was an awful noise."

"What kind of a noise? Some bear rummaging around? They get a kick out of throwing things around." George laughed. "Those fellers like to poke their noses into people's stuff. They're regular beggars. I had one try to turn my outhouse over a few nights back."

"It sounded almost like it a child. Crying."

"I think I know what that was." Joe said relieved. "You probably are hearing some coyote cubs in their den. They act like humans the way they carry on. It's creepy. Makes your skin crawl."

Instead of waking to wailing that night, a thunderstorm rattled the cab and the ground shook under her. *That's what canons do if they're exploding all around. Oh Homer!* She covered her ears and stood sentinel by the door for a second night watching for lightning strikes and praying for her son.

Martin-Twenty-Eight

A cold sober person can endure the intrusion of waking up to screeching streetcars rippling along iron rails. After an extended night of whiskey and cigarettes, the noise the last straw. *Christ almighty.* Martin moaned as he attempted to lift his head off the pillow. The squeal corresponded to the nightmare he was in the middle of, his head trapped in a vise as someone steadily increased the pressure, the screws digging more and more into his temples. He thought he was screaming but it was the brakes of a streetcar rolling into the intersection.

His shirt stank of alcohol. He'd collapsed onto the bed wearing his pants and shoes, the room spinning in the dark. The dull morning light pierced straight back into his eyes and he fell out of the bed rushing to the toilet and plunging his head into a sink of cold water. It would be a stupid mistake to get to work late and have it reported on the company records, but he had to have coffee and a cigarette or he wouldn't make it at all.

Erno and Taavi were working on the floor looking as two white shirts, and not a hint of distress. Erno's biceps bulged as he put his frame into the torque. He and Taavi couldn't have had much, if any, sleep because they had left his place after 3:00. Maybe they didn't go home at all but, you wouldn't know it from the effort they put into the rotations. It was as if Martin had dreamed up the evening's party. He didn't look up, but Taavi's eyebrows were perpetually pinched, basted together by slipknots of worry.

The Finns barely regarded him throughout the shift. Fewer hand signals and little eye contact. He expected Erno to slap him on the back at the end of the day. "Let's go to Lilly's afterwards." When he didn't, Martin caught up with him outside the works. "You want to go for a beer?"

"Naw. Got some stuff to take care of." Like Martin had the plague. Taavi wasn't around anywhere but Martin wouldn't approach him if he was. He'd disappeared at shift change. Martin tossed around the notion of going over to Lilly's on his own but if they didn't want him around, it was best he didn't push it. He couldn't read what was going on, but in case Erno had been serious during the night, and really meant for him to come up with a plan, he would.

Back at the apartment, he got out his sketches and designated each job, the locations, and the timing to get it done without mistakes. If they showed they were serious, he would be ready for them. For now, there was nothing to do but wait for them to make a next move.

He heard her footsteps come up the stairs while he fried eggs and greasy sausages that turned his stomach. The Canadian evenings were lighter longer but Eaton's Department Store would have closed earlier. He scowled at himself for wondering where she had gone after work, for considering her comings and goings.

When he was a teenager, his father had told him on several drunken occasions, after he'd come around hours after a few of his drinking buddies had hauled his dad up the four flights of stairs to their flat because he couldn't walk on his own, how to cure a hangover. The neighbors turned their righteous noses up at them on the streets, in school, and in the shops. Townspeople whispered behind their hands and gave sideways glances. Martin daydreamed of Canada and flying off into the fields to escape their condemnation.

"Greasy sausage." The greasier, the better his father enlightened his humiliated son. "Fastest way to chase away the shakes." Or the nausea and dizziness although those two factors didn't appear to be a problem for his father. Martin guarded against his own propensity toward weakness or intemperance.

A shadow breezed past the sliver of light at the bottom of his door then keys jangled and her door swished open and closed. *Dammit.* Black eggs stuck to the bottom of the pan. Nevertheless, his shoulders sagged and a weight lifted while he ate the burnt supper and debated what he could do to get the Finns out of their rabbit hole. That's what it had to be. The fear. For Taavi, it was the horror of someone getting hurt.

"Jesus, Taavi." Erno had chastised him between shots. "We could knock off a bunch of Eye-talians. How's that sound? Not bad, huh?"

If Erno was having second thoughts, Martin had to find a way to get him to say so. To invite them to his place again was ludicrous so it had to happen at Lilly's. But how?

104

By ten o'clock he had a blueprint to show them. It was deliberately amateurish and vague to counter qualms or second guessing. A professional scheme could put the men off altogether. Frighten them all the more. He wasn't convinced they trusted him or that they hadn't already changed their minds. And, if the impetuous Finns were setting him up for a fall, the sketchy plan's crudeness would seem put together at worst by an angry rabble-rouser, not a Nazi saboteur.

The Finns drank too much and that was dangerous. If they eventually agreed to go along with the plan, he'd warn them to swear off alcohol until it was finished. He'd had a headache but it was gone. His eyes still hurt from the night's drinking and grease or no grease, he felt uneasy in his gut when he went to bed. Mary Alice was dragging something across the floor of her apartment. It was nearly midnight, too late to be moving something *for Christ's sake*, and it was too heavy for her so she groaned but kept shoving whatever it was. He fell asleep before she had finished moving it.

Florence-Twenty-Nine

Early birds, the anxious crows bitterly squabbled over the destruction from the savage storm but the squirrels scurried about too busy rearranging their habitat to quibble or vent their usual frustration. If possible, the sky was more dazzling than the day before although the ridge was a mess of broken tree limbs and bushes.

Throughout the cacophony, Florence had stayed huddled in a corner wrapped in a blanket murmuring a childhood prayer. *Now I lay me down to sleep, I pray the Lord my soul to keep.* None of the spotters got much sleep for a long spell with the temperamental thunder god throwing a strident snit at their cabs over some unknowable celestial grievance.

She sipped bitter coffee while dashing around to read her gauges, called in the report, and told the ranger she was heading down to the creek as her water supply was getting low. Out of haste or tiredness she forgot her hat but ignored the rifle hanging over the doorway.

The soft side of the sun was already beginning to stew and heading for a sweltering afternoon. On the barren ridge, she wished she'd worn the hat but as it would be cooler and darker where the trail descended into the pines didn't consider going back for it. Something seemed off when she reached the woods, like a smack in the face but she couldn't pinpoint anything and credited it to the switch from light to shade. Farther down the path, however the mood grew more off-putting, an otherworldly calm, eerie quiet, the typical animal noises she'd grown accustomed to had gone mute.

It was because she was tired. She'd almost snapped at the ranger when he asked about a measurement in her report. She hoped her edginess hadn't been that obvious, didn't want to end up the foil for gossip and someone hard to work with. Heavy air compounded her fatigue. The trail wound hypnotically through patches of dazzling sun and cool shade and she wished that instead of going for water she could curl up and take a nap. Or, be like Henry. Keep a low profile immersed in detective mysteries. Pine boughs and twigs littered the trail hampering her steps. She gulped in deep breaths of the heady nectar that comes after rain sweet as the wild roses blooming along the trail.

Heaven's fireworks had robbed her of a second night of sleep. The cab jumped up like a rattled snake wriggling from the floor to its rafters wrestling to shake off its old skin. Even the windows tinkled. Features that had been insignificant, the glass insulators fastened to the legs of the bed, suddenly seemed important. How many people who came before her, people like Miss Conrad and Joe, had through trial and error devised ways to make life in the lookouts safer for everyone. Lightning bolts had shaken her awake striking at intervals up the ridge with uncanny precision and now the insulators made sense. First an electrifying flash immediately followed by a snap that shot into the cab as if someone had fired a rifle. Her ears rang long after the storm subsided. "You're a sitting duck up here, without them insulators," Henry said later.

Another night cramped on the floor catching only bits of sleep. At dawn, she'd scoured the tree-lined slopes looking for signs of a live strike in her valleys, her peaks into Glacier Park, dreading that any part of her territory might have taken a hit. The Osborne Fire Finder would make itself useful if so. She scrutinized her area through binoculars, every gulley, for dark spots, gray spots, anything that looked different from the evening and swallowing hard at the notion she'd miss a crucial clue. False smoke, "water dogs," are hard to distinguish from actual combustion. Confusing mists of bluish columns that hang in the gullies after a summer rain and fool even the experienced smoke spotter. What looks like a smoldering fire and is reported as such could turn out to be only haze and a terrible embarrassment. The smoke chasers tenting in the valleys below the lookouts would get the report, break temporary camp in a hurry and rush to the pinpointed location. They relied on the spotters to make accurate assessments.

With eyes slit against the intermittent brightness, her head still in a fog, she nearly missed the bundle lying slightly off the middle of the path. She would have stepped over it except her boot collided with it. The clump was oddly shaped but somewhat similar to the other debris left by the storm although she recognized the tell-tale yarrow leaves and their significance, and that someone who knew the plant's benefits had used it for medicinal purposes. She pushed it over with the toe of her boot and found exactly what she expected, the reddish tint of blood. Someone else was in *her* woods!

Halfway between the creek and the cab and needing water and not knowing where to hide, what was she to do? Instinct told her to run to the lookout, bar the door, get on the phone to the ranger for help. But what if someone was already there, or somewhere between her and the cab? What if nothing came of it at all? She'd look the fool and then without water she'd have to make another trip down to the creek so despite trembling hands, and knees shaking, she raced forward toward the creek.

Between tree trunks and among the thick brush she conjured eyes following her. At every turn on the path someone might jump out so the rustle near a stand of birch off to her right produced an involuntary yelp from her. She'd flushed a grouse that scolded her with its brash flutter and belligerent attitude. The fowls nested in thick brush and every time she accidentally flushed one it gave her a start. "A very fine meal." Miss Conrad's face lit up at the picture of eating a plump grouse breast.. "If you act fast enough."

Joe was wrong about the crying the night before the storm. It hadn't come from a den of coyote pups! A bloody poultice, made by human hands, had someone's blood on it. Her woods, until now filled with the clamor of opinionated birds, scolding squirrels, hammering woodpeckers, and singing breezes strumming pine boughs had gone silent because of whatever it was.

Miss Conrad had badgered, the spotters pestered, "keep the rifle at the ready," and now after the fact, her limp excuse was humiliating, that it was cumbersome and awkward to manage when hauling up water. Her heart throbbed at her temples and she was breathless. Not far from the stream at a spot where the deer crossed over a section of the path and left dainty ballerina-toe prints, she bent over to catch her breath. Fresh bear scat and droppings from the pack train already dried and straw-colored lay clumped about. But there was no sign of human footprints.

The swollen stream leaked over onto the path creating rivulets and her boots sank up to the ankles in the mud. There was no easy way to get to the creek bank with all of the broken branches clogging it. The mud sucked at her heels and any other time she would have taken her boots off and cooled her toes in the icy stream as she collected her water supply. After a quick drink and a thorough scan of the area, she started back up the trail.

The sun was pounding down at the edge of the rim the ridge when she hid in a clump of bushes listening and watching. If someone was in the cab, there wasn't a sound, not even a movement, but she wouldn't risk going up on the shelf of land where the cab was until she could be sure.

She fixed a hearty breakfast of oatmeal with huckleberries, then barred the door...some things were missing from her pantry.

Martin-Thirty

Lilly's place stank in equal proportions of smoke, sweat, and spilled beer despite a goofy-looking carved bulldog propped at the doorway to let in fresh air.

If you could call it fresh. The residue from nickel dust lodged in the sinuses and headed straight for the lungs. Hacking and continual coughs were the norm year round as were runny noses. It was as hot outside as it was at the crowded bar. "Don't you guys have homes to go to?" Three hours before closing her blouse was soaked at the armpits and her lower back and she was cranky cleaning up after their perpetual messes. She'd come to work leaving her youngest kid still struggling from an asthma attack where an older brother was assigned to watched over him.

"How 'bout I come home with you?" Erno gushed appearing half-smashed and slurring his suggestion.

"Not in a year of bloody full moons." That made him cackle and he reached to grab her at the waist but Lilly knew when to duck and twist around pushy men and Erno missed her and slipped off the barstool.

"I'm ready, Lilly, any time you are." He whistled to her back hauling himself back onto the stool. "Good looker there." He winked whenever she walked by the table and repeated it. "You think so, too, don't you?" He sputtered at Martin, begging him to agree. She must have been quite lovely ten years earlier but single-handedly running a pub, putting up with the rough crowd and raising two kids on her own had mapped her face. Martin didn't respond. "Do you?" Like it was a requirement for Erno.

"'Yeah. Sure. Quite a looker." *It's got to be hell running a place like this.* He hated drunks.

"So. You do what you said you was gonna do?" No one was near enough to hear over the din, but Erno leaned in whispering loudly and in the process knocked his beer over with his elbow. Lilly was behind the bar, heard it clang and glared at him. He didn't notice but since the glass was almost empty, he left it where it landed. Martin looked over at Lilly with a slight smile, righted the mug wiping the spill off the table that through the years had known its fair share of abuse from hard-working, harder drinking patrons. The tabletop resembled Lilly's face carved from grooves in the veneer that still emitted boozy fumes of bygone splatters.

"I'm not drunk." Another stage whisper. "It's an act. Just in case." Up close, the lines in his face were craggy furrows typical of the Finns from the forge shop with pale skin and fair hair but ruddy complexions. Martin needed a smoke.

Julia was like a younger version of Lilly, his only girlfriend. He was eighteen and so was she. Amber hair wrapped like horses' tails in thick braids that ended below her breasts, apple cheeks that looked to explode when she laughed. A contagious guffaw. Lilly pushed through smelly men, put up with their careless drinking, slipped around their wandering hands and yet her girlish giggle, generous and delicious, rang ever so often across the pub. When Martin heard it, every other noise in the pub was stifled. Julia had been right about him, said if she ever disagreed with him, he would vanish. She was quick-witted, like Lilly, not one to abide rudeness or flippant behavior, firm in what she valued.

He had been shunned by Erno and Taavi which put him in a real quandary. Looking back at how he'd gone about recruiting the Finns, he must have misread the hints and asides, been presumptive, trusting what they said. He should have broadened his net from the outset, made in-roads with the Italians whose loyalty would be more apt. After work he stayed away from the pub which suddenly seemed off-limits and headed to the storefront café with the six tables in Little Italy. Four nights in a row. The papa eyed him from the kitchen portal convinced Martin was angling for his buxom daughter because each evening he asked for a second basket of crusty rolls when she teetered over to serve him a plate of spaghetti and flashed flirty smiles.

"Why he wanna so much rolls?" Papa pushed an accusing wooden spoon into his daughter's overpainted face.

The food was reminiscent of Europe, the crisp bread evocative of his hometown Bäckerei but his purpose of unveiling potential prospects failed so when Erno tapped him on the shoulder the

111

following Friday afternoon, although cautious he was mildly encouraged. "Let's a get a beer at Lilly's after work."

Erno in a kingly manner steadied himself back onto the center of his stool, winked at Martin who took a long draw on his cigarette, and kept his "looker" Lilly in plain view of his kingdom. Taavi stood behind Martin at the dart board shooting with a vaguely familiar person but not someone they worked with at the forge.

Martin hesitated, taking his time. Smoked the fag down to the butt then cleared his throat. Taavi watched him out of the corner of his eye quickly turning away when Martin caught his glance. Taavi's competition was not a regular at the pub but was determined to win a match even though behind by two games. Martin noted the man's soft white hands. If he worked in the nickel industry, it was not with his hands.

"Yep." Martin at last answered about the plan and Erno's beamed.

"Where is it?" Erno leaned back farther, looked as though he might topple off the stool.

Martin stubbed the butt out and squinted through his self-generated smoky air. Erno tapped his fingers as if he was at the piano. The individual fingers flicked up and down against the glossy damp wood. "Not here, Erno."

"Where then?" Erno puffed, moved closer, and gave a slight nod to Taavi.

"Catholic Church. Sunday night. Don't expect it will be busy after confession." Martin's sarcasm missing its mark.

"I'm a practicing Lutheran." Erno scowled. "Not one of them damn stinkin' idol worshippers." Martin might have made a mistake in the location seeing how it put Erno off.

Taavi and the other man continued their game when Martin and Erno left. Erno threw his arm over Martin's shoulder and they ambled down the road to Erno's house where Martin bid him goodnight.

"See you soon." Erno grinned widely. "At that place." Then he grimaced.

Martin felt the eyes zeroing in on his back after leaving Erno off. The same feeling as when he'd come ashore from the U-boat. He didn't turn around. The night sky was without stars or moon, the miners in their darkened houses tucked up in their beds, and Sudbury invaded by ghosts.

Florence-Thirty-One

A few things in the larder were not where she'd left them the previous evening. Florence checked her supplies against the list for what if anything was missing. A loaf of sourdough. *Maybe.* Uncharacteristic as it might be, she wasn't sure if or when she'd finished the last one. How was it possible she would forget that? But the unhinged storm had unleashed confusion and disorder. The canister of dried fruit was not where she stored it but not much if any of it gone. The potato bag opened.

Perhaps no one had been inside the cab. That seemed likely given the force of the tempest and the pounding it gave the cab stirring up its insides and scattering the contents about. She'd risen off the floor early morning to record measurements and ended up drinking the most awful tasting coffee. It bit at her psyche as much as it did her tongue but not having slept, or having the reserves to be upset about it, she ignored the taste and completed her duties. Fred would have spit it out on first taste triumphantly gloating and adding it to the list of episodes that had become a permanent part of their history. The morning had come at her as a shortsighted blur and the coffee, sharp or not, was necessary to get the day going.

A whole bag of potatoes could have shuffled in her confined world after being upended. Even the ladder to the cupola had shifted and gone cockeyed but the gauges, the Osborne fire finder, and the phone remained intact, bolted firmly in place.

"You get a pretty good beating up there last night?" Jake, the ranger, wouldn't know where to look to find a sympathetic feeling, his main objective being that the spotters stayed on track, no matter what Mother Nature threw at them. Henry complained about the rotten egg stink. "P-U." Florence grinned and imagined him pinching his nostrils together, righteously sticking his nose in the air. The shutters on the east side of George's cabin had disappeared into the valley flapping like eagle wings as they flew away, and he wanted to go looking for them. "Stay where you are." The ranger dictated and promised him a carpenter with supplies to replace them soon enough.

The oatmeal bubbled and Florence mixed a batch of bread dough. Two small loaves would see her through the week and if part of a loaf went stale, it would get scattered for the birds to feast on although that was a defiant act given the warning about leaving food around. She was tempted to brew another cup of coffee but the day was turning into a scorcher so she ate the mush and washed her hair from some of the water she'd hauled up from the creek.

After that, she rinsed out laundry in the same water and then used that water to scrub the woodwork and mop the floor on her hands and knees, probing the cracks for pine needles and crushed gravel. By then, it was time for the ten o'clock call to Jake, the second of the day. The six o'clock morning report, before hiking down to the creek, hadn't been noteworthy despite the storm but it did verify the phone line had remained intact. If she didn't call in at the assigned times, and if there was no answer after repeated attempts to raise her, someone would be sent up although that would take over an hour.

"McGregor Lookout calling in." Her knees complained about the hardwood floor.

"Find any damage from that storm?" Jake had asked her that question at 6:00, too. Clearly, it was a familiar pattern for the seasoned ranger who knew the spotters just pulled themselves together on the first call of the day to read their gauges and scan their territories following a night of fireworks. Except George who could immediately report his shutters had taken flight because he'd watch them wing past. He hadn't circled his cab to assess the damage any more than the rest of them.

Jake was prepared to learn about more losses as the day got going. "No. Except my groceries got moved around a bit." He grunted. That first clap of thunder above the tin-roof had been like someone pounding on a metal pail with her head inside. By the time she'd eaten and washed things up, and talked to ranger, she had dismissed the notion of an intruder, Mother Nature had been her prowler.

From her location, she could see the three other lookout stations at distances ranging from five to twenty-five miles away. Joe's peak the farthest. On some days the closer cabs seemed so near she considered scrambling over rocks, cliffs, and avalanche fields to share a cup of coffee, especially now the weather was clear, the dismal fog completely lifted. The idea of finding Henry buried in a book would be worth the effort and the surprise.

The sun had sucked up the mist from the night's storm. "I can see Joe's lookout." She thought that God had no better vista on a cloudless day. "Humidity's at 42%." Strictly business. Chatty phone calls came at the end of the day for entertainment and to talk to someone other than themselves.

She reported the weight of the fuel moisture stick. She'd give more details at five o'clock. "Wind is light today. Four miles per hour from the south-southeast."

"That makes a nice change then, doesn't it?" The smoke spotters' consistent gripe was of the wind.

"Nothin' to stop it." Henry complained. "Blows right up and over them rocks." His lookout was situated on a precarious rocky outcropping, the cab held in place by eight heavy cables. Miss Conrad shared a story about a young man's first and only stint as a smoke spotter on Stark Lookout over near Alberton. He put up with the whining and groaning of the wind over the cables as long as he could then called the switchboard at the ranger station in the middle of the night to be comforted by the motherly voice of the woman attending.

"Well, you might figure how long he lasted." Miss Conrad grinned. "Not like us girls." Miss Conrad didn't seem to know fear Florence realized in retrospect.

Later, she gave the plants a good dousing, and complimented the peas and carrots on how well they were coming along. The storm had not bothered them at all. After that, she punched down her bread and ate a can of pork and beans before starting an entry to Homer which she immediately tore up after going over what she'd written. She described the storm and the lightning leaping like tongues of fire running up the edge of the ridge, and cupping her ears from the boom that rattled her teeth, and realized with horror that could be exactly what he was going through.

The entry she did write to Homer was of the garden's progress, and the discovery of a ptarmigan on the way to the latrine. *It was such a shy little thing and seemed fragile. How can such a tender thing live in this*

116

harsh setting? The other discovery, the one she didn't write about was of the wad of yarrow-stained blood she'd stepped on.

Martin-Thirty-Two

Sudbury woke to a typical Sunday morning dull gray sky acting proxy for summer light. The Canadian dawn had cracked rosy over the mining town's meteoric hole but just after Saturday night's revelers dispersed leaving the downtown barren as the inside of a crater, the sidewalks deserted but for a lackluster rusty cat that ambled into Martin's path at an intersection. It sat down in the crosswalk as he approached holding a steady look on him, silently blocking his path in the hopes of being picked up. *Scat!* He poked the toe of his shoe at the shaggy coat so it hissed at his leg and made him step around it following him with its eyes, sizing him up as he moved past.

Twenty minutes ahead of the first mass Martin slipped into the last pew of Christ the King ignoring the Mary Alice candles, the donation box, the holy water, and neglecting to genuflect. Long suffering widows donning shrouds of shapeless black dresses with dowdy scarves waddled behind him in single file.

At the altar, three beginning-to-gray women bustled about arranging fresh sprigs whispering in case God was listening. Their collective frown either a nod to their pious duty with its sacred seriousness, or a judgment on themselves for not having finished the adornment ahead of the early worshipper. With bobbing goose heads, each privately assessed him with fleeting glances.

Catholicism with all its trappings. The sensations it elicited, the memory of his fingers rippling in holy water, trying to lick them but his mother slapped him, her correcting his inadequate effort making the sign of the cross, hating the humiliation of bowing before entering the pew, the nauseating repetition of beads gliding over his knuckles. His mother always pushing him to a be the perfect Catholic. In his earnest preadolescent years he had imitated her rhythm, mimicked her devotion until the heavens opened one day and in a ray of enlightenment realized the absurdity. She wouldn't be fooled by him in the pew if she were alive now for she'd washed her hands on his ever repenting.

The massive wooden doors creaked behind him and groaned at the later arrivals followed by the echo of footsteps on the tile floor rapping across the sanctuary, and more than once, a cane tapping in accompaniment. Except for a stray cough now and again and a stifled sneeze, the grand cavern felt hollow and aptly sepulchral.

The worshippers were the silver-haired variety who resented younger people blessed with a satisfying night's rest and in consequence have no incentive or desire to attend early mass. Peppered among the mostly empty rows of pews was the occasional gentleman squeezing a timeworn tweed cap between his knees and then the two young men, not yet adults, but nearly, slumped down in their seats, one pickle green in color, the other suffocating an irrepressible laugh.

Martin trained his eyes on the blood-red flakes in the stained-glass window until a clatter from a side door alerted him of the priest who suddenly burst into the apse fluttering like an unpracticed bird flying out of the nest and possessing a surprisingly sharp beak. The cleric darted from the sacristy toward the altar his arms flapping in the sleeves of his black robe until he landed safely behind its bulk. With his back to the congregation, his head was an egg atop mounds of monotonous cloth that swallowed up the entire torso. Eye glass frames hung heavily over his ears hooding the weakness of bad eyes that only eternity would absolve.

He frowned when he turned around begrudging the mostly homogenous worshipers, the scant group of wrinkled brows, babushkas, and bald heads all of whom Martin had identified by pew location and assessed for possible motive. Martin expected Mary Alice to be at a later mass. The elderly came to negotiate a perfect confession to prepare for eternity after their final exits.

He intended to scout out the entrances and exits to the church ahead of the evening meeting with Erno and Taavi when he would lay out the plans. Ideally, he would have done reconnaissance before he suggested the church as a meeting place but the Finn had pressed him hard. Erno was fidgety at Lilly's and Martin was worried if he didn't give them something concrete they might put him off or ignore him again and he'd waste more time. How many entrances did the cathedral have? He had to know all of them which he would learn by circling the building after mass and following them down the streets to their end. Hopefully, at least two of them would terminate at the train depot.

The pasty priest was puzzled, going so far as to direct his attention toward Martin as he proceeded with the steps of the morning ritual. His peculiar presence in this milieu, tall, sober, barely middle-aged and going through the motions, kneeling, standing, reading, and kneeling again were heartening but implausible.

His stomach tightened when after the service began Mary Alice knelt beside him and smiled. She must have hearing like an owl because he'd sneaked out of his room an hour before mass, deliberately carried his shoes in the hallway slipping down the stairs in his stocking feet. He'd put his finger over the door latch and eased it quietly into place once he was out on the sidewalk. Where in the process had he given himself away?

She nodded at rosary between his fingers, tapped his hand once, the one holding it, and smiled again. She'd given it to him the time he'd gone with her to mass. He'd meant to throw it away but because he lived next to her thought it might be a mistake to act in haste. She'd been disappointed with him more than once already and if she asked for it back, the fewer lies he had to make up the better.

Tiny details. One small mistake could be a deciding factor for success and survival. He planned to leave the beads behind, had already put the rosary in an envelope to place it in her mailbox but pulled it out again that morning. It was a highly visible and convenient prop. He tore up the note from the envelope that said he couldn't keep up the pretense and was going back to join his wife.

"We'll go for tea afterward." She whispered and boldly squeezed his hand.

Florence-Thirty-Three

Florence hung wet laundry in the windows despite the wind's lethargy in the airless afternoon. An occasional breeze now and again gave a tepid tap at a shirt sleeve or collar, a begrudging attempt at cooling the room.

"Don't call 'em dog days for nothin'." In the beginning of June and in their initial evening conversations, Henry was a grammarian, impressive as a university scholar, but as the days grew longer and steamier his language gradually degenerated. If he were her student, Miss Conrad's knitted brows would unravel to hear him falling prey to Marlowe tough-guy talk.

"So. The dry season is here and this is when our work begins." George said between chirps on his mouth harp.

"Too hot to make biscuits, Flossie. Got any suggestions for something cooler?"

"Hell, I'm eatin' beans out of the can these days." They all laughed.

"Not all of us are as backward as you, George. I boil my eggs when I get up 'for it gets too hot. You can eat them all day long. Or peanut butter sandwiches. What do you think of that, Flossie?"

"That makes sense to me, Henry." The salad greens from the Missoula garden would be young and tender and ready to be picked.

The heat baked the tall, thick grasses crowded together from all the rain and the ranger fretted and laid out a schedule for the spotters so their shared boundaries would be continually supervised during the daylight hours.

"You remember all that rain you griped about? That was your summer vacation." Jake laughed but got silence on the receiving ends. He cleared his throat. "Every day from here on out assume things are gonna be dangerous. Tons of fuel drying out begging for a stray flame. If we can keep the damn fools from tossing their cigarette butts out the car windows, and lightning don't strike, we might make it to September with our noses clean. Just maybe."

Every thirty minutes since the hot spell began, Henry, George, and Florence rotated shifts on their adjacent perimeters. In June, the

121

lookouts were secluded aeries enveloped in thick fog and like snowbound farmers in eastern Montana, the spotters suffered stir-crazy notions. Monotonous days, tedious hours with little to do but read books, play instruments, or write letters.

Florence collected small bouquets of wildflowers between rainy spells. Blue lupines, early bloomers, blossomed on the slopes below the cab with a pungency that made her a head ache. Impressive in the Mason jar at the table, yet intrusive, she wrote to Homer and on a whim scribbled their tall spikes with Prussian blue, pea-like flowers. *I wonder if you could eat them.* She didn't.

Vermilion Indian paint brushes were kinder on the nasal passages, not as fascinating, squat and intricate, and harder to replicate on paper. Snowballs of fuzzy bulbous bear grass sprouted out of nowhere taller than her knees, their white heads striking but weird like cabbages on skinny poles.

Henry's spirits had sagged during the soggy weather but it had ground down on them all, and privately they had asked themselves whether they wanted to or could see the summer through. "Worse than being snowed in." George lamented.

"Did you bring books to keep you company?" Henry patted the pile at his side, rubbed them like the ears and fur of a fireplace dog.

"Hell, no, Henry. I ain't going back to school." Then added, "Sorry, Flossie."

"Are you eating hot meals?"

"What'cha mean, Flossie?"

"She means George are you cooking your spam. Right, Flossie?" She laughed.

"I mean, Henry that a hearty meal will keep your spirits up and pass the time."

"What you got in mind for us this time?" Florence talked them through the steps of Mulligan stew using the supply of canned meats and vegetables.

"How long you cook it for, you say, Flossie?"

"Make a batch of biscuits to go with it, and Henry, don't overwork the flour. That's why you're biscuits aren't turning out."

"Whatever that means." Henry grumbled.

122

She sketched the latest crop of flowers adding them to journal to Homer. On that hard chair at the small table, she drew until the light grew dim or her stomach growled or her legs barked at her from sitting too long.

She was grateful, and lucky, she wrote Homer. *People pay lots of money to go on expensive vacation holidays. I'm not but I'm independent and I cook what I want when I want and happy being left alone.* She laughed when she read it back to check the spelling and grammar but didn't change a word although Homer might see she was like a stubborn girl stamping her foot. *I'm working for a paycheck, too, come September.*

The fire danger grew like bread in the oven too long. In a matter of days, not weeks the temperatures soared, the open fields scorched to brown and the brush on the hillsides turned dusty orange. Daylight hours and surveilling in the cupola were like a slow yawn that wouldn't end. Letters to Homer became foot notes, a jot here, a paragraph in longer moments between her duties and her garden.

When a rusty puddle was all that remained at the bottom of the storage tank she set out to the creek after her early morning report. On her first venture, just past the scrappy pines below the cab a mountain goat huffed at her from the shade, his wooly coat hanging in clumps of giant fur balls. He was breathing like an asthmatic whether from having his territory disturbed or from being overheated and gave her a vague nod when she skipped past him to descend into the woods. The creek was icy, too cold to stick her toes in, but almost an exotic luxury to drink. She gulped handful after handful before spotting a delicate pink flower six inches tall, bent in the shape of a pipe. Delicate and different from the imposing bear grass it was both quiet and spunky in the monolithic wilderness. She dabbed at it to promise herself she would not pick it.

On her next trip down, the mountain goat had gone, probably to higher ground but a belligerent goose charged at her just above the creek threatening an attack. He screamed and honked swiveling his head while she stood perfectly still until he relented and stomped off into the brush. The third trip down, after the storm, she came across the yarrow bundle.

Someone had been or was still on her mountain, but no one had been in the cab and no one had been on the trail. When the supplies tossed around by the storm were back in order, she had lunch, visited her reluctant garden, punched bread dough down and jotted a note to Homer. At three o'clock she surveyed her area to prepare for her four o'clock report.

The smoke was in Joe's district and if it was real, he would have called it in already. It was either a mirage or a water dog. She scanned the valleys, the ridges, every gully, searched for anything else unusual, and then cleaned her windows.

At three-thirty, she did another check look. Her area was clear but Joe's smoke was still there and seemed even bigger. The azimuth on the Osborne fire finder was complicated and baffling but she'd been trained on it. She revolved the ring on the fire finder with its circular map of the area and adjusted the sights until the base of the smoke or whatever it was, appeared in the cross hairs of the front sight. A measuring tape running between the front sight and the rear sight gave the distance. The smoke was in the Wolf Creek drainage.

Still, she hesitated. It seemed late in the day for water dogs, and the sun had shifted. In fifteen minutes it would be four o'clock and she would be required to call in. Fifteen minutes was an eternity.

Martin-Thirty-Four

The priest gave the benediction and recessed spider-like down the aisle toward the entry with his pasty pate bobbing atop black forewings to meet his parishioners at the massive doors, coolly nodding at the unctuous repetitions of "God bless you, Father," their gratitude enough to stretch the seams on a fat man's pants. He sidestepped Mary Alice leaning across her for Martin's hand with a mixture of resignation and regard, and a tinge of pleading.

"Do you want to come to confession with me?" Mary Alice later asked spreading butter to the edges of an otherwise flavorless scone. The woman had a marvelous knack for reading the wrong signals.

Hell! Are you really that dim? "Not today." Two ladies at the next table leaned in toward them to hear what was being said.

"Another time, then?" God, she was needy.

"Maybe."

"When?"

"Jesus!" One of the women set her cup down with a clatter on its saucer. *Settle down.* "I'll let you know." Mary Alice would devour him before he escaped Sudbury.

The freewheeling cat watched the pair at the crosswalk, but because traffic had picked up, had shifted to a street lamp and was crouching behind the base. Its eyes followed Martin's polished shoes and Mary Alice's functional pumps crossing to the opposite curb before giving an indolent scratch, yawning with mouth agape, and closing its eyes.

"Aren't you coming up?" He held open the outside door, the object he had blamed for giving him away when he had sneaked out of the building carrying his shoes, its screech for some reason now in remission. She was pitiful and obvious. The cat lurking on the street corner that offered him one chance and then moved on with not so much as a thank you very much rated better.

He lit a cigarette. "No."

As it was, she'd sucked up his valuable morning intruding on his mission and then annoyed him with her recycled stale tale of the longstanding rift with her mother. Her white handkerchief collected her tears and the beige makeup that came off with them along with a bit of red lipstick. The café patrons stared hard at him like he was a callous rock letting her weep and showing no compassion.

"I just feel so guilty and that's why I can't sleep with you anymore."

"What?" She laid a motherly hand over his, patting the dejected child but he snatched it back from her grasp. "I'm so sorry. You know I put flowers on her grave every morning ahead of work and today before mass." So, the squawking door turned out not to be his enemy.

He hated tea. Too British and too colonial. Why didn't the Canadians stand up like the Americans had done? Join fight in their revolution? The crusty, stale biscuit he'd ordered not because he was hungry, but to get the business with Mary Alice over with, ground like pebbles against his molars. He lit a cigarette instead, calculating the hours before he would meet with the Finns.

"You do still like me, don't you?" Tears in her eyes. Seven hours to go. She put her hand over his watch when he checked it a second time. "I think it will just take time. You know." She raised her eyebrows smiling to the top of his head as he analyzed a stain on the otherwise white tablecloth. "To put the funeral and the shock of her dying behind me. Then, we can start again?"

"Why do you ask me that?" She put her hand over the cloth stain and then held it out for him to pick up. "Listen. I've got some things to take care of." He touched her on the forearm and but drew back as if it was a hot stove burner.

"You mean because of your wife?" The street cat had the common sense and self-respect to turn its back and walk away when he scorned it, why didn't she? She wasn't a street fighter. The feline would take what it could but it wouldn't lower itself to grovel for improbable benefits. He hated their lies. His and hers.

By meeting with her, accompanying her, running into her despite doing his utmost to prevent it, drinking foul tea with her in cafés while being examined by an untold number of eyes and ears, he was giving up precious cover. The skill at being invisible grew more improbable due to the exposure he had with Mary Alice, and he had some sympathy toward the handlers who had argued against placing him because of the unpredictable difficulties he brought to espionage.

If his cover was blown and the assignment aborted, he could endure the consequences, but at the core his failure would be impossible to accept. Precious time and Mary Alice pressed down equally and the weight of both resulted in the sharp bark he gave her in the café that drew harsh glances. She pushed at him and time evaporated something would explode if he didn't get the plan executed, and it wouldn't be a controlled eruption with fuses and detonators going off where they were designated.

Planned sequences, organization, and things in the order laid out were necessary to keep him going, to help him maintain his temper and his control. His scheme would be successful but must not be done in haste. Only she was pushing him hard yearning for him to the point of throwing off her highly valued cloak of dignity. Her desperateness was making him feel desperate.

"Why not?" She looked up to the head of the stairs then grabbed the end of his necktie from where she stood inside the foyer and he was still outside the doorway.

Halfway in and halfway out of the entrance, he reclaimed his tie but she had a grip on the end. "I've got to go. I've got to run an errand. Pick up a satchel from one of the guys." Another lie, another excuse instead of telling her to go to hell. He yanked the tip from her and the tug-of-war ended.

"You mean one of those shady guys who got you drunk that night?"

"No. It's someone else."

"You make it sound so mysterious."

She was desperate for sex, for a man, for a life, for whatever, but she wasn't dumb. God help him if she had him figured and that thought sent a chill up his backbone.

"Nothing mysterious about it." He stepped back out onto the sidewalk. She followed him halfway out. He folded the tip of his tie into his hand in case she reached for it again.

"Is something else going on that you're not talking about?"

"That's silly woman talk. Nothing's going on." He made a face and turned his back to her. "You got too much time on your hands? Making up stories to fill the time."

She winced. Took the jab and backed into the foyer as though he'd poked her with his finger.

"Will I see you later tonight?"

"No chance. I got something going already." He waved dismissively over his shoulder wishing she'd get mad at him, tell him to go to hell, like she should have. But she didn't. She smiled sadly and turned to go up the stairs.

"Maybe another time, then." He was passing the next storefront and she said it so quietly he wasn't sure what she'd said.

Florence-Thirty-Five

At ten of four she made the call. "Look the fool, if need be." Miss Conrad whispered in her memory. "They aren't paying us up there to have a nice long vacation from our weal and woes. Be bold but not reckless." Florence paced in front of the cupola windows for a full five minutes checking the Osborne and pleading for the smoke to peter out as her stove did during the rains despite coddling. Her fail proof expression when Homer talked back to her failed to stop the smoke, only aggravated it, so she got on the phone.

"Good call, Flossie!" The boys hooted and bantered later that evening. They were proud of her but each quietly held the regret of not spotting it. It was July and it was the first fire and they were itching to do the job they'd been hired for, the chance to call one in.

"I guess so." She fidgeted with the phone cord and heard along with their compliments the longing and envy. If it were Fred she'd bested she'd have apologized again and again, not that would have amounted to forgiveness, told them she was sorry for having spotted the fire before them, like it was her fault she'd snatched away their favorite toy without asking. She hadn't shown them up but she felt that way. It was the circumstances and if she was honest she'd tell the ranger she'd dragged her feet. He'd confirmed the fire was blazing out of control and she couldn't choke down her jello dessert. She should have been bolder sooner. The firefighters were pushing back against the shafts of hungry flames rabidly gobbling up dry fuel. Miss Conrad would shake her head. "Now what did I tell you, Florence? Did your common sense take a vacation?" Florence imagined the flushed woman's face, hands on hips and hanging her head at letting the teacher and the forest service down.

The fire began in a gully not visible from Joe's lookout until the smoke rose up roiling like angry clouds over the ocean's rioting waves. She waited for more news that evening and while doing so, wrote out her resignation letter. She'd delayed calling in her report because of her pride, more afraid of the humiliation of making a false alarm although she attempted to be cheerful with the boys while eating remorse by the spoonful. She didn't deserve the responsibility she'd taken on, having failed on the first attempt to meet the basic requirement.

Joe was the veteran of the peaks, level-headed, confident, and reassuring, the overbearing father who listened to them, boosted morale when they sunk into gloom or started climbing the walls out of boredom. He talked Florence through a nasty spell of anxiety over night noises. He was their cheerleader.

But Joe, the reliable pillar, who bolstered them when things grew rocky didn't catch the fire. She did. He was experienced and an expert but when he wasn't there to help she messed up. His experience and expertise couldn't help her do her job. The boys and she were a team of sorts, but each had to uphold a separate and vital role. They'd become like brothers, more family than she'd known except for Homer after her dad died, but that was in June when fires seemed fanciful and they couldn't see in front of their noses beyond the glass panes.

"Don't take no genius to know it got started from that dang lightning last night." Henry crowed, his voice deep as Robert Mitchum's. Joe told them while they grumbled through foul weather that they would see a fair amount of action before their stints were up. He wouldn't remind them, again. "Remember in June when I told you we were going to have our work cut out for us?"

They'd been slap-happy the night before the storm roared through. Too much waiting around, too much heat, too many daylight hours. They traced the path of the Milky Way, watched falling stars. "Did you just see that one over Glacier? You wish on 'em, Flo?"

She giggled. "Sometimes." A breathy reply.

Henry cracked jokes and couldn't stop laughing at them, to the point of doubling over, and Joe told him he was as contagious as the chicken pox the way he had them in tears. "You drinkin' somethin' other than water over there?" George needled.

"I ain't no disease and I ain't no heavy drinker." Henry stuck his tongue out at the mouthpiece between his wise cracks.

"No. You ain't. But it would be a doozy sickness if you ever caught one." Now Joe egged him on.

The ranger from headquarters broke in to give them an update on "Flossie's Fire."

"The worst is over. It's pretty much out except for the mop up. It was your good call, Florence. And, it didn't hurt that there was hardly no wind today." She fingered the resignation letter in her lap.

"So, what was it, then? Lightning strike after all?" Joe made an assessment but wondered if the ranger thought something was as odd as he thought it was. The fire ignited in the drainage although the lightning strikes had advanced along the ridge lines.

"Well, that makes the most sense." The ranger sounded exhausted. It would be several days before the embers and burning logs were uncovered and extinguished. "I mean what else would it be? About 100 percent sure of that the way that lightning tore through here last night. What, you think, Joe?"

"Not so sure. Anybody hanging around the back woods that you know of?" A chill went straight up Florence's back.

"What? You thinking some idiot out there started it?" The ranger sounded peeved like it would be Joe's fault if that were true. He'd been on the job since early morning and his night wasn't going to be over anytime soon. "I haven't seen much of anybody up this way the whole summer. Have you? Who'd do that, anyway?" He didn't wait for Joe to reply. "No. I'm chalking it up to the storm. That's the report. I'll catch up with you in the morning."

"You ain't buying it, are you Joe?" George asked.

"I dunno. Maybe I still got fog on the brain. Something don't seem right, though. It don't fit." He took a deep breath and slowly exhaled. "Ranger's probably right. I'm making a mountain out of nothing, most likely that ain't there." He chuckled.

"Why would someone start a fire down there, anyhow? That'd be downright reckless." Henry preferred mystery novels wrapped up tidy in happy endings.

"Wouldn't seem reckless if you was cold. When that sun goes down. How about you, George? You still sleeping under your wool blanket?" Joe guffawed. Nobody would fess up to that. "Like I said, I'm just imagining too much. Let's get some sleep. Looks like we're going to have some busy days ahead of us."

131

"I hope so!" Henry sounded as happy as the time he'd come across Dashiell Hammett in his pile of unread books.

Florence propped the only chair up against the handle. She loved her room of windows, the transparent, thin partitions of glass beyond which held a mountaintop world view. On clear nights, she personally claimed a few of the brilliant stars watched over her, and Homer. At a little after ten o'clock she got ready for bed but instead of going to the outhouse, peed into the bucket instead.

Martin-Thirty-Six

At the intersection of Elgin and Elm, Martin hustled past the forsaken lamppost, the cat having moved on to a more fortuitous corner, took a right onto Beech Street and retraced his route to early Mass. Mid-block the church's twin towers hogged the skyline with heavy-handed architectural bluntness unrepentant to Sudbury residents for the imposing monstrosity. In blooming seasons, the deciduous trees lining Beech softened the gauche exterior, but the walkway in nun rigidity led to the foundation before angling into a kinder half circle ahead of the lower staircase. A two-foot white battlement at the staircase's second tier implied that the higher one climbed, the closer one rose to purity and eternal safety.

Martin circled the perimeter three times pinpointing exits leading to the railway depot. Beech Street ran by the church before making a sharp right turn toward downtown and ended at the train station. The contingency plan would be Elgin Street. Forthright front doors spilled out onto Beech making it almost impossible to leave without being spotted. The exits at the rear of the building, a third possibility but only as a last resort, led to the parking lot and onto St. Anne's Road which didn't go toward the depot.

In a busy alley off Beech a pack of dogs bared their fangs at him while fighting over rotting food that hung half-devoured from their sloobering jaws. The stench followed him for a block. He peered into deserted alleyways looking for niches, places he could hole up. He'd go over the route again later after meeting with the Finns when places of business that used guard dogs or owners of bitchy, lap-warmers, fuzzy, spoiled yippers were put outside. He came back up on Elgin from the train station and ran into the cat at the corner of Larch eating a fish head. It stopped chewing long enough to give him a smirk. *Disgusting cat!*

Mary Alice and her damn tea and biscuits and never-ending woes, hinting and wooing and then backing away like she was dancing the jitterbug had torpedoed his initial plan, but he'd done what he wanted after all. Still, he wished he'd taken care of it earlier because his feet boiled from the hot pavement as he raced down streets, waiting while cars crawled past, cooking the soles of his shoes and swelling his ankles. He cursed his stupid cigarette addiction and its consequence of being out of breath but more than once it was the excuse to stop and study roomy storefronts. He encountered some of the same people coming and going and tipped his hat in recognition but got vacant stares in return. Did Sudbury have a moratorium on the amount of walking one was allowed to do on Sunday afternoons? He ground his molars as another such person approached, smiled a tight grin pretending to be an ordinary walker on a brisk afternoon stroll.

Something was amiss when he got back to his room. He intended to fix a light supper and gather his material to meet with Erno and Taavi and go over his plans, but had decided after second guessing he would not disclose all the key elements. Was Erno reliable? He went from hot to cold and back to hot without a blink. The Finns he'd met were a taciturn bunch, slow to make up their minds or jump into something new except in Finland where they got naked and jumped into six foot high snow banks that apparently didn't require overthinking. Even then, they wouldn't shout with pure joy or cry out in misery. Judging from how Erno had raved the night they came to his flat, then did a U-turn the following week at the forge, and flipped once more in the pub put Martin on edge. Would Erno take another U-turn? As unpredictable as he was, Taavi was worse, unnerving and wary. Martin felt like the tail-end of a swinging pendulum what with Mary Alice smothering him with a neediness that squeezed the breath out of him and Erno and Taavi changing moods more often than their underwear. He had a clean, meticulous plan, yet despite the groundwork, it was like trying to hold on to an oily bottle that could easily slip from his grasp.

He lingered briefly in front of the church after coming back up on Elgin and onto Beech debating going through the route once again before he headed back to the flat. He decided to do it later when he could see how dim the corners and hiding places were once it got darker. The Canadian summer evenings labored futilely to get to dusk. Where were the guard dogs? He had been careful not to loiter at the train depot and managed to recheck the departure schedule for that evening.

Whoever had gone through his things knew what they were doing. Someone with a trained eye although not as proficient as Martin's. If only it were Mary Alice acting out of female jealousy and on the hunt for a picture of his wife, or ferreting out if and how many children he had, trying to unearth a private secret to satisfy all the unanswered questions he would not accommodate. If only she had gone through his things, it would be a welcome and uncomplicated prospect that meant enduring only a pathetic cross-examination. However, overreaching and snooping through his things weren't part of her style despite the poorly disguised but underlying urgency to land a husband. She was too good a Catholic girl. The agent who had rifled through the room failed to see the fold of the blanket that deliberately hung carelessly off the bed frame to the floor. The space should have measured precisely six inches. Instead, it was four. Martin appreciated the appetite of his invader, inculcated from his training to perfection, the requirement to leave things just as they'd been found, as neat but no neater, obsessive yet fastidious.

He scrutinized the cutout hideaway in the floor where he stored his plans and had spread an almost indiscernible powder. There was a muddle of footprints like a fox had been digging fruitlessly at a hole to get its rodent. The intruder had gone without the prize but why? Had he left in a hurry? Had Martin arrived back and surprised him?

His stomach growled. Even the biscuit he'd snubbed in the café now seemed nearly appetizing. Through the flimsy curtains to the street below he watched for a shadow in the graying evening. Something, any movement at all that would betray a hider when the dim street lamps came on and threw out their blurry arcs. He turned on the ceiling light attempting to throw the hunter off the scent and pretending the prey was unaware of his stalker. During those precious but vapid moments he considered next steps.

135

Florence-Thirty-Seven

After midnight a breeze fluttered through the screen promptly dropping the temperature several degrees and Florence, propped up against the frame of the cot and determined to stay awake, shuffled the wool blanket up around her shoulders. She refused to sleep after what Joe had said to the ranger or rather what he hadn't said. It hung like an empty noose in the darkness. Instead of contradicting the ranger to say, "Someone down there lit that fire in the gulch," Joe only hinted at it. A siren went off in her head. The bloody bundle, had it been a warning omen? *Oh my lord.*

She'd twitched when she came across it, like a hare trapped and too far from its hole to find safety. At once she was engulfed in a coma of fear and became deaf and blind to the surroundings. Time took a long breath before the birds chirped again, had they been singing all along, and squirrels squealed at her racing over mossy, rotten logs. Someone was injured somewhere. She stepped back up against a thick tree trunk so no one could sneak up behind her. All seemed remarkably normal when she came to her senses.

That extraordinary encounter got buried from the commotion over the fire and was remembered only when Joe suggested someone was in the woods. Although it had frightened her, she wouldn't have mentioned the yarrow anyway to the spotters, that it was used to staunch blood.

"Yeah, Flossie. A grizzly got all tore up on some barb wire and rubbed up against that yarrow." That sounded like Fred guffawing when they first dated. He got into the habit after a year into their marriage of going to the bar after work with his pals. She hoped he'd grow bored doing the same thing night after night, but he didn't, and as one block of disappointment piled on top of another, she stopped expecting it. Joe and George, and even Henry, cracked open that hole long closed over revealing what she'd lost and locked inside her. Joe wouldn't want her balled up and waiting out the night, a tiny dot perched on a mountain where the weather got moody and vicious, voracious animals hunted, trees dried out vulnerable to fires, and arbitrary humans roamed.

To stay awake, she wrote to Homer about spotting her first fire, how it looked like a cloud hanging there, and about pacing and worrying about doing the wrong thing. Pitch-black darkness came before she wanted to stop writing and before the breeze started so she made up a game reciting out loud all her recipes. There were the other recipes too, ones forgotten after these many years, dishes she fixed when Homer in the fourth grade developed an affliction that Dr. Halverson couldn't identify. He turned into a spidery skeleton that miserable year and looked like he would slip away forever but an herbalist from the reservation showed her how to use plants to get his appetite back.

Where was that strapping young soldier of her now, the one with the wide back and muscled arms? Was he looking up at the inky silkscreen printed with its shimmering stars crowded around the Milky Way or streaking rebelliously across the sky?

At 5:30, the sun bathed over her face and woke her ahead of the alarm clock, a half hour before the morning call to the ranger station. She'd fallen asleep in her work clothes huddled in the corner of her bed, her bones creaking more than the cot when she got up. Not a hint of anything out of the ordinary during the night except for losing precious sleep and waking up with a crick in her neck.

"Let's talk about unwanted visitors." It was the last day of training and Miss Conrad was on a tear. Rolling her eyes, she pointed to the room across the hall where the men happily chattered about the Pulaski, a tool the women did not have to master. "Now, between you and me and the kitchen sink, if you will forgive me the sin of the proverbial cliché, are any of you girls afraid to be alone with a man?" They squirmed and looked down at their hands.

"Not in the least bit." Hattie McCloud, the woman skinny as a teenage kid standing about that tall and just as eager. Miss Conrad's speech sprinkled with strange words didn't deter Hattie.

"I'm glad to hear it." Miss Conrad grinned. "Now, what you need to remember girls is to use the word, NO!" She eyed them hard and they waited for her to say more, so she did. "No, is a powerful word *if* you mean what you say. And I mean IF!" Hattie nodded like a horse drinking from a trough.

"You need to be careful up there alone on your peaks. If a man shows up and you give him mixed signals he will think you are opening a door to him. Frankly, men have more on their minds than you want to know about." She scowled. "For them, it's a fine line between your being a gracious hostess and what he imagines you are really offering. You have the rules about how to receive visitors to your mountaintop abode and you will, of course, give any who show up that courtesy. But be cautious about falling into the trap that if you don't serve charm along with a snack, he is going to call you stuck up. It can get sticky if he thinks you are giving him special signals. If it gets that far, even the word NO will sound like you are leading him on." Florence didn't know why her head was going up and down in agreement.

Miss Conrad didn't stop there. "If you say 'No', and you don't put your clout behind it, he might ignore it believing you want to be coaxed first, and that your No really means, *Yes*. Do you understand, now?" Grace shook her head.

"But what can we do? We aren't as strong as they are." Big-boned Grace stood almost six feet tall. Hattie sat next to her and cocked her head up at the woman as if she was a complete imbecile.

"Well, that's as good as saying you can't do nothing to watch out for yourself." Hattie jumped up and her chair fell back. Standing by Grace's chair, she looked her straight in the eye. Before their summer spotting jobs ended that September, Grace would face down a grizzly, and she would be prepared and calm. She would know exactly what to do. Assume a passive stance, make no eye contact, back away slowly. A man may be a different animal but to Grace's way of thinking he was dominant and commanding and she would be just as compliant and accommodating.

The shimmering light, already threatening to be intense at 6:00 am melted away Florence's nighttime chicanery. "Crystal clear this morning. Not a cloud to be seen up here."

"Looks like a beauty today, don't it?" The ranger sounded exhausted. The breeze was light and coming from the southwest. She checked the humidity and then looked almost with tenderness for a sign of lingering smoke from her fire.

138

"Good work up there yesterday, Florence. You're an asset already, by golly."

She wished they would stop praising her. "Thanks. I'll check in at 10:00." She nearly tripped over the wash bucket on her way out the door to the outhouse. She moved the chair away from the door and pulled the handle back letting the sunlight flood through the opening. She was squinting and missed seeing the footprints.

Martin-Thirty-Eight

Daylight wheezed its last breaths when Martin spotted the edge of a jacket and toe of a man's shoe in the haze of the lamp across the street from the flat. He fried up the sausages, chewed each bite twenty times, and kept the drapes wide open. Just a working man having an early supper. If they meant to come for him, they would have already done so. They would jump him when he met up with the Finns in two hours, catch him with the plans they hadn't found in the apartment. *Not terribly clever.*

The tip of his cigarette jiggled, or was it the match? He drew on the fag, pulled the smoke deep into his lungs and held his breath until the faithful rush from the tobacco kicked in, then a staccato of puffs followed by some longer drags, squinting into the self-made fog. The air in the room was stifling but began to feel cooler as the nicotine coursed into his arms and legs. When he got to the last embers his mind was steady.

He lit a second off the first recalling the spidery padre who had thrust a hand of dough into his. Martin had was preparing to dump Mary Alice after the service and didn't expect a clammy palm enclosed in his. He brushed his hand on his pant leg letting the half-burned fag perch on his lower lip.

A car's tires squealed. Balls of light glowed around the street lamps. Other than a matching pair of red taillights trailing a lone auto, the street was dark. At the edge of the window, he searched for the government regulation shoes among the shadows. Did the agent know he'd been spotted?

Now it made sense, that night the Finns came to the apartment, Taavi a caged wolf before they'd climbed through half the bottle of whiskey, tapping his foot and knocking his knees together or staring wide-eyed and sullen. At Lilly's place Taavi was different, more overt, sometimes hostile toward Martin or sinking inside himself, not able to square whatever was troubling him.

"He all right?" Erno was eyeing Lilly's ass as it swayed past their table. He cupped his hand to grab it but she made sure to be out of reach. Lilly dodged, ducked, served beer, prayed for her kids to turn out all right, and someday to move away from Sudbury.

"This place is a dead-end pit." She said when some idiot started a fight in the place or a rowdy crowd spilled beer.

"She gotta been one hell of a looker in her day. What'd you say?"

"I dunno. Guess so. So, is he sure he wants to do this? Taavi?"

"Ah, that's just his way. Don't mind him. He's a bit off." Erno grinned twirling his finger around his ear. "His rocker. Know what I mean?" Erno nudged Martin with his elbow.

"He up for it?" Erno shrugged.

"Hell. He does his damn job, don't he?. He don't have to be told what to do." Taavi didn't make mistakes, never missed a day of work, pulled his fair share and more. Could he carry out Martin's plan? Erno beamed.

"Don't worry nothin' about him. He's gonna do fine. just fine." Taavi was winning at darts and throwing glares at them from across the room.

"He got a family?"

"Lives with his sister and her old man. She's got a brood. Too goddamn many mouths to feed."

"What about you? You got a missus?" Erno caught him off guard. Martin cleared his throat, took a puff.

"Got a wife and two kids up Timmins, way.'

"And that girl in the apartment on the side." Erno tipped his head back and roared. Taavi's head swiveled goaded by the laugh but his feet stayed cemented to the oche. "How'd you manage that? Lucky devil."

"Her mother lives with us but she's too sick to move her down here right now."

"Best of all worlds, then." Erno slapped him again. "Hey, Lilly, bring us another round." He leaned into Martin whispering. "Hell. I'd like to send my missus to Timmins. Me and Lilly could make some damn good music."

A truck backfired and its taillights shimmied past his window before disappearing around the corner. The sidewalks were silent, the street empty, no stragglers out for a late stroll, everyone tucked up and running fans full speed in their baking houses, making lunches for Monday.

His escape route, through the kitchen window and out across the roof was compromised. They must have a man up there and at least three others in the street including the one under the lamp, tucked into doorways, one or two in a parked car.

His obsolete plans flamed brilliantly in the frying pan, one page at a time, before disintegrating into useless ashes. The landlord would have to replace the cheesy utensil with another cheap one for the next renter. Martin made an occasional foray past the window to feed any stray doubt the watcher might have about him. Once, he stopped at the window for a cigarette, looked through the glass and his own reflection down into the street and sucked on a crumb of satisfaction that the agent was squirming, wondering if Martin knew. At the sink, the ashes sloshed under the running faucet before slipping into the drain. With only two pages left to burn a noise warned from outside the door. He lit the next one.

Heavy smoke consumed the room. He didn't dare open a window. The hallway was quiet again so he packed the knapsack, organized the items first on the cot. A change of clothing, his razor, and hairbrush, his flashlight, binoculars, Swiss knife, a rain poncho, and a roll of salami, hard cheese along with a few hard rolls. A carton of cigarettes and two pairs of heavy socks. Finland had been so damn cold. He held it against the country that his feet were never warm there. If he ended up in prison, he prayed that before they shot him they let him wear his socks.

The final minutes dripped away. Erno and Taavi, would be waiting unless the agents jumped him before he got to the church. He needed another way out of the building.

Florence-Thirty-Nine

Florence had one single regret. Miss Conrad gave out mountains of gold star advice for succeeding at the lookout, just one example being how to bake biscuits in an oven without a gauge. Florence's fellow spotters frequently got the shirttail ends of Miss Conrad's nuggets.

"Put a piece of bread or paper in the oven to check the temperature, Henry. I'm sorry yours got scorched. If it turns brown before five minutes are up, it's too hot."

"Dang it, Flossie. You shoulda told me that before now. I been using them cow patties for target practice on the squirrels."

Miss Conrad's lessons included plans for breakfast, lunch, and supper to assault the hum drum meals from the 30-day supply of canned goods. When it came to burying refuse, she was an Algebra teacher, laying out precise dimensions for the size of holes, and then applying practical math to measure the usage of water by the number of cups, pints, quarts and gallons needed for every purpose. Florence the gardener added to those figures to maintain her plants. Beyond nuts and bolts , Miss Conrad's assorted discussions ranged from fending off unwanted male attentions interspersed with a sure-fire method for shooting grouse which Florence had no intention of doing despite their intimidation when she accidentally flushed them out of the bushes.

With a teacher's bewildered sigh, Miss Conrad led into the topic of loneliness and what to do when it set in like it would. "It could hang on obstinate as tent caterpillars." During the school year she lived in an apartment on Brooks Street free of the gardener's many plights, a walking encyclopedia. Even caterpillar problems were taken hostage to her comparisons.

"Frankly, there is just so much you can do to combat the solitude. My advice is to ride it through with the knowledge it will end sooner or later. Try to make the most of it and do not panic! You know the old saying: there is always light at the end of the tunnel." Miss Conrad was a woman of complete sentences, rarely using contractions.

Isolation wasn't getting the best of Florence. She didn't regret the long hours without human contact, and the evening conversations were more than enough to satisfy her. Only one thing kept her from perfect joy over her post and that was lack of news from Homer. In Missoula, letters came like waves on the tide without the moon's phases to predict them. But, they came. It had been over a month since leaving Missoula and until the packer arrived next with her supplies, she had to imagine how and where her boy was. On optimistic days, she pictured him doing an important job away from the front lines. The lookouts were cut off from news about the war, and every other thing that happened in the rest of the world.

Homer was on her mind as usual as she headed down to the outhouse. The ranger had sounded brittle when she made her early report because he too had gone without much sleep. The sunlight made beads of sweat on her forehead, and she chuckled. "Every day there's something new to discover on this job." Now, she'd need the hat with the big brim just to go to the bathroom! A few weeks before it had rained and rained and an umbrella would have come in handy.

Ancient roots and the occasional rock pocked the otherwise gentle path, bending around wild grasses toward the outhouse. An ambrosia morning, sweet as honey and fresh as just baked bread and pure elixir after the vexing hours cramped up on the cot. She hummed absently trailing her hand over the tall grasses, a familiar tune she'd sung to the fellows. A flock of chickadees added to the mood peppering the rising day with dainty high-pitched squeaks.

"Gol darn it, Flossie. You got a voice as good as any warbler I ever heard." George bragged when she first started singing along with them, the others clapped and hooted.

A squirrel ran to the middle of the path in front of her carrying a pine cone twice the size of its mouth. It froze at being exposed, dropped its load and stared at her. She laughed and it scrambled off to the side but not before retrieving the pine cone.

"Pack up your troubles in your ole kit bag and smile, smile, smile." The humming turned into song bellowing from her lungs. Every week throughout her married life, Florence had dusted her mother's gramophone sitting on the shelf Fred built in the living room. Her dear mother so loved music. She squeezed an allowance selling eggs from her hens to buy records, and when she turned ill, her dad bought a bigger stack for her. "I figured if I bought enough of 'em, she'd have to like some of them."

"I just love them all." In the evenings, when her mom no longer had the strength to turn the handle Florence cranked it up. She was still able to work on her embroidery almost up to the end. Florence sat nearby doing her English and math homework, her dad labored at the kitchen table tying flies.

"Take it. Go on, take it!" Her dad insisted after she got married. He had bought the radio by then and had found a taste for baseball and the news. "You know I'm not gonna play it."

The packer was overdue. She'd followed Miss Conrad's hints so she wasn't down to crumbs and a few cans of beans, and she didn't need to shoot a bird to carry her over, but she was hungry for some news of Homer. From the cupola the trail was visible and every afternoon for the past week she watched for the pack train to ride over the rise

"I'm always chasing rainbows." She'd switched tunes and stopped to watch a hawk whose shadow moved across the path. "Out for an early breakfast, are you?" It floated like a feather along the ridge but when it spied its next meal skipping along the rocks turned and began to fly in circles, large ones at first, expert circles, then smaller and smaller. When it swooped, it didn't even touch the ground.

She didn't scream, she was almost sure, when she recalled what happened at the privy, but maybe she had. It had taken a few seconds after opening the door to adjust from the brilliant light to the darkness. A tiny grate covered a small opening and let in a pinhole of light.

She would have tripped over the shoes had she not been looking down. She jerked backwards and covered her mouth. Tears in her eyes. Did she scream? If so, it was at the same instant she turned and ran back toward the lookout. "Block the door. Block the door. The rifle. The rifle." Oh, why hadn't she listened to them? They'd warned enough times.

145

"Remember your rifle might be your best friend when you really need it."

She was ten yards away from the door when she glanced over her shoulder to find that no one was following behind her.

Martin-Forty

The hallway was quiet beyond the clatter of plates, and if he was correct, onions sizzling. With his ear pressed to the door that aroma slid through the cracks. This was shortly followed by the invasive smell of liver frying and then a decisive series of scrapes from a knife and fork against porcelain. Finally, the abrupt screech of chair legs across linoleum and then water running in the sink. He waited a few minutes longer before shutting his door behind him leaving on the ceiling light. He guessed he had twenty minutes before they put it together.

After one light tap her door flew open. A sheepish grin, the naughty boy trying to head off his mother's wrath before someone else got to her first.

"Hi, Mary Alice." He whispered. "Sorry to bother you when you're eating supper."

"Well, hello." A broad smile. That was encouraging. "No, no. I was just washing up. I'll fix some for you." The rapturous Madonna lowered her voice to match his. "Come in."

"I already ate."

"I thought I smelled sausages frying earlier."

The knapsack's bulge rammed into the doorframe jostling him against her. "What's this, Martin?" Barefaced disappointment deflated Our Lady's brief rapture.

First, a foolish grin and then an attempt at an innocent shrug before he put an index finger to his lips. "We should keep our voices down.

"Why?" There was already frost in her whisper.

"Some guys are after me." Keep to the facts as much as possible.

"It's those creeps, isn't it? That came late and drank all your whiskey. I knew they were skunks!" She sniffed.

"Yeah."

"You're safe here." She tried to separate him from his pack. "How do you know they're after you? Where are they?" Five minutes already gone. He pushed her hand away.

"And why?" She took up a dish towel, wiped the plates like they were children's dirty faces. Sweat dripped off his forehead. "You should take your coat off."

"They said I cheated at darts but I won and they don't want to pay me the money they owe me." She nodded. She irritated him. Too easy to lie to.

"They are two thugs." She tugged at his jacket sleeve.

"Did you know they were in my room today?" If she kept pulling, it would be a tug-of-war. Three more minutes gone.

"I heard someone rummaging around. Heavy footsteps on the stairs, cupboard doors slamming. Then it got quiet. I thought it was you because later I smelled something burning. Then, it wasn't you?"

"No. It wasn't me."

"What were they doing?"

"Going through my things. Looking for money." She was so damn upright. A pity she was easier to lie to than a liar. Too good for the Catholic Church and the padre who took advantage of her good will. One minute malleable as butcher paper, the next hard as a bank safe. She would pay the price for believing his lies. But he'd be long gone before that happened.

"Where are you going?" He'd reclaimed the sleeve of his coat.

Dead straight into her eyes he lied once more. "I'm going back to my wife." Just a flicker across the brow to register the stab wound to her heart, she looked back at him and didn't blink.

"Why aren't you turning them in to the Mounties instead of running away? You shouldn't let them bully you like that. They'll just keep doing this till someone stands up to them." Two more minutes gone. For a second he got mixed up about his lie.

"I'm not a chicken."

"I didn't say you were." She stuck out her chin.

Another minute gone. He wouldn't argue. He forced a smile and changed tact, murmured sensually near her ear. "Listen. You are right, darling. I'm going to go the Mounties. Just as you say. You are right. I shouldn't be running away."

A beatific grin, like that of her namesake Mother Mary down on Beech Street tucked into a cryptic alcove the woman in cement smiling absently from her vaulted pedestal. "I'm so glad, Martin. You know in your heart it's the right choice, and you won't be sorry you did it."

"But, here's my problem, sweetheart." He spoke very quietly and she leaned against him. "You see." He brushed a wave of hair back off her forehead. "They're waiting for me down on the street right now, and I can't get to the Mounties until I find a way around them."

"They're out there now? Why didn't you say so? You *really* think they're down there, now?" Softly kissing her right temple, he nodded. She shuddered. "They could break into your room tonight." Another nod and another shudder. "You have to get out of here." If his time hadn't already run out. She squeezed her eyebrows. "There's the roof. Do you think you can manage that? It's dark and it's steep." And it was dry thankfully given Sudbury's heat wave.

He squeezed her cheek. "You're brilliant, Mary Alice! Why didn't I think of that?"

"But, you don't need your pack, if you're going to the Mounties. Leave it with me."

"I have to have my flashlight if I get lost. I'd better get going." A pitiful excuse but she didn't question it or think to volunteer hers, if she had one.

The bedroom was dark and he knocked his shin on a corner of her bed. "Goddammit." He rubbed it through his pant leg. A draft rippled the curtains and a red neon light blinked from a liquor store a block away. Someone somewhere was cooking onions and garlic. Her apartment faced the alley where one of them might hide. He didn't see any movement and would have to take his chance.

She brushed up against him, smelled his body heat and threw her arms around him. He kissed her hard for a long second, pushed her away roughly and stepped around the glass and out onto the roof tiles. The rubber soles pattered like cat's paws along the soffit gradually fading into silence.

"I'll wait for you." He had blended into the shadows before she whispered and too late to hear what she said.

149

Part Two

Florence-Forty-One

As the result of environmental studies, and on-the-ground experience, plus an increased budget, the Forest Service got aggressive about fire management and added a bunch of summer spotters. Hundreds of lookouts were erected in forests throughout America. The solid D-1 design with cupola built in 1922 constructed as permanent/temporary housing was meant to withstand gale forces, drenching rains, mountains of blizzards, and bear intrusions. The six to eight inch claws on a grizzly bolstered by massive shoulder muscles and blade sharp scissors can rip open fallen tree trunks to get at a tasty dinner of insects. Black bears come with the same equipment just inches shorter and with a stunning amount of force behind them. Florence's sturdy wood door and shades fashioned over the screened-in windows mostly thwarted rummaging bears. Would they also defend against human invaders?

A pair of shoes in the outhouse! That first second, the shock turned on the faucet of adrenaline drowning out the normal, usual noises, the squirrels' chatter and arguing, a dozen agitated crows complaining, the woodpecker's urgent tat-a-tat. Do those sounds continue unabated when fear overtakes? Kicking at the heels of that terror came the crushing drive to retreat, to duck into a blind, the all-out need to get to safety.

Florence flew back up the trail. Over gnarled roots and obstruent rocks, speeding up the crooked path, past the tall grasses. *The rife. The phone. Get to the phone.* But it would be hours before anyone would reach her. The rifle on the rack above the door. *Just get to the door. Bolt it. Pull the rifle down.*

She hustled as fast as her legs could run when a sudden but contrary idea entered her head. Unbelievable as it was, just twenty yards from the cab she stopped dead in her tracks. It was insane but a sudden stone-cold rationality needed to know who was coming after her. However irrational and threatening, jarring as a chair pulled out from under her, it also pilfered the chance of getting to the cab to shutout whoever was after her.

Except no one was chasing her. The pounding noises had come from her own footsteps. She wasn't being hounded! Sweat dripped onto her shirt, the sun hammered on her forearms and scalp. She shivered instinctively wrapping her arms around her to replace her elsewhere jacket. She felt like a half-wit. Nonetheless, her hands still shook although that pair of shoes hadn't jumped out at her. If she'd taken the rifle, if she'd stayed calm hadn't leaped round and turned tail, she would know at least who was attached to them. A couple of shoes didn't walk to the outhouse on their own.

She locked the door, closed the shades, pulled the rifle down, and stuffed the pleasant red-colored finger cartridges into its eager gullet. The oxygen in the room soon would be sucked up by the heat and despite the early hour, it would be sweltering by noon with the windows boarded up.

"Well, dammit, Florence. What else did you see?" Only pointed questions the ranger would demand. Specific details.

More than her paltry explanation. "There's a pair of shoes in the outhouse."

"Shoes? What else? I can't justify sending someone up there for some damn shoes, Florence. Song and dance." Florence, the hero fire spotter demoted to wolf-crier. Miss Conrad shaking her head, a pained expression, personally injured at her shining pupil's failure.

"Don't panic. Use your head. If you get yourself in a fix, get yourself out of it." It would betray independent women who rely on their personal skills, digging down into the wells of their strengths to find the way out of whatever obstacle and doing so with wit and humor intact.

From the cupola vista she surveyed her domain for any clues of another human. The cab was buttoned down and by early afternoon it was going to be hot enough in there to burn biscuits.

Everyday noises droned around the upper level, the Clark's nutcrackers perched on the eaves above her studying her through the glass. "South southeast at 10 miles per hour," she'd reported of the breeze at her 6:00 am call to the ranger. On such a hot day, any wind at all would feel lovely but murder for a crew who had to tackle a fire.

The enemy that propelled fires across acres and acres of timber, egging it on until every resource is devoured.

Petite Hattie by this time had her first report called in for the day. Spitting distance from the Idaho border, practically straddling the divide and climbing how many times a day to get on and off her 50-foot tower with the L-six cab. Hattie, the runt of the spotters who had knocked the knees out from tall Grace during training. "Sure enough, Grace, we can watch out for ourselves." Did the mouse sway the rat? How hard-wired was Grace to her belief? The large woman shrugged at Hattie but didn't appear to take offense. What would either of them do if they came across shoes in their outhouses? What would Miss Conrad do?

Basic necessities called so she came back down the ladder to use the chamber pot, wash her face and hands and get breakfast. What she would do next she didn't know. The shaft of light from the cupola was enough to make a simple breakfast of leftover biscuits with jam. "Problems have a way of sorting themselves out when your belly is full." She missed her mother, had passed that simple advice on to Homer who never got to meet his grandmother.

Hattie didn't stumble about because of her size or let her gender slow her down. "What makes men strong?" She practically shoved her turned-up nose into Grace's Roman tilt. "It's because they think it. That's what they do. They don't ask." Hattie pointed to her temple. "We can think we're strong, too, Grace."

"It's the shoes!" Breakfast had helped. It wasn't the shoes. That's what she put together finally, the fact that no one was in them! What she had come across were soles turned up in the doorway.

"That's what's been bothering me." She called in her mid-morning report, not a peep about shoes in it. "Wind steady at 10 miles per hour."

"How ya doing up there? Long night." His way of apologizing for being short with her before.

"It's going to be a scorcher today." She smiled into the receiver, pushed her shoulders back and imagined Hattie lugging water and counting each step up to the cab. Fifty feet up!

"You got that right."

"You won't have time to load *and shoot* if it comes down to that, girls so remember to keep the safety on. You don't need to shoot yourself in the chin. That would be a bloody mess." Miss Conrad intimated they could do things the stupid way, or the sensible way- *her* way.

She clambered up the ladder for one more look around. "Maybe the packer will show up and find me dead." She shook her head and put her big-brimmed hat on. "Here we go. I love you, Homer, with all my heart." Unbolting and opening the door, for a moment she was blinded by the sun sizzling down onto the dusty ground.

Martin-Forty-Two

Two men were staked out on the roof by his flat, crudely outlined lumps due to the new moon which allowed Martin to glide behind them and over a gable onto the next roof and the next until he reached the street and dropped into the alley. Twenty minutes must have passed yet they were still watching his apartment.

He hurried through a string of alleys crossing streets to get from one to the next until he was on Beech and just a half block from the church. He darted between row of trunks thoughtfully planted lining both sides of the roadway and stopped opposite the steps leading up to the carved doorways where the oleaginous padre advanced on him that morning.

The air was thick and sticky this Sunday night, his jacket an annoying extra weight but it took up too much space in the crowded pack. Everything in it was necessary for later. It was quiet at the entrance to the church but he was early for the arranged meeting time. Low branches gave him adequate cover as he clamored up to the crutch in the trunk to better view both flights of stairs. The dully dressed old ladies that morning with their swollen ankles and clunky black shoes had pulled themselves up the steps by the handrails for early mass in pious submission.

A cat, was it *the* cat, hissed down at him from a branch above. "Shut up." He hissed back and the cat gave out a warning, "meow."

"Damn cat!" He shook the limb. "Scat!" A hiss with molten eyes, marble-sized snarled but didn't bother to move.

He'd left the radio booming with dance music in the flat. Turned it up as he organized his pack. Before he left he turned it down briefly to listen at the door. Back on then with the volume full blast. Funny Mary Alice didn't mention it.

A man and a dog jaywalked from across the street stopping directly below him at the base of the tree and wearing the distinct scent of Russian Leather. Bounteous leaves concealed his post. Martin pulled his feet up when the man lit a cigarette waiting for the dog to do its business which seemed to go on longer than forever. Between puffs the dog owner hummed. *Dritter Aufzug*. It was an accurate

154

rendition of Wagner's *Die Walkeüre* but then the cat hissed making the dog bark and rise on its hind legs to claw at the trunk. *Christ!*

"It's just a goddamn cat, Trixie, for Christ's sake. Not our type." *Trixie, of all names.* The cat hissed again and gave a ferocious spit so the man pulled on the dog's leash. "Let's go home to Mama." He waddled like overweight middle-aged men do back across the street. A good thing he went that way because Martin would have missed seeing the two burly figures coming from Elgin Street and heading toward the church. *Stupid man. Stupid dog.*

The pair arrived, but coming from where? They were maybe thirty feet from the church when one of them stopped and lit a cigarette. The flicker briefly illuminated Erno's shape. Taavi hopped around him doing a baboon's two-step. Erno suddenly disappeared off the sidewalk into the shadows behind the lower stair casing. Martin shifted to a sturdy higher branch to keep him in sight. Taavi bounced about on the sidewalk in front of where Erno went off and kept looking over his shoulders. Martin thought Erno might have ducked into the bushes to take a leak. When he came out, he nodded into the shadows before he joined Taavi on the sidewalk.

They walked to the sidewalk toward the church and Erno threw his cigarette down before they started up the first flight of stairs. He lit another when they reached the first landing and handed it to Taavi. Whenever Erno stopped, Taavi twirled or jumped around him. It was still too early. They wouldn't expect him for another thirty minutes.

Martin moved back down to the crutch for a cleaner view, and the cat spit at him again for disturbing its tranquility. At least one other man was at the front, likely two more near the stairs, one man at each of the exits. If he also counted the ones stake out at his flat and on the roof there must be ten, maybe twelve of them.

He moved quickly. The cat bellowed, fiercely offended when Martin reached the ground with a soft thud, another sleek nocturnal cat shifting from one tree to the next on the dim street. How long would it be before they discovered he'd bolted? A half hour maybe?

Erno had pretended to act casual the one time Martin was a half hour late getting to Lilly's. "Was you gettin' up the skirts of that looker at your place?" Erno slapped him on the back. Martin hadn't noticed the many gaps in his teeth. "Nice, huh?" He'd deliberately shown up late. Better to keep them off-balance. It was a fine line. Come across determined and in command to gain their trust and subtly control them by arriving late. Be unpredictable.

So, Erno would accept that he might be late. He'd allow ten minutes leeway unless Taavi got too agitated. Then, there would be the slow burn when it dawned on him that Martin knew it was a trap. Poor Lilly was going to get an earful of his venom for some time to come. She was used to men blowing off steam. She'd refill Erno's mug and give him a wide berth. Maybe the orangutan Taavi would by then stop his perpetual pulsating. If he didn't, Erno would box him a good one.

Martin creeped past a one of the pursuers in position on his haunches behind a parked sedan just before Beech Street made it's big turn toward the depot. He was smoking, waiting for a signal to go into action. Martin's ruse had worked. The people staked out at his flat, the others waiting at the church, let him know he had a twenty minute lead. Poor Mary Alice. He almost felt sorry for the interrogation she was about to face. The good Catholic caught in a web of intrigue and finding how badly she'd been duped.

A sudden cool breeze hit him in the sweaty face. If all Sudbury hadn't been snoozing, the tall man running down Beech Street with the bulky jacket flapping open at his sides on such a sultry night would raise the alarm. Keen and calculating, he raced over curbs, dips on the pavement, and stayed far from the alleys where dogs barked. He wasn't being followed. He grinned and promised himself a reward of two cigarettes as soon as he was safely away.

156

Florence-Forty-Three

Crunch, crunch. *Shhh!* Each footstep cracking like a firecracker although she was guarded putting them down carefully. Still her boots boomed out thunderous claps. Past the indolent wild grasses bending with the breeze, one hand on the nose of the rifle, the other ahold of the butt and crooked in her elbow. The path seemed changed, strangely going on longer than ever before and then abruptly dumped her with clenched stomach before the outhouse.

The Forest Service hat had dipped down her forehead as she bumped along cutting off a third of her vision. She flipped the brim up when she stopped, put her hand back on the rifle with the tip aimed at the door, and waited for the shoe owner to walk out. Her armpits prickled with sweat. A trickle crawled down the small of her back. Uneven breaths drowned out her heartbeat. She waited. Nothing happened. *What am I waiting for?*

A few more deep breaths before she stepped forward and listened. Still nothing so she poked the door with the tip of the rifle. It didn't bother to budge. This provoked her to nudge harder and it cried out a painful arthritic creak while incrementally letting daylight creep in. Successive jabs got the door open halfway and there he was. Her finger twitched on the trigger, so ready to pull it, but this day Miss Conrad prevented yet another potential disaster. The safety was still on. She was breathing hard.

Greedy daylight was slow to reveal the scene in the latrine. Florence squinted into the dusk waiting for her eyes to adjust.

"But...you're just a boy!" She announced to the walls of the tiny hut after a few seconds.

"No, I'm not." Feral green eyes flashed from the semi-darkness. He looked to be maybe ten years old. The age Homer was when Fred slugged him in the mouth for talking back. Florence had stepped in and taken a punch herself.

"You raise a hand on Homer ever again, I'm leaving with him for good." Fred cried like a baby.

"I'll never do it again."

The boy was a propped up Raggedy Andy, carrot head and all flung into the far corner to be picked up at a later date *if* by chance he was remembered and missed. The soles of his shoes still faced the door, floppy clown shoes that had been owned by a grown man who'd wisely gotten rid of them. Had the boy been upright, he would be a familiar comedic spectacle minus the clown face and goofy hat.

"But you are!" She winced, repeating herself.

"I'm not!" Dried blood on his forehead accentuated the furrows in his young brow and in the sparse daylight he squinted and shielded his eyes. He fell back against the wall when he tried to stand up to prove to her he wasn't just a boy, and yelped from the pain.

"You're hurt! How did you get here the shape you're in?" Her shock and alarm came across as criticism, finding a wounded boy in her outhouse and knowing she could have just shot him. Her hands shook and there were tears in her eyes.

"Dunno." He wouldn't look at her.

"What happened to you? How did you get hurt?" Her mind raced. How badly was he hurt? She had to get him up to the cab but he couldn't stand on his own let alone walk and he was too big for her to carry. Wisely, she didn't ask him more questions. He'd set his jaw. She'd only just had a rifle aimed at him and measured the fear in him. *In due time.*

"I'm fine." If nothing was broken he could put his arm around her neck and she could half-drag him up the path.

"I don't think you can walk on your own, can you?"

"What?" He sounded far away.

"You're not going to faint on me, are you?" She commanded. His eyes rolled back into his head. "Please don't faint." She pleaded. Thus far she hadn't reached out to touch him reckoning he could be wild enough to claw at her or bite if she did. But he was drifting off and she needed to talk to him. She reached for his hand tapping it and rubbing it. "Stay with me." She whispered it several times. "Just stay with me."

He was very still for a few moments. When he opened his eyes they were astonishing, deep green and yellow, like a cat's. She stroked his hand, talked quietly. "You're going to be all right." When

158

he was more conscious and saw what she was doing, he jerked it away.

"Stop doing that!"

"I'm sorry. It's just that you fainted."

"No, I didn't." He tried to stand up again but his legs couldn't hold him.

"Listen. I think if you put your arm around my neck I can get you up to the lookout. We can do this if we both try. What do you think? Can you do it?"

"You gonna turn me in?" He fell back down and screamed pulling his legs up to his stomach and then rolled into a tight ball. His ribs protruded from his t-shirt. He cried briefly but hid his face.

"Who would I turn you in to? What kind of trouble are you in?" He moaned. "All I want to do is to get you out of here and help fix you up. Will you let me do that?"

"Dunno."

"Well, you think about it." Her mother-tone more than her words said she wasn't going to take *no* as any kind of answer. "I've got to get back to the lookout right now and make a report to the ranger station. If I'm late, they might send someone up to check things out. You wouldn't want that, would you?"

He shrugged. Thought about it and shook his head.

"It is going to take us some effort to get you up there. As soon as I'm done making my report, I'll be back. Okay?"

"You gonna rat me out?"

"No." She whispered. "Of course not." That was the way Homer talked before he'd left. Him having her make a promise that she'd stay busy and not worry about him.

"Get a job, Mom. Just try to be happy. For me."

"I promise." She told the boy. "We'll get you up to the cab and sort this out when I come back. I promise."

Martin-Forty-Four

The *Bouclier canadien*, an enormous shield of igneous and metamorphic rock on the Laurentian Plateau in Ontario is not conducive for napping when the temperature rises on its crusty surface. Martin was able to rest until noon, but after that he was baking in his own juices. The benefit, however, was that the escarpment was unpopulated and it overlooked the railroad tracks and his one transport.

Ahhh. A freshly lit cigarette. He smiled as if it was the well-behaved child who had performed appropriately and brought praise to the family. When he made his escape from the flat, he'd calculated to this ersatz offspring the number of packs he could tote on the run. One every twelve hours. Deprivation would continually hound him and, coupled with the craving, incite him, heighten his effort to get away clean and fast. Three weeks to get out of the country *if* they didn't catch him by then. Three cartons left behind to be squandered on deficient secret agents and a most disagreeable parting.

Thus far, his plan had worked. Each evening as darkness fell, an enigmatic affair during the Canadian summer, he sped alongside the railway tracks stopping only for a cigarette after he'd covered half the distance he'd set for the night. He smoked the second when the heat basted him awake and hunger pangs twisted at his guts. He'd counted on finding drinking water as the area is dotted with lakes and cut through by rivers.

He dreaded two things. Cold feet and not being able to get ahold of a cigarette. If he was caught, would a condemned prisoner be allowed cigarettes while awaiting his sentencing followed by the execution? Morbid thoughts served their purpose pushing him to stay awake when his eyelids refused to stay open. They may have been propped open and he slept nonetheless. He couldn't be sure despite the manufactured but unpleasant image of himself blindfolded against a wall drawing in and savoring his final cigarette.

It was his fourth night on the run. He rummaged at the top of his backpack for the flashlight to see the time. Just past midnight. He shivered in his sweat. The temperature had dropped into the high forties. Hot, muggy days and chilly nights were his friends. They kept him on the move. He napped when he sensed he wasn't in danger, especially when he could camp hidden under birch or tamaracks or evergreens.

If the heat didn't rouse him, his addiction shook him out of a restless sleep. His heart raced, his fingers trembled but after a few puffs, he grew calm, almost tranquil, inexplicable for someone pursued. If he was. It didn't seem so now that he was four days away from Sudbury.

The last half of a baguette had gone stale. He broke off bits and tossed them at a squirrel that showed up as soon as he opened his pack. After a few slices of salami and hard cheese, he waited for evening to come and reviewed all the Canadian railway routes headed west and the cities they served. Canada had a lot of small towns with strange names. Carrot River, Cut Knife, Saltcoats, Neepawa, Fox Creek, Okotoks to name a few of the more unusual ones.

The first day out of Sudbury he had been twitchy, looking over his shoulder, twisting around at even humdrum sounds. Too near, too soon after his getaway and then a wolf howled. In Finland when day and night merged into ambiguity, the wolves yowled one continuous complaint for weeks.

The Walther P38 next to the flashlight at the top of the pack was loaded. A primal cry causes the short hairs at the back of the next to stiffen. But wolves are wary creatures and shrewd, master vocalists of the tundra and wilds with an uncanny ability to not show themselves. It offered up one howl followed by an echo of eerie silence and he was not fool enough to fire a round even if it had approached him. Better to wrestle it to the ground and strangle it. The lull was unnerving and he broke his recently imposed rule and had another smoke.

If he had been hunting down a spy instead of being the one hunted, he would have concentrated his resources on the shortest route out of Canada. By way of Sault Ste. Marie and across the border into the United States, or a train to Toronto where he could smuggle himself out of the country another way. It was no surprise then upon discovering he'd been betrayed to find when he got near the Sudbury

161

railway station an arsenal of agents, a gaggle of squawking geese, waddling up and down the platform. Lax fellows dressed in obvious garb, they were biding their time until commanded to take up positions. They thumped each other on the arms when they walked past each other pacing excitedly back and forth near the tracks, energized bulls let into the ring and sniffing the thrill of catching a spy.

The second day out, people were talking on the tracks below the escarpment and woke him. He was about thirty miles out of Sudbury as he'd passed through Capreol during the night. He'd put to memory the thirty-eight hamlets on the rail line between Sudbury and Manitoba. He unsnapped the leather case of his Walther and took piano wire from his pocket. He'd shoot one and garrote the other and hoped there were only two. There were and he was no more than four feet above them when he peered over the ledge. He could have reached down and pulled their hats off. As he hid on his haunches behind a hemlock tree they complained about the state of the railroad ties.

"Here they go again." One of them kicked several of the railroad ties with the steel toe of his boot. "Wild goose chase. Damn managers. They don't have no goddamn intention of changing them. Rotten as hell. Look it the shape they're in." The other wrote on a clipboard.

"I'm puttin it on the schedule, anyway." They walked along the tracks kicking at ties until they disappeared around a curve about a half mile from him. He studied the map and as it got cooler explored a half-mile radius away from the rim and came across a small lake, emptied his pockets and jumped. Like an otter, he lay on his back and floated under a sky of puffy white balls. Later he shaved using the lake's surface for a mirror.

He was three miles to the west of Leforest when he stopped for his smoke after hustling through the town. The train would pick up passengers at this stop, fifty-one miles northwest of Sudbury where he assessed the terrain. He'd gotten this far on foot and weighed the risk of hopping on the train before it got up to speed from Leforest where the tracks snaked alongside the cliffs.

162

The cigarette invigorated him and kept his appetite tame. He had the rest of the cheese and waited and listened for the train's whistle.

Florence-Forty-Five

The garden needed water. A mental note as she flew past it back up to the cab, her hat flapping against her shoulders hanging by the strap. That stray thought was necessary to steal attention from the mess behind her. A disturbing, mysterious predicament.

Adding to it, coming over the rise she had a horrible premonition. What if the packer had come, gotten to the cab ahead of her? Or what if he was coming up the trail now? She'd expected him for nearly a week and if he came this day he'd hang around into the afternoon smoking and eating her food.

"Everything okay up there, Florence?" The ranger quizzed. She always called on schedule.

"Things are just fine up here. How about down there?" She chuckled lightly and held her breath. "I haven't spotted anything suspicious. So far, at least."

She was fifteen minutes late but didn't give an excuse or say she was sorry. The motley crew of spotters along with the ranger, like radio operators learned how to read each other, identify who was on the end of the line without ever coming face-to-face by the way they paused, the length of their sentences, the words they used, the things they complained about, their brand of humor, and how they answered questions. An uncomfortable guffaw, a snide retort, a jerky phrase, a too long silence.

She'd rushed up into the cupola, did a cursory survey of her territory and breathlessly called in the report, clipping her words. This was not the patient Florence who answered with precision the measurements of her gauges, thoroughly and in great detail. The ranger annoyed her. She anxious to get the call over with, get him off the line, and ran back to the outhouse.

A fire that smoldered in one of the gulches, or on a ridge could not compare with what she had discovered moments before. The ranger prompted her. "What's your wind speed?" She read the thermometer. "76 degrees."

"Florence?"

"What?"

' The wind speed?"

"I just told you."

The kid was hurt so bad he couldn't stand up. How had he gotten himself to the outhouse then? He had been in the cab, too, she was sure it wasn't the storm.

"Florence?" The ranger's voice echoed from inside a deep well to her ears.

"What?"

"I just asked you for the third time what your wind speed is. You sure you're okay?"

"Never better. Sorry. I didn't hear you. Phone must be acting up today." She tittered. "Hardly any breeze at all. Lovely up here." Maybe she could use her belt as a strap to keep him from falling over. "Wind south-southeast at five miles per hour. Nice and calm, thank goodness." Her insides were shaking. She bit down hard on her finger and held it between her teeth.

"That's good to hear. Hey, about that fire you spotted, they're slow piecing together what happened on that. Pretty sure someone started it." Just as Joe had said but in a way that wouldn't embarrass the ranger yet opened the door to doubt.

"Do they know who it was?" Teeth marks left an impression on her knuckle. The boy could have done it to stay warm, but that didn't fit with how injured he was. He couldn't even stand up on his own. How would he have started a forest fire? He hiked up the mountain in those floppy shoes and she bet he wasn't carrying matches. Had he come into the woods on a lark, been attacked by a mountain lion or a bear and somehow wandered into her privy? Not a bit of it made any sense. And what about the yarrow?

"Florence?"

"Yes?"

"You got something else on your mind?"

"No, for goodness sake. Why?" Except for the damaged ragdoll sprawled on the floor of the outhouse, half conscious and in need of treatment now, not later.

"Well, I just told you that fire of yours was man-made. You got any idea about that cuz you're the one who spotted it?"

"What do you mean?" Was he accusing her? She glared at the receiver. *Oh, hurry up and get off the line.* "You think I had something to do with it?"

"No, no, no. Nope. I sure didn't mean you to think that."

"Well, good cuz I don't know how I could have since I am up there and it was clear over there in Henry's territory."

"That's not what I meant." He apologized again. Jesus. She sounded edgy. "The packer come up there, yet?" He change the subject. If the guy had been there, the ranger would have a chat with him. Ask him how she was doing. She'd been fine earlier that morning far as he could tell but then he'd been a bit of a grump himself.

"No. You know when he's coming?" That got her attention and her voice changed. Some nights when she was trying to fall asleep and get Homer off her mind, she'd picture the ranger and Henry, George, and Joe. The ranger must be close to sixty, the gravel voice gave him away unless he was a heavy smoker. He'd be overweight from too much sitting, probably did his fair share of drinking, too.

"I figured he'd have come and gone by now. You say he hasn't come?" She could see his eyebrows squeezing together on the face she'd created for him making parallel tracks along his forehead.

"I figured he'd be here by now too."

"How you're supplies holding up?"

"So far I'm doing okay." Thanks to Miss Conrad's practicality. Maybe the packer got paid for every trip he made and went to Polebridge or back to Columbia Falls where he spent it as soon as he got it. Cash in hand. Probably on booze. It might be a mistake not to tell the ranger about the boy but she had promised him she wouldn't say anything. She wished she knew how he had ended up in her latrine. Was he hiding from someone?

"If he don't show up by tomorrow I'm gonna track him down. Son-of-a-gun." What was she going to do with the boy when he did come? The guy pushed his weight around as it was and he wouldn't keep his mouth shut about the boy if he found out he was there.

She didn't know his name. Maybe it was Billy. She liked that name. Short for William. It was regal. If he didn't offer to tell her,

166

she'd say, "I bet your name is Marlon or Humphrey." If he smiled or made a face that would not be the right one, but if he didn't respond that would be.

"Did I tell you the temperature?"

"Three times now, Florence."

Martin-Forty-Six

Downtown Winnipeg was in a hurry. At the switching station, which covered an area a quarter mile wide, croaking and groaning freight trains loaded with tanks and weaponry jockeyed on multiple parallel tracks for a position at the front of the line. Maneuvered about like toy locomotives, they inched back and forth and with every increment the behemoths squealed when metal ground against metal. The industrious city screeched and bleated like the inside of a hive jammed full of live bodies rushing here and there. No laggards, only intent faces with noses pointed in fixed directions and moving along with economical speed. The commotion was somehow calming and without frenzy, and ordered. Martin floated along in one particular stream, his gray fedora tilted downward over his brow.

Cars clogged the traffic at the intersection of Broadway and Main in front of Union Station Depot stopping to drop off passengers. On the platform relatives and friends stood five rows deep waving their goodbyes, shaking their soggy hankies at the fresh-faced farm boys in immaculate uniforms who giggled worse than schoolgirls overt the excitement of their first train ride, plus the prodigious chance to see the world. Their naive optimism, that Canadian can-do spirit which the Allies bragged would win the war, would quickly end in Europe. Some of them only just eighteen, pimply, green, the self-congratulatory fools expected to win against the great war machinery, the superior strategy and ingenuity of the Germans, yet their raw sincerity innocent was nearly convincing.

In the crowd he was just another body to be bumped up against. He didn't stand out, wasn't displaying a sign that read SPY on his back. He relaxed his shoulders, picked out a phlegmatic intergenerational family to stand near, each of the members wearing the same inscrutable smile and individually brimming with the same high level of restraint. The youngest, a girl about twelve with thick braids held together with blue ribbons privately wiped a tear away. Martin lit a cigarette and waved at the anonymous and eager faces hanging like monkeys out the windows even after the troop train lamented as it departed from the depot platform.

168

He'd paced his stride the last fifteen miles while walking into the Manitoban capitol the previous day from East Selkirk. After a week on the rails, and sleeping out of doors, his face and hands had turned black, rough as sandpaper, worn and brittle from the soot. His fingernails indicated he dug potatoes or sugar beets to keep ends together. His eyes bloodshot, his shirt and pants filthy and ripping at the elbows and knees, his hair looking like the sweeping end of a broomstick. His long back ached for a mattress, even a lumpy one, and he wanted a satisfactory meal.

Before he got to Selkirk he spent one night and a day upstream along the Red River where he soaked in the still chilly water and washed out the extra pair of clothing in his backpack. He hung the socks and underwear on tree limbs and laid the rest out on the rocks to dry. When he walked into Winnipeg, he had dumped the coat and passed for a day laborer rather than a hobo.

By midday, he'd had a shave and a haircut. The barber was chatty and meddling, peppering him with questions while he slapped the strop with the straight-edged razor like he was slathering a slice of bread with butter. Martin's nose and eyes peeked out from a steaming hot towel. "Don't sound like you is from around these parts. "I can't put a finger on that accent of yours."

Martin mumbled from behind the towel. "I figured I'd better speak English since this is Manitoba." As if his first language was French.

"Say again?" The barber leaned over him and Martin looked up into his nose hairs.

"Where'd you say you come from?" He sounded friendly enough but snoopy. "Looks like you been sleeping rough, wherever you been." Martin had stopped counting the number of trains he'd hopped on and off after he left Sudbury in an attempt to mislead his pursuers. The federal police, Canadian Royal Mounted Police, had interred several Nazi sympathizers, and likely had a reciprocal agreement with the United States, too.

Before one of the trains he had hopped pulled into town, he'd jump off and after dark follow the tracks to the next station to check out the depots for posters of the MOST WANTED. Stark, black and

169

white photos that would make everyone, even an innocent mother, look like a criminal. So far, the Mounties hadn't posted anything posted about him because they didn't have a photo, but he wouldn't be hard to spot if they put up a written description and someone stopped long enough to read it. But everyone seemed hurried.

"I'm a mixed bag. Kinda a mongrel, I guess." The barber guffawed and offered him a cigarette from a stash on his counter and lighting it for him. "Long as you got money to pay for this here cut and shave." Martin dipped into his pocket and handed the guy the amount owed in quarters.

"Guess that's the same for most of us folks around here. My people come here fifty years ago." He pointed toward the east as if Martin should be able to guess from the gesture which country had been his ancestral home. "They was farmers. I'd a been one too if I coulda got things to grow. My dad said I was a disgrace to the whole family, but he never missed a chance once I started barbering to come to town for a shave once a week. The old fella never give me so much as a thank you even till the day he died."

He had the whitest teeth Martin had ever seen and wore his glasses half off his nose peering down like he was studying beetles or butterflies. Martin closed his eyes and pretended to rest while the barber clipped the little hairs on the back of his neck.

"There's a decent café up the road a bit. You look like you could stand a good square meal." He pumped down the chair and shook the haircloth out beside it, folded it in precise squares and placed it on the back of the barber chair. Sweeping up around the chair, he turned and pointed down the street. "The hotel down there ain't too bad either from what I hear."

Martin tipped his head. "Thanks for the tip. I'll give it a try." When he got within a block of the café and hotel, he turned onto a side street perpendicular to the main road, and walked along a quiet, tree-lined avenue with rows of neat compact houses until he was out of town. An old farmer in an even older rusted out pickup gave him a ride the next five miles.

Florence-Forty-Seven

"Halloo? The packer's Stetson bobbed just even with the top of the ridge like a puppet pulled along by strings. He materialized little by little straddling the quarter horse as he came up above the ridge, trailing a string of two mules. Florence was at the outhouse helping to get to the boy to his feet.

"Wouldn't you know it?" She groaned.

"I'll be up in a minute." She yelled next to his ear and the boy lurched backward. In a panic at the notion the packer would take it into his head to come looking for her.

"Oh, I'm sorry." She whispered putting him down again into the corner. It was nearly noon and felt like a sweat house full of flies circling the dried blood buzzing and touching down. "Don't try to move." His eyes sizzled with fear and she shuddered. She shooed the flies away. "It's just the packer bringing up supplies. He comes once a month." *Or so. The moron. Why didn't he come last week?*

"I'll get rid of him but he'll want lunch, first. Try to rest. I won't come back til he's gone." She wished she'd brought water but then she hadn't expected to have to leave him rotting there in his sweat, blood, and the dirt. The boy glared. He didn't believe her. How many times had he been on the tail-end of not getting a fair shake? How many broke promises?

Maybe he was a Billy. They hadn't gotten far enough along to know each other by name. When she'd rushed back down the trail he was in the same spot she'd left him. His eyes glazed over. *Oh, Lord.* She jiggled his arm making him moan. She kept at it to get him to open his eyes. Maybe there was more wrong with him than she could fix. She was being a fool to keep the promise and not report what was going on.

She wanted to but couldn't ignore the sting of the boy's look. She hadn't betrayed him but his eyes accused her and she felt guilty just the same, took in the blame. Whatever she told him couldn't ease him, wouldn't be enough, not the shape he was in.

"It'll take some time to unload the supplies but I'll get rid of him quick as I can." He winced. "And he won't go without lunch." She reminded. Cold spam on a dry biscuit. It felt mean. She patted his leg but he drew back recoiling. "I have a son." Trying to win the boy over. The packer was at the cab probably snooping through her things, trespassing. She cringed.

"I don't like the packer that much. The sooner he's on his way, the better." She made her face calm for the boy, another attempt to assure him he wasn't in danger. Her stomach was tight and she felt like she was suffocating. She had to get back to the cab.

"I'm Job." He'd told her that first day. "So, you're Flossie." The trailhead was still half-buried in a snowbank. The horse was stunning against the pristine white, his winter coat a shimmery reddish brown. The packer swatted the rump of the first of the two heavily loaded mules and even two feet from him she smelled the horse sweat. Job? The longsuffering Biblical character with open sores living on a garbage pile and damned to endless suffering?

This person would be bringing her supplies. She took a breath before asking, "What's your last name?"

"Lindstrom." Then she would refer to him from then on as Mr. Lindstrom.

"You on your way up, Flossie?" He hollered from up at the cab. "Need me to come down there and fetch you?" Laughter rolled down the slope. The boy's head snapped up.

"I don't like him. I'll be back soon as I can." The boy nodded. He seemed confused but didn't look as fearful now.

"I'm on my way, Mr. Lindstrom."

He was halfway down the path when she met up with him. "What you got cookin' today, Flossie?" She'd made cornmeal bread the day before and Mulligan stew. She hoped the boy would eat it for supper. If he had any appetite.

"Looks like you been babying that garden patch. You think you gonna keep them critters out when things get good and ripe?" She sat across from him at the table. Fred had better table manners. A piece of biscuit fell down the front of his shirt. "I figured you'd fix a stew or somethin for me.'" Picking up the bit of biscuit that had now fallen into his lap and shoved it in his mouth.

'Yeah. Now I've got fresh supplies in I can start cooking again." He looked out the window ignoring the insinuation.

"Goin' to take a trip to the outhouse and then I gotta head out." He'd wolfed down the last biscuit, stale or not.

'Oh!" She smiled, pushed back the alarm. He hadn't gone down there the previous trip. Why this time? He didn't light up, either.

"You sorry to see me go, Flossie?" He stepped in toward her.

"No, no." She took three steps back. "I've got to get back to work now."

"You sure you ain't lonely for a little male companionship? Up here all alone? Long summer for you on your own and I'm available and ready!" The grin was that of the man in silent movies who's just tied the beautiful young woman to the railroad tracks.

"I couldn't be any happier than I am, Mr. Lindstrom. I'm having the most wonderful summer."

He jogged down to the privy but after twenty yards she lost sight of him where the path went below the crest. What could she say when he came back up? He would hold it over her if she expected him to keep the boy's secret, and then he couldn't be trusted not to rat on her. She climbed into the cupola and paced by the windows waiting.

When he reappeared on the path, he was alone. She slid back down the ladder. "You camping out down there now?" He stood in the doorway, halfway in shadow squinting at her.

"What?" He had to have stumbled upon the boy. He would have had to step over him.

"Looks like a rat's been scrounging your potatoes. You musta seen them down there. Ain't you? You been missing any of your supplies?"

She shrugged. "Potatoes, you say?" Where had the boy gotten to? He barely had been able to move when she left him. Did that mean he wasn't there any longer? How could that be?

"And an eagle feather. You got somethin' mighty strange going on down there, Flossie."

"Goodness me. I'll take a look after you leave. Don't know what that's all about." She forced a smile.

173

"Coulda had them potatoes in a stew today." He grumbled climbing back onto his horse.

"Maybe next time." She waited until he disappeared below the ridge.

Martin-Forty-Eight

The signage, dog-eared and cockeyed, hung above the single door uneagerly advertising the entrance to the Grimes Hotel. One of several flophouses on a narrow avenue near Union Station. Somewhere in the past, the exterior had been painted gray to play down its vulgarity but failed to disguise how ugly it was.

In the center of his room, a bare light bulb dangled from a frayed chord, and while the window glass was distorted and smeared from other lodgers it had a good view over the street two stories below. He wasn't the first to use it for surveillance. His concern of being ambushed, caught in a covert trap, going down in defeat called for him to set up a post behind the fabric curtain and ignore the yellowed wallpaper peeling behind the headboard. Just another stranger among the milieu of travelers who took cheap rooms in swarming Winnipeg. Men revolved in and out of the only door all hours of the day and into the night in garb ranging from elegant, confident, and meticulous to street worn, uncertain, and drab. The Axis Powers had boosted Canada's enterprises, stimulated a thriving war industry and the city scratched to meet the demand for housing.

Within three days, Martin knew the particular and peculiar movements of each of the hotel residents. Somewhere someone was looking for him. Maybe not in Winnipeg, but it took only one person to recognize and finger him.

Men came and went on the poorly lit stairwell and he got to know their distinctive gaits along with the different creaks on the floorboards. A prehistoric attempt to muffle the sounds with carpet put down by some optimistic hotel owner had lost that battle years earlier. During its golden years, the flooring likely had been vibrant and welcoming, now it mirrored the color of the building's exterior.

His time riding the rails and living rugged on the Canadian landscape made the lumpy mattress an indulgence after waking up sweaty on sheer rock. The first afternoon he exchanged his clothing, chose a dark gray fedora, two long-sleeved shirts, two pairs of pants, dark dress slacks and a sturdy pair of dungarees, a pair of work boots and dark brown loafers. He replaced his overcoat with an anorak after the mind-blowing exposure from biting winds on the trains he'd hopped. There would be more trains to hop before he got out of Canada.

During Winnipeg's busiest daylight hours, he went to the station to see if the trains heading west were overcrowded and if they ran on time. If he got to Vancouver, British Columbia, he would sneak across the border and head for Seattle. If he wasn't nabbed by some hypervigilant patriot before then, he would follow the coastline down to Mexico and book passage either to Argentina or back to Germany. Canada's vast unpopulated interior was going to be one of his major obstacles. Too exposed for a man on the run with too few large cities to blend in and not be singled out.

A myriad of offshoots from the main train lines crisscrossed the heartlands stretching like loose threads on a loom, often these extensions seemed counterintuitive as if railroad designers sketched plans and let their pencils wander off the blueprints. Feeble arms fingered out to the remote nowhere to hamlets whose headstrong citizens required the services. He memorized even the most remote branches in case he needed alternative solutions. Any of the lines leading to the US border might be the one that would save him.

He hung around the busiest cafés, drank copious amounts of coffee, smoked, and sketched out the routes on the backs of paper napkins. Back and forth from the station to restaurants plotting and adding to his list of spidery rail lines. When he went back to the Grimes, he put to memory the growing list of secondary lines to the west of Winnipeg adding more until he'd covered the area between the city and Vancouver. Using his French novel as a prop, he drew new lines off the main course while he sipped and smoked.

But on the third day he sensed someone watching him. It was in a tight and busy café, the tables crammed together making it difficult to move about without knocking a purse or the back of a chair or someone's arm. He didn't look to see who it was but when the waitress refilled his cup he smiled and glanced over her shoulder. An elderly woman with a dead brown animal wrapped over her shoulders nodded at him. The legs of the furry creature dangled into her plate its claws reaching for her pastry. He returned her nod

176

briefly. She had been there the day before he recalled but aside from the excessive makeup and being overdressed in the day's heat she didn't stand out. Just another traveler. She was someone's grandmother waiting to meet one of the trains or leaving on one herself.

He put his pencil away, took a few more sips of coffee, and smoked another cigarette. The old woman didn't take her eyes off him. He looked out the window ignoring her gaze preparing to fend her off when she stood up and came toward his table. Would she make a commotion? Call him out? The humiliation he could not endure.

She squeezed around chairs and knocked the elbow of a woman lifting a full cup of tea to her mouth. The liquid spilled onto her lap and the woman glared. "Watch what you're doing." The old lady didn't notice or didn't hear. When she got to Martin's table, she clacked her bold red fingernails against the mosaic inlay playing an arpeggio. The lipstick matched the enamel paint on her nails and went beyond the natural lines of her lips.

"I've had my eye on you." Her voice cracked and he looked past her lips to the eyes. Cloudy and bloodshot. Maybe she'd been drinking. He'd put the book in his pack as she made her way toward him.

"Oh yeah?" She was bottom heavy. He'd push her down and be out the door while everyone had their mouths open and before they tried to chase him down. She might be someone's grandmother but she was a busy body. He wasn't about to be undone by a painted-up old woman who drank too much and drew attention to him. She was maybe five feet and an inch and that was with two-inch heels. Her suit skirt was too short, the material on the purple jacket tugged at the silver buttons across her bosom, while the only item that redeemed her wardrobe was a single strand of pearls which suited her and said she was a wealthy matron.

"I've been watching you for two days." He studied the door. The way was clear, nobody coming in or going out. If she uttered one single word. Just one. He had a clear shot to bolt. "There's something I   want   to   ask   you."

177

Florence-Forty-Nine

She was half in and half out the doorway for an agonizing number of minutes. Swaying from leg to the other. Waiting to be sure the packer was truly on his way. The horse's saddle creaked where the trail turned steep causing its human cargo to rub up against the leather from the downward pressure. Hooves paddled on the soft earth and now and again one of the beasts snorted. She waited longer than bearable before the sounds were absorbed into silence by the primeval woods.

And then she couldn't find the boy. She ran back down the trail but he wasn't in or anywhere by the outhouse. The packer really hadn't seen him. She was sure he'd lied. The sort to talk out of both sides of his mouth. That's why she'd waited at the cab until she was sure he was gone. To protect the boy.

The potatoes and feather were stuffed in the corner just as he'd told her. She hadn't noticed them what with first the shock of the shoes and then discovering the boy and his condition. How had he gotten food from her pantry and then later gotten away from the privy before Job Lindstrom discovered him?

Beyond the latrine, the land fell away precipitously where it was overrun by scree from eons of avalanches that flowed downward for twenty-five yards. A deer trail coiled at the bottom where the rubble abruptly stopped and scrubby plants scrambled to stay alive. Determined yellow flowerets poked out from the debris, dabs of butter shining up in the unforgiving terrain.

The boy had to have gone down that slope over the jagged rocks and so did she. But right away she realized it was a mistake to go feet first over the loose rubble because she went sliding over broken and sharp shards that were like falling into broken glass. She went down the rest of the way by the seat of her pants and then spat out dirt that tasted like chalk and brushed herself off, and ignored the cuts on her hands and arms.

The brush at the bottom was barbed and spiny along the animal path but wouldn't deter deer with their thick hides, just thin-skinned humans. The boy must be in worse shape now if he dragged himself

178

through these obstacles. For certain he'd think she'd turned on him, and that would force him to scrounge for another place to hide. It wasn't the packer's fault he'd gone off but it was just another reason to dislike the man. What would he have done if had come across the boy? Keep his mouth shut? Not likely unless she bargained with him. Even then she wouldn't trust him to keep his end of the deal.

Once more Miss Conrad guided from afar, probably two hundred miles away and at present whisking around her perch on some salient task. The heavy work pants, the thick boots. "It's not a fashion show, ladies. Pack your most durable clothing and wear them. Every day! We're not going up to lookouts to recline in the sun in our shorts and frilly tops now, are we?" Hattie nodded vigorously. Grace sighed and looked down at her newly painted nails. Florence had not given any thought about Grace and if she was managing her summer job.

Her hands took the worst of the brunt. She'd left her work gloves at the cab and if the boy was hiding in the bushes, he wouldn't come out if she called out for him. Straight into the thicket she went lifting her legs over the lower branches grabbing at that higher ones to keep her balance. She'd put vinegar on the pokes and scratches when they were back at the cab.

She couldn't find him. Wore the same scowl Homer dreaded when she directed it at him. "Oh, boy. I'm in trouble, aren't I?" he said. Yes, she was edge because the boy was missing and hurt, the packer had created more confusion, and on top of everything, she was shirking her one duty. What if there was smoke from a smoldering fire while she was on the hunt for the boy? Even Miss Conrad would have no sage words for this. It was a human duty to help the injured boy, but what about the cost of a fire that would destroy what she had been hired to protect? She had to get back to the cab to make her next report. If she didn't find him before nightfall, she would report him. She had to.

Back and forth in straight lines through the bushes until her hips ached and her legs were shaking. Sweat running down into her eyes. If she called out, would that scare him more? Push him farther into the woods? A dense stand of evergreens abutted the thicket ahead of her. If he was in there, she wouldn't find him. And time was short.

Whoever he was running from, his fear of that danger could just as likely destroy him. The cold, the heat, an animal, his bleeding, hunger. Any or all of them would win.

She had to call in her next report but she would come back to this spot where she left off and start again, cover as much area as she could before she gave up. She caught a whiff of fresh horse dung and that meant she was near the trail the packer had gone down a few hours before. During their training in Missoula, the instructor had warned about how easy it is to become confused in the woods, to get completely turned around. She had been sure she was on the other side of the ridge, somewhere below the outhouse, not anywhere near the trail going to the cab. If it was that easy to get lost, how would the boy ever find his way out?

She should have taken the compass and water. Another piece of advice that was recalled too late. Her throat was parched. But she'd only meant to go down to the privy where he was supposed to be waiting for her. That's where she'd left him and where she expected to get him. He'd been savvy, hadn't he? She both admired that and feared for him and more than that, felt bruised that he didn't trust her word. She wanted to be angry with him but only if he was safe with her. Give him a good piece of her mind. Or not. She wished she knew where he was and that he was safe.

She had to report him to the ranger. Let someone else have a go at it. A bigger promise to him would be to make sure he was alive and found, that he was safe. If she didn't report him missing, he could die of exposure or be mauled by an animal. The ranger wouldn't send someone out yet that evening to look for him. He would have to spend another night on the mountain. This time, without an outhouse roof over his head.

Martin-Fifty

It was a clear and sunny morning in Winnipeg but daylight would not find the Grimes Hotel before midafternoon. Martin stepped out from the dark doorway at the precise moment the car pulled up by the sidewalk.

"Is that all you're bringing?" She sniffed at his backpack as she came around the front of the car. He raised one eyebrow at her. He'd stood on the sidewalk as she pulled up then thought better of staying where he was and backed up against the wall until she finished an abysmal parking job. Two tires on the curb in front of the hotel. To begin with, the thing was the size of a hearse and matched the color of her fingernails.

He yelled at her to stop before she ran into the car parked ahead of her in a space large enough to put down a small plane. She made a face through the windshield as if that would be his fault, then shifted into reverse, but instead of keeping her foot on the brake, stepped on the gas and managed to stop within a whisker of the car behind her.

"Step on the brake!" You stupid old fool, under his breath.

If she was going to do the driving, it would be a calamity. He may have made an error by agreeing to her to her proposition. The curved black claws from her fur stole dangled off one shoulder as she came up the curb.

"You almost hit the car in front and the one behind." He bawled her out.

"Well, dearie. That's why I've hired you now, isn't it?"

She'd watched him for two days in the café. Set her mind after the first one because he looked refined and because he'd acted the gentleman when he came inside. Both times he removed his fedora. He was the appropriate man to drive her to Regina.

Her adult son had forbidden her to come to Saskatchewan by car unless she hired a driver to get her there. "You can't handle that monstrosity on your own. Take the train, Mother."

"You must be joking. You'd have me ride with those people for hours? Think of the stink and the noise. What kind of a son are you?"

He tried to be a dutiful son, to protect her from life's little inconveniences and difficulties.

"I'm driving the red dragon wagon." Her name for the car her husband left her in his will. "Don't even try to argue with me."

"Then find someone to drive it for you, Mother. You know how tired you get these days now that Dad is gone." She vacillated between abhorring and adoring the car depending on how well she got along with it on any particular day.

The husband had offered no endearing sentiments toward the end but he'd seen to it that she had no financial worries. "You better take good care of my Cadillac. Goddammit." His final words except for the very last ones. "Leave me in peace." In their forty years together, she was happy to leave him permanently in peace.

She hadn't been allowed to touch the steering wheel or even sit in the driver's seat while he was alive. He headed off her arguments by buying her a Ford Super Deluxe which miffed her when it turned out to be blue. "I told you I wanted maroon."

Because his treasure stayed in the heated garage, she donned boots, a fur coat that came down to her ankles, fashionable wool gloves and matching scarf to scrape snow and ice off her vehicle. Before he went to his office, he wiped off imaginary motes and hidden hints of dust, wiped the chrome down both before and after work. Until he was too ill to get out of bed and she hired a nurse to tend to him. She didn't bother to ask permission to drive his Cadillac when the weather turned cold and she wanted to go shopping.

She also did not distress him about the dent in the front right fender when the side of the garage got in her way. Not for a minute did it cross her mind that he wouldn't get better so she asked her son how to get the car fixed. She dreaded facing the stinging insults that would go on for months.

"I can't do that." She pouted, flatly refused when her son told her what she would have to do to get it fixed. Instead, she came up with her own solution for handling her husband once he was back on his feet although the image of him walking out to his garage and finding the dent was daunting.

"Someone backed into the car in the parking lot." He'd yell, of course.

'What the hell were you doing in the Cadillac? That's off-limits to you." She had an answer to that, too.

"I couldn't get the Ford to start because it was so cold, and you were running out of pain pills."

"I'm Mrs. Frank Baker." She'd extended a mottled hand to Martin at the café but not before she told him what she wanted. "I've found what I'm looking for." She was a coquet. Flirty smile. "You're exactly what I've been looking for." He coughed, and then coughed again.

"Too many cigarettes."

"But you may call me Mrs. Eleanor Baker." Leaned in toward him filling his nostrils with the strong scent of lavender. "I saw you at the depot, dear, looking at the schedule and I believe I know what you are planning." Exposed by a grandmother. The café door had quickly jammed up with passengers from the latest train arriving.

"From my observation, I think you are going west to Regina, aren't you?"

"What?" He coughed again.

"You may drive me there since you are."

Was this a ruse? He looked past the several people standing in the doorway waiting for an open table. How long before the police arrived? A woman old enough to be someone's grandmother teetering on spindly heels that his mother would scoff at unless twisting a frail ankle was a way to garner sympathy.

Martin saw the dent on the right fender of the Cadillac as she parked the car. As long as he did all the driving, they would get to Regina. But he quickly began to doubt that when they were on the outskirts of Winnipeg, had just the left the city limits. "You're driving too fast."

He slowed down to placate her although he'd been going the speed limit. "Now you are dilly-dallying. Why are you dilly-dallying?"

Less than hundred miles from Winnipeg she said, "Pull over. Right now. You almost hit that truck that passed us." The vehicle had pulled in front of him too early and Martin had slammed on the brakes.

"I'm taking over, now. I think you tried to fool me, Mister. You're no gentleman." He'd stopped on the side of the highway. When she got behind the wheel, she stuck out her lower lip. To think he'd given up riding the rails for what he thought would be comfort and safety to Regina.

Florence-Fifty-One

The wind had picked up to nine miles an hour, still coming out of the southwest. "Thermometer reads 86." Clipped, unfinished sentences. *Please, please don't keep me on the line. Get it done and over with.*

"Yeah. That's what I figured. Probably gonna top out at 90 up there. It's already that down here." The ranger's shirt was soaked despite a fan buzzing full blast behind him. "Not spotting another fire up there, anyway. Keep it that way." He wanted to talk. She could just tell.

"Nothing out of the ordinary." She wriggled her toes inside the boots. An annoying but soothing old habit that didn't help ease the urgency. Of all days, the ranger had to chat. A long worrisome stretch of summer lay ahead for all forest service employees. Too dry and too hot too early. They were only into July. The more he talked with her, the calmer he became but she was breathing hard.

"You okay?" Either he was antsy or he noticed she was acting different. "You're not having any trouble, are you?"

"I'm fine. I'm fine. Why do you ask?" Handing it back to him. Smiling into the receiver attempting to sound sweet while trying to figure out how to get him off the line.

"I dunno. It's gotta be this heat. Driving me nuts."

"The packer came today." Threw him a bone.

"Well, finally. Son-of-a-gun. You should be set now." She hadn't stopped to read Homer's three letters bearing the cryptic APO return address.

"He behave himself?" That was odd.

She chuckled lightly. "Well, he's okay." What else could she say? The kind of guy who crosses lines and then acts innocent or sulky if it is pointed out or worse, if it is ignored. Like the grocer. The behavior just overt enough to squeeze out a look of surprise or disgust and to make her move back a few steps.

"He kinda has a reputation in town. If you wanna know. I'd watch him. You're the first woman he's hauled supplies in for. Wouldn't put it past him. Let me know." She wouldn't put it past him either. The boy needed to be found and helped. She'd handle Job Lindstrom best she could when he came again next month. Hattie, Grace, and Miss Conrad. Any kind of men hanging around them trying to get familiar? A hiker or some packer bringing them trouble? It was a woman's plague and plight, more than commonplace, situations where they should feel safe but weren't. The grocery store, walking on city streets, or the pastor of their church. Little Hattie, big Grace, stalwart Miss Conrad, and herself. Size and shape, personality, it didn't matter whether plain or attractive, strong or weak, standoffish or kind. No matter what their qualities, being female meant being regarded as waving the white flag before the wall was breached.

With compass, work gloves, a canteen of water, and being optimistic, lots of bandages, bread and sausage, she hiked out from the trail at the cab deciding not to attempt the scree a second time. The ranger was tolerable usually, gruff at times, short-tempered, but today heavyhearted. She had a twinge of remorse for not being a little understanding. "Oh, dear. I forgot I've left compote boiling on the stove."

"Sure." He knew what she was doing.

Her hat kept the sun off her neck and face but that meant she saw more of her boots and the ground as she descended below the ridge. The air was soaked with humidity and the temperature soared. She pushed through the bushes again where she'd left off until she got into the woods and stopped to take a drink. It was late afternoon. Running out of time again.

She almost missed seeing him. He was propped up against the trunk of an old-growth tree and mostly hidden by low branches, eyes shut and lower jaw hanging open.

She choked on the water and coughed and his head turned, his eyes pinched shut. "Oh. My lord." Devil swallow the minister's admonition about swearing. Pompous mule he was. Funny time to wish she hadn't barked at Homer, called him out when he said, "Geez, Mom."

"Don't take the Lord's name in vain, Homer. I don't mean to tell you again."

"Geez is not a bad word, Mom. It's slang." He countered.

"It's short for Jesus. You don't think that's bad?"

The boy groaned but didn't move or open his eyes. "You weren't here when I came by before. You couldn't have been!" She hurled the accusation. Upset with the thought she had missed him.

She'd reported a nine mile per hour breeze but in the woods all of it got captured by the upper branches and was lost to the undergrowth beneath. It was perfect weather to be sitting on the muddy bottom of the stream sifting the jewel-toned wet gravel through her fingers and cooling down in its chillness.

He groaned when she put a wet cloth over his forehead and eyes. "Don't try to move, yet." Not that he was doing so. At the outhouse he'd pushed her hand away and she wished he was doing so this time. His lips were chapped and bleeding but he didn't cringe or moan even when she covered them with a wet cloth. Not even a tiny reaction. He was so pale. She sat shoulder to shoulder matching his shallow breaths with her own until his head rolled onto her upper arm. When he moved his tongue to seek out the water, she added more drops to the wet cloth.

Nature's other creatures rested in the heat except for the occasional chipmunk that squeaked at the vagrants occupying its tree, and a woodpecker unfazed by the temperature riddled the bark of a diseased pine. Her legs cramped sitting in the one position after a half hour, her back itched leaning against the bark but she wouldn't move. Every few minutes she dosed him with a bit more water until he gasped for air and rolled his head farther down her arm to the elbow. "Oh, Lord." He was dying on her. "Please, please don't die!" She must have shouted it.

The whole forest could go up in flames. She shouldn't have run back to the cab earlier to make her report. She would have found him then if she'd kept looking. "I won't leave you ever again." She kissed the cloth on his forehead "No matter what."

Martin-Fifty-Two

Barbed wire, railroad tracks, villages, and silos. The provincial highway ran alongside the Canadian Pacific Railway making sharp right or left turns where it came to and left townships. Chocolate colored grain elevators, prairie pillars of industry dominated the small towns' otherwise humble architecture broadcasting the word in giant letters POOL.

Flat earth and wheat fields stretching to eternity. It was ten o'clock and because he was feeling warm, began to roll the window down for a smoke. "Are you kidding me? I just spent twenty dollars at the beauty parlor." She patted the helmet of a hairdo that would take a tornado to dislodge. Her first comment since she had taken over the wheel. They could be on the moon for the monotony of the scenery, but if he suggested she drive faster, she'd intentionally slow down.

He toyed with slitting her throat. In one quick act reach over and sever the pout from the rest of the body. Or he could strangle her with the damn fox fur that forever inhabited her neck. Tie the feet in a double knot at her neck and pull it tight until she stopped gasping. She probably slept with the creature. The woman couldn't concentrate for ten minutes and he felt queasy because she kept pressing on and off the gas pedal.

They passed through the village of Brandon and in the fifty miles since she'd taken over, he'd bitten his fingernails down to the nub and stomped his right foot into the floorboard where the gas pedal would be in the driver's seat again and again. A random barn and farmhouse appeared like a pop-up toy out of the emptiness conjured by a magician's wand. Invariably a row of towering poplars concealed the solitary structures.

They'd gone through another hamlet and she must have forgotten she was sulking, because her pout flourished into incessant palaver. If she found out who he was, the old woman would tear his eyes out with those sharp red fingernails. Her son awaited her in Regina. "Eagerly." He'd better be eager if he knew what was good for him. Martin grinned out the window at the dangerous notion of committing the gruesome crime that was tempting him. She was a

188

rash that raises welts and has to be scratched despite the serious outcome.

The ton of motorized steel was more often than not left to manage itself lurching out of the lane as she fussed and picked at him. Strangling was too good for her. In a span of ten minutes she'd crossed the center line five times, grazed the shoulder three and aimed directly toward the ditch once.

"Watch where you're going!" Damn woman! He grabbed the steering wheel before the car would have smacked into a culvert.

"Get your hands off my car! You're crazy." He had a horrible sense of glee at permanently silencing her. She was foolhardy and her recklessness was going to kill the both of them. But then how to dispose of the body?

Ten days earlier he'd been in Sudbury. He wasn't a gambler, wouldn't bet on it but he may have outfoxed the agents. Each day on the run was a minor victory. So, what if he committed murder? She continued harping. They could only execute him for one crime. A murderous felony or treason.

"What are you grinning at?" How could she be that oblivious to such treacherous driving?

"I'm not grinning."

"I saw you grinning."

"Just enjoying this fantastic ride."

"Oh, don't you act smart with me." Jesus, he really was going to have to kill her.

"I didn't know I was."

You're sulking, then. I can read that kind of thing a mile away. Just like my husband. I'm going to tell my son about you. Just you wait."

Her son, poor sod. If he'd been smarter, he would have encouraged his mother to drive the beast of a car on her own to Regina. With any luck, she would have killed herself on the way. Run into a bridge or a truck. The son had moved to Regina no doubt to get a lot of distance from the henpecker.

"I thought you were different. A gentleman. Of course, I was wrong about that, too. I can't be too surprised." With this woman the switch was either on or off. "Second-rate driver. You should be ashamed fooling me like you did. You had me believing your lies." He didn't ask what lies she meant.

"My husband was the best driver. You dress like a first-rate person, just so you can fool everybody, but you're not."

"How far is it to Vancouver?"

"We're not going to Vancouver. Did you hear what I just told you? See what I mean about you?"

"I know we're not going to Vancouver. I wondered how long it takes to get there."

"I should have ignored Bobby. I should have put my foot down."

"Who's Bobby?" Whoever he was, he would be astute enough to know he'd better agree with whatever she said.

"Who's Bobby? You don't know who Bobby is? What have I been saying? He's my son! I've told you a hundred times by now. If he saw me doing all the driving after hiring you, he'd be ashamed he didn't come to Winnipeg and drive me himself."

"Well, here's a solution for you. Pull over and let me out. You can take it from here." She cocked her head at him, then looked straight ahead and clammed up for the next ten miles. The ride was easier with her mouth shut except for when she slammed on the brake every mile or two. He stared out his side of the window, wouldn't look at her because it might encourage her harping again. Maybe they would get to Regina before she opened her mouth.

Bleary from the heat and endless fields swimming past, he started to doze off but then she flipped the car onto the shoulder without first slowing down. The brakes squealed and gravel flew out from behind the tires.

"What are you doing?" He jerked to attention. Those nights when he had been screamed awake by the Abwehr were minor compared to her skill. They should have enlisted her. She was going to dump him on the side of the road after all. What had taken her this long to make up her mind?

"I'm tired. You're going to drive now! Come around and help me out." Before he got the car on the road again, her head tilted back into the seat, mouth open, and the defunct animal crawled into her lap.

Aside from the painted nails and face, the tight gray curls, and expensive jewelry, her face looked peaceful in repose, just an ordinary grandmother who doted on her grandchildren and sneaked them candy behind their parents' backs.

Florence-Fifty-Three

Winter nights in Montana are very long and very black. When the sky is clear, enormous crystals dazzle from the heavens, but most often they snuggle up behind blankets of clouds. A mile-long steel pole couldn't poke a hole through the thick cover. Summer evenings, however, are a balm that unmask the season's darkness and hold the light up in the sky late in the day. Nature's reward to those who have endured the interminable months.

"Hey, Flossie. Would you sing for us? How about Goodnight Irene?" George huffed out a three-glissando lick on the harmonica. They waited a space and then she cleared her throat the voice starting out deep and ponderous as a cello before rising up the scale to her usual soprano. They'd missed hearing her laugh at their jokes. She'd been unduly quiet until George asked her to sing. When she did, she held onto the whole notes, frugal as a miser, stringing out the vowels and turning the folk song into a lullaby, breathy and wistful. The spotters hummed along as if they were sitting around a campfire, feeling the heat on one side, too cool on the other, rotating like marshmallows or hot dogs and singing dreamy songs.

She did it for the boy sleeping on her cot. His face washed clean of pain and fear with golden late evening sun shimmering on his translucent skin. Whether or not he heard her song to him, she trusted the serenade to reach the unconscious distance between them.

The earlier evening banter behind, her music wriggled through the bravado that men have, men being men, to tug at their longing and loneliness, the places they don't go. Henry gave a stab to shift the mood.

"Hey, what's the difference between a watchmaker and a jailer?"

"Who ain't heard that one, Henry? Give it a rest."

"One sells watches. The other watches cells." Henry slapped his knee.

"It's awful dang quiet up here tonight." George blew a single note on the harmonica and drew on it holding it for several seconds.

"Whooo. Whooo. You need a feathery friend to cozy up with, George."

' Cut it out, Henry."

"How you doing, Flossie, after all that excitement from yesterday?" She let out a gasp before she understood Joe was not referring to the boy. The fire was a lifetime ago, erased from her current memory.

"Oh, I'm just fine." Too hasty an answer.

After they signed off, some nights George counted stars after she'd sung a last melody. Joe whittled a piece of wood, made a serving spoon he'd be able to use as long as he lived. Henry was too restless to read. He thought of lost acquaintances although he didn't want to, or went to sleep to an old recurring nightmare.

Joe wouldn't know about the boy. His question unnerved her, though. "I think I'm tired. Too hot today, wasn't it?" She backpedaled.

"Hot enough to grow pineapples." They laughed. Henry saved them from a serious moment.

She was dead tired, the muscles in her legs twitched from the lifting and twisting. The tiny cuts on her arms stung now from sliding over the scree, feeling worse as hurts always do when night comes.

"I think I'll say good night." The men got quiet. "Some animal got in the outhouse." She added. "Made a mess down there today. I'm all in." She lied, but not about the exhaustion.

"Shoot him, Flossie. Probably a raccoon."

"I'll try. If I can catch him at it."

"Good night, Flossie. Nice breeze coming on to cool things down. We'll all sleep pretty good tonight." She made up a bed on the floor near the boy asleep on her cot. His toes stuck out from under the cover and she pulled the blanket over them like they were cut glass heirlooms.

She couldn't fall asleep, blamed it on the moon for making the room bright as midday. This was the first chance to be alone with her feelings and go over the whole business. His breathing had been so ragged after she found him and then it was gone, disappeared. Slowly and carefully she'd been hydrating him with droplets of water, and when he stopped gasping it was because his body was readjusting, letting go of the stress. She'd screamed at him right in his ear and it roused him.

"Stop it." He mumbled at her. She couldn't believe it.

"What'd you say?" She yelled again in his ear and although his eyes were squeezed tight, he winced. "You're not dead. Are you? Thank God. You're not dead." She started sobbing and couldn't stop, snot ran out of her nose. She wiped it off on her free elbow. "You aren't going to die on me?" Demanding he wouldn't. She wouldn't let him slip away from her like her mother had. There in the bed one moment, alive and then with one final breath, not there.

"What?"

"Here. Drink some water if you can." It dripped down his chin from the canteen but he managed to get a few good swallows. His head was still partially attached to her arm. They were in the shade and he squinted when he finally pried open his eyes. How long had he been there? And how?

"Don't!" He pushed back at the canteen and lifted his head. For a few minutes longer he let her sit next to him and then tried to move away.

"How in the world did you get here?"

"We've got to get you up to the cab. Can you hold onto me?" He was four or five inches shorter than she with a small frame. He clenched his jaw and nodded.

"How did you get here?" She asked him.

"You."

"No. I didn't bring you here."

"You carried me." She shook her head. Stupid of her to disagree. He must have been hallucinating. The main thing was to get him up to the cab.

"Can you hold onto me?" He made a face like don't baby me.

"That man?"

"What man? Oh, you mean the packer?" He nodded.

"He's gone. Hours ago. Went back down the trail." It was so long ago she'd forgotten but it aroused a sour taste in her mouth.

"He doesn't know you're here if that's what you're wondering. He asked about the potatoes in the outhouse and you can explain that

194

to me later because I'd like to know." He stuck his chin out. "Sometime. Not now."

She got him to his feet. He was remarkably stable. Stood steady and on his own, but not for long. "How did you hide from the packer when he came down to the outhouse and end up here on the trail?"

"You." He was forceful. "I already told you." She hid her smile.

"No. It wasn't me." She shouldn't have said so, but it slipped out.

"You carried me." He stuck out his lower lip.

"But I've been searching for you ever since the packer left." He turned his head away. There was something fierce about him. A fire of resolve. "Here. Lean on this." She handed him a long pole from a fallen branch to use for a walking stick and helped him only when he was about to tumble over.

The moon tucked in behind an enormous cloud finally. She fell asleep to his rhythmic breathing.

Martin-Fifty-Four

Prairie towns of box-shaped buildings and flat streets lay straight enough to roll a ball from one end to the other with a single push. The somewhat impressive Capitol Theater, City Hall, and LaSalle Hotel added a bit of flavor to the otherwise monotonous Regina pancake.

Bobby's jaw was set. He ran ahead of Martin to the depot but not so fast as to lose him in the throng checking over his shoulder now and again to make sure the man followed behind. Bobby's singular decision was to get Martin the best seat on the westbound train.

"I'll manage. Really, you should take your mother home."

"I'm buying your ticket through to Vancouver. No arguments." If his mother behaved toward Bobby as she had with Martin on this trip, he had endured an unpredictable upbringing at best confused by its affluence. Martin couldn't see Bobby stamping his foot, for he would have been no match for his mother. When Martin met him, he stuttered and paused and his sentences seemed filtered through some curious thought process to gauge if the result would end up with a thrashing of harsh words. "Come on! I won't be satisfied until I see you settled." He'd taken charge of Martin's backpack without asking, pulled it off his shoulder, charged ahead up the steps into the car, found the perfect seat, and handed the pack back to him. "You'll get the best view from this angle." Anybody else, Martin would have flattened. Not Bobby.

"You ever been through the Rockies? You'll love it." Bobby's eyes glowed. He panted from trotting the distance between the car to the depot, the back of his shirt stuck to his spine. He bent to look out the sparkling window ignoring the filthy tracks in front of him and seeing only the magnificent scenery Martin would be passing through in a short time.

Martin tolerated most of the Canadians. Not Eleanor Baker, and not the Finns who weren't real Canadians anyway, but there was Lilly and Mary Alice, the barber, waitresses, people doing their jobs and getting along. Even nosy strangers wanted to be of help.

"You got some time before you get into the mountains. Take a good snooze. Boring before beauty. That's what I always say. Outside of Calgary, it's eyes wide open. You don't want to miss it." A few nearby passengers smiled at Bobby. An older woman nodded.

During her episodes of babbling, Martin had formed a mental picture of what Bobby would be like given Eleanor Baker as a mother. A life of bouncing between lavish plates overflowing with criticism and platters of donuts and cookies and cakes. The most impressive thing was how Bobby's thick gold wedding band gouged into the flesh of one of his sausage fingers. In the sunlight his scalp glistened from under thinning blond hair, and the buttons at the belly of the formal dress shirt which no doubt he wore to please his mother held on in stunning resilience, the ever-present danger of popping off with the least assistance.

Impertinent Eleanor Barker had a mean streak, and Bobby was her alter ego. For Martin who spent only one exasperating day with the woman even before meeting Bobby he felt pity for him. His eyes had blurred over saturated by the tedious landscape, and for a while Eleanor Baker snored, her head resting against the seat. Martin thought of Mary Alice on the kneeler praying in church, rosary beads flying across her wrist. If there was a god, he would gladly offer a prayer of thanks to see Regina rise on the horizon. He didn't actively consider killing Eleanor, they had endured the other's miserable company, and who knows, she might have had a similar idea, maybe of poisoning him. Had she been his mother, however, he would have stabbed her in the back with a kitchen knife or run away by the age of twelve. Or maybe both.

He and Bobby shook hands on the street near the depot when they met. Martin recognized him immediately near the curb although Eleanor didn't point him out. She nodded when he waved at her. She seemed to be pouting again.

Martin had colleagues in Germany he met for beer before holidays. But there were no pals, not like the gang up in Timmins who he stole cigarettes and smoked with on the banks of the Mattagami River when he was ten. "Care for a smoke?" Martin handed Bobby the opened pack.

They leaned against the hood of the Cadillac chatting and smoking.

"Get off my car." Eleanor rolled the window down halfway but didn't get out of the car.

"Hi, Mom." Bobby walked over and leaned into the window to plant a kiss on her check.

"Don't say hi, and don't call me Mom. You know I can't stand that. And since when are you smoking?" She shrugged off his kiss.

"Where you headed next? If you're not in a big hurry why don't you come and stay with us for a few days." Martin shook his head. One more hour with the old lady and he would kill her.

"He's not coming with us! Are you out of your mind?"

"I'm gonna buy your ticket, then. Right now. Where you going?"

"Vancouver."

"Oh, I love that city. We need to hurry, then. That's leaving soon."

"He doesn't need you to buy his ticket. Take me home. I want to take a nap." She stuck her chin out the window. The caked-on make-up was cracking, her magical hours behind her.

"Mother, the least we can do is buy him a ticket. Look at what he's done for us. Got you here safe and sound." She pursed her lips and looked through the front windshield, the lines around her lips pronounced.

"He didn't have to buy a train ticket to come here. He got a free ride from me and I'm not going into that stinky train depot."

"You just stay here, Mother, until I get him on the train. Maybe you could nap a bit. Don't you want to thank him and wish him a good trip?"

"I wouldn't thank *him* if he brought me all the tea in China. He's a fake. I'll be glad to see the back of him. For good!"

"True to form." Bobby said softly to Martin. Martin grinned but Bobby's face crumpled like an old apple. His children behaved just like her, didn't even try to be courteous.

Martin went up to the car window, but she started to roll it up when she saw he was coming toward her. He managed to say before she got it shut, "You have raised a quite a son, Eleanor Baker. He does you credit. You must be very proud of him."

"We're going to get you the best seat on the train." Bobby's voice cracked.

After the train pulled out, Bobby stayed on the platform and stared at the empty tracks.

"Did you lose something, sir?" The porter came over and looked at the spot where Bobby was staring.

"Nope. I'm fine." The horn blared from the red dragon wagon. It went on for a full minute before he turned away and walked back to the car and his mother.

Florence-Fifty-Five

A woodpecker woke her drumming on the stove pipe, her chin wet with saliva from sleeping with her mouth open. It was too early for the sun to come through the windows but when she sat up and rubbed her shoulder which ached from lying on her side too long on the floor, the boy was watching her from the cot.

"You're awake?" She whispered not wanting to rouse him except he already was. He didn't answer so she got up and folded her blanket.

"What's that?" The cot was behind her back and she had to turn around to see that he was pointing to the Osborne fire finder in the cupola.

"That's the most important piece of equipment here. It's called an Osborne fire finder." She wondered how long he'd been awake but felt relieved he was talking.

"Are you hungry?" He shook his head.

"Well, I'm not surprised. But you should have something. Just a bit to get your appetite back."

"Coffee." He said quietly.

"Did you say coffee? You're too young to be drinking that." Ignoring that she'd been doing the same since the age of fourteen.

"No, I'm not." He glared at her with the feral eyes she'd seen in the outhouse.

"I'll make you a deal. A cup of coffee if you eat a biscuit with it." He shrugged. She waited. Finally, he nodded.

The cool air thickened the room with rich coffee aroma. She knew he couldn't eat it all, but put two plump biscuits loaded with butter and honey on a plate and brought them to the cot and the caffeine loaded with powdered milk.

He ate and drank it all and licked his fingers sticky from the honey. "I'll get a rag to wipe your hands." Grinning to herself like she'd won a blue ribbon for her strawberry jam at the county fair.

She'd just gone to bed after the hellish day of finding and getting him back to the cab and was settling down when he turned on his side and the blanket slid off to reveal the wounds where his shirt and

200

pants were torn. He'd been sleeping on his back until then after collapsing in the cot. Gashes that looked like he was hit with something metal spread across his back on his neck and the back of his thighs. A gasp she couldn't cover stirred him but not enough to wake him up.

The welts had begun crusting crusted over but would cause him problems as the healthy skin tightened around them. With a very light touch, she rubbed homemade calendula lotion on them knowing he wouldn't let her touch him if he was awake. Wherever he got the yarrow, it had stemmed the bleeding.

"What does it do?" The boy rested on his elbow asking about the fire finder.

"Well, let me see if I can explain. It pinpoints where..." He had turned green. Eating too much too fast. Her fault. His sallow color and his ribs like sticks were hard to look at, yet harder not to. She should have been more careful about feeding him.

Here!" She'd rushed a pail to the cot.

"I'm fine." He growled. And he was. The nausea passed and some color came back into his face.

"I've got to call in my report. Then we will attend to you, young man."

"I don't need your...your." He didn't know the word she'd used.

He appeared to run on the lean side, but frail as he was, his appetite was astonishingly good. By the third day, he was eating potatoes softened with canned milk and poached egg and his cheeks began to glow rosy.

"Why...why does...does it have two sights?" His sores were closing up and he didn't balk at using the calendula cream, but wouldn't let her help.

"See, I rotate it here, and adjust it for distance. A couple more days and I'll show you how to do it." He was sitting up more and awake for longer stretches at a time.

"Shouldn't you be a man?" She was adjusting the Osborne and didn't turn around so he missed the look. She could have said it was because of the war but she didn't. Miss Conrad should tell him. She held all the reasons. Owned them like pieces of jewelry.

"Does it make any difference?" She asked finally.

"Women ain't supposed to do a man's job." He was just a kid.

"Aren't."

"What?"

"Never mind." He shrugged and she took up the field glasses. He was awake again when the spotters came on. He giggled as soon as they started.

Early on the spotters had fallen half in love with Florence. Each had an image of what she looked like and each thought she preferred him over the others. For George, it was because she used that lovely voice to sing along with him. For Henry, she laughed at his jokes and listened to him when he griped about the silliest things. With Joe, she asked how to keep the stove going in the rain, how to discourage a bear, how to prepare for the next storm. She'd taught all to make biscuits, how to store butter so it didn't go rancid, and how to keep the flies away.

They joshed first thing Henry starting things off with a detective quote and George stamping down on it like it was a bug begging to be squashed. Right away the boy laughed.

"Put your hand over your mouth." Florence whispered. "Or they'll hear you."

It had been sticky hot for over a week. Late in the afternoons, the rain fell gently in spurts, God turning a heavenly faucet on then quickly off. Huge dark balloons hung on the western horizon threatening to burst. Not even a kiss of a breeze to dry the clammy shirts that clung to their backs.

"It any cooler up there than it is down here?" Florence had just given the wind speed and laughed.

"You can send a breeze up here anytime." The boy listened from the cot.

"You know what that wind stirs up. Don't borrow trouble, Florence. What's your humidity?" She scrolled with her finger to her latest numbers and read them off.

"I don't like the looks of that sky over there on the Idaho border. We might get ourselves a bunch of fireworks later today if it heads our way."

"I've been keeping my eye on it." She winked at the boy and he smiled. He had perfect white teeth.

That evening the musicians played and Florence sang an Irish lullaby. "Wish we was all sitting round a campfire about now."

"You getting the blues again, Henry? We need a happy song, Flossie. You got one for us?"

"Sure." She began, "When the Saints Go Marching In," and George chased after to catch her on the harmonica and Henry and Joe sang along. The boy swayed back and forth on the cot.

The rumbles started a few hours later just as the ranger suspected. The last storm had tossed the cab about scaring her half to death. She had thought the cab was going to split in two. The boy must have been hiding in the woods that night! She shivered imagining him huddled up out in the open and pulled her bed closer to the cot.

Martin-Fifty-Six

Regina, the breathing space between incessant miles of wheat fields and acres of barley, and a temporary respite until the train picked up where the Eleanor Baker trip left off. Another hiccup on Canada's agricultural mecca.

Bobby advised sleeping to avoid more tedium so he would be more alert to fully savor the vistas of the Rocky Mountains. But a barrel-chested farmer came aboard at Moose Jaw and regularly hitched up his suspenders knocking Martin in the ribs, and took up more than his fair share of the seat. His boots were caked with dried mud and his sweat smelled of cows.

"Mighty fine weather." The seat bounced when he sat down. Moose Jaw's sprawling depot resembled a chateau in the Alps. A too elegant structure for the town's name but the people on the platform bustled about just as they had in Regina. He'd had a seat to himself but when he saw the people waiting to get on board pulled out his prop of a book which was looking tired and shabby and pretended not to hear the man. "Good for the crops this year, too." Martin nodded.

He was averse to putting up with more empty talk. "Herman Schlegel." The farmer had a paw the size of a bear and a grip of steel. "I never met a stranger yet." He slapped Martin on the back like he was smacking a hammer down and bellowed. "You and me talk long enough I'm gonna find out somethin we have in common." Throwing down the gauntlet making Martin just as intent to prove him wrong.

"You a professor or something?" The farmer motioned at Martin's book. Martin nodded dismissively.

"Don't get many of your kind up this way. That why you ain't off fighting?" It didn't sound like an insult or accusation, only an inquiry.

"I was wounded." Martin whispered.

"Where was you, then? I gotta son over there somewheres. Maybe you know him." Martin mumbled a name of a French village mentioned in his book.

"What was that?" He cupped his hand over his ear and leaned so close Martin could see the hairs on the top of his nose.

Martin repeated it. "Nope. That's not where my boy is. Heck, I don't know where he is to tell you the truth, but he ain't near there. I never heard of that place." He waved his hand in the air. "The Missus is besides herself. Cries morning, noon, and night. She's sure he ain't coming back. Hell, what can I say? Sooner we lick that loud-mouth Kraut my boy can get back here and pitch in again. It's been hell doing all the farmin' on my own. Don't know what to say to the Missus, though." He looked down at his brawny hands resting in his lap for the answer.

Martin yawned and closed his book, leaned his head into the seat, and closed his eyes but whenever the farmer moved, his boot, his elbow, even his shoulder bumped against Martin. The man fidgeted not at all used to being idle, wired to move from one never-ending job to the next.

Martin attempted to rest until he smelled tangy mustard and heard wax paper crackling. A whiff from a thick slice of homemade German sausage between two ample slices of bread transported him back to Germany, and like his strong-smelling companion, Martin hoped his country would put a quick end to the war. In Tubingen now the summer heat would be miserable and he'd be drinking a mass of beer along with the season's freshly made sausage. The gently rolling hills of the Rhineland carpeted in green were in sharp contrast to the endless miles of crops.

He must have dozed off. The train slowed down snapping him awake.

"I'm getting off at Medicine Hat." The farmer said sounding disappointed. "The wife's got a sister over here and her husband is ailing. Something ain't right in the feller's head." He tapped his temple with two bratwurst fingers. "Gotta help out when things get rough. That's what they say, don't they?" A pleading look in the hope he was doing the right thing because it wasn't what he wanted to do.

Had his wife counseled him about his duty to the family *if* he needed reminding to do what was needed as any decent brother-in-law would in difficult circumstances? Martin nodded. People like him and Mary Alice forever doomed to feeling guilty no matter what they decided. On the next leg of the journey to Calgary he hoped he'd get the seat to himself.

But the train sidled into the station and Martin spotted two men at the end of the platform who didn't blend with the somewhat smaller crowd waiting to board. It wasn't just their clothing that deceived them, but that was the most noticeable. After that, it was the posture, the way they stood next to each other. From a distance, it was obvious they didn't fit the awkward space between them and their movements were edgy. They had a job that bound them. They tried to pass themselves off as typical passengers, but they couldn't disguise their motive. He watched them watching. Agents scouting, looking but trying not to appear like they were looking. They used each other as props, shifting positions, facing each other to scan the area over each other's shoulders to cover the area.

"I'm sorry. I forgot your name." Martin spoke to the farmer's back once he moved into the aisle. Martin jumped out of the seat and grabbed his knapsack down off the rack.

"Herman. Herman Schlegel." The farmer gleamed and shook his hand again like he was grinding hamburger. Happy that Martin was offering him another chance to get to know him. How many times had he told the missus he never knew a stranger and believed it? Martin had been the first to make him doubt himself.

"You gettin' off here? From the looks of you, I'd a thought you was headed for one of them big cities."

"I've got some time and this looks like an interesting town. Think I'll get off and take a look around."

"Hell, this ain't what I'd say is the garden spot of Alberta except it's got them coulees along the river. You should take a look at them if you want to see something interesting."

"You wouldn't be able to give me a lift, would you?"

"That's a mighty good idea." Herman squeezed his shoulder and Martin tried not to wince.

"You wouldn't know a good place to stay here, by the way?"

"Say young feller. You didn't tell me your name yet. But I think I got just the ticket for you." Martin smelled the mustard on his breath.

Florence-Fifty-Seven

The storm teased, flirted, rumbled, spat out an eye dropper of rain, huffed and puffed then disappeared with its tail between its legs. That happened at one o'clock. A few hours before it had toyed around debating whether or not to cause a menace. She stayed awake in case it broke to reassure the boy but then fell asleep against the cab's wall waiting.

The aroma of coffee and feet shuffling from the galley woke her, and when she opened her eyes the boy was crossing the small space with a steaming cup, nurturing it so it wouldn't spill. She had a crick in her neck from sitting up all night but smiled and he grinned. His dazzling teeth surprised her again.

"You're up?" Making her voice sound casual, not making a fuss but it really was too soon to be on his feet. He'd had to step over her to get off the cot without waking her. "You must be feeling much better."

He'd made oatmeal. It was on the table with a spoon beside the one bowl. He waited while she folded up the bedroll. She was still dressed from the day before so ran her fingers through her hair and dabbed her eyes in the wash basin.

"Where is your bowl?" Giving him a motherly raised eyebrow. He didn't answer but then he didn't need to. She saw it in his downcast eyes. "Don't be silly. There's plenty for both of us and I'm not eating without you." He wouldn't look at her. Although it was early morning it wouldn't be long before the room heated up since there had been little rain during the night to cool things down. Moisture hung like a wet mop in the cab. She didn't mean to snap at him, hoped he didn't think she had. The day was starting out sticky and there was this annoying pain in her neck.

The dazzling light didn't lesson the feeling that something was looming. No reason for it as the signs were all good. The boy was alert and moving, out of bed and not hobbling at all. Being mulish served him well. The clouds on the Idaho border were bloated cows too leaden to move. The heads on the tall grasses below the cab stood upright as sentinels. "No wind to speak of." A dull set of figures to log in her record book.

"Sit." She pointed to the chair where the oatmeal waited. "You make a fine cup of coffee by the way. Who taught you to do that?" He looked at the wall in front of him. Not a significant word between them since they'd come back to the cab, and he wouldn't look at her. "Did you make enough for both of us?" He didn't say. "I'm going to make another bowl of mush. For me. And a cup of coffee for you." She waited for him to pick up the spoon first. "You're not going to let that go to waste, are you?" She mocked him the way she did Homer to irk him into doing what she wanted. "Mom, knock it off." Homer growled, but not the boy. He looked anxious.

"If you're feeling up to it today, I'll show you how the Osborne works." He was scraping the bottom of the bowl and if he kept eating like that, he'd soon have some meat on those sticks for bones. His elbows stuck out like slingshots.

"Yeah." At last a first word and a sideways glance with something of a smile.

Her neck ached but it hadn't bothered enough for her to lie down during the night. She must have been too exhausted and while she was sleeping the boy climbed over her and had seen to her gauges, gone up in the cupola and entered the figures into the log. Doing her job. Now, he was washing the breakfast dishes.

"This one's gonna be a scorcher. What you got up there for me, Flossie?"

"Not enough rain to measure."

"Yeah. Don't I know. A good downpour is what we need and no stinking lightning. Don't want another tempest in a teapot."

"Much ado about nothing." Florence giggled at that leftover memory from her English class. Aside from raising Homer, and a garden every year for the past twenty, the pages of her life were blank pieces of white paper.

"Don't count that storm out just yet."

"You mean there's still a chance it might come this way?"

"There's always the chance." He was chewing something, probably a donut. "Too good a chance, if the wind comes up. And if it's not this one, there's sure to be another before we're through."

The oatmeal didn't fill him up. He'd washed their dishes and was leaning on the counter. She told him to sit down and fixed him two slices of bread with butter and honey.

"Would you like some eggs?" He was chewing the last slice of toast and shook his head. "Don't tell me you are full?" He grinned. He finished his last bite with effort and trying not to let on that he had run out of steam. How long had he been up? "I really think it's about time you tell me your name." A shadow crossed his face and his shoulders tightened.

"Or, maybe not." Under her breath. That earlier glimmer about learning the Osborne flew off his face. She started humming to cut through the awkward silence.

"It's okay. Tell me in your own good time. If you want." Everything had seemed fine until she'd asked. He'd gobbled down the breakfast, he'd even sort of smiled, and he'd even gotten up before her as if he was settling in. But she crossed a line.

He slept the rest of the day. She watered plants in the morning and later when the sun was cooking them, covered them with shade cloth, and tiptoed in and out of the cab up to the cupola to survey her territory, and whispered her reports to the ranger. She left the boy alone.

"You comin' down with a sore throat or somethin? You sound hoarse."

"My throat's dry, I guess."

He slept through the evening conversation with the spotters "Why you so quiet tonight, Flossie, if I might ask?"

"It's the heat, Joe. I'm tired. I think I'll just say goodnight."

She woke to sun streaming in and the aroma of coffee.

"We need more water. I'll go down this morning and get it." He handed the cup to her, looked straight into her eyes and dared her to disagree.

"Don't worry. I'll get it." She rubbed the sleep out of her eyes.

209

"You think I'm not up to it, but I am." He dazzled her with a million-dollar smile.

"Okay. But how about we go together? Otherwise, I'm going to die of cabin fever." He smiled because she was chuckling.

"Tommy." He blurted ahead of her on the way down. The empty containers banged against each other off her shoulder. She'd gone to sleep deciding if he wouldn't tell her his name, she would assign him one. She was going to call him Bobby until he told her otherwise. If he ever did.

"Hello, Tommy. I'm Florence." She said to his back and smiled.

Martin-Fifty-Eight

Sitting on the doorstep of Medicine Hat the village of Dunmore is the eye of the hurricane to an expanse of Alberta's wheat fields. It bears the name of a long-forgotten and obscure earl who promoted the Canadian Pacific Railroad in the area. It doesn't have a bank. The granary is its vault holding the jewels of harvests in years good or meager and the singular point of interest in the banal hamlet.

Herman Schlegel's brother-in-law Ned's place was five miles farther out of Dunmore along the Crowsnest railway line. A block from the depot, Ned's wife leaned against a rusted-out pickup shading her face with her hand. She didn't wave or nod to Herman or Martin who walked toward her. Herman was thrusting a stranger on her and she looked to have about a stick's worth of energy left in her. It was so damn hot. She'd pulled her hair back into a bun at the nape of her neck.

"We're gonna give him a lift." Herman shrugged one shoulder toward Martin to punctuate. She hadn't yet said anything and didn't acknowledge Martin. They tossed their gear into the pickup bed between bales of hay and groceries.

"Jesus, woman. You load them in yourself?" Referring to the bales. Her indifferent shrug impressed Martin. None of the cheery-o Canadian good will coming from her.

Without knowing he had done so, Herman abetted Martin who used him as a wall to hide behind to get past the agents. His excuse was Herman's firm belief in the possibilities. "There ain't such a thing as a stranger. We're all connected some way. And by God, if you ain't in a big hurry, we'll see how them strings cross." Martin slid right by the agents, Herman between him and the men and after they'd gone twenty yards, he peeked to see the agents scanning the faces of the other passengers getting off.

Martin tipped his hat at the wife, wasn't sure she nodded in return, if she did it was slight enough to miss. Herman climbed into the driver's seat and she slid in on the other side between the two men. She had been milking that morning and smelled of dairy and something else pungent that was not unpleasant. She coughed and

Martin sneaked a look at her. By the size of her, she could pass for fourteen. She wiped her hands on her skirt and folded them in her lap, the inertia rattled him. He pumped his boot to the floorboard.

Herman made a mess grinding the gears to get the truck going. "Hell, woman, when's the last time someone worked on this thing?" She rubbed her folded hands together, unfolded them and wiped them on her skirt again. They looked as tired as she seemed leathered and chapped. Martin thumped his boot several times and offered her a cigarette as they bumped along, Herman not getting the hang of any of the gears. She returned a sad looking, turned-down smile, but he had pleased her he could tell. He lit one for her between Herman's hit and miss effort with the potholes and leaned over to offer one to him.

"Nope. I don't use the damn things. Sorry, Tilly." He looked in the rearview mirror at her. Martin glanced at her profile. She might have been attractive, maybe even beautiful once. She wasn't much older than he but her fading reddish hair was gray at the roots and the worry lines around her eyes and mouth had aged her badly. Her shoulders sunk into her chest like she was on half-rations.

"Listen, Tilly. I'd introduce you to this fella but I don't know his name. Yet." Herman waved at a car coming toward them. Martin grinned at him.

"Don't matter." She'd given up having things matter.

"Sure, it do, dearie. I been on the train with this fellow, how many hours now, and I wanna know who I'm talking to."

"Guess that's so. Paul Schwartz."

"Well, damn. I mighta figured. That sounds like a good German name, don't it, Tilly. Sorry for the language, Tilly." Foul language didn't appear to influence her one way or another. It would give her some relief to do a fair share of it herself.

"We is German too, ain't we Tilly? Only these days, we keep that business to ourselves. Even considered changing our name when that crazy nut got things riled up over there in Europe. What in the hell is the matter with those Germans? No telling what people, hell even the neighbors, might get up to. Call us Nazis. Hell, our people come over before the 1900's and we are as red-blooded as any damn Canadian. Ain't that so, Tilly?"

212

Tilly squinted out at the fields until Herman made a sharp turn onto an even worse dirt road. This one didn't have gravel and her legs and arms surrendered to the potholes like they were held together by a set of safety pins. Defeated is what she was. Whatever her battle, she'd given up, waved her flag of capitulation which had gained her nothing for the war kept going dragging her as it went and trouncing on her submission.

At a lone mailbox, Herman turned off the dirt road onto a rutted driveway fairly overgrown with Canadian thistles. "Them damn weeds gotta go, Tilly. You know well as me you shouldn't let 'em spread like that." Tilly didn': even blink.

The house and barn teetered on the verge of crisis, a world wonder remaining upright for some unexplained reason. "Jesus." Herman whispered. He had his own place to keep up. It would take a year to make some headway on this place. He pulled up to the wooden steps by the porch.

"I'll be on my way, then. Thanks for the lift." Martin put his hand out to help Tilly out of the pickup but she floated past him like a leaf in the wind.

"Now hold on a minute, Paul. No need you running off here before Tilly's give us lunch. Ain't that so, Tilly? She's one fine cook. What you got fixed for us, anyhows?" He winked at Martin.

"I really should be getting on."

"What's the big hurry? You said you wanted to take a look around here. Now's your chance. I bet Tilly could make up a bed for you in two seconds flat. What you say, Tilly?" Tilly said nothing. Martin looked at her and winced. There was an invalid inside that house, somewhere in a bed, and sucking the life out of a woman who should be in her prime. The railroad tracks ran near the farm. He would follow them while there was still daylight.

"Fetch us a bottle a beer, Tilly. We'll set on the porch while you fix them sandwiches. Least you can do, fella, is have a bite to eat with us. Don't want insult us, do you?" Herman squinted at him, the old farmer had outwitted him. The screen door had one bolt holding it upright. Tilly skillfully slid it open and ducked under it.

Florence-Fifty-Nine

The sun dallied overhead spilling more heat onto the once lush grasses tall now and overrun due to June's heavy rains. They crackled like grasshoppers when a deer or other beast grazed past them and broke in half. By the end of July, the moisture that had been sucked out of the woods left a tinderbox primed and ready for one spark to set them off. The spotters lived in a twisted reality, days of monotony paired with anticipation. They called in uneventful reports, but the ranger nervously sucked the tip of his thumb.

"Hey!" Tommy protested when Florence splashed him for the fun of it. The creek was silty in the spot where she sat and a few feet away from where Tommy filled the containers. He refused even to put his feet in.

"Come on. It'll feel so good. Take your shoes off and wriggle your toes in it, at least."

"No. I said I don't want to." He was exasperating sometimes. Even when something was good for him, he said no.

"Well, how about wetting your shirt before we head back? Or your hat? Would that kill you?"

"Nope."

Florence was like a kid in a sandbox funneling the sediment through her fingers. If it weren't for Homer off somewhere fighting, if she knew where he was at least and that he was safe, she would be content. She and Tommy had divided the duties up between them except for going down for water which they did together.

"I'll go get it next time." He put back his shoulders like he was going to dig in but knew she wouldn't agree, and she made the excuse of needing to get away from the cab, too.

"Besides, I'm not afraid of getting wet and melting, like you if you accidentally slip in."

"Not funny."

"Well, so you say, but it's my one chance to cool down. Who do you think went to get it before you came?" He could see through her. Easy.

"You're not foolin' me." He said just above a whisper.

214

"What do you mean?" She knew exactly what he meant. That she was worried for him. He hadn't told her how he'd gotten beat up, or found his way to the cab. None of his story. Zero. If he had, maybe it would help. She imagined many possibilities at night after he'd fallen asleep. But wouldn't ask him to confide because he wouldn't. Could her imaginings be as bad or worse than what really happened? She didn't even dare ask how old he was and that seemed a simple thing to answer, but with Tommy, it might not be. She asked him to please pass the butter, but not much else for fear he would close down as he had when she'd asked him his name. That turned out all right in the end, but she wasn't going to gamble on it turning out that way again.

They'd traded sleeping quarters once his sores closed up. She strung a rope across a corner of the cab and hung a quilt across and made up a bedroll for him. It wasn't much but it gave them a bit more privacy and he got up first always waking her with the scent of coffee in the mornings.

"I swear, Tommy. You make the best coffee, yet. What's your secret?"

"Wouldn't you like to know." He smirked. "Guess you'll have to get up earlier if you want to get in on it."

"I wouldn't dream of spoiling your fun." He was getting cocky which might be from hearing the way George and Henry niggled.

"You're singin' like a bird, Flo. What's makin' you so happy in this hot weather?" George had come across a large huckleberry patch that morning. "Got there before the bears, I'm pleased to say. I'm fixing huckleberry muffins and if you was close by, Flo, I'd bring some over."

Thankfully, the men couldn't see a blush through the phone. Tommy grinned at her. He'd had the bright idea of stuffing a corner of the blanket in his mouth in case he couldn't keep back the giggles. When supper came, he hurried through the meal and washed up the dishes so he was ready when the spotters came on the line.

"It's the cool evenings, I think, don't you?" Better than church where one should be able to find solace but can't. "And, the lettuce in my garden is almost ready to use."

215

"I'd take a dose or two of tomatoes if you get some, Flo. George is right about your singing. It makes me happy, too." Gentle Joe with a kind word.

"I think my violin sings as good as Flo."

"Henry. Give it a rest." Tommy stuck his head into the blanket.

"Hey, George, did I tell you about the man who walks into the records office to change his name?"

"Here we go." George groaned.

"The clerk asked him his name. 'Adolph Stinkfoot,' he says. 'What do you want to change it to?' 'Maurice Stinkfoot.'" Tommy smothered a giggle.

"It ain't funny, Henry, and you know it. I got a question for you."

"Yeah? What is it?"

"Why is it rich people have all the money?"

"I dunno."

"See. Guess you don't know everything, Henry."

"Not even a tickle of a breeze tonight."

"Well, that's a good sign, Joe, ain't it? You're always warning us about the wind kickin' things up."

"Silence before the storm, maybe." George was back on the harmonica making a patter like raindrops.

"You might be right about that, George. It's gotta come sooner or later."

"Something's gotta give. It always does."

"Is that a quote, Henry?"

"I'm just saying something's coming. It has to."

"Do you think so?" Florence mentally plugged her ears to the explosions of thunder that were going to come.

Later Tommy repeated to Florence what the fellows had said. Three times, as if she hadn't had enough of them the first time. The best part was how his faced glowed. If they only knew they had a silent partner. The furrows on his brow were mostly gone these days and he had put on maybe five pounds. His tendency would always be toward the lean.

His breathing was steady and deep, but she tossed and turned, plumped the lumpy pillow up, squinted at the clock every fifteen minutes finally stuffing it under her pillow after midnight. The spotters predicted a storm and she trusted Joe on that. She waited for it to roll in. The memory of metal burning during the last storm was still fresh in her nostrils.

It must have been one o'clock and she was in that twilight place of half-awake or dreaming she was awake when her husband appeared before her over her bed. He was unusually calm talking so gently with her. She reached out to him. Then the heavens exploded.

Martin-Sixty

The South Saskatchewan River begins in the glaciers of the Rockies and from there meanders over 800 miles to the northeast through Saskatchewan before dumping into Lake Winnipeg and then continuing on to drain into Nelson Bay. By midsummer the ice blocks have melted, the flood waters receded and it drifts civilly on the prairie.

It still had its winter bite when Martin dipped into it before dawn. He scrambled out much faster than he went in shaking like a dog to get the water out of his ears. Then, he did ten military jumping jacks before wolfing down the last of the sausage sandwiches Tilly had packed at Herman's insistence. If he hadn't been fully awake before that, the spicy mustard tingling the back of his tongue did the job.

He was on the road after outfoxing the agents at the train station in Medicine Hat with the help of a verbose farmer and a beaten-down woman. Too bad he couldn't make any further use of the free ticket Bobby bought him, but agents would be watching the train stops from here on out.

Bobby had also purchased a Canadian map for him. "You won't be needing this, but it'll give you something to pore over if you get bored during the trip." Bobby was too good for Eleanor Baker. She didn't deserve a loyal, caring son, without doubt a patriotic fellow who obeyed all rules, followed commands the best he could and who would be devastated, one of his worst blunders, his grand failure when he learned he'd aided and abetted a traitor.

Martin gave Tilly a full package of cigarettes on some fool whim that made one corner of her mouth lift briefly. He was going to run short on his supply because of it. In Winnipeg he'd gotten a taste for coffee again and after a night bedded down near the railroad tracks several miles from the farm, he craved the lift it gave him. It must have been close to morning before he stopped counting trains rumbling by that shook the ground beneath him.

Tilly filled a glass jar of godawful sweet tea and handed it to him before he left. The sun was getting low on the horizon and his throat dry when he took one gulp and promptly spit out the syrupy sweet liquid. Thick with sugar, something sure to be in short supply given their miserable poverty and the rationing. It was ludicrous. He growled at the fleeting memory of the prune-faced image, furious that she allowed her circumstances to crush her, caving in to dilapidation and misery. That's why he'd left. He'd sleep in the rough any day rather than stay in that blight which would quietly creep in and infect him if he lingered. He loathed all of them for their paralysis, for not fighting off the helplessness, for not pulling themselves out of the quagmire. He wanted to slap her hard enough across her pinched mouth to draw blood for wasting the sugar.

The stars were just starting to twinkle on the dirt road when he realized that Herman's friendliness was a not so subtle hint for Martin to stay on and lend a hand. He might talk about never meeting a stranger, and maybe in his mind he really meant that, but there was more to it. He didn't blame him. Even Herman who had the itch to be working all the time couldn't fix Tilly's chaos.

Tilly wasn't up to hoping or expecting any good to come into her life so she didn't move a wrinkle on her face when he said he had to move on. Her vacant eyes hung onto his back, however when he left the house and strode back over the ruts and weeds Herman had griped about when they arrived. He felt her accusing stare bore into his back for abandoning a moribund animal that wanted nothing more than to be put out of its misery.

His stomach turned at the taste of her lukewarm tea but more at the lingering after taste of her apathy. She'd let it become her master. He caught himself dumping out the liquid because he wanted but could not slap her for being stupid and wasteful. He wasted a half cup on the ground. Who was the stupid one to throw it away? Because he feared ending up in a similar stupor? The tea was refreshing, its sticky sweetness invigorating. He still wanted to slap her

He covered ten miles before nine in the morning and with his blood thickened from the exertion, put the wretched reminder of Tilly behind him. But the empty road troubled him because there were no outcroppings to hide behind for a long stretch and when he saw a cloud of dust growing ahead coming out of a side lane and heard the sputter of an engine, he made a snap decision. A truck farmer with a load of produce was the first vehicle he'd seen. Martin bought a handful of carrots, two kohlrabies, and filled the glass jar with unshelled peas.

"You on your own out here, young fella?" Martin said he was just passing through.

"Not much to look at out here on foot. Don't know why anybody'd wanna do it. You ever think about takin' the train? It'd get you where you're going without the misery." The farmer chuckled at his own wit but didn't offer him a lift.

"Maybe I'll do that." Martin laughed lightly.

"Where you headed, anyways?"

"Haven't made up my mind. I'll see where the road leads. You don't happen to have homemade sausage for sale, do you?"

"Well, son-of-a-gun, if I don't." He pulled out a cloth sack that Martin surmised was the man's lunch. "Didn't know I'd have a customer for it, today. Usually sell everything at Bow Island." He chuckled again handing it to him and leaving his hand open waiting for the money. "That'll cost you twenty-five cents."

A mile later Martin found a shady spot off the road. After he'd eaten the sausage which was hearty and delicious and some of the vegetables, he studied the map and between the heat and food he felt drowsy.

This rail route also ended up at the coast although only yesterday he thought he was done riding the rails what with Bobby's generosity. The security people would be watching for train hoppers. Maybe he'd go south to the border. Forget about Vancouver. Agents would be at every stop. Five US border crossings between Medicine Hat and Sparwood, British Columbia but any town on the way would have their police force, and then there was Fort MacLeod.

Florence-Sixty-One

In the Rockies, crystal clear skies in the morning and clouds of mares' tails by four o'clock bring downpours that come quickly and leave as fast. It's the moody clouds that sit pregnant on the western horizon, however, over the peaks of the Cabinet Range in sullen temperament heavy and distended, that on impulse blow up into a tantrum. Or, they evaporate on a whim without delivering their goods. This is the spotter's predicament. The guessing game with Mother Nature. Will it happen today? Tomorrow? What trouble will it bring when it goes crazy?

These days the ranger was eating a dozen powdered sugar donuts daily. The circular fan blew into his face but didn't stop the sweat from dripping or keep his shirt dry, nor did the donuts satisfy the gnawing in his belly. His wife mixed a teaspoon of baking soda with water until it fizzed and gave it to him every evening to calm the ulcer. "What you got for me today, Flo?"

She apologized. "They haven't shifted for three days now." The storm she'd dreamt about when Fred showed up over her bed wasn't forgotten. The sunlight eased her and the regular tasks kept her worries occupied.

"Yeah. That's what I'm hearin' from the fellas. Wish I knew. Wish I had a fire crew on standby. Can't call 'em out for no good reason." The woods were crisper than French fries. Other summers like this kept him awake at night.

"How do you do that?" It was mid-afternoon. Too warm to work in the garden so she wrote her epistle to Homer.

"What do you mean? Do what? I'm writing to my son." Her attention was on keeping the news cheerful, not allowing dark clouds to shadow across the page so she flinched when she realized Tommy was looking over her shoulder.

"No. Write like that? Can you show me?" Twenty years had honed her skill for keeping a passive face.

The boy understood the Osborne on his first attempt, something that had taken her a week to master. So, it was after that he was shown the right way to hold a pencil. She'd learned cursive in third grade on special paper with two horizontal parallel lines divided by a broken one.

"So, Flo, what do you do the rest of the year when you're not being a spotter?" Henry asked. In early June they were still feeling each other out and Henry had been easiest to figure. A wannabe detective who asked blunt questions.

"Keep the house clean and make the meals. I have my garden too and I can my vegetables."

"You mean you're a housewife?"

"Yes. I make bread once a week and when the strawberries are ripe, I make preserves. I mean, I did. But Homer went into the army and I don't know where he is." Remarkable for Henry, he heard the worry.

Joe came from Klamath Falls, Oregon. Henry from Chicago. George had bummed around growing up. "You from around here, Flo?" Joe asked quietly somewhere in the midst of George pining for something sweet after supper.

"You could make rice pudding."

"Got a sweet tooth, I gotta admit. How do you do that?"

"Make your rice then add a cup of evaporated milk and a cup of water. Add two tablespoons of dry eggs, and a teaspoon of vanilla, then bake it until its firm when you shake the pan."

"Let me write it down. Hang on."

"You can add raisins, if you like.

"I hate raisins."

She laughed. "I grew up in Frenchtown, Joe. On a farm with a few milk cows. Moved to Missoula when I got married."

"Your husband lets you do this job?" Henry bellowed but didn't add, "What kind a fool is he?"

They didn't ask about Fred. None of the men were married. When they went back to civilization people asked if they were. "It's the nature of the work." Some spotters chose the job for the independence, and its isolation, and if truth were told, bumbled and stumbled when it came to relationships. George had tried to make a go of one once, had gained a son out of the deal of whom he was quite proud, the wife a footnote buried somewhere at the bottom of his page. He didn't analyze the failure or blame himself for it, and to his credit, he didn't blame her. It hadn't worked out, that was all there was to it. "I'm not cut out for it."

Joe joked. "Hey, I'm just your typical old crotchety bachelor " He was in his fifties and had come to Montana to live the life of the mountain man. "No woman would wanna put up with that kind of nonsense." Henry was mum and they didn't pry. He wasn't shy about putting his nose in but didn't want it in return.

George was having trouble with a bear, complained of losing sleep because it tried to climb into bed with him after nearly ripping the door entirely off the hinges. He spent half the morning getting the catawampus thing back on straight. Henry griped. "I'm fed up with the quality and quantity of supplies the stingy packer hauled up."

"It was awfully warm today."

"Yeah. Sure was." Joe waited for her to say more.

"I just wish I knew where Homer was."

"Sorry, Flo. That's got a be a tough one." She didn't mention Fred, good or bad. Common sense filled in the details.

Florence drew lines on blank paper to help Tommy master the cursive letters. "Don't watch me." She was sitting beside him after explaining how to write within the lines.

"All right." She got up to make a compote, despite the heat. That's when the dream came back, her husband's phantom arrival the night before. Then she thought about when they were young and how he tried to woo her from her high school friends at the river. The girls were taking turns jumping into the frigid Clark fork, plugging their noses and screaming from the shock, and then running barefoot and screeching over the rocky bottom to the muddy bank. They took turns shouting encouragement to the next one while her future husband hid in a clump of trees watching them. He was handsome and muscular and when it was Florence's turn and she screamed as she emerged, he jumped from the shadows in his bathing suit in front of her. The girls were like a herd of deer, collectively turning to stare at the foreign creature and if they should flee. He mimicked Charles Atlas at the beach, showing off his biceps and the whole herd giggled. He clambered onto a driftwood log, pushed it into the water and made a grand effort at being an acrobat. Drifting on the current past the girls who still stood in a bunch, stretched his arms out toward Florence and kept his eyes only on her. Her friends giggled and she shivered from cold and excitement.

Tommy was dreamy that evening. So was she. When they went to sleep even the brooding clouds in the west seemed pacified. She was smiling in a dream about rice pudding when the first bolt struck and there was the noxious smell.

Martin-Sixty-Two

In 1915 a tornado cut a devastating path from Redcliff to Grassy Lake and as it headed to Calgary dumped four inches of water per hour in the Bow River. Bow Island lies between Medicine Hat and Grassy Lake and the town's water tower toppled during that storm. The metal replacement is a plump sugar bowl atop gigantic stilts that dwarfs the granaries standing at attention next to the railroad tracks.

Ripe fields hug the farming community and one road runs in and out of the heart of Bow Island. Martin needed cigarettes and since he couldn't avoid the town unless he struck out through acres of corn rows, took his chances. In Toronto and Regina, blending into a crowd was not difficult. Not so for Bow Island where strangers take a long stare and come to quick judgment, the kind of people used to make rapid and astute decisions because their livelihoods depend on gauging beforehand the moods of nature and how to handle gouging buyers.

In rural locales practical individuals bump up against the cosmopolitan, the suspicious confront the aloof. And so, on foot, this too tall, too elegant man strode past the down-to-earth businesses marking the edge of town and into the meat of Bow Island. Such as it was.

Across from the general store, the truck farmer who'd sold him the sausage sandwich had his operation set up and was arranging the last of his produce on the tailgate.

"I see you made it, then." He'd run out of peas and now plumped up the drooping carrot tops that hadn't sold yet and hung off the end wilting.

When they had met on the road, Martin tried to buy some cigarettes off him. "Don't smoke the damn things. You shouldn't either. Go to hell over it." Martin ignored the stupidity. Far more likely to get strung up because that addiction drove him into a town where everybody knew everyone else and what their business was, and were suspicious when someone was out of the ordinary, like a man wandering along the road with a backpack.

The farmer gabbed and studied the backsides of the teenage farm girls who walked from the store to the café, and gloated over whatever money was put into his grubby paw. For Martin, he was a godsend for calling out to him in public which changed him from being a total outsider. He would still be an oddity but less a threat and more a puzzle deserving of an, "Afternoon," greeting and not just a nod.

"S'pose you're in town to stock up on that filthy habit of yours." His mouth was crammed with sunflower seeds. He spit out the shells indifferent to an answer. He knew the answer.

"You have any more of that sausage?" The farmer laughed from the ball of his belly.

"That was my goll-darn lunch, fella. You wanna have my supper on top of it?" Martin bought a few more carrots and a pocket full of sunflower seeds.

"See you around."

"Not unless you're walking backwards from where you come from."

He bought a carton of cigarettes, a roll of salami, a loaf of bread at the general store, and a bottle of aspirin. The café was opposite the sleepy police station and on a police vehicle parked in front someone had drawn a sun with rays coming out of it on the dusty windshield. No egregious offenses were committed in this village. Either that or the station's manpower had been peeled off by the war.

He smoked two cigarettes and drank his tea at a window seat noting the occasional pedestrian, none of whom were curious to look at who was looking at them from inside. A handmade sign posted in the window reminded residents of an ice cream social the following weekend at the Catholic Church. Another sign, its yellowed tape peeling at the corners should have come down weeks earlier. It highlighted the events that had been celebrated on Canada Day.

After an hour, he ordered a sandwich, took a bite and puffed on his cigarette. The teenager girls had cleared out, gone home to do the milking. A pack of flies buzzed at the window trying to find a way out. The young waitress sat at the counter with her plump legs crossed at the ankles painting her fingernails blowing on each after it was lacquered. Then she applied a second coat and smacked her lips on her bubble gum.

Two screen doors, one at the front and another in the back, circulated air through the place, helped by a wheezing fan that was meant to keep the place from stifling. It didn't cool things down but pushed the air around for some relief. Who needed the Mounties? The heat put a damper on any unnecessary activity. The few people on the street looked frazzled enough to melt.

Even the flies grew listless. If he didn't move on from the café, get out of town before it got cooler someone was bound to start asking questions. He took a second bite and sipped the last of the lukewarm tea, didn't pull out the map but wanted to although he knew from memory what he needed to know. The waitress hadn't budged from the counter. After testing her nails, she gave a halfhearted wipe with a damp rag as far as she could reach.

"You'll have to finish up, mister. We close in fifteen minutes." Her hair was oily. The pimples on her chin seemed more pronounced since he'd come in. "Okay, miss. I'd like a ham and cheese sandwich."

"But we're closing." She looked up at the wall clock.

"Just wrap it up. I'll take it with me." The first sandwich had been soggy in the middle, the lettuce wilted. "No lettuce. Just mustard."

"You want a pickle with that?" She played with her ponytail, smacked her gum and wrote down his order. The pickle on the first sandwich had been delicious, in fact the best part, homemade by someone who took pride in canning, a would-be blue ribbon winner at the county fair. Crisp and juicy with the right amount of tang, not too much salt.

"I'd like two." She smacked her gum again writing on her pad. *Two pickles*! with an exclamation point.

Florence-Sixty-Three

Lightning is a giant spark of electricity that lasts about one-fifth of a second, the most dangerous and frequent of all the weather hazards, and the number one cause of storm-related deaths, twice as many as those from hurricanes, tornadoes, or flood. The super-heated air measures more than 50,000 degrees Fahrenheit, puts off an explosive shock wave of thunder typically four times hotter than the sun's surface, and from cloud-to-ground can be two to ten miles long packing a billion volts.

A spotter's job is not to measure such statistics for posterity, but first-hand experience is a remarkable teacher. Florence had been through one such storm, yet that evening before bed it hadn't seemed necessary to close the shutters hot as it was. Besides, the nightly rumbles were becoming routine. "All smoke and no fire, aye, Flossie?"

"I'll keep my fingers crossed, Henry."

"Who knows? Maybe we'll beat the odds, you think?" George pressed Joe.

"We don't get odds. But, let's wait and see. I hope you're right."

Listening to the distant rolls night after night got to be like taking a sleeping pill. Reassuring because it sounded off in the distance with the volume turned down low so when Florence considered whether or not to close the cab up for the night, it was easy enough to let it go.

When morning light broke, Tommy was sweeping up broken glass. She was moving about on the cot. "Why don't you make the coffee?" He said quietly with his back to her. "Get our motors started again." He forced a chuckle and glanced at her.

She'd vomited. Somehow found the pail at the beginning of the confusion and made it just in time. Just after the glass exploded into the cab and just after the animal-like scream that sent cold shivers up his spine. He crawled on his hands and knees sweeping with his hands until he came across her leg. Even with his hands on her shoulders the retching wouldn't stop.

"It's gonna be okay." That assurance canceled out by the next clap of thunder. The black room was off kilter as if a dog had gripped it between its teeth and was shaking the life out of it. An inky underworld seesawed between darkness and hideous chartreus as lightning hurled flames from some incendiary god demanded retribution and egging on the seasickness. The waves obliterated a chance to focus on a single point. And, the horrible odor piled on to the nausea.

"Ma'am?" Her body slipped away from him falling with a soft thud. He held her head in his lap and wiped her mouth with his sleeve, rocking her ever so gently for what seemed an eternity.

When you wake, you shall have all the pretty little horses. He sang. She woke to the lullaby that had lulled Homer to sleep as a baby.

"You okay, Ma'am?" A wave of nausea hit her again when she lifted her head but she didn't throw up. A mishmash of fusilades whistled about the cab, popping guns or booming cannons and then the climax came. A hail of small snowballs rapped on the tin roof, giant drumsticks that produced earsplitting pounding.

She was half-sitting now, and leaning against Tommy, covering her ears and whimpering. When the sun showed up, she was back in her bed and Tommy was sweeping up shards. She followed the swish of the broom with her eyes. His rhythmic movements were deliberate and purposeful like a well-oiled rocking chair.

"Watch where you put your feet!" He jerked his head up from the broom. Bits of glass sparkled like diamonds on the floor and through the smashed-in window a remarkably sweet mountain breeze drifted in. Nature returning the theft of precious fresh and pure air in apology for the rudeness they'd been forced to be a part of. Witnesses to a violent row.

She looked like she'd slept with a porcupine, the quills of hair standing at attention.

'I am." His feelings hurt because he'd tried hard not to disturb her while getting the mess cleaned up ahead of her. He'd moved his bedroll beside her cot once the storm whimpered its last and listened to her breathing. Thankfully, it had gotten steady and stayed even. The sun was just about to come over the Glacier peaks when he caught a few minutes sleep.

A sudden notion triggered her to get upright but when she did, found she needed the cot for support and plopped back down pulling the plaid Pendleton around her shoulders. It was still early. The sun had begun lapping up the night's moisture. The day was going to be muggy.

Something had to happen next on the cot, she understood but it took some time to figure out it had to do with putting on and lacing up her boots. Tommy dumped the broken glass and put the broom back and felt her eyes following him each step.

"Would you look at that." Shaking the coffee pot at her. "It didn't budge last night. Wanna make us some?"

"Oh." She hadn't figured out the boots, yet.

"Don't you want a cup of coffee?" He pleaded with her.

"Coffee?" She looked down at her boots at last. "Coffee?" Looking up at him for an explanation.

"You know. It gets you going in the morning." He moved his arms pretending to run.

"I have to put on my boots. I have to tell Fred."

"Who'd Fred?" He got it. It was the way she looked around the cab and, in her mind, collecting her belongings to pack back down the mountain. He made a pot of coffee and brought it to her.

"After you drink your coffee you need to call the ranger. He's gonna be waiting for your report." He headed up to the cupola to check the gauges and entered them in the log. When he came back down the ladder she was still staring at her boots and hadn't touched the drink.

"Drink the coffee. It'll get cold." He put his hand on her arm. "I'll make another after you drink that. Then you should call the ranger. He's gonna need your help more than ever today." He spoke flatly, kept his tone even. "Here. I'll put a little more sugar in to sweeten it." When he handed it back to her, she nodded.

Martin-Sixty-Four

Grasslands spreading from Winnipeg to Calgary are more than just 750 miles of flat, treeless landscape. Rolling hills swim across sections of the prairie like giant undulating sea monsters and several places on the plain's plateaus are massive tables large enough to seat titans for dinner. And, at their toes, escarpments wait for food scraps to fall. But hills, plateaus nor escarpments are sufficient barrier against a tornado when one decides to barrel through.

Martin bedded down in a coulee several hundred feet from the tracks and when the wind whipped up out of the west it didn't immediately nudge him awake. Ten sweaty miles from Bow Island the sun had been an overblown orange filling the horizon and he had stopped along an embankment of the Oldman River, stripped down to his underwear gasping as he plunged into the cold water. The humidity in contrast was like breathing a milk shake through a straw. Afterward, he lay on the bank smoking for a long while.

He dreamt he was going somewhere and had to do something, but whatever the objective it wasn't made clear. The land was flat and barren adding to an already pronounced sense of urgency. He wanted Eleanor Baker who was behind the wheel of the dilapidated pickup to speed up. He couldn't get a word in while she talked to him, continually used her hands for punctuation, and seemed oblivious or indifferent to the potholes that jerked the vehicle's axels which groaned. As they bounced along, she swerved into the oncoming lane and although no cars were coming, he screamed in his sleep, "Look out!" The words froze in his throat. The claws of the dead animal jumped excitedly about her shoulders. Its grapplers bounced up to her ears and its body tried to climb into her hair.

When he tried to tell her what the disgusting animal was doing, it was Tilly who looked back at him with bright red lipstick clutching the wheel with sharply pointed, bloody fingernails. A long strand of exquisite pearls hung tantalizingly over her right shoulder and her provocative smile made him gag like he would vomit. He attempted to get on his feet and run but he couldn't move, hard as he tried.

He urged his legs on, in his sleep kicking them, but they stayed rubbery and unresponsive. Tilly was now sporting the animal stole and it continue to romp and played with the pearls running them like a rosary over its paws. "Who are you?" Was it Eleanor or Tilly he pushed away? The innocent smile leered at him, taunted him. The tangle of characters perplexing him. "You're doing this deliberately." He kept trying to get his paralyzed legs to act but they wouldn't respond. He needed to set things back in order but the more he tried, the harder it became to remain in the dream.

He woke up in a sweat. The wind whipped at him drying the sweat and caking it to his skin. The dunk in the river had only washed the top layer of salt away, the rest still stuck to him. His jacket was in the pack and after he had it on, he was still cold and that was when he realized the temperature had dropped precipitously.

On flat land, the wind would have knocked him off his feet. But as he was tucked into the gulley the blast only jerked his head back when he peeked up to take a look around. Debris flew into his mouth and nostrils pocking his cheeks and forehead. He coughed and coughed to clear his throat of the grit and his eyes stung and were weeping. He shut them and sank back down into his trench and waited for it to blow over.

It didn't. Tumbleweeds and hard objects, a furry creature, corn stalks, and a rusted can sailed into the furrow, some battering him with direct hits. He threw the dead prairie gopher back out to the wind but then a fragment, the size of a softball, smacked his thigh and created a lump that started to bruise. He covered his upper torso and his head with his jacket and wasted three matches before he got one lit and puffed cigarette smoke into his knees. According to his watch, it was three o'clock, but it wouldn't tell him how long the blast would last.

A low rumble like a dog growling from the back of its throat only much louder raised the hairs on his neck. For a moment the wind had slowed down so he poked his head up over the ledge. The night sky looked like a lava pool, twisted and murky and swirling with steaming rage. Surging pots in black, white, and gray filled the entire sky over Bow Island and he suspected would be the harbinger of deadly news. The muddy clouds danced in agony, twirling madly around and against other clouds, jockeying for space. A black thread hung off one with a long tail spiraling toward the ground where it slithered along at a frightening pace. Lightning flares jumped around the cord to egg it on.

The roar stopped suddenly, making the ensuing quiet chilling as the cavern of the church in Sudbury before early Mass. Quickly he dug a hole big enough to hold the contents of his pack, covered them with dirt and stomped it all down before tucking himself into a hollow in the earthen wall and pulling the hood of his jacket tight over his head, tying it under his chin and pulling it as far as it would go over his forehead and eyes. He put the pack high on the back of his neck and pulled the drawstrings around him. And then he waited.

If it were Mary Alice, she'd be on her knees flipping beads and doing Hail Mary's, Eleanor Baker would bark at how cruelly she was being put-upon, Tilly would cower, Bobby's grin would attempt a cheerful optimism, Herman would offer a glad hand. The girl at the counter in Bow Island would smack her gum and blow on her nails, the truck farmer would court his money and sneer. Martin burrowed into the recess, his face to the dirt wall, pulled at the ties to make sure again they were tight enough, and he waited.

Florence-Sixty-Five

"What's the damage up there, Florence?" The ranger yelled into the receiver. "You there, Flo? Goddammit. Say something." Bicarbonate of soda wasn't going to see him through this day.

A part of his job was to handle reports from the spotters who at the best of times were a colorful bunch. On calm days he put up with the absurd jokes and the griping, mostly about supplies and boredom, or a bear or a raccoon raising some sort of hell.

"Can't you haul the son-of-a-gun over to Idaho someplace?" Henry lamented about a black bear that kept coming into the area. The ranger went home to his wife and said he wished they'd shut up and stop their infernal whining. "Just do the damn job you are paid to do."

"Yes, but you don't want to get on their wrong side, dear." The bicarbonate fizzing in the glass. The spotters had a lot of independence, but their freedom was inextricably bound to their peaks. Unlike the ranger who most nights got to see his family, eat a home-cooked meal that didn't come out of a can, and sleep in his double bed.

"What?" Florence mumbled into the receiver Tommy held to her ear. He pointed to the broken window. "A window." He had the log in front of him ready to point to the columns so she could dictate the report.

"What? Only one? That's it?" The ranger tapped the pencil on the desk and unzipped his pants. His stomach was killing him.

"Yes. Only one." She snapped back. Tommy looked at her and shook his head.

"No." He whispered in her ear. "Easy does it."

"Well, be grateful for small favors, then, Flo. Henry got three of them knocked out." That should cheer Henry up considerably having a good gripe that could play out for several evenings to come.

"I have the worst luck. Why is it always me?" Well, that was Henry. Poor Henry. He would complain, no matter what. As they'd come to know him over the summer, Henry would be slighted if he got hit the hardest by the storm or feel cheated if it hit the others and passed him by.

Tommy walked his fingers down the gauge report and she read off each number as he pointed to the it. He held us breath, mouthing the figures before she read them. After drinking the second cup of coffee her head started to clear, and the ranger's abrupt tone irritated her Tommy gave a relieved sigh when her voice got stronger.

"You spotters are all gonna have to be wide awake up there for the next forty-eight hours. Any sign of smoke, any water dogs, any sign of anything, don't hesitate, Flo. You call it in. You hear me? I don't care if it amounts to a hill of beans. Call it in, anyway."

"Don't call me Flo."

"What'd you say?" Tommy shook his head again squeezing his eyebrows at her.

That the ranger had the gall to remind her after she called in the one fire of the summer to be vigilant was insulting. The glassy eyes were gone and there was a spark behind them now. Tommy grinned but shook his head. Again. "Take a deep breath." He whispered. She looked at him puzzled. Who is this kid? The ranger had riled her, intended or not and helped to get her back on track.

"He's an idiot." She'd rung off in a huff. Tommy scrambled eggs while she buttered rolls and put spam on them. He laughed.

"He's just trying to do his job, Ma'am."

"If we don't get something over that window right now, we're going to get every kind of flying thing in here." A swarm of tiny insects already hovered inside the window frame where the glass should be keeping them out. The mosquitos, horse flies, buzzing insects, and who knew what else, would make themselves to home without invitation. As soon as they smelled the food or found a sticky surface. The squirrels would soon follow after they found the opening.

It was a quick breakfast and then they took the blanket used to separate their sleeping areas and tacked it up firmly around the window and made the room seem like early morning. The ranger said he would send someone up with a pane of glass if and when they got through this storm without a fire flaring up, but he said he wasn't

235

making any promises he couldn't keep. "Sure as shootin,' there's gotta be a fire somewheres."

"And if that doesn't happen, I'd be surprised, the way that bugger went through. But if another one comes on the heel of this one, you are gonna have to live with that hole a while." He rubbed his sore belly and ate two donuts. Stuffed them in one right on top of the other.

The other spotters had already reported more thunderclouds agitating in the western sky. There was a slight breeze coming out of the southwest. If it changed directions and got stronger, things could turn around very quickly.

"Keep a sharp eye out on the winds today. It's calm now, but don't let that fool you. If it whips up, as I suspect, things could shift and make trouble in a hurry."

Tommy went down alone to get water while Florence studied the ridges, the valleys, and watched the trees for signs of changes. An occasional bough swayed wistfully, but that was all.

"No changes up here." She reported mid-morning. Other than the few sluggish flies that didn't relent to the heat, the day was still and lazy. The blanket made the room feel hotter and Florence fanned herself with the log book.

"I brought some extra water for the garden." Tommy's face was red and he was huffing when he got back. "I'll take over and you can go see to your plants." He took the binoculars from her. She seemed her old self far as he could tell but he wasn't taking any chances. She'd be happy poking around her vegetables.

By midafternoon, the clouds had dissipated and the wind was little more than a gentle puff that occasionally pushed the warm air around. The few flies that buzzed around weren't worth shooing away. The mosquitos would wait until evening before they got the desire to search for food.

Martin-Sixty-Six

The sun came up behind a gossamer curtain of dust particles casting a gentle glow over the countryside and giving the sense that this day was just another ordinary one. The memory of the night erased behind welcoming oranges and fuchsia on the horizon that on a lazy morning would be inviting as a downy pillow.

When the soft light peered into the gulley, gradually edging down the wall, Martin was rolled up in a ball and it nudged him out of a dream he didn't want to give up. Lilly and he were on a picnic blanket next to the Rhine and she was feeding him grapes, one at a time, leaning over him, her breast rubbing on his upper arm. He'd spit the seeds out after each one and she kissed him every time. Her brow was smooth and unworried, her laughter rippling and girlish and he wanted to stay in her arms.

Half-sitting up, he spit out the sandy grit lodged between his teeth, his tongue rough as sandpaper and fumbled in his pocket for cigarettes. *Shit.* He'd rolled onto them sometime during the storm breaking most of them in two. He smoked two of them before he realized the hood of his jacket was tied around his neck constricting him. It had BB sized holes on the sleeves and back of it and so did his pack.

He woke up in a junk pile of broken glass, bits of wood, a dead snake, corn stalks, beet tops, and a solitary toad that hopped away when he stood up. He must have gone to sleep at the tail end of the pandemonium. The three-day old beard itched and his chin felt raw. He dug up his cache, headed to the river for another dunk, and shaved.

Near the bank a few trees had been pulled up by the roots looking as limp as the truck farmer's carrots. They flopped on their sides and the water poked at their leaves, tugging to get them into the river. Several feet away and without explanation, others stayed firmly rooted.

Lilly was still on his mind when he started again on the road. She was more beautiful in his dream than in real life, but he thought she could be that lovely again if she got away from Sudbury before it ground her down further. His hip hurt from the impact of the rock. He didn't mean to favor it but then his lower back started to ache from being in a fetal position too long.

It was getting warm and he was hungry so he had the last of the carrots and peas, and a part of the dry sandwich. The pickle hadn't held up well but the flavor was still excellent. He had changed shirts, washed the dirty one and draped it on the back of his pack to dry. The road was a gigantic dumping ground littered with beer bottles, tumbleweeds, thistles, rusted nails, pieces of farm machinery, and twisted vines from squash or pumpkin or cucumbers. The truck farmer, son-of-a-bitch, might not be as self-satisfied and righteous as he'd been the day before when he pocketed Martin's money with noticeable relish. Martin grinned in spite of his aching back and hip.

Sunflower seeds eased his parched throat as the sky's earlier agreeable rosy pink became a fiery yellow ball. The heat was just as oppressive, storm or not, as the previous day in Bow Island. The woman who'd made the pickles for his sandwiches, someone with that amount of skill should be spared from the tornado's havoc, in all fairness. She'd be nondescript, hair pulled back at the nape of her neck, a good-sized canning apron covering her everyday dress, intently bent over the steaming jars she sterilized. The hot weather was perfect for growing hefty cucumbers. Probably not great for pickling them.

In the scattered debris, Martin came across a branch to use for a walking stick with a rounded gnarled tip at one end just the right size to cup his hand over, the other end he carved to a point and although it gave him some relief he continued to dodge litter and it was slow going. He considered whether to go through Fort MacLeod since it had gone well for him in Bow Island in broad daylight.

Riding the rails was risky. Too much chance to be exposed hopping a train on the prairie and too little cover. Once he got into the mountains it might be safer.

So far, the road was deserted as far as he could see in both directions. Tilly and Herman would be picking up the pieces. The rickety screen door most likely ripped off its one hinge and Herman scratching his head while she said nothing but silently regretted the storm had not taken her away with it. Judging from the state of the road, farmers were stuck in their own lanes and digging out. Except for cheerful magpies yak yakking, it was as if the world, including prairie dogs, were dug down for the duration. The walking stick was useful for zigzagging through the clutter.

Lilly was a good woman. Strangely, he wanted to stay in that dream. Maybe all of ten or so words had passed between them while he was in Sudbury. She was steady and even, didn't hand out opinions about anyone in the pub, dodged the grabbers, cleaned up the slops. Did she hate him now? Whatever the Finns would say about him, she wouldn't join in. The feeling from the dream went along with him as he walked along. He was safe in her arms and he liked her honest laugh.

The roar of an engine caught him in this trance. It was several seconds before he could see where it was coming from. It threw up a cloud of dust behind him in the direction of Bow Island like a mini tornado gliding across the landscape stirring up what the storm hadn't already raised. Its speed didn't give Martin time to find a hiding place so he stopped and turned toward the oncoming vehicle. It was remarkable given the amount of debris that it was coming so fast. He couldn't make out the vehicle for the ball of dust, but the sound was that of a motorcycle engine.

"Jesus H. Christ. You been out in this damn tornado the whole time? Look at this mess." The guy was straddled to the bike and without waiting for a reply started polishing the chrome with the sleeve of his elbow. "Dust is enemy Number One!" He groomed the machine like a faithful and beloved horse.

Florence-Sixty-Seven

Each report that day raised more worries for the ranger. "What now?"

Tommy came down from the cupola and ran to the garden after he spotted water dogs. "I think you'd better take a look."

"That's good work, Tommy." She tried to ruffle his hair but he jumped away. "I'm pretty sure they're water dogs, but I have to call them in anyway."

"How do you know they ain't a real fire?" The light on them was changing.

"I'm not sure. It's the way they change when the sun shifts. But, I'm sort of guessing. Let's see what the guys say. Maybe I'm wrong."

Henry crowed that evening, most likely strutted around the cab with thumbs tucked under his suspenders. "You could hardly see the damn thing. Sorry, Flo. But I kept looking at this one spot, see. Hell...sorry Flo. I thought it's just another dang water dog I'm looking at like you're always saying, Flo, and it didn't amount to no hill of beans, but I kept my eyes on the dang thing, and sure enough. Where's there's smoke there's always fire." How many more times before the season was over would one of them say that?

They'd all spotted water dogs. "Better safe than sorry." They told each other. Tommy pointed out the first one and she'd hurried back from the garden. In the afternoon they spotted another around 2:00 in the hazy day.

"Dog days, Tommy."

"I guess so." It didn't take any figuring to know when a dog is too hot to do anything but lounge on the cool grass under a tree.

The ranger shouted down the telephone. Between reports, and a loaded ashtray he passed the latest on to the men on the trails waiting to be told where to head next. Henry's was the only report that came up as a real fire. The smoke chasers worked out of tents where they stayed in the woods, sleeping rough, cooking on Kimmel stoves, waiting for the call to get to the hot spots. It took all of two hours to put a damper on Henry's fire.

240

"It don't matter the size." He had to work to check his disappointment. "Hey, nobody has a crystal ball. Do they? It coulda blowed up and all hell break loose." And for several evenings afterward, they listened to him say the same thing.

"Henry, I'm gettin' to the place I'm wishing for another storm after having to listen to you every night."

"You're jealous, George. You have been from the get-go. What you got up your craw is that I thought ahead and brought books with me. I bet you sit up there in that roost of yours and twiddle your thumbs all day."

Florence didn't mind Henry's gloating. It took her mind off worrying about the next storm that would come. Tommy stuck his tongue out and rolled his eyes as Henry went on and on, and Florence laughed out loud. She couldn't help it. This was an adolescent boy doing exactly what he is so good at, mocking the overblown adult in need of a child's dose of reality. She put her finger to lips and whispered, "Shhh." Then, she giggled again.

"You got a joke for us, Flo?" George jumped at the chance to change course.

"No, no." She'd laughed. "No. I was just watching a squirrel trying to sneak in around the blanket I have up covering the broken window." She stuck her tongue out at Tommy and he grinned.

"That was about the worst lightning storm I've seen." Joe had been awfully quiet while the two competitive men rattled their swords in verbal combat. "I was about ready to head off the mountain this morning. It was worse than being stuck inside a pressure cooker." Florence stared wide-eyed at Tommy.

"Know what you mean. They can't pay us enough up here. Rattled around like your teeth or brains are going to fall out."

"Didn't know you had any brains, George." Tommy grinned.

"Anybody besides me thought they was going to bail this morning?" Was Joe testing them? Florence had managed to get on with the day, thanks to Tommy. She saw he was waiting to see if she'd say something. That's when she understood something about him she hadn't figured out before. He was used to keeping other people's secrets. Homer wasn't that much different. He'd hid the evidence of drunken bouts, made wild excuses for the bruises from beatings, and rarely brought a friend back to the house. He dove into his math and science homework, practiced basketball with the hoop Fred attached to the garage and got good enough to be a starter in high school. On weekends he helped her with chores and did repairs, always helpful and anticipating what she needed. Stayed busy at home and remained watchful.

She put her shoulders back, cleared her throat. "I sure was." Tommy's head whipped around.

"Glad I'm not the only one."

"I was this close to packing up and leaving." Florence held her thumb and forefinger apart about a half inch as though they were in the room to see it.

"What stopped you from going?" George hadn't admitted he had thought of doing the same.

"I'm not sure." Florence paused. "I guess it was the ranger. He expected me to carry on cuz that's what we're supposed to do." She winked at Tommy. "He made me think twice about running off. No whining." Miss Conrad turned her nose up at the men who couldn't make it through a whole summer. Florence had vowed to herself she wouldn't back down. But she almost had.

The spotters laughed about the whining. She glanced at Tommy and nodded.

"Know what you mean, Flo. The ranger was about busting a gut this morning. I thought he was gonna have a heart attack right over the phone. He got there ahead of me."

"When am I going to get my dang windows?" Henry asked. They all laughed which made him feel sorry for himself. They could hear him slapping at the mosquitoes who had found their dinner.

"Hang some blankets up, Henry." Florence and Tommy would sleep well. Poor Henry.

Martin-Sixty-Eight

Martin was going to kill him. He knew it even before he climbed behind him on the bike and the guy peeled out producing a shower of gravel. Knew it almost as soon as the guy rode up bringing his own dust devil with him and after interrupting a most pleasant trance. Knew it when he was still a half mile off and he recognized the engine type. Confirmed it when the guy screamed to a stop after nearly running him down.

"I coulda squashed you like a goddamn punkin." An attempt to snap his fingers failed because of the leather gloves. His cackle wiggled the bike. Engine still running.

"Looks that way." Martin laughed.

"Better believe it." He was a blemish, one of God's bigger mistakes. If you believed in some stupid invisible being hanging around in the ether that noticed or cared what the little people running around below were getting up to.

"You havin' a good time on this little ole' road?" He laughed at Martin's walking stick. "You ain't that old, are you? What in the hell you doin' out here in the middle of nowhere?" Martin at first considered whether to answer, looked him in the eyes but couldn't keep up with them. Some sort of genetic tic ran him. The guy scratched his crotch, cleared his throat several times and spit wads of something into the grass. It was like watching a heart madly pulsing on the entire surface of the skin. This was not some feckless guy out for a sporty jaunt on his motorbike. It would be a matter of when, not if, that something would set him off and he'd snap.

"This road is one big fuckin' obstacle course. I'm nuts about it. Too bad it didn't happen like that yesterday." He'd pulled his goggles up over his brown leather aviator cap after he turned off the engine looking like a four-eyed alien with moon-shaped circles indented around his eyes. His eyes were an astonishing blue but what was stunning was how feral they were darting here and there and not settling on any one thing. Martin shifted automatically to compensate for the eye movement and tried to steady them by making a focal point for the wonderers.

"I flattened about a huntert punkins back there." An impressive deer hunting knife hung off his belt in a leather sheath.

For him, the tornado was better than giving whiskey to a drunk. He and the storm seemed to run on the same parallel energy. He was thrilled at what he could demolish at breakneck speed. He petted the bike and rubbed it down while they chatted. "Pretty thing." His reflection looked back at him from the shiny chrome. A few minutes later, he started the motor again, and like a petulant child demanding attention, roared the engine.

"What the hell you running away from, Mister?" The guy ran on instinct. Whatever he smelled about Martin, it didn't fit.

Martin rested on his walking stick. His back ached, he needed aspirin.

He turned off the engine again seeing that he'd missed a speck of dust that needed his attention, once again set about polishing the chrome. Martin stood in the road not at all sure the guy remembered he was there. He jumped off the machine but caught his pant leg on the tail pipe, turned on the bike and kicked the fender with his leather, steel-toed boot. "Goddamn bike." Martin groaned under his breath.

Under his leathers, he was a scarecrow, more an adolescent boy trying out an adult swagger. He'd taken off the jacket to get to the pack of cigarettes rolled up in the sleeve of his once white tee shirt. He lit up and so did Martin.

"It's an Indian Four, isn't it?"

"Sure is. See you know your stuff."

"A good machine, is it?"

"Great. When the damn thing runs. See. I gotta adjust it all the time or it gets too damn hot." Martin watched him pull out some wrenches and tinker on the machine. The guy couldn't stop the twitching. "I'm gonna sell this piece of shit when I hit Vancouver."

"That's where you're headed?" Somewhere he'd get rid of him.

"I suppose you're looking to bum a ride."

Martin slowly drew on the cigarette. "I'd guess that bike of yours doesn't have enough juice to haul two of us. I'd bet it won't make it up those Rockies, anyway." For a second the guy's face looked like

244

one of the squashes he'd flattened. Martin threw down the challenge, prepared for the guy to take a swing at him or kick him with his boot. It worked. The numbskull turned out to be easy to manipulate.

"You joking around with me, Mister?" His eyes actually stopped darting about and he looked straight on at Martin and waited for him to answer.

Which he didn't do. At least not right away. Martin pretended to deliberate making the guy squirm while waiting for the answer, the right answer. His hands were fists but for now at his sides. Martin kicked the ground with his boot, looking off in the distance. Miles of littered road lay ahead, and where they were on this deserted stretch was not a good place to dump a body. He'd find a better place. A better moment.

"I guess I'm wrong about that. You'd certainly know better than me " Martin muttered.

"What'd I hear you say, mister?"

"Said you'd know better than me."

"You're damn right about that." The biker folded his jacket with aching detail and stowed it under the rider's seat. "Don't mess up my leather jacket, neither."

The bike lurched for the first twenty miles around and over litter, the guy aimed for vegetable matter, avoided broken glass, shingles, metal panels, and a dead skunk. Martin hugged the guy's scrawny ribs to keep on the bike trying not to breathe in the oily stink of hair product. Even if it was not intended, the biker would make trouble for him. Off the bike he was twitchy. Jerked his head like he was checking if someone was after him, and his eyes couldn't settle on one spot. Once he was back on the bike, he was all business. Martin did the math. There were over 700 miles from where he was to Vancouver.

Florence-Sixty-Nine

For three days cotton ball clouds polka dotted an azure sky. By noon, they turned into white rabbit tails before evaporating or being tacked up by pins that held them in place.

"Keep looking for them mares' tails. Let me know soon as you spot 'em." Florence and Tommy took turns scouting in the cupola. She tended the garden or wrote to Homer while he practiced his cursive or went down to the stream for water. The unease from the last storm lessened with no further warning signs, no elephants blundering about the heavens, no clues that would point to another blowout. The wind couldn't nudge a hawk's feather.

"I have an idea. Let's have a picnic." In the tall pines, the sun's glare got tamed by the thick branches and aside from flies buzzing around their tuna fish sandwiches stuffed with newly picked greens, they forgot about the heat.

"Bet I can throw a pinecone farther than you." Tommy dared.

"Probably." Sitting with her back against the tree, her eyes half-closed. She yawned.

"Show me."

"Do I have to?" Giving him a tepid look with one eye.

"Yep. Here." He handed her a big fat one.

"Okay. Not fair. Let me see the one you've got." He giggled and threw it before she had a chance to compare.

The cabs sweltered during the day and as usual Henry had an evening complaint. "I feel like a stewed prune."

"If you look anything near how you grumble all the time, that's likely true." But Henry wasn't the only one. George wouldn't give Henry the satisfaction of agreeing with him, not ever. Tempers were hot as the insides of their cabs and they snapped their numbers to the ranger who had a fan that buzzed in the background.

"You know what I'm thinking about?"

"One of the dames in your detective books, probably."

"I'm gonna ignore that remark, George. I said a hundred times already you're jealous. And that's not gonna stop till you climb off that perch come September."

"What *are* you thinking about, Henry?" Florence grinned at Tommy knowing the boy looked forward to some stupid joke.

"I'm thinkin' about sittin' in a bathtub filled with ice. That's what I'm thinkin' about."

"You gotta memory about the size of a flea, Henry. Ain't you the one who was whining cuz there wasn't no sun shining in June?"

"Well, blind as a bat as usual, George, I'm not a bit surprised you didn't notice June came and went and now it's a hundred degrees."

It was too hot to get out their instruments and Florence didn't feel like singing. The jokes didn't seem halfway funny anymore. Every afternoon the sun dissolved into steamy haze developing optical illusions that made the spotters second guess their observations. What was mirage and what was real?

Not a day went by anymore when by 4:00 o'clock thunderheads rose on the Idaho panhandle tall as skyscrapers. The spotters longed for a good downpour. Not a thunderstorm.

"Can't we have one day of rain?" Instead, for ten minutes dark shadows passed over the cabs, dropped brief but vigorous showers, and skipped away. For a half hour the air felt fresh and sweet and then the atmosphere sizzled again.

Florence and Tommy played Hearts. She was lucky if she won one time out of three. He didn't know he gave himself away when he lifted the right corner of his mouth as he got ready to pounce. She liked watching how his mind worked. He was clever. When he was puzzled, whether it was a game of cards or figuring out how the Osborne Fire Finder was designed, he held his tongue into his right cheek.

"You been pickin' any more huckleberries, Flo?" She'd collected a nice batch on an early morning outing down on a sunny ridge.

"No. I should get some for oatmeal and I could make muffins or even a pie. How about you, George? Any luck?"

"Yeah. I eat 'em by the handfuls. I sure would like a pie. Didn't cross my mind, but now you mention it, Flo, I dunno."

"It sounds good, but I don't want to heat the stove up now that I think of it."

"What else can you do with the berries? I got a real good patch the bears ain't been at, yet." George's cab sat above a gradual slope thick with huckleberry bushes.

"Vanilla ice cream. That's what you can do with them." Henry cackled. Tommy made a face.

"Next best thing. Evaporated milk." They went to bed with huckleberries on their minds.

"I'll do it. Get some for breakfast." Tommy couldn't stop thinking about them.

"Then I'll make pancakes. Watch out for the bears. One was near there last time I was out picking."

His bedroll was empty. Like a fox he'd slinked out of the cab, his footsteps too faint for her human ear to pick up in her sleep. He'd come back soon with a good crop so she doubled a batch of sour dough pancake batter.

"You had enough?" She laughed. Five dinner plate sized pancakes later stuffed with huckleberries.

"You got anymore?" Licking his lips.

"I'm running low on sour dough. How about some more bacon?" His face was filling out, less boyish, on his way to becoming a man and a handsome one at that. A few undecided blond hairs loitered on his chin, the darker ones on the top lip attempted to stitch together a mustache. Homer was fifteen when she gave him a razor set for Christmas. Tommy wasn't old enough, yet.

With their stomachs pleasantly full and a soft breeze drifting through the screens, the day was off to a positive start. They played cards in the early afternoon.

"I don't think you always play fair, do you?"

"What do you mean?" His sly grin smiling at the cards on the table.

"I mean I've got to win some of the time, don't I?" Later she wrote to Homer.

"What's he like?" Tommy nodded toward the paper. "Your son."

"Homer?" Her eyes welled up. "He's...he's." The tears fell down her cheeks and between smiles, she sobbed.

"I'm sorry. I didn't mean to make you cry." He stood up, looked at the door.

"No.... no. It's okay. It's all right. I'm...I'm...just..." The tears came on as quick as their afternoon showers.

"I think he's a lot like you, Tommy." She spoke softly. He stuck his tongue into his cheek. She smiled at him. "He'd like you just as much as I do and I hope you can meet him some day." A shadow crossed her brow. "When he comes home from the war."

Martin-Seventy

The deer knife slid almost too easily between the ribs, neatly cutting off the biker's mortality with his own weapon. First the gasp of a punctured balloon. Then sipping breaths until Martin delivered the fatal blow at the base of the skull snapping his neck, and the body slumped doll-like over the handlebars. Its arms fluttering eagle wings that slackened to a pathetic twitch and then nothing.

Like the summer sniffles coming on, the bike had coughed and sputtered as they started to ascend into the foothills. Unfortunately for Martin, the biker had pealed out from Fort McLeod and only the blind and deaf would have trouble identifying the pair. He kept a watch from the back of the bike expecting a Mountie to catch up and pull them over.

"Did you have to do that?" Martin yelled over the engine.

"Mind your own business! You buy gas next round if I don't kick you off before then."

"Sure thing."

In a Fort McLeod restaurant, the fluorescent lighting exposed every corner and shadow where even a farsighted person didn't need a magnifying glass to read the fine print. On top of that, the abundance of chrome reflected anything else that might be hidden.

Martin attempted to discourage the biker from going in when they walked by. "Why don't we get something at the store? Keep going." If the guy had an ounce of sense, he'd be stupid enough to dispute it with himself. "No sense wasting time sitting down to eat, don't you think? With all the stuff on the road."

"What's your hurry, mister. You was dawdling in the road when I see'd you." The fort wasn't crawling with Mounties as he'd imagined, but it looked like a set from a Western movie with John Wayne at the head of the cavalry flying a flag behind him on his majestic horse.

The waitress warmed to Martin. He'd gotten halfway through the door and there she was right in his face. However, the biker didn't register on her radar. She poured Martin a second cup of tea, put her hand on her hip and smiled brightly. "Where are you from? You talk like one of them foreigners." Giggling like she was fifteen.

"He's probably one of them Nazi spies we been warned about." A grin of two big front gopher teeth, knocking his knees together under the table. Did the guy ever sit still?

They zipped through the flatlands between battles with deflated and decaying fruit. With a second person aboard the engine lost power as the grades grew steeper, but the biker ignored the early symptoms as if it was a fever that could be outridden. Until it puttered to a crawl. On a solitary stretch outside of Pincher Creek where willow saplings hugged the ditch next to the road it sighed heavily and stopped.

With a surprisingly organized set of wrenches and a certain logic that didn't carry over to corral the demons running around inside his head otherwise, the biker tinkered on the engine. There was no meat on the guy so he wore his leather jacket all the time, even when they went into the swampy Fort McLeod restaurant that had one lousy squealing fan tapping at the air, to disguise his scrawniness.

"I gotta take a leak." In a single leap, he jumped up from his adjustments and pushed through the brush, the squirrels having returned to his brain.

Martin lit a second cigarette from the first and squinted into the distance. No cars coming in either direction.

"Here." He handed him a fag. "You got a knack with that bike I have to say." Gopher teeth grinned back at him.

"You know, I'm a thinkin' you ain't such a bad egg after all. A little snooty but I might take you all the way. See how it goes from here on out. Let's go." They ground their butts into the gravel.

It took no more than an instant. As the biker jumped onto the starter pedal Martin pulled the knife out of the sheath hanging off the guy's hip and in one smooth motion, thrust it in and then twisted it into the vital organs and he sank with a lethargic drop onto Martin who cracked his skull and pushed him away. When the body gave a final jerk, Martin reached around to feel for a pulse in his neck. There wasn't one.

The air was thinner due to the elevation and the sun more intense. He squinted into the glare checking in both directions for traffic. No car noises from either direction.

When the twitching subsided, he pulled the heap off the handlebars steadying it against his shoulder so it wouldn't tip the bike over before he got the kickstand down. Thankfully, the incision was clean, an oval of deep red an inch wide at the entry point and very little blood at the exit to trace.

But the dead man's pant leg caught on the exhaust nearly pulling the bike over with it, and Martin grabbed tighter and the protruding knobs from the backbone bulged under the jacket. A girl's charm bracelet would fit around his wrists. The boots alone weighed at least five pounds. Free of the bike, Martin carried him like a baby but for the reckless legs and arms that bounced and quivered uncontrollably. So far, no vehicle had come by. He hastened to get the body to the spot he'd scoped out while the motorcycle was getting repaired.

The earth was hard. Not an ideal burial ground. A bear or a mountain lion would soon unearth a careless or hastily completed grave and on its tail, a flock of carrion crows would announce the death to all travelers, circling in between dives to tear way any remaining flesh.

If there was someone who cared about the guy, there was a chance a missing persons' report would be filed and would include the make of the bike and a description of its owner. If he had told anyone where he was going or when he would arrive at his destination, they might be searching for him fairly soon.

The Rocky Mountain giants imposed when paired against the boring landscape as if a magician had waved a wand to cancel out the unimaginative prairie. Bobby wanted Martin to experience the grandeur of the Alpen peaks that rose ahead dwarfing men and forests, rivers and beasts, and hogging all of the panorama. Silver-tipped monsters that enticed travelers while luring with the fragrant scent of mountain air and ponderous evergreens. Except for the one that was dead.

Florence-Seventy-One

Sunflowers hugged the wall just as she'd imagined back in the spring when she applied for the spotter job. Now they were higher than her knees. The deer, maybe one of the mountain goats that climbed across the ridge, or some other herbivore had discovered them and bitten the budding heads off. In the garden, Columbia ground squirrels tormented the lettuce until Tommy gerrymandered a cage that kept some creatures out and the plants in.

High elevation with too little between the ground and the glaring sun meant that the plants that promised early every morning to be bountiful standing at attention before her, reneged on that vow by noon and shriveled up. Lack of good soil and the short growing season added to the hurdles. Then, there was the extra effort of hauling water from the stream. In June, the water in the tank seemed ample enough to last the whole summer.

Worms bored into the radishes. She should have added chunks of egg shells in the holes when putting the seeds down. Even so some bulbs were still good and had the right amount of bite, not too bitter with snow-white centers. She would have been harvesting a second crop about now in Missoula. Too late at this point to add shells. The carrots were stunted but sweet. Not enough soil for them to push down into. She was munching on one when hoof beats echoed off the ridge catching her like a mouse between its hole and its tormentor.

She had been flipping pancakes earlier, Tommy was setting the table and waving a fork punctuating every word he said. "I won fair and square. You just ain't very good at Hearts. And I'm gonna beat you again and again."

'Not if I stop playing. And don't wave that fork at me." She teased. He wore the same mischievous grin between bites and waved the fork. Tommy more than compensated for wilting lettuce, runty carrots, and wormy radishes.

Peels of his distrust got discarded as the weeks went along. One layer at a time. Little signs that revealed more of who Tommy was. Fragments like those of the broken window coming back together to make a better picture of him. He didn't see it in himself how he opened up, piece by piece, some of the bits running together all at once, others at the edges still waiting to come on stage.

It had started one day at breakfast with him repeating Henry and George's jokes between bites. She saved her politeness comment about chewing first and talking later for when he'd grown stronger roots. Stale even when the spotters told them, she mustered a laugh for each one because she felt his eyes on her. Each joke was a test and she knew it.

That evolved to a game of hiding things from her, like her binoculars or her hat, and then he'd yell. "You're not even warm." He watched her, pushed to see what it would take for her to get mad at him.

"You just wait." She threatened grinning at him.

"What for?" Sticking his tongue out.

"I'll do the same to you sometime when you aren't expecting it."

The temperature had dropped several degrees during the night. "Think I'll make a pie today." The Pendleton draped over her shoulders while she made the batter. "That's if you're in a mood to go get more huckleberries." If not, she'd open a can of peaches, drain the juice, and use them instead.

"Then it's pie for supper." He grinned and she grinned back and he went to put on his cap and grabbed his bucket.

"Back in a flash."

"Watch out for bears." She sudsed a few bits of laundry in the dishwater and dumped the rest over her lettuce. He was gone longer than usual.

The packer jabbed the spurs into his animal just below the ridge. His brilliant idea to catch Florence by surprise which he did. She stood up looking around for Tommy.

"Hey, Flossie, it's your lucky day."

"Not a minute too soon!" She yelled. Warning Tommy if he was close enough to hear. The packer's head jerked back with a grin mistaking her intent.

"Well, hello now." He leered. She looked beyond him to the ridge. "Coming up to fix that broken window of yours. Unless you got a better idea 'bout how to spend the afternoon." If he'd been closer, he'd have heard her groan.

The dust hadn't settled yet and a second person appeared riding in behind him. The ranger had said someone would come up a while back. He hadn't said when or that it would be the packer. She thought sure Henry would get his windows fixed before hers. The way he held forth in the evenings as if he was carrion fodder for mosquitoes, and likely nagging the ranger with at least the same amount of drama if not worse.

They'd gotten to the place they didn't notice the blanket much although it blocked out some of the light and part of the view. It was almost worth going through another storm if she wouldn't have to put up with the packer.

"Brought you some more company, Flo. Case you're feelin' lonely. Hell, I can't figure how you make it up here without a man to cuddle up to at night. What about them bears? Ain't you afraid of them?" The other one waddled past her. She could have been a rock as much notice as he gave. The packer didn't bother to say who he was and she didn't ask. No sign of Tommy.

"You at least thinkin' of fixin' us some coffee, maybe? Poor fellows like us, up before the cock crows just so as we can get you a window in today?" They lifted the glass plate off the mule. He got a kick out of setting her on edge. He didn't miss the fact that she was looking behind him for something.

"This feller here," he pointed to his bandy-legged helper, "Ain't had a decent breakfast in about a month. Just look at him." She did and the hair on the back of her neck stood on end.

255

Martin–Seventy-Two

Spits of rain pattered onto the leather jacket, pinged off the boots and bounced off the back of Martin's neck as he pulled the goggles back from the stony eyes that in life had been an undeserved color of turquoise, too erratic to look at let alone admire. Next, he unbuckled the strap of the aviator cap away from the still warm neck.

The sun broke out during the sprinkle and a gentle rainbow hung over the nearby cliff. The biker hadn't gotten the pot of gold in this life, and in death Martin unceremoniously peeled the leather cap back which fit as snug as a woman's rubber bathing cap. The red hair was astonishing, thick and luxurious as a horse's mane, brighter than the coloration weaving through the cliff.

The semi-circular bluff formed one side of a bowl. The opposite side fell away beyond the highway into a ravine. Martin had located a spot carved out over a millennium of downpours that hallowed out a nearly ready-made grave in a depression deep and wide enough for the corpse. With neither a shovel nor pick he loosened what soil he could with the toes of his boots, but that raised more dust than dirt. Since there was a good quantity of rock in the dry bed, he gathered a sizable mound in a matter of twenty minutes until the grave began to resemble a large mole hill. The flaming red hair was the first part to get covered up.

A single car passed by while he worked. From the other side of the brush, he heard it slow down and scope out the bike and hid behind the willows until the engine revved and it went on.

You have a girlfriend or someone in Vancouver?" Martin asked casually at the café in Fort McLeod, the biker for the moment somewhat settled across from him and the type of environment where with anyone else you might have a conversation.

"You lookin' for a place to hole up?" The eyes landed on a glass case with pies and cakes inside. "Hey. Give me a slab of that apple pie, would ya?" He glanced at the waitress. "And you're payin'." He waved his knife at Martin.

"Sure thing."

Martin didn't make it past the first question to find out if anyone was concerned or waiting for the biker to arrive in Vancouver.

"You shoulda seen the way them punkins exploded." The waitress rolled her eyes. "Bet you never done that."

"I squashed a tomato on my bicycle." She countered.

"Not the same. Not the same. Boom." He threw his arms out, a cigarette between his index and third finger. "Boom!"

The grave looked too much like a grave so he spent another precious fifteen minutes carrying and placing more rock to extend the length of the mound until it resembled the pile he'd just disassembled. On top of that, he cut willow branches and heaped them in haphazard fashion over it.

While the guy monkeyed with the bike, Martin had found the place to bury him and was sizing up his chances of getting out of Canada afterward. He didn't have enough information about the biker. If the guy was reported missing, the window of time could be very narrow to get across the border once he got to Vancouver. Especially since the Indian cycle was fussy and had the tendency to balk. Looming ahead were the grand Rocky Mountains and the problem the bike seemed to have with the altitude would slow him down. Any stop along the way would increase the risk as the motorcycle was a magnet for the curious.

A different route would get him across the border and into Montana, but once inside the United States without a map to guide him, he would be traveling blind. The Canadian map indicated a thread of a road running parallel to the Rockies on its western front to a border crossing. He would have to stay on the main road through Crow's Nest where the highway made a big loop south and the road diverged. From there he had to decide to continue toward Vancouver or go south into Montana.

The aviator cap was pungent and still damp from sweat. Nevertheless, he pulled it down over his ears, buckled the chin strap, and hoped the guy didn't have lice. The engine purred promising to behave when they climbed into thinner air. The biker had coaxed it back into operation.

He was such a paradox. Tending to mechanics with the gentle touch of a new mother and her baby but when some grease landed on his goggles, he crudely spit on the lens and wiped it with his oily rag. Martin grunted.

"What? You a snob or something? Afraid of a little spit?"

"No, no. I was watching that storm cloud heading our way."

"That's nothin'. A few teardrops for the dead and gone."

And you'll be one of them sooner than you know.

The biker held the goggles up to the sky. "Damn thing is when you get grease on 'em, you gotta have soap and water to ever get 'em clean again." He held the lenses up to the sun and wiped some more.

"Sounds good, don't it?" The engine hummed

"Like I said. You've got the knack." The biker put the goggles on and grinned.

"I sure as hell do. Listen to that." He revved the engine and he roared when the noise reverberated off the cliff wall.

Martin hopped on behind him. The right moment came just after the biker stretched his leg over and straddled the machine. He was looking at himself in his rearview mirror and giving himself a gopher grin.

"Ain't I just a goddamn genius?"

"Not for long." The engine roared.

"Hey. What'd you say?"

It was quick and clean and if the world was sane, they'd thank him for getting rid of the blight. Too many were like him, cluttering the earth, polluting pumpkins that needed to be squashed, run over, obliterated, or knifed.

The goggles were filmy. He sped off looking into a fog. The rainbow was gone, the sun behind gloomy clouds that might soon turn menacing.

Florence-Seventy-Three

She yelled in order to warn Tommy that the packer and his team had showed up, and then realized he might already be back at the cab. The path leading to the door was out of sight from the garden. He could have come back and gone inside to pick through the huckleberries before they got too warm.

She ran ahead of the packer and the bow-legged one up to the cab. "I'll get the door for you."

He wasn't inside. But that relief was immediately replaced by another dark thought. Where was he? With the two men inside her mountaintop retreat the room felt alien, a place of tawdry wallpaper and peeling paint, not where she would want Tommy to be practicing his cursive "M's".

There were no huckleberries on the narrow counter so he must not have circled back. If he came up by the trail, he'd know the pack animals had been through. He'd slipped away the last time the packer came. Even after all this time spent with him, she wouldn't know where to start looking if he hid himself away.

The two men got the glass panel up the rocky slope to the cab but the packer's earlier smirk when he showed up turned to a frown. "You ain't gonna forget to give us somethin' to eat, are ya? Last time was pretty measly if you recall."

"I'll get the coffee going and make some sandwiches." But first, she pulled out the pots and pans and covered the table with them so there was no space to sit and eat and loiter.

"What you up to now?"

"Save your charm for the President of the United States if he comes to call." Miss Conrad tittered. Don't waste your time or eggheads and moochers."

"The ants have been coming in. Cleaning out the shelves today."

"Breakfast was a damn long time ago." Determined to see he'd gotten his message across.

"Coffee's almost ready. You go ahead and get started and I'll bring it to you."

"And somethin' good to eat. You ain't got some of them huckleberry muffins the boys been talkin' about, do you?"

So, word about her had gotten around. The short one pulled the blanket off the nails and the ripping sound made Florence cringe. "He's in a damn hurry." The packer nodded toward him. "Says he ain't gettin' paid by the hour. Hell, who is?" There was this ugly look about him she'd seen as soon he dismounted and headed for the mule to unstrap the pane of glass. The packer swore at him. "Damn him. He's in hurry." He'd cut the packer's gab short and made him hustle over to carry the other end. Once inside it was propped up against the wall.

"Seems mighty lonely up here." He saw Tommy's bedroll. "Maybe not, though."

"My back's been bothering me at night. It helps to sleep on the floor." Her throat would blister if she let her anger blow.

If he'd come alone, it would have been at lunchtime. He'd watched her wiggle her ass, for his benefit that time she'd fed him and he had a cigarette ogling her as she shuffled around the miniature kitchen. She didn't sit down at the table with him.

The short one seemed familiar. She couldn't say why. There was a sense that she knew him but that was not possible. His hands, the way he worked his arms, the fixed facial expression scared her. She didn't want to have her back turned from him but she couldn't stand to look his way.

The packer was no gentleman. He was uncouth, he intruded, and not that different from the neighborhood grocer or the minister she kept at a distance. This man repairing the window was not anyone she'd trust to take no for an answer. She couldn't dismiss the notion that he was familiar to her. She couldn't have met him but she sensed that in some way she knew him.

When the glass was in place and they were finishing it, she brought them huckleberry muffins. The bandy-legged one had tacks in his mouth grunted. "I got my own food." It was the way he didn't look at her, not because he was shy, for that would have had uncertainty in it, maybe some gruffness or awkwardness. The face

260

was hostile and frightening, as though he hated her, saw something in her he couldn't stand. He didn't hide the cruelty.

"I ain't got none, though." The tracker grinned.

"Well, here you go, then."

She was in the cupola and didn't hear the packer climb up until she felt him behind her breathing on her neck. When she spun around their noses nearly collided and her binoculars bumped him in the chest.

"What do you want?" Her eyes burned through him and the heat and her snarl made him jump back. The short one was below pounding a nail into the window frame.

"I'm wondering if you spotted a brat hanging around up here." Attempting to regain some leverage.

"What?" Her heart dropped.

"You seen a kid somewhere round here through them field glasses of yours? Some little shit come knockin' on your door?"

"What are you talking about?" Was he on a fishing expedition or did he know something?

"That fellar's boy run away 'bout a month ago." He pointed down to the bandy-legged man. "Damn kids don't appreciate nothin' these days. Even when its handed to 'em on a silver platter." Biting back the urge to tell him to go to hell, she wondered what he would know about that.

"Where'd he go?" Florence took a deep breath. That's why he'd seemed familiar. He and Tommy shared some traits.

"If we know'd that, we wouldn't be askin', now would we?"

"Who's asking? You or him?" She pointed toward Tommy's pa.

"Well, hell. Does it matter if it's him or me?"

"It would if it was my kid. Who should I contact if I spot him?"

"Well, you can call me just about any old time." He smirked.

Tommy came back around suppertime. Florence and her binoculars surveyed every inch of territory as far as she could see until then. The men had been gone for three hours but they'd left behind what felt like a dirty bag of laundry. Tommy didn't laugh much that evening at Henry or George's jokes. After they'd signed off and Florence was in bed, he paced past the windows looking out at the dusky world.

Martin-Seventy-Four

In Blairmore he pulled up to the blue pump at the Chevron station to top the tank off although the needle pointed at three-quarters full. Even through the smeared goggles he could see the sketch of himself on display in the window twenty yards away. Whoever rendered the drawing had made a remarkably good representation of him.

"IF YOU SEE THIS MAN..." The letters yelled. In smaller print but still quite large, it screamed, "If you come across him, or have some information concerning him," etc. He kept the goggles on and hopped off the bike and with a casual swagger walked toward the building.

"Hey, Mister, you seen that poster?" The mechanic came around the corner out of a repair stall wiping his hands on a red rag. Martin was just going inside and happened at the second to be standing next to the poster so he turned to cover it with his body.

"Yeah. I was just looking at it. Guess you know what's going on."

"Don't know nothin' about it other than them Mounties was by here this morning. They sure is fired up. Damn Nazis. I'd kill the son-of-a-bitch with my two hands. Strangle him."

Martin nodded. "That's the truth. What direction they come from? The agents?" Were they ahead or behind him? How had they gotten to the gas station without coming across him?

"Well, that's a good question, feller."

"How do they know he's around here?"

"Hell if I know."

"What's he wanted for?" Don't ask so many questions.

"He blowed something up over there in Quebec or some other place. All I know is they'd better catch the creep before I do." He turned on his heels still wiping the grease off his hands. He looked back when he was near the corner of the building. "Them police is useless. They can't never find a damn needle in a haystack. They should ask me. I'm a pro at pickin' out faces. I could find that son-of-a-bitch like this." He snapped his finger and thumb together. "Put a bunch of 'em in a line-up and I'm your man. That's if they wanna hire me and pay me what I'm worth. That ain't never gonna happen." He chuckled and disappeared behind the wall.

He had the perfect disguise with the aviator cap and the goggles on. "Hey, fella. You goin' on to Vancouver?" The guy behind the counter wore a striped blue and white jumpsuit with a white oval spot on his chest and the name, Earl, written in it.

"That's right, Earl. I'll take a pack of cigarettes." He was clean-shaven in the photo which helped further disguise him since he was sporting a few days stubble.

"They're looking for some Nazi." Earl pointed at the poster. Fresh news and welcome as fresh meat.

"Yeah. I saw that." He counted out a handful of change and avoided eye contact.

"You ain't come across him, have you? Where'd you come from?"

"Regina."

"Hell, you come along way on that spindly thing. What do you think of them machines?"

"It's all right. Doesn't do so good on the hills." Earl laughed.

"I coulda told you that. This guy they're looking for, just so's you know ahead of time, got off the train in Medicine Hat. They think he's headed to the coast."

"How do they think he's going to get there?"

"Well, now that's the big question, ain't it?" He squinted over the rim of his glasses. "They think he's hoofin' it, or else he's on the rails somewheres." He threw a pack of cigarettes on the dirty counter.

"They have any idea where he is now?" Martin stared toward the poster.

"Them buggers, far as I can tell, don't know but they're out looking for him everywhere. All the train stations. They think he was going to Calgary but they lost his trail after Medicine Hat. Went cold as a cucumber. They're putting up signs everywhere. Sooner or later, someone's gonna remember seeing him."

"Sooner the better, I guess."

"Damn right about that. We don't need no stinking Nazis causin' trouble in Canada."

"I'll keep an eye out."

264

"You do that, fella. Maybe you'll be the one to catch him. If you do, stop back here and I'll fill your tank for free."

"That'd be something, Earl."

"You look like a strong fellow. About his height, too. Hell, maybe you're him." He laughed at his joke.

"I guess no one's come forward. Nobody's spotted him, yet."

"Matter of time. Matter of time. There's always someone somewhere. Luck and timing. That's what I always say."

"You don't know the direction the police are headed, do you? I mean, maybe I could give them a hand if they're going to Vancouver."

"That's right friendly of you. Lord knows, the way they operate, they is in dire need of help. You volunteering?"

"If it would help, yes, I would."

"They're like a two-headed cobra far as I can tell. Going every which way. I'll tell them you're looking to help if they stop back here. I'll say they just have to find the guy on the bike who's gonna be stranded somewhere between here and Vancouver and tinkering with that machine." He laughed.

He passed a stand of road maps near the door and hesitated. In addition to Alberta and British Columbia, there was one of Montana.

"You don't need a map, fella. It's straight as you go to Vancouver." He laughed. "You can't miss it cuz there ain't no place else to go. It's a curvy son-of-a-bitch but it'll get you there soon enough. That bike don't break down."

"That's good to know. Thanks, Earl. I'll be seeing you."

"If the crick don't rise." Earl wiped the dirty counter with his dirty rag.

Martin waved to the mechanic who was watching him from the bay and slowly pulled away from the pump. Earl was looking at him, too, through the blurred window.

Florence-Seventy-Five

She separated the leaves and stems from the mushy huckleberries. "You must have come across a good patch." Brushed a stray hair back off her forehead with purple fingers.

"I guess so."

"No bears?"

"Nope."

"I'll boil them up into syrup and make pancakes in the morning." Sweat rivulets ran down his dirty face. "We're having beef stew for supper. How about setting the table?"

"I ain't hungry." She didn't have to ask when he came back, his face a sickly white under the streaks of dirt. She knew he'd seen his pa.

"How about some chocolate pudding, then? Your favorite." He had his back to her and was hanging up the ripped blanket over his corner. She bit her lip in regret for not washing the dead biting and flying critters and the dust and pine needles, or having repaired the holes his pa made in it.

Even the aroma of frying onions didn't work its magic. Like them or not, they have the power to stimulate the appetite. If he was the slightest bit hungry, which he had to be since he hadn't eaten since breakfast unless he'd filled his belly up with huckleberries, that smell should have done the trick. Any moment she expected to hear a rustle from behind the curtain and him sticking his head around it. But it was quiet as a coffin.

Should she push it with him? "How about some rice and beans?" To nudge him. He hated them she'd found out after he'd stopped being timid and compliant as though he had no preferences. When he objected, and did so vigorously, it was like winning the grand prize at the fair and it happened because she'd run short of supplies.

"Ain't you got any more of them muffins?" The packer angled. She didn't like Tommy's pa at all but they had one thing in common. Neither of them liked the packer.

266

"Three off them aren't enough?" She'd glared, told him he'd eaten all of them and wouldn't let on about the ones she was saving when Tommy got back later.

"Well, then, how 'bout another cup of coffee to wash it all down."

"I'm running short. I'll get you a glass of water." Tommy's father grunted.

It was a bit of a desperate idea, to tease Tommy about the rice and beans. To get him to react and just maybe he'd retaliate with a joke.

The stew didn't have enough salt although it seemed heavily seasoned when it came out of the can. She had to coax the chunks of canned meat down and gnawed on the baby carrots from her garden that went down like sticks of wood. Sitting alone while Tommy stayed behind the curtain was worse than having Fred across the table from her sulking because his beef was stringy. She studied the pattern on the hanging blanket, its dull plaid, washed out red stripes, and mentally sewed up the tears.

"You're mighty quiet tonight, Flo."

"I...I think the heat is getting to me."

"Yeah. It's downright debilitating. I get cross-eyed by afternoon. Can't tell a mountain goat from a rock anymore unless it moves. Then, I wonder if it's the rock moving." George often sounded like a girl when he giggled. Florence saw Tommy's blanket move slightly. Like a breeze tapped at it.

"They come over there to fix your window, yet?" Henry gloated.

"Yes. They put it in today. When did they fix yours?" He didn't answer.

"Henry? Flo asked you a question."

"The ranger says they're comin' up here tomorrow." He mumbled

"Well, all right you sorry bunch. Who's got a good joke, tonight?" George wasn't the only one feeling Henry's pout travel across the phone line. "Nobody? Here's one. What'd the moron use to keep his feet warm in winter?"

"I heard it before." Henry groaned.

"A toe-ster." Tommy snickered from behind his wall.

"Lame."

"God sake's Henry, lighten up. What we don't need is no wet blanket." The heat was tugging away at their good spirits one wave after another.

"I hear the wood burning." Joe said. "We're a quiet bunch tonight.

"I'd like to sing if you're all agreeable." Tommy had shown a bit of life behind the blanket.

"You can do that anytime, Flo. You know that. What you got for us?"

She hummed the first few measures. Soft and slowly like a gentle cooling breeze. The words came next, still easy and quiet and then she switched the rhythm up. "Don't sit under the apple tree with anyone else but me. No. No. No."

"Flo's got her swing on." The boys weren't but two steps behind with their instruments.

Tommy crawled out from behind his curtain and by the time they finally called it a night, they'd stopped counting the rounds or the number of songs.

"You got a song to go to sleep by tonight, Flo?"

"When you wish upon a star, makes no difference who you are…" No matter how she was feeling when she sang that, it made her cry.

"Thank you, Flo." Henry spoke first. "Here's to a good night for all of us." The sun was going down a fraction earlier every night now.

Florence scrambled eggs and set the leftover muffins down on the table. "I saved these for you. You know I missed you today."

He nodded and wiped his top lip with his sleeve still moist from the water.

"We've got some things we need to talk about, but they can wait until tomorrow."

"Like what?"

"Well, for one, I know who that man was that came up with the packer today to fix the window." She wished she could make him feel safe again. The thought of him sent shudders up her spine.

"They asked about you. If I'd seen you." He stared at her like a caged animal. "Don't worry. I'm not going to say anything. You must know that." She waited until he nodded. "We are going to make a plan tomorrow so we're ready if this happens again."

Martin-Seventy-Six

Ten miles out of Blairmore, two cars passed him heading east. At the speed he was traveling, chances were slim a vehicle would catch up to him. He'd passed through Coleman after which an oncoming semi flew by throwing a gust that knocked the bike sideways.

Stray vehicles had peppered his progress since leaving Tilly's farm and he'd gotten back to the main thoroughfare. At the depot platform in Medicine Hat the agents stood out like rabbits in a chicken coop emerging from hidden burrows. They'd leapfrogged his travels somewhere between Sudbury and Alberta. For weeks he'd journeyed across prairie lands swivel necking on lonely stretches of highways or in crowds or on trains or in cafes. His haughty air kept most of the snoopers at arm's length except for Eleanor Baker.

Why did the agents turn up in Medicine Hat, of all places? They had come up empty-handed in Sudbury that night at the church. Erno and Taavi missed their chance to become heroes, and Erno would have the chance to raise his estimation in Lilly's eyes. Of all the people Martin had met, she'd be the one to hold her tongue.

The secret service failed to rout him. Instead they'd come away with a good stab in the eye despite a surplus of men on surveillance. Their logical next step would have been to track him down to the border in Quebec, and when they didn't nab him there, to alert Montreal. When that turned out to be a cold trail, they had a few choices. Give up the search and go after more promising prospects, assume he'd fled the country from under their bruised noses, or throw money and manpower toward the West and maybe recoup their bungle.

He'd donned a porkpie hat hopping the rails in Quebec, switched between a homburg and a fedora in the cities, added and subtracted a mustache and beard. But now they had an accurate facial image and sooner or later the handful of people he'd had dealings with would help pull the pieces together. A waitress who served him tea or coffee and a sandwich and flirted only to be left disappointed, or desperate Tilly who could repair a lot more than a screen door with reward money, or an attention hogging Eleanor Baker who'd delight in flipping around her dead fox's paws in an interview. Or even someone he'd asked directions of, the barber, maybe the night manager in Regina, another boarder he met on the stairs in the hotel, a driver he'd hitched a ride with, someone he'd passed on the sidewalk, or a clerk who sold him cigarettes.

The posters were being circulated along the route to Vancouver and he was breathing like an accordion running short of air. Rationing in Canada due to the war effort meant less fuel and rubber and fewer automobiles traveling along the highways. The pinch was felt in everything from meat and sugar to coffee. Even used string got rewound. Herman had a wad the size of a baseball in his overalls. Coffee got stretched by adding chicory. Even in wheat country fillers were added to flour, pies and cakes were replaced by fruit crumbles and only made for special treats. For Eleanor Baker patriotism meant having her yo-yo expectations and desires met, but for most people, a moral rightness was palpable. Ordinary folks had pride and were determined to do their patriotic duty by staying home and only bringing out their vehicles for necessities and business. Doubling down by combining one activity with another to preserve fuel and rubber.

"We wanna give our boys over there the best we got."

The acrimonious Bow Island truck farmer got a bigger fuel allotment because he hauled his produce to market. If his business wasn't taken out by the tornado and he'd seen the poster of Martin, he'd be at the head of the line to report on Martin and holding his grimy hand out.

Eleanor would jump at the opportunity for notoriety, bask from the attention. "I knew he was a Nazi the minute I let him in the car."

"Why didn't you report him then?" They'd get lost trying to follow her through an impossible labyrinth of unconnected sentences to explain.

"Terrible man. Terrible." Vigorously shake her head, the pearls fluttering on her bosom and she'd claim it was a miracle she'd survived his manhandling. That's why she hadn't reported him. He'd frightened her so badly. "Rude and disrespectful." But Martin guessed she'd be too self-absorbed to provide a comprehensive description. Her accusation of his terribly driving wouldn't help the authorities. He almost felt sorry for the men expecting helpful information from that interview.

Bobby wouldn't forgive himself. Betrayed yet again, but he'd take on the guilt, say he was responsible. He'd abetted the traitor. Probably plead with them to put him in jail to ease his distress over his crime.

When Tilly came for Herman at the train station, she must have come to town with the ration coupons she'd saved. On that same run, she handled all her town errands, although Martin didn't recall groceries or livestock feed in the pickup bed. Herman carried one bag into the farm house. There weren't enough agents or the manpower to search from farm to farm and not likely Tilly would be in town again very soon to see the poster. If anyone needed the reward, it was her.

Or, Mary Alice. She'd have been crying when they interviewed her. Erno had collaborated before the planned ambush. As a good Catholic, Mary Alice would have laid out the truth before God and country while doing her utmost to be precise. Her humiliating interview likely held in a small room with no windows with three men smoking nonstop while she described his intimate characteristics. Despite her virtue they would not be gentle with this susceptible woman.

He'd deceived her, but she'd made that possible, in fact, invited it. Thus, like Bobby, she would despise her culpability. So soon after her mother died that she had to add another guilt of fostering the tie with a Nazi.

Taavi's description of him would come through the prism of his clouded emotions. Taavi the shadow figure, not only dark, but inaccessible.

Martin had gassed up in Blairmore, a short distance from Coleman, nestled in the foothills of the Rockies between the border of Alberta and British Columbia and on the way to Crowsnest Pass at an elevation of 1358 meters. He'd cross the Continental Divide which was enough reason for the gas station manager to joke about the bike.

"See if that tricycle makes it to the top. It's not that much of a pass unless you're doing it on a toy."

With a full tank and a stash of cigarettes he fairly sailed over the summit. A sightseer, as Bobby envisioned him, would coo and whistle at the sight. Martin sped around the curves and twists following the highway as it looped south until the turnoff to the mining town of Corbin and the Montana border crossing.

Florence-Seventy-Seven

It rained. A real rain, not the frivolous afternoon shower they scoffed at and grumbled about because it made them feel sticky and short-tempered. Tommy returned to the cab before it decided to turn into a three-day storm. The packer and his partner were halfway down the trail by then, the odor from horse droppings heightening their descent.

"You got back just in time, looks like." His tee-shirt clung to him, his hair determined to frizz. "Here's a towel. You can put this on." Handed him the plaid shirt she'd washed that morning.

Like clockwork, the afternoon shower that typically dripped and moved on after five minutes every day, didn't quit. Instead, a steady stream of beads collected swelling into puddles near the cab, and the droplets tinkled like fragile wind chimes on the tin roof. By the second day, the mist was bear-hugging the cramped room making it a cozy den.

"I'm going to make pies!" The oven already heated after making baking powder biscuits for breakfast. "I'll make cornbread, too. We can have it with our Mulligan stew."

A blanket of fog hung beyond the ridgeline. "You wrapped in a cocoon up there, Flo?" The ranger chirped between bites of chocolate donut, his fan gone silent in the background.

"Well, it's a welcome break from going down to the crick." Tommy had been with her a few weeks before he claimed the job and happily left Florence to tend to her carrots and lettuce and write to Homer.

"Okay. Pies are in the oven. Now I want to talk with you, Tommy." His stomach was full, he'd put a bucket out to catch the rainwater, swept the floor, shook out the blankets, and just sat down at the table to start practicing his cursive, determined to make his way through the alphabet. He didn't look up.

"I know this can't be easy for you. It must have been a shock yesterday." The surly man, Tommy's pa, was a miser who withheld the most basic courtesies, avoided eye contact, snarled at her muffins.

But it went deeper than that. He made her feel like she was standing at the edge of a pool of boiling hot tar.

"You've been such a great help here. And I know how much you like to go for water. Here's the problem. The truth is since yesterday things have changed. We can't pretend they haven't, can we?" He gripped his index finger around the pencil and bit his lip.

"You can't stop me."

"From what?"

"Getting the water."

"No. You're right. I can't stop you. But do you want me to worry about you every time you go down?" His head bobbed up. "I didn't think so." Someone, somewhere had shown him a gentle side. Either that or it was in his nature to be kind. He hadn't spoken of a mother or aunt or even an uncle.

Since the weeks of his convalescence, he had started calling her Ma'am. "Call me Florence." He was healing fast and making himself useful as though that was necessary for him to be allowed to stay.

"I've made you breakfast, Ma'am."

"Call me Florence." The word made her feel like Fred owned her and as though the boy was holding a ten-foot pole between them. "Call me Florence." Every day he slid into his old habit. The name Florence got stuck on his tongue.

She mothered without him knowing that was what she was doing. Or so she thought. He responded by fetching water, making her morning coffee, logging the first readings of the day, washing dishes, and things she didn't even notice. She'd come down from the cupola to find columbine or fireweed in a mason jar at the table.

The packer told her Tommy's pa had been scouting the area. Talking to people around Polebridge and on the trails and saying that Tommy was a runaway and a thief and should be turned over to the authorities. "He might be looking for you." That was the most she would say, not the rest lest he get it into his head that if his pa was hunting for him and he'd go after him for a showdown.

"You don't need them today." Tommy pointed to the binoculars hanging from the strap around her neck. They had grown like another limb, permanently attached to her, but on this day they were of no use in the thick curtain of mist. The puddles growing from small ponds would be small lakes if the rain kept up.

"Do you want to know where I hid that day?"

"Sure." The pies were almost done filling the room with a tangy sweet aroma.

"I found a cave. In the rocks." He was a clever boy.

"Will you show me where?"

"Sure. Sometime." His tongue now in his cheek. He'd gotten to the "p's."

The rain felt confining and the fear of not being able to protect Tommy, and that merged with keeping her son safe in the war. Homer had left on a rainy day, confident, but he didn't swagger. His broad back looked so capable, so ready to fight the enemy.

So many rainy days in her life with longing for something that had no name or face. The heavens overflowed pouring out their own sorrows which fell heavily upon her shoulders.

When Homer started high school, she discovered a hole inside her that happened when the rain came. Another hole was her mother's grave stone, more a plaque the size of a dinner plate with grass encroaching each year. She wanted to lie down on it, to rest in her mother's arms.

The hollowness of rainy days invited her into a strange darkness like a summer fruit urging her to take a delectable bite. She started looking forward to rainy days, welcomed them, and waited for them, but then Homer would arrive home from school and the shadows slipped away.

That familiar melancholy was settling on her again. Tommy yelled. "The pies are burning!"

Martin-Seventy-Eight

Clouds of smoke rings circled the peaks, then the sun came out again and the afternoon was going to turn into a scorcher. His scalp prickled inside the aviator cap. The Indian Four was acting feisty in the altitude and heat, erratic as its former owner. He prodded it to keep going.

"She's worse than a damn woman." Some of the last words out of the scrawny fellow's mouth. He'd given it a good kick. "For luck." He laughed. Martin believed it wasn't the contrary machine that was fitful and excessive. It was its persnickety rider. But then the bike threatened mutiny with him, and he ended up pulling off the road but didn't kick it.

The pavement sizzled and the motorcycle sputtered coming around the loop. Maybe just a hiccup, he hoped when the road dipped down into the valley and branched off the main highway. He eased back on the throttle.

The mining town of Corbin lay ahead on an unpaved road, yet in the few miles he'd covered, there were more vehicles than he'd seen all day. A railroad spur weaved through the mountains out of the Crowsnest and a long line of hopper cars snaked past him going up to the main line filled with coal.

Just after the road split off from the main highway, the road turned to gravel. The bike now had two reasons to complain, heat and grit, and Martin had to find a speed that suited the conditions, not too fast or slow either of which had its hazards.

Wheezing from the dusty powder, the bike gasped and spurted until Martin gave in and pulled off to the side. Tucked in the valley below, Corbin was like a rural town in the Austrian Alps except there were no bright green hillside pastures or cowbells echoing off the slopes. In their place, wide swaths of land had been torn open exposing an extensive strip-mining operation.

He pushed the bike several feet back off the road in a stand of pines to repair it. The tool kit was a blunder of miracles. Not just put together, but well organized having been maintained by a man who lurched and fluttered until he had a wrench in his hands to ground him.

A raspy vehicle sputtered up the road from Corbin. It sounded cranky from the work it had to do to climb out of the valley floor. The brake screeched when the car was almost even with him although it was traveling at best ten miles an hour.

"Need some help there, fella?" He yelled as though Martin was a half mile away. Two squalling kids stopped fighting in the back seat and hung out the window gawking at Martin.

"I'm okay. Thanks."

"What'd you say?" The man leaned farther out the car window and cupped his ear. His arm was the size of an elderberry sapling hanging below his shirt sleeve. The towheads behind him scrutinized Martin, she had a pink bow in her hair, his eyes bugged from behind thick glasses.

"Just resting." Martin pointed to the sky.

"Yeah. This damn heat's a killer. That machine of yours giving you the business? I can repair just about every damn thing God created."

"No, no. Just a bit of tuning and staying out of the heat for a bit." He pointed at the sun again.

"Well, if you're sure you're okay." He waved and shifted into first gear then inched away up the road, the car whining as loud as the kids.

It was sprinkling when he got the bike running again puckering the dirt, but there was not enough moisture to hold down the dust. Still, it felt refreshing on his face. Even the bike obliged by humming along in a cheery mood.

Corbin was a pitiful place. Maybe it had flourished at one point in time, like a pretty woman until the luster faded and interest dried up. A pall hung over it as it did in Sudbury, except that here were mountains rising up from its roots and it didn't reek with the godawful stink.

Sudbury and Mary Alice in her gloves with matching shoes and purse. Lilly as worn down as this town over worry about her kids. He passed the dilapidated buildings. Whatever Corbin's history, old age was not settling on it kindly. To one side of the road, set back a bit, was an overgrown grave yard. The heads of the tall grasses tickled the letters of last names. He read the names of Johann, and then Maria. Bit by bit, the mossy headstones were giving up the fight against extreme winters and scorching summers.

The rain stopped later and the sky remained gray and brooding before the temperature dropped and a light drizzle started. Only a few hours earlier he'd been sweating. He pulled off to put on the leather jacket and noticed a vehicle in his rear view mirror a half mile behind him. After he'd left Corbin there'd been little traffic. He took his time with his jacket waiting for the car to catch up and go by him, watching it in his mirror. It either wasn't moving or going so slow it seemed like it wasn't moving. It was then he realized it was not going to pass him so he gunned the bike and took off.

The bike was a frolicking colt on the curves, wanting its head, to take the reins and break free. Twenty miles later, Martin stopped for a cigarette straddling the bike. The rain had just started again when the car showed up in his rearview mirror once more crawling along about a half mile back like a sheepdog herding cattle.

Florence-Seventy-Nine

"What do the birds do when it rains?"

"Is this a trick question?" He was finishing the last line of lower-case q's. She was starting a new paragraph to Homer wondering how much she should tell him about the encounter with Tommy's pa.

"No. It's not." He pouted.

"Oh. Sorry. I thought you were teasing me. What do they do? The birds?"

"Do you hear them?"

"No. What am I supposed to hear?"

"That's it. You ain't hearing nothing, are you? Get it?"

"Maybe they're holing up like we are. Eating huckleberry pie and staying dry." A distracted grin. He'd disturbed her mid-sentence laboring over her words to find the right balance. A newsy, upbeat letter, nothing to jar or alarm Homer. Tommy didn't laugh.

"I'm done." He flashed the paper in front of her.

"And look at those q's. You've got beautiful handwriting. Getting better all the time." He grinned. She hadn't noticed the freckles before.

"Maybe when I get 'em all learned I can write a letter to Homer like you do."

"He'd like that. Two for the price of one." She could have hugged him. He flipped the paper over and drew more lines.

"Next comes R and r." They both thought that funny.

"Railroad crossing railroad cars, can you spell it without any r's?"

"What?"

"You've never heard that one? It's a joke." She explained.

"Oh. That's kinda funny." It was his turn to be distracted. Something else was on his mind. "What'd you think of him?"

"Who him? My Homer? You'd like him a lot. I know you would."

"No. I mean my pa." He asked stone-faced.

"Oh. I thought you meant Homer." Sipping in a breath, she matched his look. "Well, to tell you the truth, he wasn't friendly with me." Treading carefully. People might not like, might go so far as to hate, their family, but then turn on the someone who says something against them.

"You didn't like him, neither?" The grammar. She'd let it go, put off correcting it because he was making good headway with his writing. *One thing at a time.*

The windows were walls of mist. After three snug days, the cab felt like a damp wool sweater clinging to the skin, the space too cramped for more than one person. And like Homer, Tommy picked the exact moment to ask the wrong question. She wouldn't lie, but the truth was bound to be painful no matter how it was cushioned.

His eyes pierced hers just as Homer's had after Fred hit her and slammed the door and escaped to the Elbow Room. Tommy was mute, waiting for her to say what he already knew.

Homer had waited, arms crossed, a righteous stare with a religious black and white clarity. When he became an adult, he'd understand why she hadn't left Fred then. "Never mind." She told Homer.

"What do you mean, never mind? Someday I'm going to give him what he deserves. Some of his own medicine." That's what Homer had said, and that's what she thought she read on Tommy's face. He didn't take his eyes off her.

She wished she could tell him she was sick of being cooped up inside and didn't that sound ridiculous after all the griping and the weeks and weeks of heat? Or wouldn't he like to tell her some of the lame jokes from the night before? Or would he like to have rice pudding instead of huckleberry pie for a change? And how many days of water in the rain barrel could they count on once the weather turned? Maybe he wanted to try his luck and beat her at Hearts? And maybe the birds stopped chirping because there was nothing to sing about when the sun didn't shine.

"No. I didn't like him." It really was that simple and he knew it without having to ask. His brow went tortured, crimpled lines in the middle. "I wondered how a man like that could have a son like you."

"Why?"

"Am I wrong or is he the one who beat you?" Tommy hung his head and she couldn't hear what he answered.

"What did you say?"

"It was my fault." His voice too soft for her to be sure that's what he'd said. *Oh, my God.* Under her breath. She gripped the table leg.

"What was your fault?" Steady, even voice. *Don't go overboard.* She held back the rage.

"He said I let the chinchillas out of their cages?"

"Did you?"

"No." Apparently i was enough that Pa said he'd done it.

"So, did you get them back?"

"No. They'se worth a lot of money."

"What happened to them?"

"I dunno."

"And your dad beat you for that?" Her voice very level and even softer, still gripping the table leg.

"He said I had it coming anyways. And I wasn't gonna come out of the chicken coop for a long time."

"But you say you didn't do it. Did you tell him that?"

"Didn't get to. They cost a lot of money." *And what about a boy's life?* How much was that worth to that despicable man who put a window up after he ripped the blanket off because it was in his way?

"You ran away."

"I don't remember nothin' about that. I was dreaming somebody carried me off. When I woke up, that's when I was in your outhouse."

"But who would have done that?"

"That's what I'm saying, Ma'am. It was a dream. Oh, and there was this feather."

"Yes. A feather." And a yarrow bundle, some potatoes. The rain stopped and a few minutes later the sun glistened on the droplets pressed up against the windows.

"How did you get to the outhouse?

"Must a followed the trail up, I guess."

"Just look at that." She got up from the table and opened the door. A Clark's nutcracker hopped up to the entrance. "The birds are back."

"Guess they finished eating their huckleberry pie." He teased.

"I don't know how you got here, either. I'm just glad you did. Think I'll make rice pudding. That sound good to you?"

Martin-Eighty

They took the bait in Sudbury and because of that one gaffe Martin slipped out of their trap leaving a cold trail behind. Or, maybe he hadn't. At some juncture they suspected he'd gone west and had at least two reasons for going after him although he didn't have the opportunity to destroy the nickel plant. First, there was the national threat to security and the need to curtail any further plans he might have to inflict chaos somewhere else in Canada, blow up a troop train, or a railroad bridge, a manufacturing plant. The second reason was to hang the provocateur. They'd been knocked down, outsmarted in Quebec and if it were him, would want to get in the last punch.

Bloodhounds picked up his scent in Corbin and had been playing cat and mouse with him for the last two hours. Either that, or it was a carload of hoods who wanted to steal the bike before he got to the border and as a bonus, go after him. The road threaded along a corridor between two monolithic ranges, aping the river's path, twisting and then unexpectedly opening up into broad valleys. It was a strange, rugged land, wilder than Finland, more savage.

"Me and Taavi are fed up with how they run things at the plant." Erno the performer. Hard to picture him a bona fide government agent, informer, that was more likely. Toying with Lilly, was that a part of his act, too, or purposely meant to distract Martin? She would not have been a part of it. Would she? Taavi wasn't savvy enough to pull it off on his own. Or was he? Was that all part of the strategy?

Mary Alice and the rest could describe his obvious habits. The way he held his cigarette, or cocked his head, or the hitch in his walk. One thing they couldn't do was mimic his speech. He was part chameleon changing accent, dialect, vocabulary, even the way he formed his sentences as he traveled across the country. With Eleanor Baker, he had been sophisticated and aloof until that evolved to pure disdain. With Billy, collegial and informal, and with Herman, a bit pedantic and deserving of a professor as he claimed when asked why he wasn't in the war. With the truck farmer, his conversation mimicked the fellows at the nickel plant. That may have been a mistake. The farmer was a sly one. A con spotting another con and only too willing to expand on the details of meeting Martin.

The bike leaped like a gazelle, fluid and effortless past thick stands of pine trees and meandering overgrowth. Massive green curtains inked the roadway in places with overreaching canopies and bike and man zoomed through a kaleidoscope of shadows and sunlight almost missing the nondescript signpost halfway hidden in the tall grasses. The throttle was wide open and he jerked the brake back. The distance between him and the pursuers had expanded or contracted depending on how the many potholes pocked the ground or rain had left channels across the road. For the past ten miles he'd slowed down and waited three times for the vehicle to reappear in his rearview mirror. *Know your enemy and his whereabouts.*

He smoked and chewed the edge of a budding mustache, his attention riveted on the rearview mirror and the sun dipped halfway behind a dark cloud. He felt the heat dissipate from the leather jacket. The summer heat didn't hold for long. His beard was beginning to look like the famous Barbarossa.

That gaunt man in the creaky car with the rambunctious children in the backseat who offered to help him repair the bike, had he identified Martin from the poster the whole population of Canada must have seen by now? He sucked the last drag on a cigarette. He kept the engine rumbling until a flicker in his rearview mirror a half mile behind materialized and the car slammed on the brakes and was swallowed up in a billow of dust that ate the entire vehicle except for the chrome on the headlights and the grinning Pontiac grill. More dark clouds rolled over the peaks and even without the sun glimmering, the headlamps gaped and the metal mouth sneered.

He flicked the butt and throttled the engine again and the tires spit out gravel behind him. It was a miracle he saw the sign at all. He was almost there. Then the rain started pelting, splattering against his goggles. He had to stop to clean them, but that was no better and he ripped them off his eyes letting the rain smack him in the face.

The border would be near. The road was churning into a chocolate cake batter of mud. No cars, no vehicles since Corbin except the one following him. There was a fair chance this would be a sleepy border crossing much like the small roads between Switzerland and Germany with one guard, at most two.

He stopped again. The bike was grinding and whining. The mirror drizzled and fogged up when he wiped it. He couldn't make out if they were behind him. They'd have a better chance in the vehicle than he did on the bike with windshield wipers and thick tires.

"Jesus, Mary, and Joseph." He started again, but the bike slipped in the slosh and in order to keep it upright he used his feet. He was nearly at the border when the curtain of green fell away and opened up onto a broad field. Traffic in both directions funneled into a single lane and a barricade of a white horizontal pole awaited. The station was at the end of a clearing that was both broad and flat enough to land an airplane. A sign said, "Trail Creek Crossing, the border between Canada and the United States of America." It looked like a setting from Zane Grey's, *Riders of the Purple Sage,* an outpost and a throwback to the Wild West days. Two solitary huts hugged the edges of their respective countries, on the Canadian side the Maple Leaf drooped pitifully from its flagpole as the rain got heavier. The American stars and stripes put on a good face as if to say it was tougher than any weather a storm could bring. It would be upstanding and searching for a puff of wind to fluff and rival its northern neighbors.

Except for the flags, the place seemed deserted. Not one car was coming or going across the invisible boundary separating the two countries. The insignificant barrier was all that indicated a frontier and two sleepy patrol cars snuggled next to their respective huts in semi-retired repose.

Florence-Eighty-One'

"I thought you'd have trouble trying to get the *S* right?" A gentle breeze pushed through the cab making it pleasantly cool and they were like two ducks their heads bobbing at the table over their writing. Homer would get a kick if he saw the two of them. Soon Tommy would be writing to him, she promised, when he got all his letters mastered.

"Naw. It's like sliding on the ice only with your fingers instead of your feet."

"Slippery, you mean? You do have a way of saying things."

"What d'ya mean?" He frowned.

"You make the letters out like they are humans going about their business." He cocked his head.

"Is that okay?"

"You bet it is. I like it. I've never thought writing the alphabet could be so much fun."

"Hey. Now I can write my name." He'd gotten to the *T*. "But how do I make the *y*?"

"It's easy. Like the tail of a monkey." He scratched his armpits.

"That's an animal. Not a human." He teased.

"I've been thinking." She said but then stopped. He was mouthing the letter *y* along with his hand drawing the squiggle. She didn't go on so he put his finger on the spot where he was writing and looked up at her. He had a smudge on his index finger and thumb.

"Well, I gotta say that was a pretty short amount of thinking." Tittering at her. Sometimes he sounded like an old man the way he said things.

"It was, wasn't it?" She smiled then turned to look out the window. Every day she wrote to Homer about the changes at the lookout. The progression of flowers coming into bloom and fading, the many moods of the sky from ponderous to radiant, the varied sounds of the wind sometimes soft as a mother's breath in the trees and at the cab, the meddling birds and their several songs, and the types of animals that came around. Or the spotters' jokes and their stories, or how much Tommy complained about rice and beans. But maybe that's what Homer was eating wherever he was. She almost scratched that part out, but he'd be used to eating them if that was the case.

At the beginning of June, the spotters were feisty as young pups looking for the next toy to toss in the air and chew up. Then came the many days of rain and tedium mixed between angry storms, sweltering afternoons, thieving bears and campy humor and all that was giving way to thoughtful and sober observations. The banter wasn't gone completely. It was still there when Henry got it into his head that he didn't get his fair share of whatever was important to him at that moment.

"You're like the runt, Henry. The last one to the trough and there ain't nothin' left but a potato peel."

Their spirits sagged in the heat and from the monotony so it was no surprise when the tone of their music changed. George's lively music eventually grew soulful and he played, *So Long It's Been Good to Know Ya*, while the others hummed along as if they'd been waiting for him to do it.

Evenings later he was the one who started singing which was another twist since Florence was the unofficial designated singer in the group. *"I Ain't Got a Home In this World Anymore."*

"And ain't we all glad about that." Henry crowed but there was the underlying sense that things were going to change. Tucked up in the mountains and hidden in the mist in June, September was a blurry future and something to be faced at a later time.

"Speaking of that, Flo, what will you do when this job is done?" Joe had kept to himself more lately, like he was chewing on something so when he asked it seemed to come out of nowhere.

"I don't know." Ice water in the face although she knew he didn't mean to make her heart race or her temples pound. A friendly question, not friendly fire. The summer was getting away from her wrapped up in the cocoon of a cab. When Tommy came along, the future on the plate to be picked up later.

"Well, Flossie, you any good at typing?" George asked gently.

"I used to be." Tentative as a baby deer moving a few feet from its mother.

"You could talk to the ranger. They's looking for typists, I heard. Over in Idaho. I guess they're looking for people to work in the boxing plant there, too. Maybe no jobs in Missoula though. That where you're heading back to? Probably wouldn't work for you."

If she went back to Missoula. Why should she? Homer was gone. Her dad dead and gone. The lookout her only other home, but answers hadn't dropped from the heavens like pinecones. The one decision she'd made on her own before she applied for the lookout job was to marry Fred. Look at how well that turned out.

"I'll ask the ranger." If it was a fact and there were jobs in Idaho, she'd move and take Tommy with her. If he wanted to go.

Tommy had run away. She had run away, too. They had reasons and they weren't so different. She'd see to it that Tommy went to a proper school and came home to rice and beans if that's all she could afford, but she would watch out for him no matter what. As long as Tommy was with her and Homer could find her again and come home to her in one piece.

"Okay. I've got something important to say." Tommy was looking at her resting his chin on his fist as a fleeting shadow crossed his face. "I've been thinking about what we're going to do next. I mean after we wrap it up here at the lookout."

"You mean you and me?" He pushed his spine into the back of the chair, shoulders poised and looking at her, unsure like a ten-year-old waiting for Christmas if there's a present for him. Taking his chin off his fist, he pointed at her and then himself.

She nodded. "Yes, I do mean you and me." It wasn't a sigh or chuckle, something in between and a pencil smudge on his chin.

Martin-Eighty-two

At the edge of the clearing, and from what he could make out through the drizzle, the crossing station looked wrapped up and put to bed. He tapped his fingers on the handlebar and wiped the rain off his cheek with his arm.

Probably shut down because of gas rationing. Only an outside chance of arousing a surly guard out of the hut, tearing him from his solitude, resenting the intrusion on his exclusive territory. Or some smug prick with an inflated attitude about duty or hyped up sense of patriotism. He'd seen it happen in the small border towns in Germany, an aggressive officer's innate meanness brought out when a nervous man fumbled with his papers, the guard baring his teeth because fanaticism was encouraged. A perfect place to act out a bully's dark spirit.

Craggy peaks ahead mimicked those he was leaving behind. The two countries, identical not fraternal twins, separated by an imaginary, fabricated line.

After weeks of hopping trains and hiding, lying, sneaking, manufacturing disguises, misleading, and even killing, *hell, he'd survived a tornado*, the napping border crossing seemed tepid, an almost second-rate ending to his aborted attempt in Sudbury. Sure, the car was on his tail, a mile or so behind, but he'd shake that off like a wet dog when he slipped round the flimsy barricade to get to the other side.

As much as he could make out, the space between the barricade and a cement pedestal seemed narrow, but the bike could squeeze between them without alerting the guard, if there was one on duty. No traffic was coming through. There hadn't met up with a car coming from the American side since he left Corbin.

The ground sponged up the rain fast as it came down so he'd set down his boot to stabilize the bike but it sank farther into the mud while he puzzled out his next move. Everything seemed straightforward and once across the border, if the rain slowed and the road was maintained he would put miles behind him before dark due to the headlamp which was as good as a firefly against an inky sky.

The stalkers hadn't edged into sight in the rearview mirror. Yet. Then a sudden buzz, a thrill up his spine when it came to him that they'd been setting him up. Herded him like a sheep dog to get him to the border where they wanted him. The way they creeped after him, crawling along inching around the curves stalking him from the edges. Yes. Yes. A deep breath and a tingle of elation at the revelation. Who was hunted, who the hunter? They'd have to catch him before he got across, and on the bike he had the advantage.

He scanned the empty field again. The rain pelted the skullcap, the leather jacket, ran down his neck, and emboldened him. Deader than a mortuary, this place. Did his pursuers think they could intimidate him pushing him to the border? That he'd turn around and raise his hands in surrender? He laughed out loud.

He needed a cigarette. Instead, he gunned the throttle and aimed it into the open space. The bike leaped like an antelope out of the mud. In seconds he'd be in Montana.

In those few seconds, he discovered too late as the machine thundered past the Canadian hut, the unmistakable whiff of smoke. He kept moving toward the border, spotted the slow coil of smoke on the American side above the stovepipe. He had mistaken it for fog. Shit!

Between two countries and he was a sitting duck. Chased by one and enemy to both.

Mud held on like sticky dough making the tires wobble. He struggled to keep the bike steady, or else, he was doomed. It tried to pull him and the bike down and he dug in with his feet. The Americans heard him coming and erupted from the hut in full-weather gear to get into formation in front of their barrier and aim their rifles on him.

Curtains of rain battered the road turning it into sloppy soup. Enemies ahead, enemies behind. He'd led them on a grand chase. A fine piece of work. They were salivating now, at last cornering their prey, inches away from victory. His government should be pleased for the amount of resources Canada had to use to catch him, but they would only consider his Sudbury failure.

They watched in awe, the Canadians and the Americans, as he attempted the impossible, inching forward, lifting each cemented foot to remain upright.

"Son of a bitch." Behind him, the Canadians yelled. "Stop." Their hut swarmed with men flying out as if it had been poked with a stick. One Mountie worked to get his suspenders up after he made it out the door. Another, with only his socks on, leaped like a rabbit through the mud to get into formation.

"Don't shoot. Don't shoot." They yelled to the Americans. They'd need to interrogate him, first.

The bike waddled toward the finish line, fifty feet ahead to the American side. Either he made it, or he'd be planted there in a murky grave. In his dream he hadn't been able to move his legs. Paralyzed and numb. Now, he willed his legs to keep going. Ahead, the guards had him in their sights. Behind him, the rifles pointed at his back.

Five Americans lined up in front of the barrier which seemed absurd and he laughed. A belly laugh. "Jesus." The Allies sure knew how to waste good manpower. No wonder they would lose the war. One sharpshooter from either side could do the job in an instant and by rights, the Canadians should have the first shot.

"Goddamn it. Get it over with." A shot in the back far superior to pacing like a caged wolf in a cell with cold feet and no cigarettes waiting for the moment he heard them walking down the hallway to take him to his death. The unreachable United States stood behind armed men and a pathetic white pole a few feet in front of him.

He'd been seduced, maybe fooled himself, having come so close to freedom and that everything seemed possible. He'd convinced himself the border was unmanned when he came into the opening. He fabricated his own story that of an inept American commander who made the worst possible choices, lax in his duty, a poor tactician. But he had imagined wrong. The station wasn't after all a low priority due to the requirements of manpower for the war.

"Halt!" The Canadians kept screaming at him like he was a dog off the leash. Unconsciously, he tensed his back muscles to reduce the target.

"What the hell!" He screamed then and revved the engine aiming it toward the soldiers at the American barricade. "Let's get it over with. Shoot me, you fucking bastards!"

Florence-Eighty-Three

"$210. We broke our backs for that this summer."

"You got a gripe, Henry?

"You know I do. It sure ain't gonna break the bank when I get back to civilization."

"No. But you got free room and board thrown in for nothin'."

"What you gonna do with all that money, Flossie?"

"Don't you stick your nose in Flossie's business, Henry. All you done this whole time is whining and complaining. How much suffering did you do over there on that rock of yours? Dollars to donuts you've already gambled away that $210 you're counting on."

A tapestry embroidered with pillow clouds in pink and orange hung in the evening sky. August hadn't decided yet if it would go out a scorcher or bring on an early snow. Rain wasn't holding them hostage anymore, rendering their jobs obsolete, but the brown and tall brittle grasses had perked up from the last dowsing. Was there governmental logic to continue spotting?

"And how do you figure in that pea brain of yours I'd a done that, George? Playing poker against myself? Sorry, Flossie."

Tommy giggled. Florence gave him the warning eyebrow and put her librarian finger to her lips.

"I know." Tommy whispered. He put his own finger to his lips and mouthed, "Shhh."

"Joe, do you think there's any chance of a fire starting now after all the rain?" They had dutifully reported back to their gauges and Osborne once the fog lifted and they could see beyond the ridges once again.

"Fair question, Florence. Wouldn't seem like it from the way things look so fresh right now, but yeah. There's still a chance, especially if we get some lightning storms."

"What a summer." Henry grumbled. "Spent the damn summer waiting around for nothin' to happen. Sorry Flo. That's what we been doing holed up on these rocks."

"Here we go. Again. You know what, Henry? I think we've all had about a belly full of your ranting about nothing."

292

"I ain't bellyaching, George, and I don't appreciate you making a mountain when I've got something to say. I'm stating a fact. Plain and simple."

Florence chuckled. They were an odd tribe of grumpy moods and optimism, diligent and fussy, practical and musical, thoughtful and intelligent. Henry saved them from the need to complain in silence. George delivered the harmony, Joe was the rock, steady and solid, and Florence gave comfort and directions for her recipes. When they picked up their conversations each evening, without asking, they knew who was upset or brooding, or lonely. They wouldn't meet face-to-face, but she had a picture for each of them, was fairly certain she could guess their features and would recognize them if she saw them on a street in Missoula. Joe was the puzzler. He listened to everyone, held back except to remind and caution and encourage.

"Do you think we'll ever meet?" She pictured Homer walking away, his strong back blurred by the droplets on the window pane. These men and Tommy were her people now.

"Well doggone it, now, Flo. That's a dang good question." Then silence.

It was solitary work on mountaintops for three months and generally done by men who had to account only for their own company. They were amiable and mostly considerate, and kept their private feelings behind barbed wire fences and so did she. They did the job they were paid to do, and she wasn't one to talk about Fred behind his back.

George hadn't told them he planned to head to Idaho to work in a lumber mill come September 15th. Nor Henry who hoped to line up a stint as a bartender either in Columbia Falls or Kalispell. Pouring drinks and pretending to sympathize with tribulations and woes trumped working outdoors in the winter for him. Joe had a fulltime job with the forest service waiting for him down in Missoula at the beginning of September.

Endings were like mosquitoes, meant to be brushed off or swatted if they got under the skin. The lookout summer was one of a series of gigs. After they finished the work on the mountain, it was off to the next job and the next until summer rolled around again and for three months, they watched for fires…if they decided to come back.

She loved the three and their ways. Henry's complaints had the opposite results arousing laughter and wit. The music energized and calmed them. Joe kept them steady and on track. They were better than brothers although she didn't have one to claim. When winter came, would their vivid moments together see her through the dark days and nights she saw ahead? Would she be able to laugh then, ride through the twists and turns coming her way?

At first her mountain perch had been strange and remote. It took time to realize that absolute isolation and silence were anything but that. In Missoula she shut out truck engines belching early in the mornings, or people chattering on the sidewalks and downtown, gates squeaking and brakes squealing, the radio soaps and dramas. She and Homer listened to Roy Rogers and Dale Evans after supper.

The town noises changed to quixotic breezes in the pines, and incessant flies buzzing. Birds, as Tommy pointed out, kept quiet during storms otherwise their cacophony was pretty constant, squirrels chastised her when she interrupted their business. One of her favorite sounds was water tinkling off the rocks and around downed trees at the stream.

The abundant spirit, the generous if unpredictable character of her mountain asked much of her and did not drive her away. She'd stayed on as the steward to the magnificent slope despite her ups and downs, accepted and went along with the dictates of its wildness and sometimes violent nature. She chopped wood and broke ice to have water. She gave a feeble attempt following Miss Conrad's advice to supplement her supplies with fishing, but the fish ignored her. She didn't like fish all that much, anyway.

Demanding and wondrous, this interlude would soon come to its necessary end and they'd hike off the mountain for good, surely before the first snow. Laughter and terror, learning to improvise and adapting, teasing and heartache, those were the features of the tribe she'd joined and would hold dear. She would be all right, no matter where she and Tommy went after they left the cab.

Martin-Eighty-Four

Truckers made up the volume of traffic at the Trail Creek Border Crossing and relatives who lived on one side or the other sneaked items through Customs that were hard to get. Bedding was one of those valuable commodities. A variety of other crossers to this remote outpost included backpackers, hikers, sportsmen, or poor map readers. One wrong turn in Columbia Falls and they ended up miles from their intended crossing at Eureka on "this terrible road to nowhere." As if it was the border guard's fault for its condition, certainly not their fault for not being able to follow directions. Nature-lovers, exhilarated or exhausted after a strenuous expedition shrugged off the inconvenience of the jarring ride, relished it, in fact, as part of the adventure. Some days only a single car came through.

Gas rationing had affected leisure travel, the thirty or so cars on a sunny day before the austerity measure, dwindled to a dribble. Prior to the war, the border guard signaled cars through with a dismissive wave gnawing on an apple or eating a sandwich.

"Where were you born?" A scrupulous and exacting guard would ask, and if he didn't like the answer, he'd order everyone out of the car. Otherwise, the monotony could be excruciating.

Truckers snaked their rigs around the many bends along the North Fork River overfed by glacial runoff and still hungry. It was a dusty and potholed road when the weather was good, rutted when it wasn't, slick and treacherous when it had eight or more feet of snow lining the banks that had to be plowed for the sparse local population. Three more well-traveled routes across the borders from Western Montana handled the bulk of visitors to Glacier National Park.

Eleven miles south of the Canadian border sat the cardinal red Polebridge Mercantile, a two-story affair plunked down in a large open field, the first or last outpost on the road depending on the direction. A sign posted near the front door read, "We have everything you need. If we don't have it, you don't need it." The nearest real town was Columbia Falls thirty-five miles to the south, and that took two hours to reach when the roads were good.

"Keeps the riff raff out." Locals preferred their own company to God or man. Winter could come in September or maybe not until Christmas. A couple of cords of wood wouldn't see them through if temperatures slid to minus twenty to thirty degrees and the mercury stayed there for weeks. Late spring snow flurries flew and the woods rang from the axes of men and women chopping fuel for the following winter. The Canadians and Americans alike proudly and publicly boasted of their raiding parties to the other side of the border. Any tree fair game as long as they could get to it and justified because of Mother Nature's harsh consequences. In the North Country an artificial boundary was no more barrier than a fallen log other than having been put in there by intrusive governments.

The area leans up against the spine of the treasured Glacier National Park, a rare find, a hidden jewel abundant for trout fishing and hunting elk, deer, moose, and bear, and the fantastic views of glaciers and expansive vistas. On the Going-to-the Sun highway, Flatlanders gasp at the too narrow road and the sheer drops at the abrupt edges. "Who in their goddamn right mind would live here?" Wealthy wheat farmers from the Dakotas or Iowa stomped their brakes berating relatives stupid enough to have moved to a place where you can't see the sun rise or set because of all the interference. After they returned to their prairie lives, they showed photos atop real glaciers where they threw snowballs. "In the middle of summer! Can you just believe that?"

Martin gunned the bike knowing full well what would happen next. The wheels would spin and grind down and his blood would spill and swirl in the chocolate earth. Not a bad way to die.

"Stop. Stop. We will shoot!" But the bike responded finally showing some mettle. The odd contraption had balked going uphill and now it broke loose from its reins. Now that it was too late. He was a dead man against the five rifles marked on him. The bike flounced and sashayed like an exotic hoofer swooshing through the mud like a grinning jokester.

The noses of five rifles followed his action, dancing, weaving, turning to say in step with an erratic partner. He didn't have a chance of making it alive. Why hadn't they already fired on him? Were they

296

waiting for someone to bark the order? He was twenty yards from them and they didn't shoot. The bike dipped and curtsied and he stayed upright atop a bucking bronco. They were young and uncertain boys. He saw it in their eyes. They hadn't killed, yet.

When the bike sobered up, he was no more than ten feet from them. Their rifles hadn't made it back to target as he charged at them, aiming for the weakest link. The one with doubt in his eyes. The one who would jump back instead of firing. One already lowered his rifle. Did he think one of the others would pull the trigger?

It was hard to decipher what happened first. Events came together at the same moment and the episode was over almost before it began. Details slid into each other, a blur as to whether he charged at the waffling recruit before an out-of-control pickup truck loaded with firewood crashed through the barrier coming from the American side. Just as he closed the gap between them at the border, a vehicle that hadn't been there and then it was, leaped out of nowhere silent as a sled because the engine wasn't running and they didn't hear it coming. All ears were tuned to the bike's engine when the truck with a will of its own got to the gate ahead of him and he ducked to avoid the chopped pieces of wood for potbelly stoves that flew and scattered. Two soldiers were splayed out in the mud where the barrier had been and where his own blood should be.

Martin kept going. Through the demolished barrier and around the limp bodies, bullets whizzed past and there was a sting like a wasp on his upper arm. The bike ground through the sludge leaving a furrow in its wake. When it sputtered to a stop, he was a few miles inside the United States boundary.

Florence-Eighty-Five

Pine scent is freshest just after dawn before the heat gradually sucks it up into thin air. She let the sweet air fill her lungs and hummed and waited guessing which of Tommy's jokes would come next. The woods droned, the morning light glazed the yew and fern. Tree roots and rocks hid in the shadows on the path that would twist an ankle if she went dreamy and didn't watch her step.

If only he'd be quiet for a blessed few minutes! She was to the point of covering her ears. He chattered over his shoulder chirpy as a chipmunk, the needle stuck on what he thought the funniest of the jokes from the spotters' arsenal. The men's humor hadn't moved on from age twelve which was appealing and annoying. The energy of the adolescent boy is contagious.

He stopped suddenly and she almost ran into him. He couldn't help it, bending over with tears running down his face.

"Get to the punchline." His stomach ached from laughing. "Spit it out." It's driving me nuts, she would have added but tedious as it was to take in yet another moron wisecrack and pretend she hadn't heard it how many times before, she rolled her eyes and gave a weak smile.

"How about this one?" She told a joke Homer had told her. It hadn't been funny in the kitchen after school. His humor ripe as her tomatoes.

"Mom, do you get it?" He was laughing hard until he saw her puzzled look.

"Sure. Sure. I get it." She wasn't sure she had, and if she did, it didn't seem funny. She didn't do the joke any favors in the retelling, but thought that since it came from Homer it must be good for another boy of that age.

"What's so funny about that?" Tommy was moving down the path and stopped short and turned to face her, his hands on his hips, like she was hopeless.

"I don't think you have the knack. I like Henry's jokes better." Well, he would, wouldn't he? It must be something about male humor. Who would have ever thought of Tommy getting mouthy with her? The boy who addressed her as Ma'am and how long had that gone on? Well, she'd let him tell her all the jokes he wanted and she'd try her best to laugh at them all. No matter how often she heard them, just as she'd done when Homer told them.

She'd started packing the rifle. "In case that bear comes back." Instead of, in case your pa just happens to show up sniffing around for you and growling. Truthfully, a bear had tried to get into the cab one night recently.

"You ever shot anything with that?" He looked at her sideways. She couldn't fool him, although the bears were hanging around more, most active in the early mornings and late afternoons. "Make a bunch of noise. Why don't you? Humming ain't going to cut it. They's practically blind, you know."

"Isn't. Isn't." Now that he'd mastered cursive, she'd begun correcting his grammar.

"I know."

"I know you know." He didn't know if she could react in a split second, though, get the thing pointed in the right direction, pull the trigger at the exact right time.

"Why don't you give me the rifle?" He'd do it. If he spotted the old man, he'd grab the rifle from her anyway. She wouldn't do it, shoot him, but he would. Aim for his eyes and pop him a good one before he ever knew what hit him. His pa might be a sloppy hunter, slow and noisy. Tommy passed out when he started slapping him with chains.

"There's always a first time, you know. Just because I haven't shot anything, *yet*. You think I can't do it? Hmm." She stuck her tongue out at him. He shrugged. Before Tommy had shown up, she'd heard scratching and huffing around the cab. She moved her cot in front of the door. One morning she set up empty tin cans on some fallen logs near the edge of the slope. On the first shot she sent one backward over the cliff. She hit more than she missed that day. She even told Homer she had a pretty good eye. She had gotten used to the night rackets, could even identify what animal caused what noise, a pack rat or a badger, or a bear, and the rifle was above the door.

In three weeks, they'd close up the cab, a week ago the heavy rains stopped and the late afternoon sprinkles failed to return. It had gotten hot again. Itchy hot. Stifling heat that made them snap at each other. Midafternoons were the worst for the spotters. The ridges went hazy and the spotters hated not seeing what they were supposed to see.

"What about you, ole' deadeye?" Was it because of the rifle that he suddenly turned sullen?

"Shoot a grouse on the fly. Bet you ain't done that, neither."

"Haven't. Haven't." He remembered the grammar when he wanted to. "I bet you can. I wouldn't be surprised."

"You wouldn't?" She missed his intent. "I can hit anything I darn well want to shoot."

"You had a lot of practice, have you?" Fred and Homer hunted for a buck up Blue Mountain in the fall. They returned after it was pitch black even if there was part of a moon and the sky was clear. The headlights emerged from the dark, the truck turned into the driveway with a dead body hanging off the hood, antlers dangling between the headlamps.

She could see her breath when she went out to the truck, her plaid jacket draped over her shoulder. Bent over to look at the pitiful, beautiful creature. Homer and Fred were efficient moving and hanging the dead beast up to clean it out, remove the hide, its innocent eyes staring at nothing.

They didn't say who shot it. Which one of them had wronged the animal. She didn't want to know. If it had been Homer then maybe he was a good enough shot to survive the war.

"Why don't I pack the rifle, now?" Tommy put his hand on the stock.

Martin-Eighty-Six

When the downpour turned to a drizzle, the bike whimpered. When the rain stopped, so did the bike. It went another ten feet buckling under him and he fought to keep the handlebars steady and upright and then it went entirely limp with a single mutter, the mud gripping the tires, holding it in place.

The gutsy thing's spirit drained. *Damn machine.* He didn't kick it or slap the handlebars as the previous owner would have done, instead cursed when he climbed off and pushed it through the muck to the side and then jumped back on and stomped down on the pedal. *Come on, you damn piece of shit.* Hard as he came down with his heel, not even a groan from the engine. He was starting to get sick to his stomach and needed a smoke.

Where were the border guards who should be rabidly pursuing him? The evening sky had turned prematurely gray and the rain had stopped but black blobs of clouds hung overhead. He listened for sirens, for engines to be screeching and what he heard was the bike wheezing and squeaking at him when he tried to revive it.

He'd give it a few minutes and try again. Temperamental thing. Maybe it would snap out of it after its latest protest. He'd dump it as soon as he found something better.

Not even a spark of life. He jumped on the pedal. No grinding or lurching. *Come on. Damn it.* He gave it a few minutes more. Why wasn't he hearing their cars bouncing up the road? What was taking them so long? One more try and he had to get it into the woods, but that would leave a trail. Then he smelled the gas fumes.

He'd looked the tank over and hadn't found a hole. He felt around where the mud hung thick and felt a tiny nick, no bigger than the head of a needle. The bullet must have hit the tank at an angle, enough just to notch it and it kept going for a few miles before the fuel drained out. They wouldn't know they'd made a hit.

It started raining again before he got into the trees and a hundred yards from the road where he was swallowed up in branches and vines that grabbed hold of and clung to the bike's pedals. A sliver of daylight remained hidden behind the crowns of the ponderosa and tamarack. He had to dump the thing far enough from the road. Cover its chrome so it wouldn't catch the light if they found his tracks. Gratefully, the rain would make it harder to find the trail he was leaving.

They must be searching for him. Unless the pickup turned over and blocked the road and they couldn't get their vehicles around it. A piece of the bike's headlight and part of the handlebars peered out from the bushes like a deer with antlers. He grabbed his backpack. There was a bullet hole in it too. What had stopped it? With the bike well hidden, he headed deeper into the dark woods. If they didn't come across it, this would be its unmarked graveyard. A better burial than its owner under a pile of rocks.

It grew dark and the terrain was covered with small bushes and was steep for a while then dipped down, then up again. Up and down and around trees, lifting his legs over and over. Rain ran down his neck. He kept going. Too soon to stop and not safe to use his flashlight. A cigarette was out of the question. He chewed on a reed of grass.

At one point, he came upon a meadow on a ledge overlooking the way he'd come. The sky was clearing and an almost full moon slid out from behind a cloud. The road curled around the woods swirling like the chocolate in the German cake his mother made for the priest twice a year. Some chipmunks rattled at him and then an owl hooted. Three times.

Why weren't there any vehicles parked near where the bike broke down and the trail he'd left behind? There should be two at least, and flashlights should be flickering where he'd begun climbing. Keep your enemy where you can see them, second guess their strategies, outthink them when they show a hand. Maybe they'd already spread out, three or four dropped off, others dropped off farther along the road. Had they come across the ruined bike?

The moon dipped behind a cloud. He started climbing again and pulling himself over the undergrowth then stumbled on a massive root beneath an old growth tree. It was the first dry spot since Corbin when the bike broke down and he'd been sweating. The last thought before he fell asleep was of the faces of the two towheads in the back

302

seat hanging halfway out the window looking at him as if he was an exotic specimen in the zoo.

Shivering woke him or maybe it was because the moon glowed too brightly in another part of the sky. He piled some dry leaves and made himself a bed and crawled into that mound and smoked. The last cigarette he'd had was in Canada.

It was cozy as a grave if they found him there. The pistol was ready. He'd hear their footsteps before they were on top of him and it would be quicker than the cyanide pill in his kit.

In his burrow, he was a kid again in Timmins. It was fall and he was leaping into a pile of leaves with his pals. If they'd seen the wild man at the border hours ago, they'd have cheered on his wallowing in mud up to his shins and screaming.

"You come out without a scratch." Their grins proud and victorious.

"Dare you to do it again." Crazy sons-of-bitches, those kids were. The guard he'd aimed the bike at had flinched. Was he the one who got the shot off that took the bike out? It should have been him. Madder than hell he must have been. The bullets whizzed close enough to take off his ear but he kept going. They hadn't got him. The boys in Timmins loving it and what's her name in Sudbury would say if he just believed in God, he'd know it was a miracle.

He was half in and out of sleep, very drowsy and comfortable when he first felt a shooting pain in his arm.

Florence-Eighty-Seven

In early July, the edges of the stream were like a bathtub filled and overflowing. Now the tub was half full despite the torrential rain days a few days before.

"Yessire! I got another one!" She could just make out his ankles and bare feet on top of a large rock that jutted like the figurehead on a ship's bow over the water and the wriggling, undersized fish on the hook. The stage whisper couldn't conceal his delight despite the distance between them. She was a bit farther downstream dipping her toes in and out of the water and he wasn't about to scare a fish off letting them know he was there.

He disappeared off the rock and she heard him darting through the bushes searching for another dark pool where the fish might be hiding. He'd caught six fish by her count. A few minutes only, and if no nibble, he moved along the stream to the next spot, staying well back from it so the fish couldn't spot his shadow. Undergrowth crowded the bank as did drooping tree limbs.

This was their second trip down since she started packing the rifle. "I still don't get why you won't let me take it." The set of her jaw told him it was no use arguing but he did anyway. She wasn't going to get a shot off fast enough the way she hauled it.

"Is that thing even loaded?" He'd tucked some cartridges in his pocket before they left.

"I'm beginning to think you don't have much faith in me." She teased and stopped to show him the extra ammo she carried in her pack. "Yes, it's loaded. And...ta da, I have the safety on in case you didn't notice." He had.

They'd gone earlier than the other times because he wanted to take the rod and said the fish would bite better before it got too hot.

"What difference does that make?" He snorted. "What'd I say?"

He shook his head. "You ever catch anything with that?" He took the rod off the wall the evening before where it had hung all summer catching dust and being a decoration.

"Who likes fish?" She made a face and he returned it with his best adolescent scoff. It was amazing she'd managed to live so long before he came along.

"Well, they're tasty, for one thing." She made another face. "I bet you haven't fried them in cornmeal, have you?" She shrugged. "You'd love them if you did."

"I don't want to cut off their heads." She scrunched her face up. "Ugh!"

"I don't believe it." That was as funny to him as his moron jokes. "Leave the heads on 'em. Just throw then in the pan after you've cleaned out the guts."

"You mean fry them up with their eyeballs staring at me? No thank you! That sounds like murder." He was still laughing, thought she was pulling his leg. "I'm glad you're enjoying yourself." She sniffed.

He readied the rod that evening, wiped it down, put on fresh line in preparation and listened to the spotters' sarcastic exchanges. "I've got to thinking I better start writing my life story to keep myself awake up here."

"Well, now, Henry, that's two things I didn't know you could do."

"And, just what's that George?" He'd set himself up and was ready with a comeback.

"Well, first off, Henry, I didn't know you could think. That's the biggest surprise of all. And second I didn't expect you'd learned how to write, yet." Tommy loved it. He was slipping the line on the rod and quietly giggled.

"You're just jealous cuz you ain't had an exciting life like me to write about."

"Yeah. Like right now. Pretty exciting up here, ain't it? I can't wait to read all about it. Let me know when it comes out in the comics."

The air felt heavy when they headed down to the water. Even after two cups of Tommy's coffee, it was like walking in a fog. At the stream, he hopped around the rocks to get the containers filled before he threw his line in. When she finished topping the last one off and turned to have him put the cap on, he'd scampered off and was rushing through the undergrowth like a bear rustling in the woods.

She didn't expect he'd catch anything. She really didn't want to eat fish and was fairly certain he'd have about as much luck as she'd had with the pole. It had to be the pole's fault for her bad luck.

With the water level down, she tested it with her toes and gasped at the surprise. After so many hot days the stream should have heated up. In and out with her toes until she plunged her feet in and kept them there as long as she could. In the stream, pebbles glistened in the shallows sparkling like multi-colored gems, greens and blues, golds and reds.

The gravel made raindrops splashes on the water as she sifted them through her fingers with one ear listening to Tommy move through the thickets and voicing his triumphs. Half in and out of the sun, the water chilling her toes, a simple, perfect moment.

The girls, she and her friends at the river, her lungs aching from the cold water. Long ago, another happy time. Laughing like Tommy at his jokes, holding each other up, huddled in a circle. Complete and perfect. Now her toes were turning purple and yet there was sweat at the brim of her hat. All those in-between years, the obscure time except for Homer and now Tommy. Like finding a missing sock and tying it to its pair after a life of separation.

Her feet were throbbing and the boots didn't warm them up at first. They would on the hike up. She whistled for Tommy.

"In a minute." He was somewhere behind the verdant curtain waiting for the next fish to strike. She whistled again ten minutes later.

"We've got to get going." When he emerged, his face was beet red. "You got too much sun."

"I don't care." He shrugged. "Wanna see all my fish?" She'd leave the salve out when they got back to the cab.

Martin-Eighty-Eight

Someone shouted and it was very close by. He sprang out of the leaves which flew up with him spinning and falling back down, a few landing on him while he tried to make out where the voice was coming from. His shirt was sopping wet and he didn't know why, nor could he figure out why he was under a tree. *Easy. Take it easy.*

His temples had cymbals on both sides banging together and he tried to get up and run but his legs were stuck in the leaves. But run from what and to where? He didn't know why. Skewers of light pierced through the shade of the tree's canopy and the bed where he'd fallen asleep and was dreaming of men dressed in black with black capes wearing goggles aiming long knives at him. Backing him into a corner. He waved the cyanide pill at them. But why would he do that?

Brittle leaves clung to his damp hair, some caught between his collar and his neck and itched, but he was too troubled about the jacket on the other side of the tree to do more than scratch. Above him the skullcap peered down at his head like a bat hanging upside down from a branch.

His eyes weren't in focus and the jacket was a spy lurking in the bushes. *Just try it. Go ahead. Try it,* he'd hidden the gun somewhere in the leaves and fumbled in them. His head was going in circles, his eyes whizzing like pinballs between his ears. *Good god.* After he finished throwing up whatever meal he last ate, he fell back among the leaves and waited for the eyes to slow down.

He needed his jacket. What was it doing on the other side of the tree when he was feeling so cold? Someone, he didn't know who, had gotten mad at it, yelled at it for making him sweat and lobbed it and the skullcap. His brow glistened like a man digging a trench. The sweat trickling into his ears. *Jesus Christ!* His voice hoarse. Even his teeth hurt, but the nausea was easing up now that his stomach was empty.

When he woke again, sunlight was stabbing him in the eyes. *For the love of god.* He rolled over onto his side. It was different pain now and he was sweating again. Someone asked him why he was lying there. Shouldn't he be on the move? He should have been gone before daylight. *What time is it?* The backpack was just out of his reach and he yelped in pain when he stretched for it. Was he awake or was this a dream? He couldn't tell anymore but he saw the jacket moving. He was sure of it.

Dewdrops of sweat dotted his bare skin, the jacket blanketed over him when a noise woke him. Not boots pounding the ground, just a slight sound little more than a whisper in the branches, enough to make him scoot back to the tree trunk to steady the pistol because his eyes kept moving around. He heard heavy breathing, like someone winded from climbing too fast, so close it was practically in his ears yet there was no sign of anyone coming. That was before he realized he was the one panting.

The breeze, his breathing, and a squirrel barking indignation at either him or the skullcap that had horned in on his branch or both, and his twitchy eyes. He mopped his forehead with the sleeve of his jacket and felt the stupid cap staring down on the back of his neck making mean faces at him. It would be only too willing to betray him when they came by. That's what they'd see first, alien eyeballs hanging down. He had to get the smirking thing off the tree, as obvious as a cairn for any tracker or hiker. *You're not going to get the best of me.*

He steadied himself against the trunk and lunged for it, but fell back without laying claim to it. It snickered at him. What he needed was a long stick. He'd give it a good whack and wipe the sneer off it forever. He poked around in the leaves to find something long enough, ended against the trunk again, perspiration pooling in the folds of his neck. His arms felt heavy as two bags of cement and he needed to shut his eyes.

It was raining, wasn't it? Or was he dreaming? When had it stopped raining? Someone yelled again and he bolted up from the trunk only to get knocked back down. The pain shot into his elbow and up into his neck, his eyeballs pounding into his skull. A bloody lower lip because he refrained from crying out to not give himself away, and then finally realizing he'd been shot and he was the one doing the yelling.

The hole in the upper sleeve of his jacket where the bullet went in and another where it went out matched the holes in his arm. There was very little blood in the two wounds because the slug had cauterized the perfectly round openings.

Got to get moving. On your feet, old boy. He mashed up aspirin, four of them, and mixed them with his saliva since he'd emptied the canteen. They must have found the bike by now, and his trail. The powder coated and tickled the back of his throat and he hacked up half the pills and waited for the pain to pass.

Beads of sweat peppered his brow. Even the insides of his nostrils burned. *I've got to find some water.* He thought he said in more lucid moments when it was quite clear to him that he'd been under the tree for more than a day. Maybe even two. When had the rain stopped?

He woke up shivering. It was still daylight, but just what day was it? The jacket was on the other side of tree again, as if it meant to fool him by impersonating a spy hiding in the bushes watching him. It wouldn't work. The aspirin helped some. He favored the arm, put his good arm in one sleeve and draped the other over the swollen shoulder. Then he found a good stick, long enough to yank the skullcap off the branch. When it hit the ground, the smirk went down in defeat. The sturdy stick and he set off to find water.

Florence-Eighty-Nine

The back of Tommy's neck was pink as the fish flesh. "You're gonna love them!" He'd called her down from the cupola for lunch. The sunburn salve at the end of the tiny counter was there if he decided to swallow his pride. Knowing Tommy, he'd tough it out.

"He's staring at me." Tommy expertly tackled the bones of his second fish. He put down his knife and glared at her.

"Just try it, at least. Here. I'll take the head off so you don't have to look at it."

"Ohh. Poor fish."

She'd logged measurements while he clanged below her at the stove. He was whistling, *I've got rhythm.*

"Three water dogs." She called down over the ladder.

"What do you think? Trouble?"

"I'll keep my eye on them this afternoon. Don't think they're anything to worry about. For now. I think it's going to hit ninety today." Damp curls clinging to her temples.

"I shoulda cooked 'em on a campfire. That's when they taste the best anyway."

"Yeah. And it wouldn't heat the cab up. Just imagine if we had a fan." She waved a blank piece of writing paper in her face.

"This is going to be the best lunch you ever had." The muscles in his back tensed for her argument. The cornmeal crackled.

"Is that a promise?" An attempt to be jovial, but her stomach stood ready to revolt when he put the head on his own plate, with the other two. She held her breath to keep from smelling the stink of fish fried in lard but the odor permeated the cab.

"I don't think he liked that."

"Actually, it was a she." Tommy had found the eggs when he'd gutted the fish.

"Oh. That makes me feel so much better." Killing a mother.

"I'll keep my eye on them." She'd assured the ranger. "So far it doesn't look like much." He was gulping something liquid.

"It's the humidity. Joe's got 'em, too." It was root beer. The bottle gurgled whenever he tipped it up.

"I'm sending someone up anways. Odd you and Joe are seeing 'em near the same spot." Her early attempts with the Osborne, of second guessing every reading, once a nearly unworkable partnership, was distant history as she rattled off the coordinates. "Like chocolate chip cookies." She told Tommy. "You make them enough times you don't need a recipe anymore."

"You ain't made any since I been here."

"Haven't." His deliberate choice of words when he wanted to jab her.

"You bring me chocolate chips and I'll make you those cookies."

"I gotta say, Flo, you keepin' on it up there. I could use ten more like you." As the end of summer grew closer, he was becoming more human. The days leaned into fall, and the odds favored them if lightning didn't strike or some idiot throw a lit match out the window of a car, or start a campfire in the woods. The ranger had caught up on his sleep and his wife had gotten hold of a good piece of beef and made sandwiches with lots of mustard and onions.

She was giving the poor fish a good attempt poking it with her knife. "Here. Just pull the skin back. Now, look at that!" The fleshy inside looked almost pleasing. She put a bit on her fork and held her breath when she bit down.

"Um. This is good." At the third bite.

"Watch for bones." A railroad track grin across his face.

"Could I have another one?" They ate the lot and wished for more. "Next time we go down, let's go earlier." She'd fish if they had two poles. "Could you show me how you do it?"

"I'll show you." That evening while he listened to the banter, he put the equipment on the floor in separate piles. "You need all these things." No wonder she hadn't caught any fish. It wasn't simple. He rattled off the names for bobbers, the hooks, the line, the reel.

"It's not a pole. It's a rod." He explained what lures were. "Don't worry about that. We'll get some worms from your garden like I did this time."

"You got anymore water dogs, Flo?" George and she watched over adjacent sections

"Earlier this morning. I didn't figure they were much after awhile. You know how it is when the sun hits them at an angle."

"Good. Cuz I didn't see nothing out of the ordinary on my end."

"How about you, Joe?"

"Same thing here. Looked like it could be something this morning. Then it went away."

"Those fellas down there in the camps must be about bored out of their minds. You gave them something to do anyway." George envied the men living the whole summer in tents and waiting to be called up. They didn't live in cushy cabs with a sturdy roof or a place to store staples and cook meals and get a visit from the packer with fresh supplies. But they got to move around, weren't locked down to a single location.

They cut down trees and cleared trails when they weren't on the hunt for a fire, shored up places where runoff had washed away or eroded the paths, and waited for the call to rush to a fire or some suspicious activity. The back breaking work was meant for fit, strong young people, but they were in short supply with the war on. Older, slower men who still had good legs and strong hearts filled in wherever they could be found.

"Thank you, Tommy." The sun was setting earlier now. She said quietly from her cot. Behind his curtain, he grinned. He'd taught her about the fishing equipment and he would show her how to fish. She'd eaten the fish he'd cooked up and liked it.

"I'll dig up worms tomorrow. We can keep them in the cooler until we go down again."

Martin-Ninety

Dawn unfolded and the creek babbled less than a foot from where he lay. He rolled onto his side and dipped a hand into the frigid stream letting the water coax and drag it along with the flow before slaking his desert of a thirst using his hand for a cup. Droplets salted his beard.

In that half-light, the sun checked its wardrobe from the wings of a triangular peak before coming onto the morning stage. The mountain seemed so close he could put his finger on the tip. Its celestial head suspended with no supporting body to hold it up, cut off at the neck by the numerous and thick riparian bushes clustered along the bank. Repetitive chatter from the brook pleaded for him to close his eyes again, to stay where he was, leave behind the many cares the world brought.

When had he ever smelled air this succulent, or tasted sweeter water? Divine yet earthy, the life force flowing next to him unaware of human woes and miseries. It held back raging waters in the spring until powerful energy leaped over boundaries and brought down trees and brush.

Nearest him, the water tinkled against pebbles in a shallow spot gentle and insistent as the bells during Mass that divided the service into bearable segments. That world was interspersed with pungent incense smoking up the cathedral, stinging the eyes, with the stale odor of melted candlewax, and Sulphur from extinguished wicks. Old ladies wearing dark, ankle-length dresses, and veils. Mary Alice's fine-spun gray hat with its coy nod to a truncated veil.

For a time, he was mesmerized, his mind wandered aimlessly, wayward and balky. Fourteen again. His mother waiting outside his bedroom ready to hand him the neatly ironed church clothes. "Quit dawdling. We will be late." He wouldn't budge from the other side of the door. Put his chair against the door and after her cajoling with no result, she threw the clothing with the hanger against the door scraping it and running out of the flat slamming the door.

The stream was his enchantress, luring him and making his brain sluggish. "Come on. Let's blow smoke rings together. I bet I can make bigger ones than you." Charming him there while he lay on his back, the sun warming him inch by inch as it pulled its cover over him. That half-awake nonsense, the residue from too much sleep, the hazy lull that tempts one to slide back into the dream world when a harsher reality looms.

The stream sang for a while, then scolded him for being such a sour puss. "Lighten up. Look around you. Have you ever seen a more glorious day?" When he was a child in the days before he was dragged from fluorescent Timmins to solemn Germany and just before falling asleep, he'd put his legs up against the wall, and whistle. He felt that if he really wanted to, he could fly. The creek whispered as his mom had done from the other side of the door, "Schlaft gut." He'd trusted her then. That was before he started hating her and he still did sleep well.

He'd gotten to a creek somehow and managed not to tumble into it. His clothes were dry and he must have discovered it there in the dark. He remembered stumbling and feeling confused. That's why he'd stopped. Fearing he was going around in circles.

Had he heard the water running? Is that why he stopped? How long had he been there?

He looked up to see if the skullcap was staring down at him. Oh, yes. He'd been under a very large tree. It had been raining. It wasn't raining now. He'd been so thirsty and there was that other thing. What was it? Something awful. He'd swallowed bitter aspirin, spit it up again, and a spy, yes that was it, a spy was watching him, hiding from him in the bushes, but he saw him. He saw him! When he tried to knock something off a branch, he couldn't do it and fell back down. But he'd gotten up again. When was that?

Underneath him, the earth had the odor of a weeping basement. The sun crawled up the backside of the mountain breaking suddenly over the crest and in that moment, silence, a hush as if a heart missed a beat. That's what woke him up. The noisy stream wasn't even whispering.

The world's engine went from park to drive and the motor of the universe restarted. Leaves rustled, the creek again burbled, Martin drank and drank until his lungs felt they would explode, and he dallied, beguiled by the stream and the sun stretching out like a lizard.

Until he heard the footsteps. Lying on his back, he was more a spider than a reptile moving only his eyes. Right and left, back and forth. The feet continued to shuffle and because his ears where on the ground, they sounded too close for him to stay where he was. He lifted his leg and pulled the knife out of his boot. There was a splash. Then another.

Opposite him, on the other side of the creek, a magnificent 4-point buck stepped into the water with its two front hooves. The majestic beast in its kingdom didn't appear shaken when it spied Martin at the same second it lifted its head. The pair locked eyes before the animal dipped its nuzzle in again and took another sip. And snorted. Martin didn't move, not even his eyes and when it was done, it lifted its crown of antlers to check again. A statue, sculpted in plaster, it stared at Martin across the bank. Then, it coolly turned and shuffled back into the brush. Oher noises of the woods came awake as if the deer had pushed them from their slumber.

Martin stuck his head into the stream and drank like the deer lapping the water with his tongue. When he finished, he shook like a dog. His stomach growled, but the bits of bread in his pack had hardened and were moldy.

Florence-Ninety-One

The cot was most inviting between four and five in the morning. A fact that Tommy ignored when he yelled at her to wake up.

"Stop yelling. I can hear you." Covering her ears.

"I'm not yelling. Come on. Get up or we're gonna miss 'em for sure." She squinted at him across the semi-dark room. He was dressed and waving the can with the few worms he'd dug up.

"I'm coming. Give me a minute." Slowly sitting up and shaking her head to clear it. Why does a bed smell its freshest before dawn, she wondered as the pillow pleaded with her to lay back down where her head had left a depression?

Once she was up and, on her feet, the two of them bustled about the cab like they were late to feed chickens. "Hurry up!" She prodded because she'd caught his fish fever and was putting the eggs and spam on bread and wrapping them in cloth napkins. "Morning snack." She waved them at his back, but he wasn't the least bit interested in food. That would come later. They'd decided to skip breakfast and make an early start while the fish were hungry and eager as they were. She finished the last bit of coffee while he rechecked the gear which he'd packed and repacked the previous night.

"In a minute." He squeezed his eyebrows together. "You'll be sorry if I forgot something, you know."

"I don't know what you could possibly have forgotten. You've been fussing over it all for two days."

It was light enough to see the ridges when she took all the readings, wind speed, thermometer, precipitation. The tamaracks, quiet sentinels on the edges of her domain were just hinting at gold although the temperatures had dipped only slightly at night. Sunlight peered out between the peaks painting stripes across the tops of the ridges and promising another scorcher.

"Looks like another hot one." The ranger mumbled something in response. She was pretty certain she'd heard two burps as she read her numbers off.

"Right now, it's nice and cool down here in the pines, but I smell the heat coming on. No breeze to speak of. You got any of them storm clouds you need to keep an eye on?"

"Clear as a bell far as I can tell. I'm going to head down for water." She almost said, *we. We are heading down for water*. Since Tommy's pa she'd been keeping the boy close by making up two-bit jobs when the real ones were done. They locked horns over it some days. He knew what she was doing. Keeping him like a prisoner

"I wanna collect rocks. On my own." He was a bloodhound when they went for water, nose down so as not to miss an odd geometric shape or unusual color. "Just look at that one." Weighted his pockets down and required a needle and thread afterward to fix the holes. He propped his prize finds up against the cab next to where her wimpy sunflowers drooped.

"I think you're going to be a geologist someday."

"What's that?"

"Well, I don't know much other than they study rocks to find the minerals and whatever else is in them." She shrugged. "That's how they decide where to dig. You know. For mining."

Some days were better than others. Maybe he wouldn't give her lip. He wrote to Homer on those days. He'd stop his pencil and put his finger where he'd left off asking her how to spell a word. Other times he'd go to the edge of the cliff and pitch rocks down on the scree. He'd flinch over the petty things she asked of him, his ears turning red. "That's stupid." She had him take all the cans off the shelves and wipe them down. He was resentful but did the chores knowing she was watching out for him.

"Maybe throw a pole in the water while I'm down there today." The ranger burped again. This time right in her ear.

Tommy looked up from his gear and whispered, "Rod." She waved him off.

"I didn't know you were a fisherman, Florence. If you get down there sooner than later, you might still catch something. They'll be hiding in the dark pools. Probably not any more interested in eating than we are." The ranger chuckled. Tommy made a face and whispered under his breath, "What does he know, anyway? "

317

"Wouldn't mind being out there myself. Put some trout on the supper table for a change. Let me know how it goes." He signed off.

"You finally ready? We're not taking a trip around the world, you know." She had her big brim hat on, one impatient hand on a hip, waiting in the open doorway. "Hurry up. You're going to let the flies in."

"Don't stand there with the door open, then." He grinned walking by her. When did he get to be such a sass? She stopped herself from hugging him.

"Just remember not everyone's as nice as me." Raising her eyebrows.

"You gonna pack the rifle, too?" The crewel dangled off her shoulder crammed with their food on the arm she used to carry the weapon. She hadn't forgotten it, walked under it on the way out the door but didn't take it down. The rascal got her, relentless he was, like mosquitoes looking to find a way through the screens into the cab.

It flopped off her other arm as she stepped around rocks like one of Tommy's fish.

"Here. I'll take that. And, just so's you know, you don't pack lunch in a crewel."

"But that's just common sense." He swung the rifle over his shoulder.

"You wanna be a real fisherman or one of them touristy kind that don't know a pole from a rod or where to go to look for fish, or how to keep em on the line if they get a bite?"

"I want to be a *real* fisherman. Like you." She laughed. "But I don't see why I shouldn't use the crewel for our lunch. Seems practical if you ask me."

"Because it's stinky. You want to eat something that smells fishy?"

"What? Since when are you fussy when it comes to fish? I thought you *loved* the smell of them." She grinned under her hat and brushed past him on the trail.

"I love 'em." He hollered behind her. "I love 'em, but not when I'm not eating 'em."

318

Martin-Ninety-Two

He was sweating and his arm was twice its normal size when he woke again but this time there was water to wash down the aspirin. Black flies bigger than honey bees buzzed at him administering nasty bites on his bare skin, greedy man eaters that pursued him until he moved farther downstream where fish, miniature missiles, burst up through the surface snapping up bugs before slipping down and disappearing into the liquid world. They left circles on the water that expanded to the size of dinner plates and got swallowed up in the pool.

His arm was healing too slowly. It wasn't festering, but it pulsed, angry red, and felt hot. He'd awakened in full sun and couldn't tell if this was still his first day at the stream or if he'd slept through another night. Had a day passed since the deer stared him down?

In spite of the pain, he was hungry. For fish. The stealthy trout hid in the dark below the surface when they weren't making a splash and gave themselves away with loud smacks at the surface. Hard to believe something that small could make such a commotion and disappear that quickly. Underwater they were U-boat silent.

He'd improvise something, cut a sapling, attach a string to it from his pack, smack another of the carnivore biters for bait, but he had to wait until later when he didn't feel so hot and tired. Lying back on his elbows on a rock above the stream, his feet dangling off the edge, he gnawed around the moldy spots of bread and threw the spoiled bits back into the water. Like a bunch of mosquitoes, they swarmed and fought over the crumbs. Deceptive creatures, seemingly placid otherwise. Their greediness fascinated him, their eagerness and hostility with every morsel he tossed at them, even anticipating his next throw which he did emptyhanded.

The sun followed him, fingered the tops of the plants near where he rested, the analgesic began working and the bread coated his stomach. A cigarette helped too, the heaviness eased from the damp that had been dogging him since he didn't know when because days and nights melded together and he didn't know how long he'd been in the woods. It had clung like insect paper, another irritant among his other difficulties.

Rain pelted down on him. That he remembered. When had that stopped? It was after he'd left the bike behind, wasn't it? Climbing and climbing in the dark. Slipping over wet leaves, mud and more mud, dried mud still on his boots. And mountains that kept cropping up. Square peaks of granite walls, toothy ones like an alligator's bottom jaw, gentle mounds interspersed to mitigate the harshness.

The mother tree had protected him, kept him dry. He'd slept in her arms, but for how long? The rain pattered on the leaves and he was safe. It was the thirst that drove him away from its refuge. They hadn't found him, but that didn't mean they weren't looking for him. He didn't know where he was. His pursuers must be in the area and they would know the landscape.

He had to get a move on. The longer he stayed in anyone spot, the easier for them to find him. But the rock was a natural heater collecting and holding more and more warmth as the sun grew higher, although it made his arm ache more. Judging from the sun's angle, it was about eight in the morning. He deliberated about when to start out again. He needed food badly and he needed more rest. A nap until it got cooler, a few fish, and then he'd follow the stream down. It had to intersect with a river or some other outlet.

The hunger pangs hit him again so he lit a second fag, suddenly feeling terribly thirsty. After he drained the canteen and refilled it, he closed his eyes to think things through. He was west of the Continental Divide so the water's flow would be to the West. Until he came across a town and could get hold of a map, or talk to someone who could give him directions, he'd follow the stream, let it lead him.

He didn't know how far he was from where he'd left the bike. If he'd gone in circles, easy enough to do even with a compass and a clear head, he might have end up near where he left the bike. Judging from the sun's direction, it made sense to follow the stream. At some point he'd have to intersect with a road, a highway, or a village of some kind. Hopefully, the Americans wouldn't have had the time to post WANTED signs.

This was rugged territory. He hadn't heard a car engine or a truck motor. Certainly, no human voices, just the shuffle of a thirsty beast and its snort.

He'd stick with his plan to get to Mexico via the coast highway and ship out from there. He'd follow this stream while it meandered in a southwesterly direction. It should lead him to a river and a river would lead him to a highway or a railroad.

He sucked the last bit of life out of the cigarette, tossed it in the stream, missed the fish snatching at it like vultures. The warm air made him sluggish and then the sun was on his face. It was Eden without the snake, free of sin. He wriggled his toes, lifted his arms over his head and stretched. He was still lying prone when he heard voices somewhere nearby in the woods. Like a cat, he turned on his side in the direction of the sound.

Two people showed up on the opposite bank several yards down from he'd had a face-off with the deer. A mother and her son with a fishing pole.

Part Three

Ninety-Three

Thirsty dragonflies or damselflies, maybe both, skimmed over the still pools. Like miniature blue helicopters they stopped abruptly, tapped the water, signaling food to the eager trout, and zoomed off. A contest of speed and agility between fish and insect.

"Look it how they're jumping." Tommy led the way through thick brush to get to one of the holes he'd fished out of last time, and because his gear was set to go, he immediately threw out a line.

"How'd you know this is where they'd be?" She said too loudly.

"Shh! I'll tell you later." He hopped around willows letting the line drift, his shoes made squishing sounds in the mud.

"Okay." Holding back her excitement. She had a decent seat on a log to see what he was doing.

"You do it, this time." He carried his shoes in one hand and in the other a squirming worm.

"Ugh." She grimaced. "Like it or not, you have to do it." In less than ten minutes he'd brought in two fish and he made it look simple. She'd just do what he did. Breakfast was in the crewel which she'd dropped under a tree up from the bank on one of the deer trails.

"I don't like this part of it." He rolled his eyes.

"Here. I'll do it for you. This time only." A mixture of pride and disdain in his voice. "Do you make a face and say 'Ugh," when you dig 'em up in your garden?"

"I don't skewer them. That's one thing I can tell you." He laughed out loud. "They're good for the soil. I bet you didn't know that." Putting her hands on her hips. "I cover them back up and pat the dirt down." She wouldn't go so far as to tell a teenage boy that she apologized for unearthing them.

"Nothing to putting bait on after you've done it a couple of times." He cast the rod dropping the hook precisely where he wanted midstream in a still, dark spot. "Here. You take over and hold it like I showed you. Remember?" He was her coach examining her stance. "Now look how you're standing. See how you've got your feet?"

Exasperated with his slow learner he put his shoulder against hers and stayed there.

"I can do it." She checked where her hands were on the rod, looked down to her feet and shifted them as he'd told her, and then the tip of the pole bobbed. He'd prepared her for that and she should have known what to do next.

"I got one. I got one." And then promptly lost it. He closed his eyes and shook his head.

"What did I tell you? You have to give 'em a second. Watch the end of the rod. Let them poke around on the bait until they decide they're going for it and then wait for them to bite down good and hard until you got 'em on good. That's when you jerk it back." He pulled the line in to see if she'd lost the hook, too. "It's not gonna be easier now that you yelled and let the fish know where we are."

"I forgot." Now remembering the lesson he'd given her at the cab.

"Went right out the window, didn't it? All of it." Reminding her of how her dad bawled her out because it was her fault the horses had gotten into the clover. He waited for it to sink in "Take your time. Remember? You messed up because you couldn't wait, could you?" Just as he'd done at the cab the night before, he went through the whole thing again explaining the art form of the sport, the dance, the negotiation.

"I know. I know. You already told me." She nodded impatiently while he threaded another worm onto the hook.

"You didn't lose this, anyway." Showing her the tackle. You gotta be patient, Ma'am." Now he was being formal with her again. "Don't get so excited. See that hole over there?" Pointing to another deep pool nearby. "That's where the fish are." She nodded and watched him cast the line exactly where he aimed.

When her rod jerked a second time, she yanked hard enough to snag the line on a fallen log blocking the stream. When he pulled it out it was a wadded ball and she heard him mumble something.

"Maybe I'm just no good at this." It seemed easy when she watched him.

"You don't get good if you don't keep trying." That's what she'd told him those afternoons when he was scrunched over the table, his

323

tongue twisting as he dragged a pencil across paper practicing his cursive and the tails wouldn't go the right way.

She smiled at him from under her hat brim. "You're right. You know what? I think we should've had breakfast first." Raising her eyebrows hopefully. He rolled his eyes.

"You mean eat the smelly sandwiches that you stuffed in the crewel?" He plugged his nose, but started laughing. "Real fishermen don't think about eating. Not till they're done."

"What do they think about then? You're jealous because you didn't think of it first." She taunted. He looked serious. She poked him with her elbow. "Don't be so gloomy this morning. I promise I'll do better after we eat. I will catch a fish! Come on." She'd left the rifle along with the crewel in the shade.

"I'm gonna restring the line. You go ahead."

"I'll bring it back down here. We're going to need some place to put all the fish we catch, and afterwards we have to fill the canteens."

Martin had first seen them coming out of a clump of willows. They would have spotted him on the rock if Tommy hadn't been intent on pointing out the best fishing holes. One of which was about ten feet from where Martin was. He'd slid off the rock and gone into the bushes by then.

"Now let's see if you can point out some of the good spots." While she looked around, he made the first cast, and could have snagged Martin, but the boy was an expert. He plopped the hook exactly where he wanted it into the dark water.

324

Ninety-Four

Giant water-logged timbers washed down yearly in the spring runoffs. Massive, uncompromising rocks regulated the stream's course that carved out S-shapes around the immovable objects, for living waters adapt and move on as nature dictates. At an advantageous bend upstream from where the woman and her boy were fishing, Martin crossed to their side and managed to stay well out of sight. When they quit for the day, he'd tail them, have them lead him out to a road or maybe even to a town.

Twenty feet from the stream, he caught the glint of the steel rifle barrel leaned up against a tree. The rest of the gear thrown down off the trail. Strange the pair had left all of it this far up from the bank unless they thought they were the only ones in the woods. Or, because it didn't belong to them and someone else was around.

When he heard a footfall, he jerked around, but there was no one so he grabbed the sandwiches, stuffed them into his pack along with the crumbly biscuits, and dried fruit. The smaller of the canteens was perfect, wouldn't weigh him down much. He found a hiding place among the prickly shrubs.

Tommy's feet had to feel like ice because his were pants sopping wet from having to go out on the log to get her broken line. Maybe after he'd eaten something he'd laugh about her clumsiness. "I gotta fix this mess." He griped. The hook was lodged in the wood and he kept trying to unwind the line, but the tangle was a hopeless ball of trouble. "We don't hardly have any time left to fish." He grumbled.

"Okay. I get that you're upset with me." She attempted to look sorrowful and upbeat at the same time. A new round of freckles crowded out the ones already on his nose and cheeks.

"We lost some good chances. That's all." And there went his big fish fry. It was getting too warm for the fish and for them and there was fire spotting and reports to do. "Let's catch some while we still can."

"I'll do better next time." Giving him her best smile. "Promise. It just takes practice."

"I don't care about the sandwiches."

"I know. But we have to eat. We're going to haul water up. Let's make a deal. Every time we come down for water we'll bring the pole from now on."

"Rod."

"Right. We'll bring the rod every time we have to get water. Pretty soon we'll be sick of eating fish."

"Not in a million years."

"Okay. Not in a million years. Anyway, I'm going to get our stuff. We'll have our eggs and I'll fill the containers while you fish for a bit. Just as long as we leave in time to turn in my report. You'll probably catch a bunch before I even get back here." Maybe fishermen never got enough fish. When was enough enough? Tommy could spend the night sleeping at the stream so he could have his pole in the stream before the sun came up.

She was glad he didn't argue with her. Tell her he was going to stay and fish whether she liked it or not. She didn't complain about her duties. Not like Henry calling them his ball and chain. She wished they could stay and he could fish to his heart's content. He blended with nature's other elements at the stream rooted in it as the plant life, mottled like the rocks he hopped on and between, liquid as the water.

In a clump of willows on the path, she turned to watch him doggedly working on the bungle of line but he didn't look up to see her grinning. It was a good that he didn't since his fuse was short at the moment. It was almost exquisite, an ideal way to view him, a window on the boy, half-man and his inner workings. How he'd come to her was a mystery, but not something he asked about. Even small children ask how they got there. It wasn't the same of course, and it could be that he didn't want to know. That fierce will and stubbornness were two things she was adjusting to the longer they lived together.

There had to have been someone who taught him how to fish, what places to look for them, how to maneuver the tackle. It couldn't have been his pa, her mindset wouldn't permit it to be the man who lurked in the shadows of her fear. She wasn't afraid for herself. The packer was the kind to grin and grab you by the throat. Tommy's pa possibly being on the prowl worried her, that sometime he would show up and tear the boy away. If the two of them could hang on until the summer job ended, and if she could keep him safe until then. *If.*

She came across the open crewel. The food was missing. "What in the world?" Was it a packrat? Wouldn't it have torn the crewel up and left the napkins littered around? And where was the canteen?

Then, she gasped. *Tommy's pa! It has to be.* Feeling his breath on the back of her neck it was reflex to reach for the rifle propped up against the tree. But it wasn't there! She pushed through the brush to find it but it wasn't there, and she couldn't turn around. Couldn't stomach coming face-to-face with him. How stupid of her to walk away from the gear. Tommy was in an all-fire hurry to get to the stream to find out where the fish were biting, and she'd hurried behind dumping everything to keep it cool and out of the mud.

But the rifle? She wouldn't have left it, run off without it. Would she? She couldn't have. Knowing that she had to keep an eye out for Tommy's pa. Why couldn't she remember where she left it? The missing lunch made sense. A packrat or raccoon. But the rifle?

In her mind, she tried to remember her steps, to imagine where she'd put it down. What that had felt like, certain she'd propped it up against something. Down at the stream, wasn't it, where she leaned it against a boulder being careful not to plant the butt in the mud. She refused to let it be Tommy's pa. No, she told herself. *His eyes are not staring at my back. I'm conjuring up things. I hate that man!*

Then she sighed calmly. "Of course!" Tommy must have gone back for the rifle and carried it down! She had been weighted down with the straps from the canteens and crewel. He must have come back for it!

Ninety-Five

If she yelled down, "Tommy, do you have the rifle?" He'd heckle, roll his eyes, shake his head, and he would remind her about it for weeks. "You just had to go and scare the fish away didn't you?" That aggravating kid she played cards with who deliberately threw her off, asked her as she deliberated over what card to use next, how she made her apple pie crust, or what kind of grades Homer got in school. She'd lose every time and he'd relive her errors regular as a cuckoo clock.

"Uncle! How many more times are you going to bring *that* up?" Him waving his pointer finger at her and smirking. Downright gloating as only a teenage boy can.

"Never!" The devil in his look.

"Well, I'm going to have to go down and eat crow about the rifle." A part of her hoped she would find it on the way down. Is there a spotter who doesn't talk to themselves by three weeks into the job? Maybe it was a habit already in place before they got to the mountains for the summer. The empty crewel bumped against her shoulder while she poked the toes of her boots into the bushes looking for the canteen. "It couldn't have gotten far. Maybe it was a raccoon." Or a bear dragged it off.

"What in the world?" She gasped. The barrel of her rifle glinted out at her from the bushes just off the path. How had it ended up there? Was she that careless because Tommy was an all-fired hurry to get to the fishing hole? Surely, she would have said something, reminded him of his lectures on handling the weapon. "That's not like you, Tommy." But he wouldn't have tossed it down. The goosebumps broke out like hives on her arms. It must be his pa! It felt like Fred just had dropped an ice cube down her back.

Her rifle nosing out of the clump of waist-high shrubs. She gritted her teeth, ready to kick him, clenching her fist. *Please no. Don't let it be his pa.* He must not know yet Tommy was at the creek or he wouldn't be after her. She should scream to the boy. *Run as fast as you can, Tommy.* But her mouth wouldn't move to make the words.

Only a few minutes earlier, she'd turned above the stream to admire Tommy, watched his tongue working as it did when he struggled at untangling her jumble of a line. If she had gone straight up the path, she would have caught Martin stealing the sandwiches and the rifle. A few seconds earlier and they would have collided.

She'd smiled coming up the path thinking about the boy. If she'd measured his height when he first came, drawn a line on the doorjamb, by now he'd grown at least an inch. The things he hadn't gotten from books and in school he'd he made up for in the most useful ways. Even before he'd given her all the directions on catching fish, he'd explained why the Osborne worked the way it did. This helped her understand the mechanism when before she'd simply followed the steps to get the results.

But the crewel was empty. Robbed. Martin was squatting behind a leafy screen as she sorted it out, standing over the basket, hands on hips. "A lousy packrat. Or was it a badger? Well, that's a fine kettle of fish." Her irony lost on her.

Martin pushed through the brush trailing the butt end of the rifle and warned her with a finger to his lips shaking his head. She didn't scream. Strangely, for a brief second she felt relieved. Martin had guessed she was the boy's mother, but she must be his older sister. Across the stream her face had been in shadow under the straw hat. Now, she held onto its top to look up at him, then her eyes latched onto her rifle. The muscles in her jaw tightened again and her eyes were steel balls, but he caught the faint sigh and the slight sag to her shoulders.

The boy was all spider arms and legs with a running mouth and he would scamper as soon as he saw his chance. "Keep your mouth shut." Martin warned her waving the barrel and prodding her toward the stream. A lifetime ago she was quibbling with Tommy about losing a fish, looking forward to eating eggs and spam, and collecting water. Ludicrous as it was, she came close to saying, "Why don't we share the sandwiches?" Then, she laughed out loud.

"Stop it!" They were just above the stream.

She laughed at the wrong times. It was a trait that made Fred even more angry when he yelled at her about his supper or some concocted argument.

"You're makin' fun of me!" It was her fault he hit her, not his.

Now a metal barrel was pointed at her back and she was afraid she would giggle and not be able to stop. It started as a tickle in the back of her throat that wouldn't stay there and pushed itself up into her mouth. She cleared her throat several times and pressed her lips together to hold it in.

With Fred it always ended badly. "Stop it. You stop it right now." She couldn't stop. Only after the fists came out on her, in the stomach or the kidney, often both, but not in the face, never the face. Only then it stopped and the crying started. "You was just begging to get smacked, wasn't you?"

"Keep your mouth shut." Martin commanded, but not like Fred. His accent, the low tones were more serious than a slap across the face with a wet cloth.

Tears rolled down her face. Like Tommy who doubled over when he heard or told spotter jokes. Without warning, Martin's face contorted and he flipped the rifle butt into hers waving it less than an inch from her mouth. Wolf eyes penetrated hers, remote, and cold. Both man and beast and foreign.

Like the sobs from a child told to stop whimpering, her heaves of laughter had to go through their death throes until they ended in one final moan. The ugly cylinder of the barrel, its black, sinister eye gaping at her, seemed less dangerous than the man holding it on her.

Whoever he was, he wasn't after Tommy, thank goodness. "What do you want?" She demanded. A certain stubbornness rose in her. Maybe he didn't know Tommy was with her and he could be diverted away from the boy. Her sunburnt face, the encroaching wrinkles, the snippets of gray hair from under her hat belonged to a fiercer woman than the one who'd come up the mountain in June.

"Let's go." He waved the weapon toward the stream.

Ninety-Six

"Hey, I caught five since you left. What took you so long?" His eyes fastened on the bobber as she came up behind him. He'd moved farther downstream. "We *are* eating fish for sure tonight!" The edges of a grin almost met at the back of his head, the letdown from her disappointing attempt and her failure to follow his precise instructions to bring in a fish had vanished. Above the shirt collar, the back of his neck burnished cherry red. Only minutes ago, that would have been one of her concerns for the day.

"See that!" The bobber dipped below the surface and he jerked the line back whipping a wriggling fish up on land. Immediately, he poked his finger and thumb into the tobacco can of Prince Albert to bait the hook with another worm.

The rifle bore into her spine. "You watch how I'm doing it so you get it right next time. Okay?" *Oh, If only there is a next time. If, please God, he doesn't act cocky.*

The mud squished up between his toes keeping him steady. Dragon flies dipped and drank near his line, and his skinny arms flitted like translucent wings as he cast the bobber into the inky pockets. He rocked back on his heels to complete each cycle. The bobber's red stripe danced along the water's surface, ducking and bouncing according to Tommy's instructions. The tackle didn't know he was gawky and awkward.

"Get on there, you slimy sucker." The worm struggled, gave a valiant effort to be defiant before it got skewered in three places. If he happened to turn around, he wouldn't see Martin tucked in the brush. "Would ya look at that? They're waiting for me to throw the worm at 'em." A school swarmed where he'd thrown the line in before.

"Quit pushing me." Florence snarled over her shoulder baring her teeth at Martin.

"You say somethin?" Just like Homer when he was concentrating on his homework, half listening. "Who you talking to? The man in the moon?" He laughed and pulled in the next fish.

"I know. I know." Talking to herself was her bookmark, a place holder when she went over to to-do list, and a way to keep company with herself. A reliable crutch, it highlighted the difference between being alone from being lonely.

"What'd you say was in the sandwiches?" He skewered a fresh worm.

Tommy would expect a smart aleck remark. "I thought you weren't interested in eating?" He'd been so busy nosing through his tackle in the half-light that morning, almost fretful that he'd come up short forgetting something essential.

"Answer him." Martin rebuked clearing his throat.

"I'm starving. Wow! Look at that. Another one. That makes six, now. Oh boy, oh boy. I bet your mouth is watering." Martin prodded the rifle into the small of her back. She turned halfway round and pushed it to the side. "Don't do that again." He could shoot her, but she wasn't going to be bullied.

"What'd you say?" He planted the hook farther out.

Martin poked her again. "Answer him, I said."

"I said fried eggs and spam. Don't you remember?"

"Can't you bring them down here? I'm right in the middle. They're biting like crazy. Come on and see what I caught."

"I don't..." She stuttered. "Want...to get my boots muddy." Martin punched the end of the rifle between her shoulder blades.

"That's a new wrinkle. Take your boots off, then like me." The worm got swallowed by the stream's mouth and disappeared below the surface.

"Then my feet will get muddy. Resolving to keep Tommy at a distance and away from the man pushing the rifle into her.

"You're pulling my leg, aren't you? I know what you're doing. Trying to get out of filling the canteens. But I'll do it so you can keep your tootsies dry." He laughed and wriggled his naked toes figuring she had her eyes on him which she did. "You at least gonna help haul the water back up to the cab, ain't you?"

Aren't. She said under her breath. "Who's going to haul all those fish back?" Trying to keep the fear from rising in her throat.

"And you gonna hog all them sandwiches for yourself? I'm starving." The bobber's spirit was sagging. He wiggled the line to bring it back to life, but the fish nudged feebly at it. He cast farther out.

If she went down to him, the rifle would follow. If she didn't, Tommy would come up soon enough. Either way she couldn't protect him and didn't know which was less dangerous for him.

"I thought you wanted to fish. I'll wait until you call it a day." He missed the angry bite in her voice that wasn't meant for him. "We'll have to start heading back soon, anyway." The tip of the rifle dug into her spine once more. "You about ready to go?"

"Look at that! Another one. Holy smokes. This one's a doozy. See that?" The tip of the rod dived suddenly. Tommy jerked the pole and waited. When the rod dipped again, he was sporting with the creature, first pulling just enough, then letting the line back out a bit, luring and easing off. Advancing and retreating until he brought to shore. Holding it up over the water dangling on the line, it was twice the size of the other fish.

The adolescent changing voice squeaked with joy. "Would you look at that!" Mud between his toes, freckles leaping off his sun boiled skin, and a hefty silver fish squirming on the hook before he turned and it took a moment as the scene sunk in. Before his body stiffened to catch up.

Ninety-Seven

"What's going on up there? Not like you Florence to be late reporting in." The dry air sucked the moisture from their nostrils, the cab stifling because in their haste at dawn they'd forgotten to close the shutters and the heat had seeped in.

Martin's breath on her neck added to the suffocating sensation. "I told you I was going down for water." She snapped.

"That you did. That you did." It was awkward, him repeating himself.

The phone's ringer had wailed out over the ridgeline chastising them on the loop as they came up from below.

"I've got to report in." She lengthened her stride.

"I'll be listening to everything you say. Don't think you can fool me." The ringing was so loud it hurt her ears. Martin ordered Tommy to the chair then moved next to her fixing the rifle on the boy.

At the stream, Tommy had twirled around grinning like crazy, the fish on the line and then he saw the man with the rifle. He stood in the same spot holding that fish up and for the life of him couldn't put it down. He looked at Florence, waiting for her to explain, then at the stranger and all the while that fish dangled in the air and Tommy's mouth invited in the flies.

"Fill the canteens." Martin threw them at Florence's feet. "Get going. You, kid, put your boots on." The big fish by this time doing anemic flops over Tommy's head. The rest of his lifeless catch on a string floating in the water.

"Can I get my other fish?" He squeaked nodding toward the string.

They marched single file. "We'll figure it out." Florence whispered. "Somehow." She reached for his hand.

"Stop talking. Keep your hands to yourself."

Tommy hauled up the canteens and Florence kept swallowing so she wouldn't gag on the smell coming from the crewel on an empty stomach and the sun beating down. The effect of the single cup of coffee had long worn off.

Tommy held onto his prize fish, still hooked on the line because Martin hadn't let him gut it. Dangling at the end of his rod, its struggle was over.

"I've got to get back to the cab and report in."

"Report what?" Florence told him the situation before Tommy decided to concoct some made-up story. "I work at the lookout and I have to call in on time." The man holding the rifle needed to think he could trust them. If they didn't cause trouble for him, maybe he'd be gone soon enough. She wished Tommy understood what she was doing and wasn't glaring at her.

But Tommy, as Florence guessed, had his own idea of how to get out of the fix they were in. It started slowly, the limp he manufactured, and even seemed believable.

"Don't do it." She whispered under her breath.

"I gotta rock in my boot."

"Keep moving." Martin poked him in the ribs.

"Stop that!" Tommy curled his hands into fists.

"Tommy. Knock it off!" She shook her head, but he kept limping.

"Get moving." Five hundred yards later Tommy deliberately tripped over a root coming down hard enough to bloody his knee while somehow managing to keep the prized fish from hitting the ground. She went to help him, but Martin pushed her away. *What does he think he's doing, stupid kid? She wanted to yell at him. Let me do it my way.*

"Get up." The ranger might put two and two together or the other spotters. She'd say things in a different way, laugh oddly and at the wrong times, talk too much, anything to give them enough clues to make them wonder.

The ranger sounded testy when after he pointed that she was late she barked back at him. She'd apologize, she promised herself, when this was over. He was terse even on the best of days, but he'd always been fair with her. Didn't talk down to her, lump her in the ditsy female category, and even on occasion in his off-handed manner, praised her for her work.

"No water dogs?" There'd been no time to survey her territory. She answered with a straight out lie.

335

"Nothing to report up here."

"That so? Wish that made me feel better, but it don't." She heard the ice clinking in a glass as he swallowed something. "Henry says he spotted something fishy near your area. You haven't seen nothing over there in his direction?" She reached for the field glasses half-tripping over Martin's leg in the process.

"Hold on a minute and I'll check again." Sure enough, there was something and it didn't appear to be a water dog. "Oh, my gosh!" Tommy jumped up to look but Martin was on him slamming him back down and the stool slid out from under the boy.

"What do you think you're doing? Stay away from him. You hear me?" Florence left the field glasses and the phone and went to Tommy.

"You leave him alone. Don't you ever touch him again." She whispered hoarsely.

"What's going on up there, Florence?" Martin seared her with his eyes.

"Answer him. Now!" He panted.

"I...I tripped over the stool is all. Got ahead of myself looking for what you said Henry saw."

"So, you see anything at all?" He took another swig and held his breath, waiting.

"Hold on a minute." She swallowed hard. All these months surveying, calling in reports, fretting when something looked the least bit odd or out of place. Now she had just told a lie saying things were fine, but they weren't and she hadn't been there to catch it. Oh, how Henry would gloat now.

"There's something."

"What is it?"

"I'm not sure. I'm going to take another look." Whatever it was, it was growing, which was strange as the breeze had as much life as Tommy's fish that was still on the hook, on the rod thrust into the corner.

Ninety-Eight

"I have to go to the toilet." Since Martin's invasion two days earlier, they'd lost their independence and privacy. They went to the latrine together and otherwise stayed tethered to the cab. Florence kept her mind on Homer and tried to ignore the stink from the three sweating bodies.

Martin had her lay out all the particulars of the job. "How often do you report? Show me your procedure." The phone, visitors, who she talked to regularly, her logs, what information she passed on and to whom.

"That's the Osborne fire finder." Martin pointed at the strange device. Tommy groaned as she attempted to explain how it worked.

"Why is your son here?"

"My son isn't here!" Then realized he meant Tommy. Tommy laughed out loud.

"He...he... Oh, he's learning the ropes. Seeing if he wants to be a spotter when he's old enough."

"What's he do?"

"He...he makes some meals and cleans up. Takes care of things that come up."

Martin eyed Tommy. "Is that so?"

Tommy shrugged. "Yeah. I guess so."

"Why'd you say he isn't here when he is?"

"He...he, well, he likes to stand on his own two feet."

"Oh, yeah? If you're thinking of trying something stupid boy, don't. That is *if* you don't want your mother to get hurt." Tommy nodded.

"He won't!" Florence snapped.

"Same goes for you." Florence nodded.

"I won't." She kept her eyes down and her mouth shut.

Martin didn't sleep. If he napped, they didn't see it. Not even in the heat of the day when dreaminess overtook the cab. Beyond the scope of the job, or preparing meals and keeping things tidy, the walls seemed to be closer than ever.

337

The vegetables were at their peak and it was Florence's favorite moment when her labors showed results, but with Martin and Tommy crowded into her private space, and a rifle eyeing her movements, she couldn't dash out to mother her plants. Tommy and she wrote to Homer and played Hearts and followed the life of Henry's fire that the fire fighters couldn't get put out, although the wind was not aiding it.

"You sure missed that one, Flo." Henry shined that evening. Florence tapped her boot against the leg of the chair.

"Lay off, would you, Henry? Don't pay him no mind, Flo." Don't look like no big deal down there, anyhow."

"You're saying that cuz plain and simple you are a old jealous fart, George. Sorry, Flo." She shook her head. Martin kept his eyes on her. One word, just one and he'd rip the phone out of the wall. He figured she wouldn't say anything to endanger the boy.

The boy's face lit up when the spotters came on that evening and the disappointment from the trip to the stream faded. Florence spent the whole afternoon watching the fire and calling in the latest report.

"Can I make some lunch?" They'd gone without breakfast and then there was the commotion about the fire when they got back to the cab. Florence was too worked up to feel hungry and Tommy was pinned to the chair feeling his stomach go around and round. Martin nodded and followed him into the galley.

"No knives." Tommy put the prize fish in the white enamel basin on the tiny countertop and if he'd been a girl, he would have cried because he had to toss it out but not near the cab where a bear would feast on it. He dumped a can of beans in a pot to warm.

Martin had eyes everywhere. The cab fitted one person but two could manage fairly well. Not three. Tommy filled bowls with leftover cornbread, looked at his feet when he handed Martin his. Florence picked at hers standing over the Osborne table when she wasn't pacing past the windows with her field glasses. The glacial German wolfed his down as if someone had stolen *his* breakfast.

Their eyes discreetly watched him. He put the empty bowl down and sat on a chair with his back to the wall. Florence was tormented over not spotting the fire. That wouldn't have happened if she'd kept the rifle with her, hadn't swallowed Tommy's eagerness like it was a feast of chocolate cake.

Tommy eyed her as she moved about. She was a bird hopping to and from the nest. "I'll take over. Go ahead and finish eating." Martin shook his head and pointed him back to the stool.

"You just keep sending those reports, Florence." The ranger told her mid-afternoon without a hint of blame at missing the signs of the fire. "The men think they'll get a handle on it. Might be out before tonight." She was close to tears and sank against the window sill.

The long, late afternoon shadows stretched out the pines making them seem longer than they were tall. Martin let Tommy practice his writing. The boy looked like a kindergartner the way he held the pencil.

"I need to water the garden." Martin turned as if just discovering she was in the room. There had been few words between them but by her tone, she let him know she wasn't asking permission.

"Where is it?" She pointed out the window. "Let's go." He motioned to Tommy whose mouth was forming a capital "F."

"We need the water." She nodded to the canteens dumped by the fishing pole. Martin signaled Tommy to get them and she saw the blood stain on the shoulder of his shirt. Not the maroon color of old blood, but not bright red or oozing. Caked on. Of course, she'd missed seeing it. After facing down the barrel of the rifle, she'd kept her eyes to herself when she could.

He hadn't taken his jacket off earlier so she couldn't have seen it. In the sweltering room, the three humans added more heat to an already overheated cab. With his jacket on, he had seemed human. Her thinking was that he would be gone soon enough despite the fact the rifle was constantly aimed on them. Surely, there wouldn't be any reason for him not to be on his way.

Her knees felt like they would give way under her. She had been foolish thinking he was simply a thief who needed food and whatever he could steal from them. Suddenly, he became as sinister as the insomniac eye of the rifle barrel.

"Let's go." He saw it in her eyes. "I said, let's go!"

Ninety-Nine

Henry's fire smoldered for a week, stagnating but steadfast. The fire crew dug a three-foot-deep trench around its perimeter and removed all the provocative fuels. Yet, it lived on acting the cornered rabbit, then when the men started packing up thinking it safe to leave it belched back to life like Lazarus and spewed out arcs of flame. A skeleton crew staying on to babysit, grumbling at the lousy luck of being kept away from real action and chewed on their mustaches waiting for the fire to take its last gasp. The bulk of the crew hiked off to other sites yet to be classified.

Sail boaters on Flathead Lake some sixty-five miles to the south put up their spinnakers pleading for even a slight breeze, while at the station the ranger stewed and unwrapped the third melting Baby Ruth of the day. If Mother Nature meant to hold back for the big event it would be a real whopper with the meadows and open fields of waist-high grasses that crackled like newspaper. The woods were a gigantic matchbox and the ultimate target for a single bulls' eye lightning strike, a careless cigarette butt, or one mindless camper cooking fish over an open fire and abandoning it to die out on its own.

"My fire." Like it was his newborn, Henry delighted in the daily update that brought his fire to the forefront. George and Joe were diligent as firefighters, too on those insufferable evenings, ready to extinguish the flames of bragging.

"Sluggish." The ranger said in part relieved by the progress of Henry's fire, but mostly irritated and suffering from his ballooning hemorrhoids. "You watch it and keep the reports coming." Chiding Florence and Henry. "Any sign of life from up there, you get it called in." That was rhapsody to Henry's ears and a satisfying substitute for his detective novels and for keeping him at his observation post looking through field glasses into the black darkness, watching for a spark. At 3:00 am the excitement waned and in distress he had to leave his post to make coffee.

"Don't make no sense to me." George spoke for all of them, except Henry, at the decision to leave a tiny crew down there guarding it. "If

I was you, Flo, I'd spend my time spotting everything else. Forget what the ranger says." Florence didn't say a word. She'd been too quiet since Henry reported "his" fire, the man who gobbled up Phillip Marlowe's attitude ferreting out crooks, like it was a stack of pancakes. But Henry couldn't spot hurt feelings. The other boys did what they could to buoy her disappointment.

"Remember that first fire? The one you called in, Flo?" George encouraged.

"I do." Martin poked her to get her to answer.

"How about you singing us one of them lullabies tonight, Flo?" Joe's voice glassy smooth as McDonald Lake on a calm day.

Martin's eyes on her, his breath on her neck when she was on the line. His beard thicker now, looked redder as the evening sunlight caught the lower jaw in its sinking path, rubbed against her cheek. He signaled her to go ahead. She recoiled at its scratchiness.

"Yeah, Flo. You ain't sung for us in a long time. How long's it been Henry?"

"How in the hell would I know." The binoculars glued on his fire as the sun's tail dipped behind the peaks.

"Sorry, Flo." George's pattern that started in June to protect her from the men's language. Some unspoken and sappy notion these men had that girls grew up and went momentarily deaf at a curse word. Women were half the blame for putting up an innocent front to any marriageable male that they were safe, prim, fresh. When George apologized for Henry because that's where the cursing usually came from, she was touched. They were like the caring brothers her friends had growing up. George's support was a glass of lemonade on a hot day before knowing she was even parched.

Henry didn't change. George continued to apologize over the summer, but her shoulders tightened with every, "I'm sorry, Flo." Singled out and separated like a dunce, not a part of them and they didn't even know they did it. It was the right thing, the polite thing, the manly thing. She was a *woman* spotter they had to watch over, be on their good behavior with, and like the poison ivy that spread over her arms the summer of her eighth grade, the invasive itch inching up the elbows, a remedy was needed.

Then Martin showed up. Every movement, every step put in a measuring cup, observed, calculated, and poured out. A trip to the toilet accompanied by two spectators. The sharp objects in the kitchen stuffed into the jute sack after dumping out a month's worth of onions. Tommy wouldn't miss them until he took his first bite of Mulligan stew. The enforcer stood over her. She couldn't fathom how he stayed awake watching them even while they slept.

"Damn it, George." She suddenly sobbed. "Would you just stop apologizing for once?" Henry sucked his breath in so hard you could hear it on the line. Then he whispered out loud, "Jesus, Flo. I guess that means you ain't gonna sing no lullaby tonight." Henry thought that would make them laugh, but they didn't.

After a long pause George said, "I'm sorry, Flo." Someone gasped, maybe Joe.

She took a deep breath. "No, no. I'm sorry boys. Don't know what got in to me tonight." She swallowed the sobs, but they kept coming. Hiccups would come next. Martin reached for the phone.

"Maybe another time, then?" She barely heard Joe.

"Maybe." She whispered, but only to herself because the line went dead.

One Hundred

It didn't knock her flat, but his fist on her jaw left the receiver swinging at the end of its noose.

"Fred." She whimpered. The crack rattled her skull sending her eyes lurching away from the blow and she doubled over to vomit.

"Here!" Tommy moved too quickly to be stopped, flew off the stool and grabbed the white enamel basin with the red trim and shoved it under her mouth, and just that quick turned and charged Martin's stomach snorting with his head lowered like a bull. Martin coldcocked him in one move, a thud like he'd hit a punching bag. She grasped at her stomach as if she'd taken the blow. That was followed by a quiet, airy sound as light as Tommy's notebook fluttering and falling to the floor with a muffled thud.

"Oh, no. Tommy!" Wiping her mouth with her sleeve, blood dripping from her nose. "You bastard!" His back was to her and she peppered it with her fists coughing and choking from the blood. He brushed her off, nothing more than a horsefly, grabbed her arms holding them up over her head. She spit on him and saw the venom in his eyes when he raised his fist at her.

It didn't matter. The line was crossed. Fred had knocked her around many times and she absorbed all of it. It was her deal with him. As long as he kept his hands off Homer. She'd leave him if he ever touched the boy. There was no distance between calm and chaos because Martin didn't give them the chance to steel themselves to his violence. Blood trickled down her chin and Tommy was a heap of discarded laundry in the corner.

"Don't you touch him again." Her growl speckled with blood accented the front of his shirt. He let go of her and retreated a few steps from it and the sticky fingers. Her warning slurred past a tongue of plump, swollen sausage, that of a drunkard speaking. He stepped back in to block her from moving toward the boy.

"Get out of my way." A pummeled face looked up at him, sneering, daring him to hit her again "Let me by!" He raised his fist, and then pulled it back.

"Don't try anything!"

"He's unconscious you idiot." As she pushed past him, the acrid tobacco breath brushed against her cheek. The bloodshot eyes followed her to the lifeless bundle.

"Tommy, Tommy." She murmured lifting his head onto her lap like it was a ripe cantaloupe. He sighed, a tender child in the middle of an enchanted dream. The sometimes furrows in his brow were wiped clean, the worries erased, no drunken pa chasing after him, hunting him down, no looking over his shoulder, permanently watching his back.

His limbs had somehow tangled when he went down, an arm under a leg, the other leg holding them hostage. She uncoiled them, delicate threads that could unravel the whole body if she was too hasty, murmuring, "Open your eyes, Tommy," gagging again on her own blood. She swallowed it and wiped her face with her sleeve.

The moments passing were captured in a vacuum. Maybe an hour, or a minute or ten when he finally moaned. She held her breath. He moaned and squinted. Florence was over him, holding his head, his eyes demanding they stay closed. He scrunched up his face and pried them open and blinked them repeatedly like flashing caution lights.

"You're awake." Salty tears mixed with blood dripped onto his face and he pushed her away and tried to sit up.

"Don't!" He fell back into her lap.

"Are you all right?" The color was coming back and he stretched his legs out. His memory was returning too and the reason for her bleeding, but not why he was lying on the floor.

"What happened?" She put a blanket under his head nodding toward Martin.

"Oh, yeah." Tommy's face turned red. He had failed as David against Goliath. Useless. He'd let her down. His face contorted in an expression she didn't recognize, a victim's look, greedy for revenge. She used her body as a curtain between the boy and Martin so the gunman did not see what she'd read in Tommy's face. Then, like a hungry newborn colt, the boy bolted up, his hands folded into fists, his mouth squeezed into hatred.

344

She tried to stop him, but a stabbing pain shot through her eye. "Leave it." She shouted shaking her head to push past the pain. His mouth was set. "Leave it. Not now, Tommy. Not now."

"Listen to your mother!" Martin growled dancing a quadrille away from the boy.

"Who are you? What do you want with us? Why don't you leave us alone?" Florence snapped. Her head was splitting. She was unrepentant, furious. He could break her neck in a second and the boy's but she egged him on anyway, taking the attention away from the boy. First her, then the boy. He'd take over their shelter and their food and have a brief respite.

Except that he needed her to stay in contact with the ranger and the other spotters. She knew Tommy was her weak link and that Martin would exploit it at the right moment.

He sat back down on the chair as if he'd come back from an evening's stroll, the bright ember sparking from the end of the cigarette, steady, unrelenting. He gauged Tommy's rage, a boy his age bound to do something foolish.

When she lay down on her cot, the crashing pain smashed inside her head and the room circled round and round. The one regular thing was the blink from his cigarette, a beacon in the dark. She had to puke, pushed it down and made herself breathe slowly in and out and ached for the aspirin in a cubby by the sink. She was too mad to cry.

One Hundred and One

Tommy banged the coffee pot as the diagonal morning fingers of light scurried across the stovetop, the clanging like the church bell's knocker against the bones inside her skull. It was peculiar for him to wake her this way. With Tommy living there her first taste each day was the scent of coffee brewing. Either it was her aching head bolting her to attention or Tommy was working himself up to the boiling point and that would end in something disastrous. *Oh, God. Don't let today start like this.* Goose bumps surged from her toes up to her arms.

She had managed the early nighttime hours without aspirin by pressing her hand against the drumming inside her head and counting the throbbing heartbeats. Gradually the pain and queasiness backed down and instead of the pitch-black cab, now the sun filled the room. There was no solace now that the pretense was gone. She'd spent how much of the night watching the bursts of flame from the corner where he puffed on his cigarettes. Surely, he had to sleep sometime. Tommy whimpered in a dream but didn't seem to be in pain, then rolled onto his side and smacked his lips and his breathing grew even.

Squirrels climbed to their railroad yard on the tin roof during the night, crisscrossing and rat-a-tat-tatting from one end to the other on needle sharp claws. It was vexing and reminded her of her yearly climb into the attic during the bitter cold months carrying baited traps that could snap a finger with one wrong move. The monotony of the scampering squirrels and the flaring embers from the cigarettes helped her drift off sometime during the night while clutching her boot to her chest. Did she really think she could beat the intruder off with it? It ended up as her pillow.

In a dream, she and Fred and Homer were visiting a quaint European city. The train had deposited them into a cobblestone city square filled with immaculately painted historic buildings. Fred massaged her back and laughed about the cricks in their necks from craning to see the cathedral spire, its foundation sucked up most of the town's center.

"Makes me dizzy." Fred rubbed his own neck.

"Come on. Let's climb up there!" Homer pointed to the gnomes waving from the bell tower like floating black dots above.

"Oh, I don't know about that. Why don't you go ahead?" Florence looked with longing at an empty bench nearby.

"No!" Homer insisted. "We'll do it together or not at all." The hundred or more cement steps wrapped inside solid walls up the spiral staircase. Fred called out the steps by number, rapid as bullets flying. After twenty of them, he stopped for breath and the final count when they reached the top was unknown and forgotten by the view. "Oh! How wonderful." She squeezed her back tight against the wall and away from the parapet.

"Aren't you glad we did it?" Homer shouted over the medieval city. Florence peeked at the red roof tiles and row after row of chimneys from her perch. Fred marveled at the tricky corners with odd bends and angles that had mastered the elevation and steep walls.

Homer called out the names of distinctive buildings, his face shining as he rattled off their histories, the construction dates, and the influence of each architectural period. The guide book was his assistant when he was uncertain of facts or dates.

The sky suddenly became foreboding, the wind whipped her scarf and the belt on her raincoat, teasing the ends. Fred put his hand up to hold his bowler on tight. There was the smell of rain before it rains, and something else, something ominous. She looked at Fred. Homer was telling a story of the local Burgermeister who'd started a beer drinking rivalry centuries earlier. Homer's anecdotes to this point had made them laugh and wonder, but now she and Fred exchanged a glance. He nodded and they pretended to listen to Homer, though in her dream, Florence questioned whether Fred recognized as she did, the urgency.

"Something ain't right." He whispered walking past her, she was still holding onto the wall. Homer's nose was inside the guide book and he was flipping pages to check his facts.

Fred's ruddy color, the robust, outdoor man used to working in bitter storms, turned ashen. She was confused. Was it a premonition? Was he sick, did he have a cramp? His heart? The bravado on the

347

steps coming up and then quickly going silent. Too much belly, too much beer, a smoker since he was ten. He looked her in the eye and she knew it wasn't about him when she saw the fear that he shared and didn't want Homer to see.

"We need to leave!" It felt like a scream as she said it because it hurt her throat, but Homer either didn't hear her or he chose to refer to his source book about some detail that now seemed ridiculous. "Let's go!" She screamed again and pulled on Homer's jacket. He pushed her away. "Don't do that!" He yelled down at her. He seemed so tall, taller than she realized. He towered over her and scowled.

Whether it was Tommy's clattering or the dream petering out, she didn't know but it lingered even when she smelled the coffee. If she could go back to sleep as she wished and finish the dream, she'd get Homer out of danger. She felt the taste of it, over the flavor of the coffee. The taste of danger and her eye started to ache again and the memory of being hit. Maybe he'd broken her nose. The blood caked in her nostrils had dried during her sleep and it stuck to her skin like glue. Her jaw hurt, but her nose seemed all right.

She got up on her elbow to take the cup and whispered to Tommy, but it was Martin instead.

One Hundred and Two

"Here!" He barked pressing the heated cup at her, the vapor grazing the bottom of her chin. She tried to pull up the blanket, but she'd fallen asleep on it and the one loose corner wasn't long enough to cover her or the blood-coated shirt front.

"I don't want it." She turned her head away from the only other man to ever approach her bed. Fred would kill him.

"Take it." It was a small dog's bark, somewhere between an order and a request. She tugged once more on the corner of the blanket to no avail and smelled tobacco mixed with sweat and something else, something earthy and herbal, like sage or thyme. She turned her head away.

Upright now against the bedpost, she studied a knothole's dark eye in the floorboard that a ray of sun was heading toward and would soon expose. His breath was on her neck again, his skin too near hers. Although they'd squeezed together in the cab for days, they'd kept invisible lines between them despite the trips to the latrine, changing clothing, or washing up.

His forearm was a mat of bronze curly hair. "Drink it." He held the cup in his palm, the piano fingers wound around its curve, and he cleared his throat to stifle a cough. Absurd as it was, she began counting again. To herself. The knotholes on the floor and the walls. Thirteen of them while he stood over her. Would he hit her again if she didn't take the cup? Before drifting off during the night, he had smoked five cigarettes, a puff once every minute, firefly sparks in the dark. She knew because she counted to sixty in the pauses. He was like a clock.

Eternity came and went. The first knothole was overtaken and laid bare, the relentless beam moving on to ferret out other boards, other knotholes. He had hit her once, smacked her dignity and her jaw, knocked Tommy into a senseless puddle, and now had made her a mug of coffee.

Fred left her face alone, he'd just edge up to the line, a fictitious electric fence holding back his knee-jerk mad dog temper. He never went for her head, or struck Homer, and wouldn't know what to do with a coffee pot.

The man with no name watched. Ever since he'd shown up, he owned their every move, trespassed into their thoughts, foresaw before they did what they would say or do. A calculator, he added up things to get to the bottom line, but didn't let them know when he got to the total.

Old feelings returned, the building blocks long ago fixed one brick at a time from living with a husband who got lost somewhere along the way inching along and veering off course, growing more belligerent as his path became more and more overgrown. She tried to push it away, that familiar gnawing and the memory of the many moments when she had prepared, plotted to keep Fred calm.

But that's the trouble with old problems left unresolved. They pop up like a teenager's pimples. The heat, the stagnant air, the inertia, not knowing what strategy was needed or what would happen next, made it all come back in full force and with it the sense of a paralysis that had held onto her in her previous life. At the lookout, that bundle of feelings had evaporated by July, went away like steam from the kettle that disappears into thin air. Now, here they were again. She'd duped herself thinking she had become a whole a new person, and now she was back to playing cat and mouse and this time it wasn't with Fred. She feared for Tommy who, like Homer, would have his own ideas. She tried to pass signals to him. A raised eyebrow, or puckered lips, a quick shake of the head. *Duck and stay down.* Homer might agree to do what she asked, but Tommy didn't have the history she and Homer shared or the private code.

She took the coffee. She had to, felt helpless as if she was down with the measles and it was required. Whatever his motive, he wasn't blubbering and bawling like Fred and the outcome of what came next would not rest on whether or not she took the coffee.

The steam stung at her nostrils making her eyes water. The first sip bit her swollen tongue and the heat felt soothing. Another sip. She swished it around her mouth as it cooled while he stood over her waiting for her to empty the cup. It was by far the best tasting coffee she'd had, but she'd keep that to herself.

The boot meant to protect her during the night ended up under the cot and before she retrieved it, she ran her fingers through her hair, wiped the dried blood off her face. He rinsed out the utensils. Tommy was breathing through his mouth, snoring away on his blanket. Martin poked him with his boot. "Time to get up." He wasn't gruff, nor was he gentle. Florence held her breath until Tommy sat up with a blank look. He didn't have his go-to-battle face on. She needed to go to the bathroom.

"We're going down for water." Martin told Tommy to his back while he sautéed onions and garlic for the scrambled eggs. The smell wafted up into the cupola and her mouth watered. Her tongue felt better, not so thick, and the salt would help. She'd take an aspirin for the headache.

"Okay." Tommy grumbled scraping the breakfast onto plates. Florence heard the anger waking up in him.

"You want to take your fishing gear?" Florence nearly slipped off the last rung on the ladder, would have if she hadn't been holding on.

Tommy rubbed his eyes, confused and looked at Florence to give him a nod or a frown. She didn't know what to make of it either. A slight shrug. If he was messing with the kid all the cemented building blocks would fall out from under her. She held onto the ladder when her feet were back on the floor in the cab.

"All right." Tommy smiled down at the three plates.

"You get your things together." Martin took the plates to the table.

They would be getting a late start. Tommy wouldn't have enough time to fish because she had to be back to report on Henry's fire.

"Just fifteen minutes." Martin answered the question she had yet to raise. "No more." His expression blank. "Tell the ranger you're going down for water."

351

One Hundred and Three

Five minutes at the stream and Tommy had pulled in five fish. "Just look at them, Ma'am!" The intruder had burrowed between them in their relationship, pierced their easy familiarity, stolen it from them like he'd taken their picnic lunch and rifle. He observed the pair from a stump.

Halfway into the stream, she submerged the second canteen. He waved the dangling catch on a string over his head, shimmering silver flags. Florence caught the defiance, the canny jab not calling her by name, the barely veiled hostility, what was he thinking? She chuckled to mask her dismay. As usual, he leaned too far over on the boulder, so sure of himself, no fear for the rocks below or a mad man either. Last night one punch had knocked him senseless, left her with a bruised and swollen face, but apparently Tommy wasn't finished with round one.

Her bare toes tunneled under the yellow, green, red pebbles in the chilly water numbing her feet while she considered the rifle. How Tommy had fussed at her, scowled at how she handled it. It wasn't that long ago, but it was another century.

"You plannin' on killing one of us?" He'd badgered her. "Nothin' to play around with, you know? Didn't nobody teach you?"

"Anybody."

"Huh?" His carelessness would have been fodder for Miss Conrad who would target the protégé, rooting her point home, no dilly dallying because the matronly teacher would not play the smart Alec to him in the next breath as Florence often did.

He grinned from atop the boulder and her heart fell into her stomach. Martin saw every glance, every inch they covered between them for he was the third corner of the triangle. The constant sentinel.

"You watch. Next one's gonna be a whopper!" As if it was that simple, catching fish when she was sure he was planning the attack on the man holding a rifle. Was she reading too much into what Tommy was saying?

Random puffy clouds like a quilt wadding up the lavender sky assured a day with no thunderstorms. The liquid morning was heating up, and there was no trace of a breeze. The woods slept on, the stream tinkled, a steady patter beating against logs making its way through and over fallen brush butting against ungiving rocks. The flies, like the intruder, never slept.

"I'll believe it when I see it." She laughed in spite of the clenched stomach, pulled off her hat and tossed it onto the bank before plunking her face into the stream and keeping it in. The throbbing in her head stopped right away, her eyes and nose burned from the cold, the ripples lapped at her face cleansing away the last bits of dried blood. For a moment she was like the fish submerged in this water world free from the turmoil above as long as they didn't bite on an inviting hook. She gasped and came up shaking her hair and cocking her head like a dog. Martin's eyes followed her. Bareheaded, she finished filling the canteens and let her hair air dry in the sun.

The pulsing ache was back in her head. His footsteps were directly behind her when Tommy whooped and hollered. "Holy smokes. Would you look at that!" His pole bent almost in half. "I told you I was gonna get the whopper. Didn't I?" A brief flicker on Martin's face.

Tommy was half dancing. "Pay attention to what you're doing" She shouted and then the pole went straight. From her angle, the scrawny silhouette stick figure straddling a dark boulder, held onto a stick that stuck out over the stream. The tackle appeared to be intact, not snagged on a drowned log.

"What the heck?" Tommy wailed. Martin looked at his watch, his lips gripping a cigarette,

"Let's go."

"For goodness sake, give him a minute." Martin's head snapped around so she must have said it out loud. Tommy began reeling in and then the end of the pole took another deep dive.

"Look at that!" Tommy hollered. "It's still on there!" The fish jerked to life, angry as a tuna leaping three feet out of the water overpowering the rod.

"Come on, Tommy. Reel it in." Florence rooted. "Don't lose it now."

The pole shimmied and shook and it was yanked again. Then again. The rod was no match for the creature flying out of the water like a missile that could in one single jerk split it in half. Tommy's toes dug into the rock scraping the skin raw underneath and with his bony arms tucked tightly against his body, he held on.

It was a game. It was war. When the fish stopped jumping Tommy snorted like he'd just outsmarted it in a game of Hearts. The line went limp and he let out some line then reeled it back a bit to see if the hook was firmly set. The fight was gone, but it was still on the line. Tommy fed out more line, reeled it back in, gradually bringing the line closer to shore.

He was in shadow, but in sunlight he would have that haughty grin, his victory smirk, a well-deserved triumph. "I'm gonna land him and I'm gonna fry him up. Hey, he won't fit in the pan, will he?"

"That could be a problem." She laughed. Martin cleared his throat.

"We could feed an army on this one." The fish was at the bottom of the boulder now, ten feet below him. He only had to reel it up out of the water. "This is gonna be the best supper you ever had." He promised, reeling in the line, but two feet above the water the fish came to life again. The game wasn't finished after all.

"Look out!" Florence screamed as Tommy started to slip off the edge of the boulder. The mad fish gyrated at the end of the line. "Let it go!!" He would not. One foot dangled like it was a puppet's leg attached to a string off the edge.

"Let it go!" Martin commanded. Tommy kept sliding and grabbing for a handhold with one hand, the rod still in the other. "Let it go!" Martin and Florence yelled at the same time.

Tommy   held   on.

One Hundred and Four

It had happened before, wishing hard for something, even getting on her knees and praying for God to intervene, or being driven to search the sidewalks for an upturned penny as a sure sign, or hearing a promising buzz from a hummingbird in her garden before it fluttered off to another flower. Generally, God and hummingbirds failed to deliver even the most elemental wishes and other people got to the pennies ahead of her. If by chance a prayer here or there was answered, the intervening time between the wish and its outcome left it potent as a used up firecracker.

And she wasn't even wishing to get the rifle back. All she wanted was the intruder gone and to pick up where they'd left off before he came.

"Just look at what you did." Tommy would berate. "We had our chance and you blew it." Of course, he'd say that because it wasn't his stomach up in his throat. It was hers watching him slip off the boulder toward the rocks. He'd have passed up the rifle, too, if he'd seen her in trouble. Sure, she could have grabbed it off the pathway as she ran to help him, bent down and picked it up, slipped the strap over her shoulder and aimed it at Martin's back. Instead, she sped over it to get to Tommy before he crashed and she was right on Martin's tail sliding over mud and slippery roots.

A breeze came up after they got back that pushed the stifling air out of the cab and cleansing as a floor freshly scrubbed with Clorox. Tommy couldn't for the life of him sit still while working on his writing. Up off the chair, back down again looking at Florence. She squeezed her eyebrows together and mouthed, "What?" He jerked his head.

She poked at the fish during supper after Tommy banged the sizzling frying pan against the stovetop, greasing spitting out, while humming in monotone. Like a toothless old lady, she teased the flesh away from the fish bones with her fork and thought of her gentle uncle who when she was a kid had gotten a bone stuck in his throat and ended up in the hospital. What would they have done to get it out, she wondered?

The wind started picking up. "That'll cool things down." A tiny chill came on when it started banging the window frames against the screens, and she put her jacket on.

It turned out Tommy hadn't been in danger at the stream. From where they had watched, he seemed to be sliding onto the rocks. There was the other thing, too. Martin had screwed up leaving the rifle to help Tommy. He sat cross-legged on the floor in Tommy's previous favorite spot, before Martin cold-cocked him, and wolfed down a good-sized bite of the boy's monster fish and scowled wiping his greasy hands on his pants.

Florence didn't look forward to a repeat performance with the spotters that evening. What if she had taken the rifle? Would she have shot him in the back? What if he had gotten to Tommy before she stopped him? Would he have tossed the boy over or used him as a shield?

It just happened there was a ledge below and when Martin got to Tommy he was reeling in his catch. They thundered onto that boulder and he snapped at them. "Stop it! You'll scare him away!"

Martin growled and turned on his heels almost knocking her onto the ledge when he brushed past her and Florence knew he wouldn't make another blunder. Tommy gutted the mutant fish and arranged his tackle and the minutes dragged past. She wouldn't tell him about the rifle. He was head-over-heels with his catch, anyway. "Just look at the size of him, Ma'am!"

"Let's go!" Martin snarled from the bank pointing the rifle's mouth at the canteens lined up ready to be packed up. Tommy's head was full of fish talk on the way back. He chattered on and on. "Do you remember the first one I caught? I thought that one was the whopper. Boy, was I wrong." He giggled. "Did you see how I was playing the big one?" Florence nodded. "Honest? Did you really see it?"

"Enough! Shut up about it, kid." Tommy whimpered. He went silent, but ten minutes later he couldn't contain himself. "I didn't never think about them fish being so big."

"Double negative." They'd gone over that point when he was drafting letters to Homer. This must be what it was like for Miss Conrad and her students. It was stupid and senseless now anyway.

They ate too much of the fish. Tommy dredged it in cornmeal and added a lot of grease to the pan. The smell of it turned her stomach, but she smiled as he fried up the last pieces. "Here's another one." They shook their heads.

"You're late." The ranger grumbled. Too long sitting in the same spot day after day.

"Would you believe I ran into a bear?" It was easy to lie when it could be worse. You could get slugged.

"Well, hell, girl. Did you take your rifle?"

"Sure did." Martin smelled of grease. "It was a mother bear, though. Didn't want to get between her and the cub."

"Damn it. You shoulda shot her. I'd better send someone up there, then. Get rid of her before she shows up and makes more trouble." Martin breathed hard on her neck.

"Oh, she took off after a bit. Not the least interested in me. I think she was headed to that huckleberry patch on the south side of the ridge."

She couldn't get the rifle out of her mind. If she had to do it over, if she had fifteen chances to do it over, nothing would change.

Martin had grabbed what he thought was a flailing arm, the size of a twig. The boy was sinew and no meat. The arm that was still connected to the rod. He would have gone over and into the rocks holding onto his tackle.

"Stop it!" Tommy bellowed. The fish stopped wriggling when he pulled it up on the ledge.

One Hundred and Five

"So, Flo. What happened with the bear?"

"I chased her over your way, Henry. To keep you company." That should have gotten a chuckle.

"What bear?" Tommy asked in his fish-whispering voice. "Oh, *that* bear." He giggled.

"Quiet." Tommy made a face. "Don't." Florence put her mouth away from the receiver.

"You watch what you say tonight." Her tongue was thick and numb and her temples throbbing. Did he really think her that stupid? The spotters filled in the blanks from what they picked up on the line but they didn't ask her. "Hey, Florence, why you talking like that? Like you're gagging on a tongue depressor."

"Well, son-of-a-gun, Flo." Henry sounded irked.

"Oh, for cripes sake, Henry, can't you take nothing with a grain of salt? Flo is teasin' you, ain't you Flo?"

"Uh huh."

"Leave it to you to get your knickers all tied up about some bear that's probably hightailed it over to Glacier by now. You know how fast they run?"

"Spare me your version of the facts, George.

"Faster than your pickup."

"What do you know about my pickup? I can get it up to 70 and no bear is gonna keep up with that."

"That so?" George let the fact dangle. "You worried that bear is gonna take a shine to you? That ain't gonna happen. Florence was just trying to do you a favor. Fill the lonely nights." George chuckled.

"I haven't seen anything over here. Maybe she's headed your way, George. What do you say to that?"

"Better have your rifle ready, in any case." Joe cautioned.

"Sing us a song, would you, Flo?"

"Good idea, George. We're down to the last two weeks and we're sure gonna miss your music, ain't we fellas?" Joe who had kept things upbeat all summer long. He sounded like he had just run out of spunk. "You planning on coming back next year, Flo?"

"I don't know. I'll just have to see, I guess. What about you?"

"I'll be back. Turned in my request for this lookout."

"Haven't made up my mind, yet." No need to read Henry's tea leaves. June had gotten to him. He about cracked up with the fog closing in so tight he felt the breath squeezed out of him. The weather had been hard on them all, but for Henry, even when the days warmed up and the sun lifted their spirits, the suffocating reminder lingered.

"Wind's coming up over here. You getting any of it? Hang on. I gotta close the window." George's cab sat on the flat surface of a boulder that towered over the valleys. No trees grew around it to act as a barrier to the weather so he had the least protection from the elements. It was the bellwether for the other cabs. "Anybody else feeling the temperature drop, yet? Almost chilly over here. We could be in for a big one tonight."

"We could go out in a blaze of glory. If all hell breaks loose. Sorry, Flo." Henry had only one wish before the season was over and that was to spot a raging fire.

"Your fire's pretty much out from what I've been watching." She'd observed it faithfully as she'd been told to do and it wasn't smoldering any longer. She hadn't needed to call in frequent updates for a few days.

"I don't know." Henry clung to the hope it might still blow up, but the men had broken camp and moved on.

Florence felt lightheaded all that evening as though she was seeing through gauze, a curtain in front of her eyes. She was queasy as well, and that had gotten worse since she'd eaten the greasy fish. Tommy belched frequently and tittered when he did. His prize catch hadn't set well with either of them. Martin's smoke made the air feel close with the windows shut.

They trooped single file to the outhouse before the daylight completely faded. The days were getting shorter and trooping single-file down the path in the dusk accentuated a longing she'd buried after Martin arrived. Maybe it was because of her sick stomach, but she pined for something. Something that was fading away, disappearing. She feared it had to do with Homer, or Tommy.

George had warned of a storm, but the sky was crystal clear. Venus twinkled over the peaks, the moon rising as a giant orange ball. She felt like throwing up, had been nauseated the night before. This could have carried over, the after effects of being hit in the face. Her nose felt sore, and she had a blue-black smudge under her left eye, and her cheek was swollen and red. It had felt so good to put her head in the icy stream, but now her face felt on fire and her head pounded at her temples. Her shirt clung to her back and in her armpits although the wind felt chilly.

Martin was unwelcome, breathing and existing at the edges of their lives. He smoked, he drank, and he ate so he must be human. If he ever slept, or used the bathroom or washed himself, they didn't see him do so. He seemed more phantom than real, except when he spoke and that was only commands. He was always there, more spirit than man as if he could see through them, what they were thinking before they thought it, and he didn't sleep. His presence forever in the room with his eyes eternally on them. Florence observed him, in return. He must know although she pretended to be looking elsewhere if he saw her looking at him. She oddly felt she was a trespasser guilty of snooping.

During the night the vomiting began with the first clap of thunder. Lightning came on its heels confounding the room with twisted light and the wind rattled the windows and shook the roof. She barely had time to hang her head over the bed and aim for the bucket beneath it. Afterward, she lay back on her cot. Her lips were dry and she wanted a glass of water, but it would come right back up.

Among the storm's noise, she heard Martin's breathing, slow and deep. The smell of cigarette smoke turned her stomach. Her knees ached and her elbows and shoulders felt like they were on fire. Her eye sockets pounded and the lightning strikes were coming faster now, slicing like sharp knives. The nausea started coming back.

Then, Tommy was retching.

One Hundred and six

The clanging phone, one step ahead of the day's light, punctured the night's malaise. Martin stopped pulling on his beard when it blasted into the room, the wearisome waiting finally over. The contraption was anything but subtle, its wailing irritating in the calm times and at others, disruptive as religious zealots' insistent knocks at the front door.

It was a petulant child screeching, demanded the spotlight, threatening if it were neglected. He didn't move to get up although he'd spent the night enduring the sounds of retching and waiting for dawn to come. He'd bit his lower lip waiting for it, one time before dawn he got up and stood staring at the ungainly wooden box, face-to-face with it, snarling into its ugly black receiver. The dead-pan look it returned seemed boringly disinterested. What a smug enemy.

Florence daily was mother to its demands. She answered it, rushed to its cradle, responded to its first wail so its cry would be cut short. Otherwise, the clang would continue to taint the unpolluted solitude on the mountain top. But today she didn't answer it.

He willed it to stop, but it took ten rings to relent. He went over to it. Nose to nose, he counted each bark and winced when one tone ended but was then followed by another. The skin on his neck and face turned tomato red. *Shut up,* he ordered after the third ring taking the clamor as a slap in the face, deliberately taunting him and refusing to be silenced by his snarls. *Go ahead,* it seemed to respond with each new ring. Finally, it went silent again making the room feel listless and benumbed. He lit another cigarette. The reprieve lasted barely a few minutes, long enough only to take one or two deep breaths before it once again blasted into the room. The first incursion had been obnoxious, this time it burst into the cab ever more strident and intrusive. He cursed when it began again, swung his arm back to smack the thing clear off the hook but stopped short, stepped away and lit a second cigarette from the unfinished one. His hands shook when he backed away from the contraption and he paced until it became silent again. He was trapped.

The sun climbed above the ridge and he recorded the readings Florence routinely made for her report. The measurements were in line with her usual figures except for the wind speed which was completely out of whack. He noted it, retook it to be certain that it had grown stronger since her last report. It hadn't subsided since the night's crazy storm. In fact, it was shrieking like an angry bird through whatever cracks and leaks it uncovered in the cab.

He'd meant to flee during the night. When he had come across the pair at the stream, he hadn't intended to take them prisoner. A miserable mistake, certainly a waste of precious time from the get-go. He craved sleep, he needed to unload his hostages. They were pale as if they were dead in their coffins, probably would appreciate a bullet in their brains. But these weren't bodies that could be buried in nowhere Canada. He would pull the phone out of the wall. They were too sick to stop him and that would buy him a good head start. He was running low on cigarettes.

Each ring of the damn phone was like a stab. The idiot box spit at him and he slapped it hard enough to hurt his hand, but he didn't disconnect it.

Florence and her son had puked up their insides all night long even when there was nothing left for them to bring up. He should have ducked out right when it started. They were moaning and retching away. The storm had confounded kicking things around for hours making the cab sway and keeping things off-kilter. He could have made a good distance before first light. It might be days before they recovered while he was feeling grand except for being cooped up like a chicken and needing to sleep.

Pink light creeped into the eastern windows, primeval and chaste after the storm's antics, like a deceitful mother hiding behind her gospel truth. The rosy glow would ease his way down the path to the stream littered with fallen logs and broken branches and he would follow it out. Sooner or later it would lead to a road and by the time Florence reported him, he'd be out of the mountains altogether and on a train or hitchhiking to the west.

He might have a ten hour start and would have had more if he'd left while the storm was sweeping its dragon tail over the landscape.

A fool's choice, but when he saw the ponderosa quiver and bend into themselves, he wouldn't take the chance. The wind slapped the rain into the window panes before the hail came, and the pandemonium competed with the gagging and the stench inside. He'd lived through a tornado in Canada before this.

"Damn!" She moaned, squeezing her eyelids against the rosy light like a doll dumped by an angry girl. The bruise under her eye was turning as yellow as her skin. The phone blared behind his back and he shot a glance at his pack loaded with tins of spam and dried fruit and peanuts from the larder waiting next to a canteen and the rifle.

She didn't have the strength to lift her head or keep her eyes open. He was sick of them, of the constant proximity, the perpetual watching, being on guard. He should have killed them before now, torn the phone out, dumped them off the cliff below the outhouse. Let an animal devour them before they were ever found.

"Answer the damn phone." He whispered into her ear leaning over her because she was flat on her back. He'd lost track of the number of times they'd thrown up. The storm was gone by the time they stopped. The phone jangled again and she smiled as if she was in the midst of a blissful dream.

The sun crawled from the foot of the bed up to her hands gliding up toward her mouth that had the shape of a perfect heart. The air was already thick and sultry which made the stench oppressive and he rushed to open the windows and smelled something burning.

The phone stopped and before it started again, he put a cold cloth on her forehead. The sun moved up on to her face and she mumbled that she had to get up. "The phone."

"That's right. You have to get up now and answer it."

One Hundred and Seven

"Goddammit! Answer the phone!" He yelled over her but her hands shook too much to cover her ears. Six rings before he swept her off the bed and hauled her over to it, threw her on the chair. On the tenth ring, he yanked off the receiver and shoved the piece to her lips. "Tell him you're sick!" He mouthed the words in her face.

"What the hell is going on up there, Flo? You all right?"

"I...I."

"Well, Jesus, woman, say somethin'. This ain't no time to dilly dawdle. That storm knocked the socks off everybody and it's worse than that. We got a bad fire comin' across and you're gonna get stuck if you stay up there. I don't know why the hell you haven't gotten on the phone before now. You get off the mountain right now!"

"What?" Her head fell back into Martin's hands.

"Eight, nine." He'd counted as he ran with her in his arms across the room. She was heavier than she looked. Muscular and taut, not like the wimp with the motorcycle whose ugly dead eyes stared him down every night.

"Damn it, Florence!" The ranger spit into her ear. "Where you been? You're head up in the clouds? This is the third time I been ringing you up. I don't have time for this. I figured you had enough brains to get out of there by now. You even see what's coming your way?"

Martin held the receiver to her ear. "Talk to him." She was in the process of sliding off the chair, liquid as water. He let go of her chin and caught hold under her armpit with one hand before she slipped onto the floor. It took some skill to hold the receiver near her face with his other hand as she cascaded. She mumbled. "Leave me alone."

"What'd you say? Listen, Florence. You there? You hear me? God dammit woman, you're gonna be in a bucket of trouble you stay where you are. Wind's gone berserk up there at George's and it's pushing the fire your way over the ridge. If it keeps up and it sure as hell looks like it's going to, you better get out of there now. It could be there by noon. The other fellas are gone already. You hear me? You get out of there now."

364

"What?"

"Dammit. Florence. I ain't got time for this. You listening to me? Where's your damn head? I gotta go. I'm up to my ears down here. You watch it. You gonna get into real bad smoke before you get down to the crick. Wet a hanky and tie it on your face like they told you in training and get down and out to the road. Don't try to be no hero. You gonna get trapped up there. We can't get you out if you stay."

"What?"

"Cut it out, Flo! What the hell is the matter with you? You okay?"

"Okay." She squeezed her eyes tighter. Sunlight stabbed at them if she tried to open them. She moaned and her head thumped against the wall. Martin propped her mouth back up to the receiver crooking her neck in his elbow still holding the receiver to her ear.

"When you make it to the trailhead, hold up there. Someone'll show up sooner or later. Trucks are coming up and down the road regular now. Just wave one of them down and they'll get you out to Columbia Falls. Get going. This is it. I'm signing off for good." Martin let her go and her forehead smacked back into the wall. She snuggled up to it making it her pillow.

The windows clapped like fervid spectators against their hinges and smoke rolled into the room. He'd dismissed the haze as he took the readings, attributed it to mist rising from the downpour, but there had been whiffs of smoke even then. From the cupola viewpoint, giant balls of charcoal clouds tumbled over each other hiding the ridgeline.

She laughed out loud snoozing against her wall with a beguiling smile, her eyes pressed tight against the pinkish light that was gradually turning gray. It is pure ecstasy and relief after the upheaval and infinite moments of nausea have passed. The bliss of peace and amnesia. She tugged at the bottom edge of her shirt thinking it was a blanket and tried to pull it up only to reveal her ribs and stomach. As fit and healthy as she was, it would not be enough to survive the blaze barreling toward the cab.

Christ. It was the phone's fault. He'd waited too long and wasted his chances to get away. How in the hell was he going to get through that black curtain of smoke and flame? After he got to the stream where would he go?

The boy groaned and coughed. "Don't hit me again." Martin cringed. He had to walk past the kid and his stinking blanket to get to his pack. "You ain't gonna do that no more, Pa." His fists punched at something invisible in the air. He coughed again and rolled over onto his side. "I ain't gonna take no more beatings from you. You mean son-of-a-bitch." He buried his head into the pillow and was quiet then. The air whistled through his nostrils and he purred like a satisfied cat.

The pack was stuffed with bulky canned goods and rifle cartridges and it was going to slow him down. The ranger told Florence to go to Columbia Falls. That's where he'd head. Follow the trucks coming back from the fire. Florence still huddled against the wall, her brow furrowed now against the nonexistent sunlight blocked by a wall of smoke. The mouth slack, like Tommy's, the smile gone.

He left the door ajar.

One Hundred and Eight

"Hey. For cripes sake!" The truck's brakes belched out a cloud of dust, the rear tires spitting up bits of gravel. "What the hell!" There was barely space enough for two vehicles to pass as the road snaked up the mountain at a hairpin where it met up with the trailhead. "For the love of God! I nearly ran her over." He bit down on his tongue hard enough to make it bleed when he saw it was a woman lying in the shallow ditch. "I'll be goll darned." He slammed his hand on his thigh the dust flying off his pants when she groaned and moved an arm like she was trying to lift something. At least she wasn't dead.

Mufflers backfired, brakes squealed, horns honked, guys shouted nonsense as they rushed past the scene. The trucks roared up the road like they were in a Demolition Derby hauling in men and equipment. Tucked in between the vehicles coming down, ambulances wailed on their way to the hospital with their injured, either from smoke inhalation, heat exhaustion, or because they'd been caught in a wall of exploding fire. Fresh-faced fighters hooted and cheered on the way up, a clump of bone-weary faces in the back of a pickup covered in grit didn't open their eyes or wave.

"Are you nuts?" Trying to stop his hands from shaking.

In her nightmare, the ruckus from the traffic added to her desperation to run away from a fire, but her legs were made of wood. She tapped on them slapping to pump them up and finally resorted to lifting them one at a time to take a single step and stay ahead of the fire that was going to trap her, but they hung like broken tree limbs. It was the ground quivering from the truck's engine thunder that made her open her eyes to face what she thought was the fire rumbling, and it had caught up with her. Then the truck door creaked and a pair of boots stomped toward her. She squinted up at a hat like hers hovering above her, government regulation.

"Good grief! You couldn't figure out a better damn place than this? You coulda been killed. I nearly run you over!" His mouth twitched. She tried to get up, fell back on her elbows because her eyes were spinning like she was on a merry-go-round. She fixed them on the solid thing in front of her, a truck wheel that fascinated her. The rest of her face was behind a bandana.

"You okay, lady?" He said gently. She couldn't hear him over the other noises until he squatted down next to her and yelled it.

"I'm...I'm fine." As the dizziness faded, her legs became real again and she wanted to run. "Where's the fire?"

"Up by the crick?" She shook her head.

"No. The FIRE!"

"It's still burning up at the crick." He didn't get why she wouldn't take his word. "You all right lady?"

"How did I get here?" She bolted up talking through the bandana part that stuck on her tongue.

"Can you take a few sips of this?" He pointed to the canteen strapped over her shoulder and offered to open it.

"The fire's not here?"

"No. They're getting it contained now. I'm pretty sure. Sorry for how I spoke to you. Scared the hell out of me, frankly."

"You need some help, fella?" A truck carrying a batch of enthusiastic guys slowed down.

"It's okay. Thanks."

Her hair was a mass of porcupine quills and she wasn't wearing boots or shoes, just socks, looked grayer than death, a real mess, but she wasn't dead thanks to her red plaid shirt. It was the red flag that saved her, got his attention.

Plump snowflakes of ash drifted down and cast a wintry hush over the trees and brush. Another vehicle passed and whipped it all up again swirling it into a string of minor blizzards.

He pointed to the water that dribbled down her chin. "You probably ought to keep your face covered." It was her bandana. When had she put it on? Miss Conrad came center stage for just an instant. "Here. Let's get it wet again." It helped her breathing.

"What you doing up this way, anyhow?" His hands still jittery. "You been camping out in the woods? Got caught in that storm?"

Three months on a lookout, alone and solitary except for the packer and an occasional hiker. Two times a day to talk to anybody other than a ranger. He wished he'd been gentler when he found her. He'd been away from people too long.

She brushed the ashes off her arms and pants and tried to stand up. "I don't know where my boots are."

"I'll look for them." He shook his head and coming back empty-handed after scouring the nearby bushes. "They're not anywhere I can see. Any idea where you left them?" At the cab, but that didn't fit. Her feet weren't torn or raw from hiking down without wearing them.

"I don't know."

"Guess it doesn't matter, does it, long as you're safe? Real smart wearing that bandana. Smoke could kill you before you even had a chance to swallow gallons of ash." He laughed.

"How long you been here? You should really drink some more water." He didn't wait for her to answer. Her throat tickled even after she drank, and her lips felt like dry oatmeal.

"I don't know." He looked puzzled. "I mean I don't know how I got here and I don't know for how long."

"What do you remember?"

"What do I remember? I...?"

A truck barreled up the road and he jumped up to move his vehicle off to the side. "Everything okay here, buddy?" Ten more guys heading back up to the fire.

"Yeah. What's the latest? Where you headed?"

"They almost got the line dug around the fire up by the crick. Some guys didn't make it. Got hit when the fire exploded and trapped them up there. We're heading back up there now."

One Hundred and Nine

They looked like foiled bank robbers behind their bandanas sitting in the ditch. A lull in the hurricane of rowdy vehicles woke up her recollection of the cab being slapped around like a haunted house and feeling sicker than a dog. "Oh." Her stomach turned and she gagged.

"You feelin' sick? You okay?" He reached for his canteen.

"Yeah. Yeah." She brushed the water away and her eyes bulged above the cloth. She jumped up. "Tommy. Where's Tommy?"

"Who's Tommy?" He jumped up beside her.

A mud-caked truck crept toward them off the mountain carrying five charred bodies recovered up at the creek. Glassy-eyed, the two men bringing them back pulled the sorrowful transport up next to the ditch.

"Did you find a boy? Did you?" The bandana slipped down to her chin.

"Nope." A flat voice answered. "We know who four of them are. Don't know the other." A fire leapt over the trench they were digging, caught them in the flames. The screams echoed down the canyon. There was nothing the others could do but cover their ears.

"These fellows was fire fighters." He pointed at the bodies wrapped in tarps in the back. "They ain't found no boy far as I know, Ma'am. Sorry." He ground the gearshift into first rolling the truck forward. "Gotta get going. Where'd you last see him? The kid?" He hollered over the engine but didn't wait for her to answer.

"In the..." She spoke to tail lights before they got swallowed up in the dust.

"In the what?' The man who'd nearly run her over asked.

"I don't know." *In the cab.* Tommy was wearing a half-moon grin and humming over the stove frying his enormous catch. She remembered the smell of grease that made her stomach turn before she took the first bite. He'd added too much grease to the pan. She felt a wave come up again, ready to heave in the ditch.

Tommy was a juggler, flipping the pancake turner in mid-air to toss the monster fish. Martin watched his antics, but looked through him to something invisible. She'd had her qualms about the fish, smiled straight into Tommy's eyes when he strutted toward her balancing the steaming plate shoulder height beaming, his chest puffed out like a city dude donning a cowboy hat and boots from his back-country vacation in Montana.

"Look at the feast you made!" She wouldn't handle his fallen face is she turned down his prize. The fish had liberated him somehow from their captivity, opened a secret escape door. If she'd hesitated a heartbeat, he would have guessed and she couldn't muster words to talk her way out. She took the first bite. He waited. "It's delicious." She swallowed hard. Martin ate everything on his plate, wore his poker face at the table and lit a cigarette.

Before she'd eaten half of it, her heart was pounding in her gut. She had a knot the size of a ball in there. First, the storm with all its artillery, and then her head hanging over the dish pan. Both went on for hours.

There was an angry voice. Someone had yelled at her to answer something that had been pushed into her face. Light stabbed into her eyes, and she was dreaming she was sliding off the boulder where Tommy caught his big fish. When the noise stopped finally, it turned night again and a very nice wall held her head and gave off a comforting woody scent.

At the ditch, a cloud of dust mixed with ash had not settled from the tracks of the makeshift hearse before several trucks barreled by. Two of them were ferrying ten men each in their truck beds, the others hauled tools, but none of the vehicles slowed down despite the potholes from the summer rains. The eager and fresh recruits laughed and hooted on their way to becoming the next forest service heroes. Not even a hearse could dampen their spirits.

She and the man moved farther off the road. A few haulers slowed down and yelled out to see if they needed help. Florence's companion waved them on. "We're doing okay here. Thanks. Good luck up there."

"Tommy!" She jumped up and he caught her by the waist just as headed face first into the ditch. "I have to find Tommy." She cried.

"Don't think you want land in there again." He chuckled holding onto her like a sack of potatoes.

"Where's Tommy?"

"I'm not sure. Who's Tommy?" Her legs were shaking, and he kept a grip so she wouldn't nose dive. "Maybe you should sit down for a bit?" She held onto his arm.

"I'll be fine in a minute." She snapped.

"I can see that." Her fingers made imprints on his arm.

"Where's Tommy?"

"I don't know where he is. Who is Tommy, again?" He apologized.

"Who are you?" She let go of his arm, pushing it away, but he stayed close enough to grab her if she started to go down again.

"Better if you put the bandana on. You sure you don't want to sit down for a bit, yet? I've got a sandwich in the truck."

"I'm not hungry. She pulled the kerchief up, the taste of greasy fish still stuck to her tongue.

"Is Tommy your son?"

"No, no. Homer. Homer's my son." His ignorance was wasting precious time.

"What?"

She didn't feel dizzy when she glared at him as if he was deaf. "I just said, *Homer-is-my-son*. Tommy I'm taking care of. Or, I was." She'd promised him. She'd watch out for him. Tears dripped down her handkerchief. "I lost him." She didn't know where or when. "I'm going back up and look for him."

"No. No. Where do you think you're going? You can't do that!"

"The cab!" He was thickheaded as a mule.

You're not...?"

"I've got to." So, this is what the woman with the beautiful voice looked like. Shorter than he imagined, and grayer but somehow younger looking than all her wisdom.

"I've just got to find him." She didn't have enough liquid in her to shed that many tears. He handed her the canteen, but she pushed it away.

"You are, aren't you? You're Flo!" His pupils the size of gnats.

"What? Who are you?" She gasped. Caught. She couldn't have turned Tommy in. They'd return him to his pa to be kicked around

372

Leave it to the ranger to find her. He'd dock her salary for sure and not take her back next season, but what did that matter without Tommy.

"You never know who you're gonna find in the middle of a forest fire, do you?" The outside corners of his eyes crinkled and that's when she recognized the laugh.

"Joe? Is that you, Joe?" His voice didn't come across that deep on the phone line. The drawl, though, that was the same, and the way he had to inspect each word before it passed his lips.

"But...but you're my Joe." She whispered behind the bandana.

"Um." He put his arms straight out from his shoulders like a helicopter getting ready to take off.

"Why aren't you at your lookout?" Her brows squeezed together.

"They called us all off when the fire blew up. Don't you remember?" His arms went down. He kicked his boot into the gravel as a batch of trucks streaked past. He kicked the gravel again. "I'll be goll-darned." He whistled. "I'll be goll darned. Florence." It was a prayer.

One Hundred and Ten

A forest service truck barreled off the mountain ahead of a tunnel of dust, but they didn't hear it or see it until it got to the hairpin. Joe jumped back from his truck, almost dropping the binoculars.

"How do. You folks got a problem, too?" The driver jammed on the brakes, just short of them. "Sorry. Didn't mean to near run you over. In a big hurry."

For three months, in fog, in snow, pelting rain and hail, and during sticky days the spotters sized up each other. They figured things out between words and jokes, the gripes and teasing. Discovered a mutual distaste for spam, dried fruit, and powdered milk. As the days fell into each other, piled up one after the other like bricks, they advised and counseled about bears, cooking, storms, and raw loneliness. They were individual pages to be read like the weather gauges they read. They sang and made music, grumbled over stupid jokes, argued, lamented the heat and the tedium, bragged and hooted, grew morose over disappointing news.

Joe toed the gravel with his boot as Florence dusted off her sleeves and retied her bandana. He pushed his hat back then forward, couldn't make up his mind where he wanted it. "We're okay." He hung the binoculars around his neck. "How they getting on with the fire up there?"

"Looks like they got a handle on it cuz the wind's died down. Messy terrible business up there. You heard about them bodies, I expect." They nodded. "Hey, you wouldn't know who this here boy I got belongs to?"

"Hello, Ma'am." Tommy's head crawled up over the steering wheel.

"Where's your bandana?" She gasped crossing the gravel in her bare feet to get to the door on the far side. Even his freckles looked pale.

"Why'd you leave me?" he pushed back.

"I don't know. I don't know." He pulled away from her arm.

"Where'd you find him?" Joe asked the driver. "She's been worried sick about you, son." He looked over the steering wheel to Tommy.

"Don't look like it."

"Doesn't." She couldn't help it. She should have been a school teacher like Miss Conrad, except she'd have to put up with all the lip. Otherwise, it didn't seem a half bad idea.

"Got the stuffing knocked out of him, but he's gonna be fine. Sure glad I came across you. Found him in a clearing below the crick. Don't know how he got there. Do you?"

"No. Do you know, Tommy?" He scowled at her.

"You ain't missing nobody else, are you, Ma'am?" Like a failed Mother Goose who couldn't keep track of all her children.

"No. But, was there anybody with him when you found him?"

"Nope. Looked like he got dumped there."

"You had the good sense to get down below the fire, son." Tommy gave a weak smile and Joe winked at Florence.

"When they hauled out them five guys nobody could identify the last one. You don't know nothin', though, I guess. They'll figure it out sooner or later. Thought your boy was a goner when I found him. Lucky I found you, too. I gotta get back up there."

"He's nothin' but a pile of bones." He flashed a dirty look at Florence. "Don't worry, none. Your boy's gonna be okay once he's out of this dang smoke. What was he doing up there, anyway?" He didn't wait for an answer. "I'm heading back up. Good thing I didn't have to haul him clear out to the police."

She shivered. "Thank you! I don't know how to thank you!" He revved the engine and made a U-turn that churned up the dust.

"Take care of your kid. That's how you thank me. Gotta go!" He ground the gears and took off.

"Sorry, Flo." Joe said under his breath.

At the beginning of June, snow piles lined the Polebridge Road all the way into Canada. In places it had been as high as picket fence, or higher. Large patches of white sheets lay over the meadows, the damp air crisp and thick with pine-scent, and the roaring dragon of the North Fork echoed down the canyon.

In late August, it was an altered landscape, muted, subdued, and untended. Weary trees bowed after the heavy rains, the promise of glorious warm days, bountiful sunshine, and bright lush growth. Ash and dust weighted down straggly, thirsty bushes dressing them up as ghosts. The river ran flat and sluggish, hardly murmuring a tune and dulled of vibrant color.

She'd been all nerves coming up from Missoula, afraid that Fred could track her down and ruin things for her, plus plagued that the forest service had more confidence in her than she deserved. Her companions that morning in early June were men she wouldn't see again. They joked and smoked while she sat in the far corner of the truck feeling guilty for not making Fred's coffee.

The door slammed in the face of the summer to end it. A forest fire shut it up and she didn't even know that until she woke up in a ditch by the side of the road. Maybe Tommy knew something more. When he got to feeling better, after his grudge passed, understanding his blaming her and believing she left him behind. They would sort it out. They had to.

Joe negotiated the pitted road and the majority of monster potholes. He looked like Tom in *Grapes of Wrath* except for the graying temples and the mountain man's beard. Her teeth chattered from the bumps, but she wanted to scream at him. *Turn the truck around and take us back!* Tommy was drooling and muttering in his sleep on her shoulder.

Joe smacked into a hole that jolted Tommy awake. "Where is he?" He yelled. She stiffened. A distinct line left by the bandana showed where the grime began. "The...the...that man?"

"What did he say?" Tommy's head bounded on her shoulder, and the late afternoon sun lit up his face so she shielded it with her hand. The guy who brought him down in the truck wasn't wrong. He was a bag of bones.

"What? Nothing." She sighed before she started to cry. When she started sobbing, so did the hiccups.

"I'll pull over." As soon as they could get to Columbia Falls maybe they could get a cup of coffee. "Here. Have some water."

"No. Don't stop." Squeezing the words between hiccups.

"Okay." He pulled the visor down and his face looked two-toned.

"It must have been mighty hard."

"What?" Between sobs and hiccups.

"Strange things happen on the mountains, Flo. You get us spotters in a room and nobody'd ever say so, but we all got some lousy story to tell. Maybe you'll tell me the one that's got you so upset, sometime."

Where to begin? On the day in spring when she left Fred, or when she found Tommy bloody and half-dead, or the man who took them hostage? What was the beginning? "Your eyes." She answered a few miles later.

"What's wrong with them?" He peeked into the rearview mirror.

"Nothing. Nothing's wrong with them." She'd stopped sobbing now and smiled. "What did you put down when you filled out the Forest Service Application?"

"What do you mean?"

"You know. The color of your eyes. Mine are blue." His had specks the color of marigold blossoms.

"I dunno." He laughed. "I think they call 'em hazel. Hey, you know what would be real nice about now? If you would sing one of your songs before we get to town."

They had driven out from under the ashy cloud and the sun was drifting toward the horizon much as it had on those many evenings when the spotters made their music. The sky gradually turned from a burnt orange to a fiery fuchsia. It looked like it would be a clear enough later to see the North Star with its Big Dipper and Orion.

www.ingramcontent.com/pod-product-compliance
Lightning Source LLC
Chambersburg PA
CBHW021130260626
47169CB00005B/1536